A NORTON CRITICAL EDITION

Maria Edgeworth

CASTLE RACKRENT

AUTHORITATIVE TEXT

BACKGROUNDS AND CONTEXTS

CRITICISM

Edited by

RYAN TWOMEY

MACQUARIE UNIVERSITY

W · W · NORTON & COMPANY · *New York* · *London*

W. W. Norton & Company has been independent since its founding in 1923, when William Warder Norton and Mary D. Herter Norton first published lectures delivered at the People's Institute, the adult education division of New York City's Cooper Union. The firm soon expanded its program beyond the Institute, publishing books by celebrated academics from America and abroad. By midcentury, the two major pillars of Norton's publishing program—trade books and college texts—were firmly established. In the 1950s, the Norton family transferred control of the company to its employees, and today—with a staff of four hundred and a comparable number of trade, college, and professional titles published each year—W. W. Norton & Company stands as the largest and oldest publishing house owned wholly by its employees.

Copyright © 2015 by W. W. Norton & Company, Inc.

All rights reserved
Printed in the United States of America
First Edition

Library of Congress Cataloging-in-Publication Data

Edgeworth, Maria, 1768–1849, author.
  Castle Rackrent : authoritative text backgrounds and contexts criticism / Maria Edgeworth ; edited by Ryan Twomey, Macquarie University. — First edition.
        pages cm. — (A Norton Critical Edition)
  Includes bibliographical references.
  ISBN 978-0-393-92241-7 (pbk.)
  1. Administration of estates—Fiction.   2. Landlord and tenant—Fiction.   3. Rural conditions—Fiction.   4. Poor families—Fiction.
5. Rich people—Fiction.   6. Ireland—Social life and customs—Fiction.
7. Domestic fiction.   8. Edgeworth, Maria, 1768–1849. Castle Rackrent.
I. Twomey, Ryan, editor.   II. Title.
  PR4644.C3 2015
  823'.7—dc23

                                                                2014023125

W. W. Norton & Company, Inc., 500 Fifth Avenue, New York, NY 10110
wwnorton.com

W. W. Norton & Company Ltd., Castle House, 75/76 Wells Street, London
W1T 3QT

1 2 3 4 5 6 7 8 9 0

Contents

Criticism

Preface

One of the most interesting aspects of Maria Edgeworth's *Castle Rackrent*, and arguably one of the reasons it continues to be read more than two hundred years after its first publication, is the complexity of decoding Thady's narration while grappling with the competing textual voice of the English editor. This complexity allows for a multitude of readings and interpretations of the novel, very few of which have gained precedence in the critical scholarship. In part, this is due to the correspondingly complex political milieu in which the first edition of Edgeworth's novel was published. *Castle Rackrent* appeared anonymously in January 1800 on the eve of the Acts of Union (1800), which saw the Kingdom of Great Britain united with the Kingdom of Ireland, creating the United Kingdom of Great Britain and Ireland. The lead-up to this historic event had a profound impact on the political and social landscape; and the proposed Union also altered the publication history of *Castle Rackrent*, adding to the complexity of Edgeworth's text, a text that is now considered the "first truly Irish novel."[1]

Another first attributed to *Castle Rackrent* is that it heralded the arrival of the regional novel while also having a marked influence on the historical novel. In particular, the influence of Edgeworth's work on Sir Walter Scott's historical novels is well documented, as is the friendship that grew out of the respect they had for each other.[2] Scott recognized that Edgeworth's narrative achievement lay in her production of realistic characters set in recognizable locales. The change in topographical focus from generalized settings, such as London and Bath, to a specific sense of place has led to Maria Edgeworth being credited as the first regional novelist in English. As Walter Allen argues in *The English Novel* (1958):

> Maria Edgeworth gave fiction a local habitation and a name. And she did more than this: she perceived the relation between the local habitation and the people who dwell in it. She invented, in other words, the regional novel, in which the very nature of

---

1. James Cahalan, *The Irish Novel: A Critical History* (Boston: Twayne, 1988), p. xxii.
2. See Sir Walter Scott on pp. 99, 101.

the novelist's characters is conditioned, receives its bias and expression, from the fact that they live in a countryside differentiated by a traditional way of life from other countrysides.[3]

The regional focus on Ireland and the Irish way of life in *Castle Rackrent* was unusual enough to necessitate the inclusion of a glossary. When the first edition, equipped with editorial footnotes and preface material, was with London printer Joseph Johnson in 1799, a last-minute decision was made to provide the reader with a glossary that would aid as a further explanatory apparatus for the main text. As the manuscript had already gone to press, and as it was the tradition to print the preliminary material last, the Glossary was included as part of the preface material, rather than in its traditional position after the narrative.[4] The late inclusion of the Glossary reflects the period in which the novel was published—a period of high political tension felt by Maria and her father, Richard Lovell Edgeworth.[5] The concern was over the portrayal of Ireland and the Irish inhabitants exhibited in the pages of *Castle Rackrent*, given the close proximity to a union with Britain and the fact that the novel was to have a largely English readership.

This anxiety was not prevalent during the relatively peaceful years of 1793 and 1796, the most likely period during which the first section of *Castle Rackrent* was written.[6] Yet after the Irish Rebellion of 1798 and the push for a union with Britain, both Edgeworth and her father were acutely aware that any negative portrayal of the Irish, even if satirical, could have a deleterious effect on the way the English viewed Ireland and the slated Union. *Castle Rackrent*, like other texts written by the Edgeworths, started out as family entertainment, the consumption of which was originally confined to the domestic sphere. The publication of *Castle Rackrent* at the turn of the century, however, meant that what had previously been available to a select group was now widely disseminated and available for public scrutiny.

Yet any reading that the Glossary was included as a last-minute reaction to the political climate and concerns surrounding the impending Union is not as straightforward as it first appears. While Edgeworth undoubtedly wished to portray her Irish characters sympathetically, the manner in which she went to their defense is

---

3. W. E. Allen, *The English Novel: A Short Critical History* (London: Phoenix House, 1954), p. 98. See also Allen on pp. 113–14.
4. Subsequent editions saw the Glossary moved to the more usual position at the end of the text.
5. See Jacqueline Belanger on pp. 131–32.
6. For more on the composition of *Castle Rackrent* see Brian Hollingworth on pp. 125–28.

curious. In the "Advertisement to the English Reader,"[7] the preface to the Glossary, we read:

> Some friends, who have seen Thady's history since it has been printed, have suggested to the Editor, that many of the terms and idiomatic phrases, with which it abounds, could not be intelligible to the English reader without farther explanation. The Editor has therefore furnished the following Glossary.

While modern readers of fiction are accustomed to a host of linguistic idiosyncrasies, the eighteenth-century reader would have found Edgeworth's use of dialect in *Castle Rackrent* disruptive. Yet the justification for including the Glossary to explain the unintelligible idiomatic phrases uttered by Thady seems peculiar when one views the manner in which the words and phrases are glossed. The high proportion of glosses are dedicated to providing sociological information rather than proffering definitions for a specific use of dialect. Even when the gloss receives a simple definition, such is the case with *Whillaluh*, a "lamentation over the dead," (p. 64) readers are still given an extensive account of the Irish funeral song and the behavior exhibited by Irish mourners when attending funerals.[8] It is difficult to believe, therefore, that the Glossary was included simply as a tool to aid in the comprehension of the narrative when so much additional information was provided for the reader.

Deciphering the reason the Glossary was included as a last-minute addition is further problematized by the facetious nature of many of the glosses. If it was Edgeworth's intention to assuage a negative reading of Ireland by the English, the humorous, tongue-in-cheek approach much of the Glossary takes seems disingenuous. Part of the reason for this approach, however, can be attributed to the fact that *Castle Rackrent* was to be read as a representation of the past, a bygone Irish era. The preface to the novel explains that these are "tales of other times" (p. 7), while the title page announces that the Hibernian novel is "Taken from facts and from the manners of the Irish Squires before the year 1782" (p. 9). In this instance, the notion that the Glossary was included to help allay any reservations the English may have had in uniting with their Irish neighbors is supported by the historical frame through which *Castle Rackrent* is to be read. This reading of the Glossary seems most plausible as it allowed Edgeworth to distance herself from her narrative. By setting *Castle Rackrent* in the past, Edgeworth was in a position to acknowledge that some of the events and actions that take place between the pages of her novel *had* taken place in Ireland, consigning them to a

7. The preface to the Glossary was titled "The Advertisement to the English Reader" in the 1800–15 editions. See n. 2, p. 63.
8. See pp. 64–66.

past history that was distinct from the reformed modern Ireland ready for union with Britain.

This is further supported by Edgeworth's choice of 1782 as the line of demarcation for her novel. Edgeworth was signaling an important historical turning point both for her personally and for Ireland politically. Seventeen eighty-two was the year that the Irish parliament demanded, and was granted, legislative independence and the same year that Maria, at the age of fourteen, arrived in Edgesworthstown, her father's Irish estate in County Longford. It was also during this period that Edgeworth first came into contact with her father's steward, John Langan (the source of the narrator, Thady), whose use of Hiberno-English and odd Irishisms Edgeworth and her father quickly learned to mimic.[9] Although Edgeworth claimed that Thady was the only character "drawn from life," it was not the only real-life source she had at her disposal when writing *Castle Rackrent*. Edgeworth also had to hand *The Black Book of Edgeworthstown*, written by her grandfather Richard Edgeworth (senior). The text chronicled the family's history from its arrival in Ireland in 1585. Written in the middle of the eighteenth century, it recounts the often dubious actions of the Edgeworth gentry. As W. J. McCormack noted, "There is no doubt that *The Black Book of Edgeworthstown* . . . is of compelling relevance to any reading of *Castle Rackrent*."[1]

Yet any reading of the novel requires us first to grapple with the ambiguous nature of Thady Quirk's narration of the main text. Arguably, more has been written about Thady and his narration of *Castle Rackrent* than any other aspect of the novel. This is owing to the inherently equivocal nature of Thady's retelling of the Rackrent affairs. Julie Nash writes: "Is Thady an ignorant servant, stupidly loyal to undeserving masters and unfair to his own hardworking son? Or is he a shrewd manipulator, claiming a loyalty he doesn't feel while damning the Rackrents with faint praise? Perhaps both characterisations tell a partial truth."[2] The possibility of reading Thady's narration in (at least) two competing ways is an inherent part of Edgeworth's *Castle Rackrent* and something that all readers must negotiate for themselves. The complexity of Edgeworth's narrative structure, with a seemingly unreliable narrator juxtaposed with an English editor's footnotes and Glossary, accentuates her ambiguous authorial intention, allowing readers the freedom of multiple textual interpretations.

9. See the letter to Mrs. Stark on p. 86.
1. W. J. McCormack, *Ascendancy and Tradition in Anglo-Irish Literary History from 1789 to 1939* (Oxford: Clarendon Press, 1985), p. 104. See also McCormack on pp. 115–17.
2. Julie Nash, *Servants and Paternalism in the Works of Maria Edgeworth and Elizabeth Gaskell* (Hampshire, UK: Ashgate Publishing, 2007), p. 79. See also Nash on p. 187.

To aid in the interpretation of *Castle Rackrent* this Norton Critical Edition includes a number of sources that discuss the issue of Thady's narration and the production and inclusion of the paratext (the footnotes and glossary). Yet this is only one of a number of areas of critical scholarship on *Castle Rackrent*. The selection of articles and book chapters included herein survey many of the ongoing debates in the field, from Edgeworth's unique use of dialect to examinations of her patriarchal affiliation and the paternalistic social model identifiable in *Castle Rackrent*. I am grateful to the authors of these materials for allowing me to reprint their work. In addition to these sources, a selection of Edgeworth's juvenilia titled *The Double Disguise* is printed with the text of *Castle Rackrent* for the first time, giving readers a unique glimpse of Edgeworth's literary development.

A Note on the Text

This edition uses the 1832 Baldwin & Cradock publication of *Castle Rackrent* that appeared as part of a collected edition of eighteen volumes titled *Tales and Novels by Maria Edgeworth* (1832–33). Since its first publication by Joseph Johnson in London in 1800, the text of *Castle Rackrent* has undergone no major editorial change. This is due in part, no doubt, to the quality of Edgeworth's original composition of the tale. In 1836 Edgeworth commented on the manuscript of *Castle Rackrent* that "there was literally not a correction, not an alteration made in the first writing . . . It went to the press just as it was written."[3] A second London edition and a Dublin edition, published by P. Wogan, followed shortly after the first edition in 1800. A third London edition appeared in 1801, with Maria Edgeworth's name appearing for the first time on the title page. Three more editions were published between 1804 and 1815, and in 1825 a collected edition of fourteen volumes titled *Tales and Miscellaneous Pieces* was published.

For the 1832 Baldwin & Cradock volume of *Castle Rackrent*, Edgeworth worked in conjunction with the publisher to correct errors introduced in previous editions and to make minor revisions. The 1832 edition marks the largest change to the text in the editorial history of her novel due to the adoption of a more modern and familiar style of punctuation. The 1832 text abandons the use of parentheses within lines of dialogue to indicate speech—for example, the use of (said she) and (says he), along with the omission

---

3. Maria Edgeworth to Mrs. Ruxton, January 29, 1800; quoted in Marilyn Butler, *Maria Edgeworth: A Literary Biography* (Oxford: Clarendon Press, 1972), p. 290.

of Edgeworth's heavy reliance on dashes to punctuate her writing. The 1832 publication of *Castle Rackrent* offers a text that is recognizable to the modern reader and offers the added benefit of being the last edition to have been edited and reviewed by Edgeworth.

Illustrations

The Text of
CASTLE RACKRENT

TALES AND NOVELS

BY

MARIA EDGEWORTH.

IN EIGHTEEN VOLUMES.

VOL. I.

CONTAINING

CASTLE RACKRENT;

AN ESSAY ON IRISH BULLS;

AN ESSAY ON

THE NOBLE SCIENCE OF SELF-JUSTIFICATION.

LONDON:

PRINTED FOR BALDWIN AND CRADOCK;

J. MURRAY; J. BOOKER; A. K. NEWMAN AND CO.; WHITTAKER,
TREACHER, AND ARNOT; T. TEGG; SIMPKIN AND MARSHALL;
SMITH, ELDER, AND CO.; E. HODGSON; HOULSTON AND SON;
J. TEMPLEMAN; J. BAIN; R. MACKIE; RENSHAW AND RUSH;
AND G. AND J. ROBINSON, LIVERPOOL.

1832.

Preface[1]

The prevailing taste of the public for anecdote has been censured and ridiculed by critics who aspire to the character of superior wisdom: but if we consider it in a proper point of view, this taste is an incontestible proof of the good sense and profoundly philosophic temper of the present times. Of the numbers who study, or at least who read history, how few derive any advantage from their labours! The heroes of history are so decked out by the fine fancy of the professed historian; they talk in such measured prose, and act from such sublime or such diabolical motives, that few have sufficient taste, wickedness, or heroism, to sympathise in their fate. Besides, there is much uncertainty even in the best authenticated ancient or modern histories; and that love of truth, which in some minds is innate and immutable, necessarily leads to a love of secret memoirs, and private anecdotes. We cannot judge either of the feelings or of the characters of men with perfect accuracy, from their actions or their appearance in public; it is from their careless conversations, their half-finished sentences, that we may hope with the greatest probability of success to discover their real characters. The life of a great or of a little man written by himself, the familiar letters, the diary of any individual published by his friends or by his enemies, after his decease, are esteemed important literary curiosities. We are surely justified, in this eager desire, to collect the most minute facts relative to the domestic lives, not only of the great and good, but even of the worthless and insignificant, since it is only by a comparison of their actual happiness or misery in the privacy of domestic life that we can form a just estimate of the real reward of virtue, or the real punishment of vice. That the great are not as happy as they seem, that the external circumstances of fortune and rank do not constitute felicity, is asserted by every moralist: the historian can seldom, consistently with his dignity, pause to illustrate this truth: it is therefore to the biographer we must have recourse. After we have beheld splendid characters playing their parts on the great theatre of the world, with all the advantages of stage effect and decoration, we anxiously beg to be admitted behind the scenes, that we may take a nearer view of the actors and actresses.

Some may perhaps imagine, that the value of biography depends upon the judgment and taste of the biographer: but on the contrary

---

1. The preface was likely to have been written in consultation with Richard Lovell Edgeworth, Maria's father, very late in 1799. In the first edition of 1800 and the first Irish edition (Dublin, 1800), the preface was directly followed by the "Advertisement to the English Reader" and the Glossary. See Jacqueline Belanger, "Educating the Reading Public," on p. 131.

it may be maintained, that the merits of a biographer are inversely as the extent of his intellectual powers and of his literary talents. A plain unvarnished tale is preferable to the most highly ornamented narrative. Where we see that a man has the power, we may naturally suspect that he has the will to deceive us; and those who are used to literary manufacture know how much is often sacrificed to the rounding of a period, or the pointing of an antithesis.

That the ignorant may have their prejudices as well as the learned cannot be disputed; but we see and despise vulgar errors: we never bow to the authority of him who has no great name to sanction his absurdities. The partiality which blinds a biographer to the defects of his hero, in proportion as it is gross, ceases to be dangerous; but if it be concealed by the appearance of candour, which men of great abilities best know how to assume, it endangers our judgment sometimes, and sometimes our morals. If her grace the duchess of Newcastle, instead of penning her lord's elaborate eulogium, had undertaken to write the life of Savage,[2] we should not have been in any danger of mistaking an idle, ungrateful libertine for a man of genius and virtue. The talents of a biographer are often fatal to his reader. For these reasons the public often judiciously countenance those, who, without sagacity to discriminate character, without elegance of style to relieve the tediousness of narrative, without enlargement of mind to draw any conclusions from the facts they relate, simply pour forth anecdotes, and retail conversations, with all the minute prolixity of a gossip in a country town.

The author of the following Memoirs has upon these grounds fair claims to the public favour and attention; he was an illiterate old steward, whose partiality to *the family*, in which he was bred and born, must be obvious to the reader. He tells the history of the Rackrent family in his vernacular idiom, and in the full confidence that sir Patrick, sir Murtagh, sir Kit, and sir Condy Rackrent's affairs will be as interesting to all the world as they were to himself. Those who were acquainted with the manners of a certain class of the gentry of Ireland some years ago will want no evidence of the truth of honest Thady's narrative: to those who are totally unacquainted with Ireland, the following Memoirs will perhaps be scarcely intelligible, or probably they may appear perfectly incredible. For the information of the *ignorant* English reader, a few notes have been subjoined by the editor, and he had it once in contemplation to translate the language of Thady into plain English; but Thady's idiom is incapable of translation, and, besides, the authenticity of his story would

2. Margaret Cavendish (1624–1674), Duchess of Newcastle's biography of her husband, *The Life of William Cavendish* (1667), and Samuel Johnson's (1709–1784) *An Account of the Life of Mr Richard Savage* (1744), both vehemently defend their subject.

have been more exposed to doubt if it were not told in his own characteristic manner. Several years ago he related to the editor the history of the Rackrent family, and it was with some difficulty that he was persuaded to have it committed to writing; however, his feelings for *"the honour of the family,"* as he expressed himself, prevailed over his habitual laziness, and he at length completed the narrative which is now laid before the public.

The editor hopes his readers will observe that these are "tales of other times:" that the manners depicted in the following pages are not those of the present age: the race of the Rackrents has long since been extinct in Ireland; and the drunken sir Patrick, the litigious sir Murtagh, the fighting sir Kit, and the slovenly sir Condy, are characters which could no more be met with at present in Ireland, than squire Western or parson Trulliber[3] in England. There is a time, when individuals can bear to be rallied for their past follies and absurdities, after they have acquired new habits, and a new consciousness. Nations as well as individuals gradually lose attachment to their identity, and the present generation is amused rather than offended by the ridicule that is thrown upon its ancestors.

Probably we shall soon have it in our power, in a hundred instances, to verify the truth of these observations.

When Ireland loses her identity by an union with Great Britain, she will look back with a smile of good-humoured complacency on the sir Kits and sir Condys of her former existence.

1800.

3. From Henry Fielding's *Joseph Andrews* (1742), the country parson and pig farmer. Squire Western is the father of the heroine in Fielding's *Tom Jones* (1749).

CASTLE RACKRENT;

AN

HIBERNIAN TALE.

TAKEN FROM FACTS,

AND FROM

THE MANNERS OF THE IRISH SQUIRES

BEFORE THE YEAR 1782.[4]

4. The year Edgeworth arrived in Ireland; the same year as Irish Independence (see
pp. x, 205). "Rackrent": an excessive or extortionate rent. "Hibernian": Irish.

Castle Rackrent

Monday Morning.°[5]

Having, out of friendship for the family, upon whose estate, praised be Heaven! I and mine have lived rent-free, time out of mind, voluntarily undertaken to publish the MEMOIRS of the RACKRENT FAMILY, I think it my duty to say a few words, in the first place, concerning myself. My real name is Thady Quirk, though in the family I have always been known by no other than "*honest Thady*,"—afterwards, in the time of sir Murtagh, deceased, I remember to hear them calling me "*old Thady*," and now I'm come to "poor Thady;" for I wear a long great coat*[6] winter and summer, which is very handy,

---

* The cloak, or mantle, as described by Thady, is of high antiquity. Spencer, in his "View of the State of Ireland," proves that it is not, as some have imagined, peculiarly derived from the Scythians, but that "most nations of the world anciently used the mantle; for the Jews used it, as you may read of Elias's mantle, &c.; the Chaldees also used it, as you may read in Diodorus; the Egyptians likewise used it, as you may read in Herodotus, and may be gathered by the description of Berenice, in the Greek Commentary upon Callimachus; the Greeks also used it anciently, as appeared by Venus's mantle lined with stars, though afterwards they changed the form thereof into their cloaks, called Pallai, as some of the Irish also use: and the ancient Latins and Romans used it, as you may read in Virgil, who was a very great antiquary, that Evander, when Æneas came to him at his feast, did entertain and feast him sitting on the ground, and lying on mantles: insomuch that he useth the very word mantile for a mantle,

'—— Humi mantilia sternunt:'

so that it seemeth that the mantle was a general habit to most nations, and not proper to the Scythians only."

Spencer knew the convenience of the said mantle, as housing, bedding, and clothing.

"*Iren.* Because the commodity doth not countervail the discommodity; for the inconveniences which thereby do arise are much more many; for it is a fit house for an outlaw, a meet bed for a rebel, and an apt cloak for a thief. First, the outlaw being for his many crimes and villanies, banished from the towns and houses of honest men, and wandering in wastes places, far from danger of law, maketh his mantle his house, and under it covereth himself from the wrath of Heaven, from the offence of the earth, and from the sight of men. When it raineth, it is his pent-house; when it bloweth, it is his tent; when it freezeth it is his tabernacle. In summer he can wear it loose; in winter he can wrap it close; at all times he can use it; never heavy, never cumbersome. Likewise for a rebel it is as serviceable; for in this war that he maketh (if at least it deserves the name of war), when he still flieth from his foe, and lurketh in the *thick woods* (*this should be black bogs*) and straight passages waiting for advantages, it is his bed, yea, and almost his household stuff."

---

5. The symbol ° indicates an entry in the Glossary (pp. 63–77).
6. Edgeworth cites *A View of the Present State of Ireland* (1596) by Edmund Spenser (1552–1599). For scholarly annotations to Spenser's passage see Elizabeth Sauer and Julia Margaret Wright, eds., *Reading the Nation in English Literature: A Critical Reader* (New York: Routledge, 2009), pp. 34–35.

as I never put my arms into the sleeves; they are as good as new, though come Holantide[7] next I've had it these seven years; it holds on by a single button round my neck, cloak fashion. To look at me, you would hardly think "poor Thady" was the father of attorney Quirk; he is a high gentleman, and never minds what poor Thady says, and having better than fifteen hundred a year, landed estate, looks down upon honest Thady; but I wash my hands of his doings, and as I have lived so will I die, true and loyal to the family. The family of the Rackrents is, I am proud to say, one of the most ancient in the kingdom. Every body knows this is not the old family name, which was O'Shaughlin, related to the kings of Ireland—but that was before my time. My grandfather was driver to the great sir Patrick O'Shaughlin, and I heard him, when I was a boy, telling how the Castle Rackrent estate came to sir Patrick; Sir Tallyhoo Rackrent was cousin-german[8] to him, and had a fine estate of his own, only never a gate upon it, it being his maxim that a car was the best gate. Poor gentleman! he lost a fine hunter and his life, at last, by it, all in one day's hunt. But I ought to bless that day, for the estate came straight into *the* family, upon one condition, which Sir Patrick O'Shaughlin at the time took sadly to heart, they say, but thought better of it afterwards, seeing how large a stake depended upon it, that he should by act of parliament, take and bear the sur-name and arms of Rackrent.

Now it was that the world was to see what was *in* sir Patrick. On coming into the estate, he gave the finest entertainment ever was heard of in the country: not a man could stand after supper but sir Patrick himself, who could sit out the best man in Ireland, let alone the three kingdoms itself.° He had his house, from one year's end to another, as full of company as ever it could hold, and fuller; for rather than be left out of the parties at Castle Rackrent, many gentlemen, and those men of the first consequence and landed estates in the country, such as the O'Neils of Ballynagrotty, and the Money-gawl's of Mount Juliet's Town, and O'Shannons of New Town Tullyhog, made it their choice, often and often, when there was no room to be had for love nor money, in long winter nights, to sleep in the chicken-house, which sir Patrick had fitted up for the purpose of accommodating his friends and the public in general, who honoured him with their company unexpectedly at Castle Rackrent; and this went on, I can't tell you how long—the whole country rang with his praises!— Long life to him! I'm sure I love to look upon his picture, now opposite to me; though I never saw him, he must have been a portly gentleman—his neck something short, and remarkable for the

---

7. Halloween, October 31.
8. First cousin.

largest pimple on his nose, which, by his particular desire, is still extant in his picture, said to be a striking likeness, though taken when young. He is said also to be the inventor of raspberry whiskey, which is very likely, as nobody has ever appeared to dispute it with him, and as there still exists a broken punch-bowl at Castle Rackrent, in the garret, with an inscription to that effect—a great curiosity. A few days before his death he was very merry; it being his honour's birth-day, he called my grandfather in, God bless him! to drink the company's health, and filled a bumper himself, but could not carry it to his head, on account of the great shake in his hand; on this he cast his joke, saying, "What would my poor father say to me if he was to pop out of the grave, and see me now? I remember when I was a little boy, the first bumper of claret he gave me after dinner, how he praised me for carrying it so steady to my mouth. Here's my thanks to him—a bumper toast." Then he fell to singing the favourite song he learned from his father—for the last time, poor gentleman—he sung it that night as loud and as hearty as ever with a chorus:

"He that goes to bed, and goes to bed sober,
Falls as the leaves do, falls as the leaves do, and dies in October;
But he that goes to bed, and goes to bed mellow,
Lives as he ought to do, lives as he ought to do, and dies an
    honest fellow."[9]

Sir Patrick died that night: just as the company rose to drink his health with three cheers, he fell down in a sort of fit, and was carried off; they sat it out, and were surprised, on inquiry, in the morning, to find that it was all over with poor sir Patrick. Never did any gentleman live and die more beloved in the country by rich and poor. His funeral was such a one as was never known before or since in the county! All the gentlemen in the three counties were at it; far and near, how they flocked: my great grandfather said, that to see all the women even in their red cloaks, you would have taken them for the army drawn out. Then such a fine whillaluh!° you might have heard it to the farthest end of the county, and happy the man who could get but a sight of the hearse! But who'd have thought it? just as all was going on right, through his own town they were passing, when the body was seized for debt—a rescue was apprehended from the mob; but the heir who attended the funeral was against that, for fear of consequences, seeing that those villains who came to serve acted under the disguise of the law: so, to be sure, the law must take its course, and little gain had the creditors for their pains. First and foremost, they had the curses of the country: and sir Murtagh Rackrent, the new heir, in the next

9. A traditional song included in John Fletcher and others, *Rollo, Duke of Normandy*, or *The Bloody Brother* (written 1617, revised 1627–30, published 1639).

place, on account of this affront to the body, refused to pay a shilling
of the debts, in which he was countenanced by all the best gentlemen
of property, and others of his acquaintance; sir Murtagh alleging in
all companies, that he all along meant to pay his father's debts of honour, but the moment the law was taken of him, there was an end of
honour to be sure. It was whispered (but none but the enemies of the
family believe it), that this was all a sham seizure to get quit of the
debts, which he had bound himself to pay in honour.

It's a long time ago, there's no saying how it was, but this for certain, the new man did not take at all after the old gentleman; the cel-
lars were never filled after his death, and no open house, or any thing
as it used to be; the tenants even were sent away without their whiskey.° I was ashamed myself, and knew not what to say for the honour
of the family; but I made the best of a bad case, and laid it all at my
lady's door, for I did not like her any how, nor any body else; she was
of the family of the Skinflints,[1] and a widow; it was a strange match
for sir Murtagh; the people in the country thought he demeaned himself greatly,° but I said nothing: I knew how it was; sir Murtagh was a
great lawyer, and looked to the great Skinflint estate; there, however,
he overshot himself; for though one of the co-heiresses, he was never
the better for her, for she outlived him many's the long day—he could
not see that to be sure when he married her. I must say for her, she
made him the best of wives, being a very notable stirring woman, and
looking close to every thing. But I always suspected she had Scotch
blood[2] in her veins; any thing else I could have looked over in her
from a regard to the family. She was a strict observer for self and servants of Lent, and all fast days, but not holidays. One of the maids
having fainted three times the last day of Lent, to keep soul and body
together, we put a morsel of roast beef into her mouth, which came
from sir Murtagh's dinner, who never fasted, not he; but somehow or
other it unfortunately reached my lady's ears, and the priest of the
parish had a complaint made of it the next day, and the poor girl was
forced as soon as she could walk to do penance for it, before she could
get any peace or absolution, in the house or out of it. However, my
lady was very charitable in her own way. She had a charity school for
poor children, where they were taught to read and write gratis, and
where they were kept well to spinning gratis for my lady in return; for
she had always heaps of duty yarn from the tenants, and got all her
household linen out of the estate from first to last; for after the spinning, the weavers on the estate took it in hand for nothing, because of

---

1. In keeping with Edgeworth's convention of employing descriptive character names, the
   assertion made by Thady is that Lady Murtagh was avaricious (see the following note).
2. A reference to the stereotype of the Scottish being frugal and a continuation of Thady's
   dislike of Lady Murtagh due to the restrictions, financial and otherwise, she placed on
   the estate.

the looms my lady's interest could get from the Linen Board[3] to dis-
tribute gratis. Then there was a bleach-yard near us, and the tenant
dare refuse my lady nothing, for fear of a law-suit sir Murtagh kept
hanging over him about the water-course. With these ways of manag-
ing, 'tis surprising how cheap my lady got things done, and how proud
she was of it. Her table the same way, kept for next to nothing; duty
fowls, and duty turkies, and duty geese,° came as fast as we could eat
'em, for my lady kept a sharp look-out, and knew to a tub of butter
every thing the tenants had, all round. They knew her way, and what
with fear of driving for rent and sir Murtagh's lawsuits, they were kept
in such good order, they never thought of coming near Castle Rackrent without a present of something or other—nothing too much or
too little for my lady—eggs, honey, butter, meal, fish, game, grouse,
and herrings, fresh or salt, all went for something. As for their young
pigs, we had them, and the best bacon and hams they could make up,
with all young chickens in spring; but they were a set of poor wretches,
and we had nothing but misfortunes with them, always breaking and
running away. This, sir Murtagh and my lady said, was all their former landlord sir Patrick's fault, who let 'em all get the half year's rent
into arrear; there was something in that to be sure. But sir Murtagh
was as much the contrary way; for let alone making English tenants°
of them, every soul, he was always driving and driving, and pounding
and pounding, and canting and canting,° and replevying[4] and replevying, and he made a good living of trespassing cattle; there was always
some tenant's pig, or horse, or cow, or calf, or goose, trespassing,
which was so great a gain to sir Murtagh, that he did not like to hear
me talk of repairing fences. Then his heriots[5] and duty-work brought
him in something, his turf was cut, his potatoes set and dug, his hay
brought home, and, in short, all the work about his house done for
nothing; for in all our leases there were strict clauses heavy with pen-
alties, which sir Murtagh knew well how to enforce; so many days'
duty work° of man and horse, from every tenant, he was to have, and
had, every year; and when a man vexed him, why the finest day he
could pitch on,[6] when the cratur was getting in his own harvest, or
thatching his cabin, sir Murtagh made it a principle to call upon him
and his horse; so he taught 'em all, as he said, to know the law of landlord and tenant. As for law, I believe no man, dead or alive, ever loved
it so well as sir Murtagh. He had once sixteen suits pending at a time,
and I never saw him so much himself; roads, lanes, bogs, wells, ponds,

---

3. The Board of Trustees of the Linen and Hempen Manufacturers of Ireland was formed
   in 1711 to oversee the linen trade.
4. Recovering goods, chattels, or land.
5. A legal custom restoring equipment and livestock to a lord following the death of a
   tenant.
6. Determine.

eel-wires, orchards, trees, tithes, vagrants, gravelpits, sandpits, dung-
hills, and nuisances, every thing upon the face of the earth furnished
him good matter for a suit. He used to boast that he had a lawsuit for
every letter in the alphabet. How I used to wonder to see sir Murtagh in the midst of the papers in his office! Why he could hardly
turn about for them. I made bold to shrug my shoulders once in his
presence, and thanked my stars I was not born a gentleman to so
much toil and trouble;[7] but sir Murtagh took me up short with his
old proverb, "learning is better than house or land."[8] Out of forty-
nine suits which he had, he never lost one but seventeen;° the rest
he gained with costs, double costs, treble costs sometimes; but even
that did not pay. He was a very learned man in the law, and had the
character of it; but how it was I can't tell, these suits that he carried
cost him a power of money; in the end he sold some hundreds a
year of the family estate; but he was a very learned man in the law,
and I know nothing of the matter, except having a great regard for
the family; and I could not help grieving when he sent me to post
up notices of the sale of the fee-simple of the lands and appurtenances[9] of Timoleague. "I know, honest Thady," says he, to comfort
me, "what I'm about better than you do; I'm only selling to get the
ready money wanting to carry on my suit with spirit with the Nugents
of Carrickashaughlin."

He was very sanguine about that suit with the Nugents of Carrickashaughlin. He could have gained it, they say, for certain, had it
pleased Heaven to have spared him to us, and it would have been at
the least a plump two thousand a year in his way; but things were
ordered otherwise, for the best to be sure. He dug up a fairy-mount°*[1]
against my advice, and had no luck afterwards. Though a learned
man in the law, he was a little too incredulous in other matters. I
warned him that I heard the very Banshee† that my grandfather

---

*   These fairy-mounts are called ant-hills in England. They are held in high reverence by
the common people in Ireland. A gentleman, who in laying out his lawn had occasion to
level one of these hillocks, could not prevail upon any of his labourers to begin the omi-
nous work. He was obliged to take a *loy* from one of their reluctant hands, and began the
attack himself. The labourers agreed, that the vengeance of the fairies would fall upon
the head of the presumptuous mortal, who first disturbed them in their retreat.
†   The Banshee is a species of aristocratic fairy, who, in the shape of a little hideous old
woman, has been known to appear, and heard to sing in a mournful supernatural voice
under the windows of great houses, to warn the family that some of them are soon to
die. In the last century every great family in Ireland had a Banshee, who attended regularly; but latterly their visits and songs have been discontinued.

---

7. Grappling with the issue of servants accepting their role in the social hierarchy was
something that Edgeworth had attempted in her juvenilia. See *The Double Disguise* on
pp. 103–10.
8. Samuel Foote, *Taste* (1752).
9. Minor properties, rights, or privileges (including improvements) that pass in possession along with the main property. "Fee-simple": an estate in land of which the owner
and his heirs have unqualified ownership.
1. "Loy": a spade (mentioned in the footnote).

heard under sir Patrick's window a few days before his death. But sir Murtagh thought nothing of the Banshee, nor of his cough with a spitting of blood, brought on, I understand, by catching cold in attending the courts, and overstraining his chest with making himself heard in one of his favourite causes. He was a great speaker with a powerful voice; but his last speech was not in the courts at all. He and my lady, though both of the same way of thinking in some things, and though she was as good a wife and great economist as you could see, and he the best of husbands, as to looking into his affairs, and making money for his family; yet I don't know how it was, they had a great deal of sparring and jarring between them. My lady had her privy purse—and she had her weed ashes,° and her sealing money° upon the signing of all the leases, with something to buy gloves besides; and, besides, again often took money from the tenants, if offered properly, to speak for them to sir Murtagh about abatements and renewals. Now the weed ashes and the glove money[2] he allowed her clear perquisites; though once when he saw her in a new gown saved out of the weed ashes, he told her to my face (for he could say a sharp thing,) that she should not put on her weeds before her husband's death. But in a dispute about an abatement, my lady would have the last word, and sir Murtagh grew mad;° I was within hearing of the door, and now I wish I had made bold to step in. He spoke so loud, the whole kitchen was out on the stairs.° All on a sudden he stopped and my lady too. Something has surely happened, thought I—and so it was, for sir Murtagh in his passion broke a blood-vessel, and all the law in the land could do nothing in that case. My lady sent for five physicians, but sir Murtagh died, and was buried. She had a fine jointure[3] settled upon her, and took herself away to the great joy of the tenantry. I never said any thing one way or the other, whilst she was part of the family, but got up to see her go at three o'clock in the morning. "It's a fine morning, honest Thady," says she; "good bye to ye," and into the carriage she stept, without a word more, good or bad, or even half a crown; but I made my bow, and stood to see her safe out of sight for the sake of the family.

Then we were all bustle in the house, which made me keep out of the way, for I walk slow and hate a bustle; but the house was all hurry-skurry, preparing for my new master. Sir Murtagh, I forgot to notice, had no childer;* so the Rackrent estate went to his younger

* *Childer:* this is the manner in which many of Thady's rank, and others in Ireland, *formerly* pronounced the word *children.*

2. Money provided to servants to purchase gloves. "Privy purse": money for personal expenses. "Abatements": most likely a reference to the tenants requesting a reduction to the cost of their leases.
3. Property used to provide for a woman after her husband's death.

brother, a young dashing officer, who came amongst us before I knew for the life of me whereabouts I was, in a gig or some of them things, with another spark along with him, and led horses, and servants, and dogs, and scarce a place to put any Christian of them into; for my late lady had sent all the feather-beds off before her, and blankets and household linen, down to the very knife cloths,[4] on the cars to Dublin, which were all her own, lawfully paid for out of her own money. So the house was quite bare, and my young master, the moment ever he set foot in it out of his gig, thought all those things must come of themselves, I believe, for he never looked after any thing at all, but harum-scarum called for every thing as if we were conjurers, or he in a public-house.[5] For my part, I could not bestir myself any how; I had been so much used to my late master and mistress, all was upside down with me, and the new servants in the servants' hall were quite out of my way; I had nobody to talk to and if it had not been for my pipe and tobacco, should, I verily believe, have broke my heart for poor sir Murtagh.

But one morning my new master caught a glimpse of me as I was looking at his horse's heels, in hopes of a word from him. "And is that old Thady?" says he, as he got into his gig: I loved him from that day to this, his voice was so like the family; and he threw me a guinea out of his waistcoat pocket, as he drew up the reins with the other hand, his horse rearing too; I thought I never set my eyes on a finer figure of a man, quite another sort from sir Murtagh; though withal, *to me*, a family likeness. A fine life we should have led, had he staid amongst us, God bless him! He valued a guinea as little as any man: money to him was no more than dirt, and his gentleman and groom, and all belonging to him, the same; but the sporting season over, he grew tired of the place, and having got down a great architect for the house, and an improver for the grounds, and seen their plans and elevations, he fixed a day for settling with the tenants, but went off in a whirlwind to town, just as some of them came into the yard in the morning. A circular letter came next post from the new agent, with news that the master was sailed for England, and he must remit £500.[6] to Bath for his use before a fortnight was at an end; bad news still for the poor tenants, no change still for the better with them. Sir Kit Rackrent, my young master, left all to the agent; and though he had the spirit of a prince, and lived away to the honour of his country abroad, which I was proud to hear of, what were

4. Most likely the cloths servants used to polish cutlery. The point Thady is making is that Lady Murtagh took everything with her when she left. "Gig": a light, two-wheeled one-horse carriage. "Spark": a fashionable young man.
5. Inn. "Harum-scarum": reckless. "Conjurers": magicians or wizards.
6. In the 1832 (and previous editions) this was displayed as "500*l.*" All occurrences have been emended to the modern pound sign. "Circular letter": a letter addressed to a number of recipients.

we the better for that at home? The agent was one of your middle
men,* who grind the face of the poor, and can never bear a man
with a hat upon his head: he ferretted[7] the tenants out of their lives;
not a week without a call for money, drafts upon drafts from sir Kit;
but I laid it all to the fault of the agent; for, says I, what can sir Kit
do with so much cash, and he a single man? but still it went. Rents
must be all paid up to the day, and afore; no allowance for improving tenants, no consideration for those who had built upon their
farms: no sooner was a lease out, but the land was advertised to the
highest bidder, all the old tenants turned out, when they spent their
substance in the hope and trust of a renewal from the landlord. All
was now set at the highest penny to a parcel of poor wretches, who
meant to run away, and did so, after taking two crops out of the
ground. Then fining down the year's rent° came into fashion; any
thing for the ready penny; and with all this, and presents to the
agent and the driver,° there was no such thing as standing it. I said
nothing, for I had a regard for the family; but I walked about thinking if his honour sir Kit knew all this, it would go hard with him,
but he'd see us righted; not that I had any thing for my own share
to complain of, for the agent was always very civil to me, when he
came down into the country, and took a great deal of notice of my
son Jason. Jason Quirk, though he be my son, I must say, was a good
scholar from his birth, and a very 'cute lad: I thought to make him
a priest,° but he did better for himself: seeing how he was as good a
clerk as any in the county, the agent gave him his rent accounts to
copy, which he did first of all for the pleasure of obliging the gentleman, and would take nothing at all for his trouble, but was always
proud to serve the family. By-and-bye a good farm bounding us to the
east fell into his honour's hands, and my son put in a proposal for it:
why shouldn't he, as well as another? The proposals all went over to
the master at the Bath, who knowing no more of the land than the

---

* *Middle men.*—There was a class of men termed middle men in Ireland, who took large
farms on long leases from gentlemen of landed property, and set the land again in small
portions to the poor, as under-tenants, at exorbitant rents. The *head landlord*, as he *was*
called, seldom saw his *under-tenants*; but if he could not get the *middle man* to pay him
his rent punctually, he *went to his land, and drove the land for his rent*, that is to say, he
sent his steward or bailiff, or driver, to the land to seize the cattle, hay, corn, flax, oats,
or potatoes, belonging to the under-tenants, and proceeded to sell these for his rents: it
sometimes happened that these unfortunate tenants paid their rent twice over, once to
the *middle man*, and once to the *head landlord*.

    The characteristics of a middle man *were*, servility to his superiors, and tyranny
towards his inferiors: the poor detested this race of beings. In speaking to them, however, they always used the most abject language, and the most humble tone and
posture.—"*Please your honour; and please your honour's honour,*" they knew must be
repeated as a charm at the beginning and end of every equivocating, exculpatory, or
supplicatory sentence; and they were much more alert in doffing their caps to these
new men, than to those of what they call *good old families*. A witty carpenter once
termed these middle men *journeymen gentlemen*.

---

7. Cheated.

child unborn, only having once been out a grousing on it before he went to England; and the value of lands, as the agent informed him, falling every year in Ireland, his honour wrote over in all haste a bit of a letter, saying he left it all to the agent, and that he must set it as well as he could to the best bidder, to be sure, and send him over £200 by return of post: with this the agent gave me a hint, and I spoke a good word for my son, and gave out in the country that nobody need bid against us. So his proposal was just the thing, and he a good tenant; and he got a promise of an abatement in the rent, after the first year, for advancing the half year's rent at signing the lease, which was wanting to complete the agent's £200 by the return of the post, with all which my master wrote back he was well satisfied. About this time we learned from the agent as a great secret, how the money went so fast, and the reason of the thick coming of the master's drafts: he was a litle too fond of play;[8] and Bath, they say, was no place for a young man of his fortune, where there were so many of his own countrymen too hunting him up and down, day and night, who had nothing to lose. At last, at Christmas, the agent wrote over to stop the drafts, for he could raise no more money on bond or mortgage, or from the tenants, or any how, nor had he any more to lend himself, and desired at the same time to decline the agency for the future, wishing sir Kit his health and happiness, and the compliments of the season, for I saw the letter before ever it was sealed, when my son copied it. When the answer came, there was a new turn in affairs, and the agent was turned out; and my son Jason, who had corresponded privately with his honour occasionally on business, was forthwith desired by his honour to take the accounts into his own hands, and look them over till further orders. It was a very spirited letter to be sure: sir Kit sent his service, and the compliments of the season, in return to the agent, and he would fight him with pleasure to-morrow, or any day, for sending him such a letter, if he was born a gentleman, which he was sorry (for both their sakes) to find (too late) he was not. Then, in a private postscript, he condescended to tell us, that all would be speedily settled to his satisfaction, and we should turn over a new leaf, for he was going to be married in a fortnight to the grandest heiress in England, and had only immediate occasion at present for £200, as he would not choose to touch his lady's fortune for travelling expences home to Castle Rackrent, where he intended to be, wind and weather permitting, early in the next month; and desired fires, and the house to be painted, and the new building to go on as fast as possible, for the reception of him and his lady before that time; with several words besides in the letter, which we could not make out, because, God

8. Gambling.

bless him! he wrote in such a flurry. My heart warmed to my new lady when I read this; I was almost afraid it was too good news to be true; but the girls fell to scouring, and it was well they did, for we soon saw his marriage in the paper to a lady with I don't know how many tens of thousand pounds to her fortune: then I watched the post-office for his landing; and the news came to my son of his and the bride being in Dublin, and on the way home to Castle Rackrent. We had bonfires all over the country, expecting him down the next day, and we had his coming of age still to celebrate, which he had not time to do properly before he left the country; therefore a great ball was expected, and great doings upon his coming, as it were, fresh to take possession of his ancestors' estate. I never shall forget the day he came home: we had waited and waited all day long till eleven o'clock at night, and I was thinking of sending the boy to lock the gates, and giving them up for that night, when there came the carriages thundering up to the great hall door. I got the first sight of the bride; for when the carriage door opened, just as she had her foot on the steps, I held the flam° full in her face to light her, at which she shut her eyes, but I had a full view of the rest of her, and greatly shocked I was, for by that light she was little better than a blackamoor,[9] and seemed crippled, but that was only sitting so long in the chariot. "You're kindly welcome to Castle Rackrent, my lady," says I (recollecting who she was); "did your honour hear of the bon-fires?" His honour spoke never a word, nor so much as handed her up the steps—he looked to me no more like himself than nothing at all; I know I took him for the skeleton of his honour: I was not sure what to say next to one or t'other, but seeing she was a stranger in a foreign country, I thought it but right to speak cheerful to her, so I went back again to the bonfires. "My lady," says I, as she crossed the hall, "there would have been fifty times as many, but for fear of the horses and frightening your ladyship: Jason and I forbid them, please your honour." With that she looked at me a little bewildered. "Will I have a fire lighted in the state room to-night?" was the next question I put to her, but never a word she answered, so I concluded she could not speak a word of English, and was from foreign parts. The short and the long of it was I couldn't tell what to make of her; so I left her to herself, and went straight down to the servants' hall to learn something for certain about her. Sir Kit's own man was tired, but the groom[1] set him a talking at last, and we had it all out before ever I closed my eyes that night. The bride might well be a great fortune—she was a *Jewish* by all accounts, who are famous for their great riches. I had never seen any of that tribe or nation before,

9. A dark-skinned person.
1. A servant who attends to horses.

and could only gather, that she spoke a strange kind of English of
her own, that she could not abide pork or sausages, and went neither
to church or mass. Mercy upon his honour's poor soul, thought I;
what will become of him and his, and all of us, with his heretic blackamoor at the head of the Castle Rackrent estate! I never slept a
wink all night for thinking of it; but before the servants I put my
pipe in my mouth, and kept my mind to myself; for I had a great
regard for the family; and after this, when strange gentlemen's servants came to the house, and would begin to talk about the bride, I
took care to put the best foot foremost, and passed her for a nabob[2]
in the kitchen, which accounted for her dark complexion and every
thing.

   The very morning after they came home, however, I saw how things
were plain enough between Sir Kit and my lady, though they were
walking together arm in arm after breakfast, looking at the new
building and the improvements. "Old Thady," said my master, just
as he used to do, "how do you do?" "Very well, I thank your honour's
honour," said I; but I saw he was not well pleased, and my heart was
in my mouth as I walked along after him. "Is the large room damp,
Thady?" said his honour. "Oh, damp, your honour! how should it
but be as dry as a bone," says I, "after all the fires we have kept in it
day and night? it's the barrack room° your honour's talking on." "And
what is a barrack-room, pray, my dear?" were the first words I ever
heard out of my lady's lips. "No matter, my dear!" said he, and went
on talking to me, ashamed like I should witness her ignorance. To
be sure, to hear her talk one might have taken her for an innocent,°
for it was, "what's this, sir Kit? and what's that, sir Kit?" all the way
we went. To be sure, sir Kit had enough to do to answer her. "And
what do you call that, sir Kit?" said she, "that, that looks like a pile
of black bricks, pray, sir Kit?" "My turf stack, my dear," said my
master, and bit his lip. Where have you lived, my lady, all your life,
not to know a turf stack when you see it, thought I, but I said nothing. Then, by-and-bye, she takes out her glass,[3] and begins spying
over the country. "And what's all that black swamp out yonder, sir
Kit?" says she. "My bog, my dear," says he, and went on whistling.
"It's a very ugly prospect, my dear," says she. "You don't see it, my
dear," says he, "for we've planted it out, when the trees grow up in
summer time," says he. "Where are the trees," said she, "my dear?"
still looking through her glass. "You are blind," my dear, says he;
"what are these under your eyes?" "These shrubs," said she. "Trees,"
said he. "May be they are what you call trees in Ireland, my dear,"
said she; "but they are not a yard high, are they?" "They were planted

2. A British person who amassed great wealth in India during the period of British rule.
3. Spyglass.

out but last year, my lady," says I, to soften matters between them, for I saw she was going the way to make his honour mad with her? "they are very well grown for their age, and you'll not see the bog of Allyballycarricko'shaughlin at-all-at-all through the skreen, when once the leaves come out. But, my lady, you must not quarrel with any part or parcel of Allyballycarricko'shaughlin, for you don't know how many hundred years that same bit of bog has been in the family; we would not part with the bog of Allyballycarricko'shaughlin upon no account at all; it cost the late Sir Murtagh two hundred good pounds to defend his title to it and boundaries against the O'Leary's, who cut a road through it." Now one would have thought this would have been hint enough for my lady, but she fell to laughing like one out of their right mind, and made me say the name of the bog over for her to get it by heart, a dozen times—then she must ask me how to spell it, and what was the meaning of it in English— sir Kit standing by whistling all the while; I verily believed she laid the corner stone of all her future misfortunes at that very instant; but I said no more, only looked at sir Kit.

There were no balls, no dinners, no doings; the country was all disappointed—sir Kit's gentleman said in a whisper to me, it was all my lady's own fault, because she was so obstinate about the cross. "What cross?" says I; "is it about her being a heretic?" "Oh, no such matter," says he; "my master does not mind her heresies, but her diamond cross, it's worth I can't tell you how much; and she has thousands of English pounds concealed in diamonds about her, which she as good as promised to give up to my master before he married, but now she won't part with any of them, and she must take the consequences."

Her honey-moon, at least her Irish honey-moon, was scarcely well over, when his honour one morning said to me, "Thady, buy me a pig!" and then the sausages were ordered, and here was the first open breaking-out of my lady's troubles. My lady came down herself into the kitchen, to speak to the cook about the sausages, and desired never to see them more at her table. Now my master had ordered them, and my lady knew that. The cook took my lady's part, because she never came down into the kitchen, and was young and innocent in house-keeping, which raised her pity; besides, said she, at her own table, surely, my lady should order and disorder what she pleases; but the cook soon changed her note, for my master made it a principle to have the sausages, and swore at her for a Jew herself, till he drove her fairly out of the kitchen; then, for fear of her place, and because he threatened that my lady should give her no discharge without the sausages, she gave up, and from that day forward always sausages, or bacon, or pig meat in some shape or other, went up to table; upon which my lady shut herself up in her own room, and my master said she might stay there, with an oath: and to make sure of her, he turned the key in the door, and kept it ever after in his pocket. We none of us ever saw or heard her speak for seven years after that:*4 he carried her dinner himself. Then his honour had a great deal of company to dine with him, and balls in the house, and was as gay and gallant, and as much himself as before he was married; and at dinner he always drank my lady Rackrent's good health, and so did the company, and he sent out always a servant, with his compliments to my lady Rackrent, and the company was drinking her ladyship's health, and begged to know if there was any thing at table he might send her; and the man came back, after the sham errand, with my lady Rackrent's compliments, and she was very much obliged to sir Kit—she did not wish for any thing,

---

* This part of the history of the Rackrent family can scarcely be thought credible; but in justice to honest Thady, it is hoped the reader will recollect the history of the celebrated lady Cathcart's conjugal imprisonment.—The editor was acquainted with colonel M'Guire, lady Cathcart's husband; he has lately seen and questioned the maid-servant who lived with colonel M'Guire during the time of lady Cathcart's imprisonment. Her ladyship was locked up in her own house for many years; during which period her husband was visited by the neighbouring gentry, and it was his regular custom at dinner to send his compliments to lady Cathcart, informing her that the company had the honour to drink her ladyship's health, and begging to know whether there was any thing at table that she would like to eat? the answer was always, "Lady Cathcart's compliments, and she has every thing she wants." An instance of honesty in a poor Irish woman deserves to be recorded:—Lady Cathcart had some remarkably fine diamonds, which she had concealed from her husband, and which she was anxious to get out of the house, lest he should discover them. She had neither servant nor friend to whom she could entrust them; but she had observed a poor beggar woman, who used to come to the house; she spoke to her from the window of the room in which she was confined; the woman promises to do what she desired, and lady Cathcart threw a parcel, containing the jewels, to her. The poor woman carried them to the person to whom they were directed; and several years afterwards, when lady Cathcart recovered her liberty, she received her diamonds safely.

At colonel M'Guire's death her ladyship was released. The editor, within this year, saw the gentleman who accompanied her to England after her husband's death. When she first was told of his death, she imagined that the news was not true, and that it was told only with an intention of deceiving her. At his death she had scarcely clothes sufficient to cover her; she wore a red wig, looked scared, and her understanding seemed stupified; she said that she scarcely knew one human creature from another; her imprisonment lasted above twenty years. These circumstances may appear strange to an English reader; but there is no danger in the present times, that any individual should exercise such tyranny as colonel M'Guire's with impunity, the power being now all in the hands of government, and there being no possibility of obtaining from parliament an act of indemnity for any cruelties.

---

4. "Conjugal imprisonment": a possible real life source for this event (mentioned in the footnote) is retold in an obituary of Elizabeth Malyn (Lady Cathcart, 1692?–1789) in *The Gentleman's Magazine*, 70 (1789), pp. 766–67. Lady Cathcart, the widow of the eighth Baron Cathcart, married Colonel Hugh Macguire in 1745. According to *The Gentleman's Magazine*, "The Hibernian fortune-hunter [Macguire] wanted only [Lady Cathcart's] money. Soon after she married him, she found that she had made a grievous mistake, for that he was desperately in love, not with the widow, but with the 'widow's jointur'd land'" (p. 766). When she refused to part with her fortune, the colonel abducted her and transported her to Ireland, where he kept her confined until her death. In a 1834 letter to Mrs. Stark, however, Edgeworth wrote that while she was aware of Lady Cathcart being "shut up by her husband," Colonel Macguire had no resemblance to Sir Kit and all Edgeworth knew of Lady Cathcart was "that she was fond of money, and would not give up her diamonds" (see the letter to Stark on p. 86).

but drank the company's health. The country, to be sure, talked and wondered at my lady's being shut up, but nobody chose to interfere or ask any impertinent questions, for they knew my master was a man very apt to give a short answer himself, and likely to call a man out[5] for it afterwards; he was a famous shot; had killed his man before he came of age, and nobody scarce dared look at him whilst at Bath. Sir Kit's character was so well known in the country, that he lived in peace and quietness ever after, and was a great favourite with the ladies, especially when in process of time, in the fifth year of her confinement, my lady Rackrent fell ill, and took entirely to her bed, and he gave out that she was now skin and bone, and could not last through the winter. In this he had two physicians' opinions to back him (for now he called in two physicians for her), and tried all his arts to get the diamond cross from her on her death-bed, and to get her to make a will in his favour of her separate possessions; but there she was too tough for him. He used to swear at her behind her back, after kneeling to her to her face, and call her in the presence of his gentleman his stiff-necked Israelite, though before he married her, that same gentleman told me he used to call her (how he could bring it out, I don't know) "my pretty Jessica!"[6] To be sure it must have been hard for her to guess what sort of a husband he reckoned to make her. When she was lying, to all expectation, on her death-bed of a broken heart, I could not but pity her, though she was a Jewish; and considering too it was no fault of hers to be taken with my master so young as she was at the Bath, and so fine a gentleman as sir Kit was when he courted her; and considering too, after all they had heard and seen of him as a husband, there were now no less than three ladies in our county talked of for his second wife, all at daggers drawn with each other, as his gentleman swore, at the balls, for sir Kit for their partner,—I could not but think them bewitched; but they all reasoned with themselves, that sir Kit would make a good husband to any Christian but a Jewish, I suppose, and especially as he was now a reformed rake;[7] and it was not known how my lady's fortune was settled in her will, nor how the Castle Rackrent estate was all mortgaged, and bonds out against him, for he was never cured of his gaming tricks; but that was the only fault he had, God bless him.

My lady had a sort of fit, and it was given out she was dead, by mistake: this brought things to a sad crisis for my poor master,—one of the three ladies showed his letters to her brother, and claimed his promises, whilst another did the same. I don't mention names. Sir Kit, in his defence, said he would meet any man who dared to

5. Challenge to a duel.
6. *Merchant of Venice* 5.1.21. "Stiff-necked": obstinate.
7. A stylish man with questionable morals.

question his conduct, and as to the ladies, they must settle it amongst them who was to be his second, and his third, and his fourth, whilst his first was still alive, to his mortification and theirs. Upon this, as upon all former occasions, he had the voice of the country with him, on account of the great spirit and propriety he acted with. He met and shot the first lady's brother; the next day he called out the second, who had a wooden leg; and their place of meeting by appointment being in a new ploughed field, the wooden-leg man stuck fast in it. Sir Kit, seeing his situation, with great candour fired his pistol over his head; upon which the seconds interposed, and convinced the parties there had been a slight misunderstanding between them; thereupon they shook hands cordially, and went home to dinner together. This gentleman, to show the world how they stood together, and by the advice of the friends of both parties, to re-establish his sister's injured reputation, went out with sir Kit as his second, and carried his message next day to the last of his adversaries: I never saw him in such fine spirits as that day he went out— sure enough he was within ames-ace[8] of getting quit handsomely of all his enemies; but unluckily, after hitting the tooth pick out of his adversary's finger and thumb, he received a ball in a vital part, and was brought home, in little better than an hour after the affair, speechless on a hand-barrow, to my lady. We got the key out of his pocket the first thing we did, and my son Jason ran to unlock the barrack-room, where my lady had been shut up for seven years, to acquaint her with the fatal accident. The surprise bereaved her of her senses at first, nor would she believe but we were putting some new trick upon her, to entrap her out of her jewels, for a great while, till Jason bethought himself of taking her to the window, and showed her the men bringing sir Kit up the avenue upon the hand-barrow, which had immediately the desired effect; for directly she burst into tears, and pulling her cross from her bosom, she kissed it with as great devotion as ever I witnessed; and lifting up her eyes to heaven, uttered some ejaculation, which none present heard; but I take the sense of it to be, she returned thanks for this unexpected interposition in her favour when she had least reason to expect it. My master was greatly lamented: there was no life in him when we lifted him off the barrow, so he was laid out immediately, and *waked* the same night. The country was all in an uproar about him, and not a soul but cried shame upon his murderer; who would have been hanged surely, if he could have been brought to his trial, whilst the gentlemen in the country were up about it; but he very prudently withdrew himself to the continent before the affair was made

---

8. On the verge of. An "ames-ace" is the lowest throw at dice; therefore, it is worth nothing and is seen as unlucky.

public. As for the young lady, who was the immediate cause of the fatal accident, however innocently, she could never show her head after at the balls in the county or any place; and by the advice of her friends and physicians, she was ordered soon after to Bath, where it was expected, if any where on this side of the grave, she would meet with the recovery of her health and lost peace of mind. As a proof of his great popularity, I need only add, that there was a song made upon my master's untimely death in the newspapers, which was in every body's mouth, singing up and down through the country, even down to the mountains, only three days after his unhappy exit. He was also greatly bemoaned at the Curragh,° where his cattle were well known; and all who had taken up his bets formerly were particularly inconsolable for his loss to society. His stud sold at the cant° at the greatest price ever known in the county; his favourite horses were chiefly disposed of amongst his particular friends, who would give any price for them for his sake; but no ready money was required by the new heir, who wished not to displease any of the gentlemen of the neighbourhood just upon his coming to settle amongst them; so a long credit was given where requisite, and the cash has never been gathered in from that day to this.

But to return to my lady:—She got surprisingly well after my master's decease. No sooner was it known for certain that he was dead, than all the gentlemen within twenty miles of us came in a body, as it were, to set my lady at liberty, and to protest against her confinement, which they now for the first time understood was against her own consent. The ladies too were as attentive as possible, striving who should be foremost with their morning visits; and they that saw the diamonds spoke very handsomely of them, but thought it a pity they were not bestowed, if it had so pleased God, upon a lady who would have become them better. All these civilities wrought little with my lady, for she had taken an unaccountable prejudice against the country, and every thing belonging to it, and was so partial to her native land, that after parting with the cook, which she did immediately upon my master's decease, I never knew her easy one instant, night or day, but when she was packing up to leave us. Had she meant to make any stay in Ireland, I stood a great chance of being a great favourite with her; for when she found I understood the weathercock,[9] she was always finding some pretence to be talking to me, and asking me which way the wind blew, and was it likely, did I think, to continue fair for England. But when I saw she had made up her mind to spend the rest of her days upon her own income and jewels in England, I considered her quite as a foreigner, and not at all any longer as part of the family. She gave no

9. Weathervane.

vails[1] to the servants at Castle Rackrent at parting, notwithstand-
ing the old proverb of *"as rich as a Jew,"* which, she being a Jewish,
they built upon with reason. But from first to last she brought nothing but misfortunes amongst us; and if it had not been all along
with her, his honour, sir Kit, would have been now alive in all appearance. Her diamond cross was, they say, at the bottom of it all; and it
was a shame for her, being his wife, not to show more duty, and to
have given it up when he condescended to ask so often for such a
bit of a trifle in his distresses, especially when he all along made it
no secret he married for money. But we will not bestow another
thought upon her. This much I thought it lay upon my conscience
to say, in justice to my poor master's memory.

'Tis an ill wind that blows nobody no good[2]—the same wind that
took the Jew lady Rackrent over to England brought over the new
heir to Castle Rackrent.

Here let me pause for breath in my story, for though I had a great
regard for every member of the family, yet without compare sir
Conolly, commonly called, for short, amongst his friends, sir Condy
Rackrent, was ever my great favourite, and, indeed, the most univer-
sally beloved man I had ever seen or heard of, not excepting his great
ancestor sir Patrick, to whose memory he, amongst other instances
of generosity, erected a handsome marble stone in the church of Castle Rackrent, setting forth in large letters his age, birth, parentage,
and many other virtues, concluding with the compliment so justly
due, that "sir Patrick Rackrent lived and died a monument of old
Irish hospitality."

Continuation of the Memoirs
of the Rackrent Family

History of Sir Conolly Rackrent

Sir Condy Rackrent, by the grace of God heir at law to the Castle
Rackrent estate, was a remote branch of the family: born to little or
no fortune of his own, he was bred to the bar; at which, having
many friends to push him, and no mean natural abilities of his own,
he doubtless would, in process of time, if he could have borne the
drudgery of that study, have been rapidly made king's counsel, at
the least; but things were disposed of otherwise, and he never went
the circuit[3] but twice, and then made no figure for want of a fee,

1. Tips.
2. See *The Double Disguise* on p. 110.
3. Court. "Bar": law. "King's counsel": to the crown in commonwealth jurisdictions. Known
   as the queen's counsel in the reign of a female sovereign.

and being unable to speak in public. He received his education chiefly in the college of Dublin; but before he came to years of discretion[4] lived in the country, in a small but slated house, within view of the end of the avenue. I remember him bare footed and headed, running through the street of O'Shaughlin's town, and playing at pitch and toss, ball, marbles, and what not, with the boys of the town, amongst whom my son Jason was a great favourite with him. As for me, he was ever my white-headed[5] boy: often's the time when I would call in at his father's, where I was always made welcome; he would slip down to me in the kitchen, and love to sit on my knee, whilst I told him stories of the family, and the blood from which he was sprung, and how he might look forward, if the *then* present man should die without childer, to being at the head of the Castle Rackrent estate. This was then spoke quite and clear at random to please the child, but it pleased Heaven to accomplish my prophecy afterwards, which gave him a great opinion of my judgment in business. He went to a little grammar-school with many others, and my son amongst the rest, who was in his class, and not a little useful to him in his book learning, which he acknowledged with gratitude ever after. These rudiments of his education thus completed, he got a-horseback, to which exercise he was ever addicted, and used to gallop over the country while yet but a slip of a boy, under the care of sir Kit's huntsman, who was very fond of him, and often lent him his gun, and took him out a-shooting under his own eye. By these means he became well acquainted and popular amongst the poor in the neighbourhood early; for there was not a cabin at which he had not stopped some morning or other, along with the huntsman, to drink a glass of burnt whiskey out of an eggshell, to do him good and warm his heart, and drive the cold out of his stomach. The old people always told him he was a great likeness of sir Patrick; which made him first have an ambition to take after him, as far as his fortune should allow. He left us when of an age to enter the college, and there completed his education and nineteenth year; for as he was not born to an estate, his friends thought it incumbent on them to give him the best education which could be had for love or money; and a great deal of money consequently was spent upon him at college and Temple. He was a very little altered for the worse by what he saw there of the great world; for when he came down into the country, to pay us a visit, we thought him just the same man as ever, hand and glove with every one, and as far from high,[6] though not without his own proper share of family pride, as

4. The age when a person can manage his or her own affairs. "College of Dublin": Trinity College.
5. Favorite.
6. Arrogant.

any man ever you see. Latterly, seeing how sir Kit and the Jewish
lived together, and that there was no one between him and the Castle Rackrent estate, he neglected to apply to the law as much as was
expected of him; and secretly many of the tenants, and others,
advanced him cash upon his note of hand value received, promising
bargains of leases and lawful interest, should he ever come into the
estate. All this was kept a great secret, for fear the present man,
hearing of it, should take it into his head to take it ill of poor Condy,
and so should cut him off for ever, by levying a fine, and suffering a
recovery to dock the entail.° Sir Murtagh would have been the man
for that; but sir Kit was too much taken up philandering to consider
the law in this case, or any other. These practices I have mentioned,
to account for the state of his affairs, I mean sir Condy's, upon his
coming into the Castle Rackrent estate. He could not command a
penny of his first year's income; which, and keeping no accounts,
and the great sight of company he did, with many other causes too
numerous to mention, was the origin of his distresses. My son Jason,
who was now established agent, and knew every thing, explained
matters out of the face to sir Conolly, and made him sensible of his
embarrassed situation. With a great nominal rent-roll, it was almost
all paid away in interest; which being for convenience suffered to
run on, soon doubled the principal, and sir Condy was obliged to
pass new bonds for the interest, now grown principal, and so on.
Whilst this was going on, my son requiring to be paid for his trouble, and many years' service in the family gratis, and sir Condy not
willing to take his affairs into his own hands, or to look them even
in the face, he gave my son a bargain of some acres, which fell out
of lease, at a reasonable rent. Jason set the land, as soon as his lease
was sealed, to under tenants, to make the rent, and got two hundred a-year profit rent; which was little enough considering his long
agency. He bought the land at twelve years' purchase two years
afterwards, when sir Condy was pushed for money on an execution,
and was at the same time allowed for his improvements thereon.
There was a sort of hunting-lodge upon the estate, convenient to
my son Jason's land, which he had his eye upon about this time;
and he was a little jealous of sir Condy, who talked of setting it to a
stranger, who was just come into the country—Captain Moneygawl
was the man. He was son and heir to the Moneygawls of Mount
Juliet's town, who had a great estate in the next county to ours; and
my master was loth to disoblige the young gentleman, whose heart
was set upon the lodge; so he wrote him back, that the lodge was at
his service, and if he would honour him with his company at Castle
Rackrent, they could ride over together some morning, and look at
it, before signing the lease. Accordingly the captain came over to
us, and he and sir Condy grew the greatest friends ever you see, and

were for ever out a-shooting or hunting together, and were very merry in the evenings; and sir Condy was invited of course to Mount Juliet's town; and the family intimacy that had been in sir Patrick's time was now recollected, and nothing would serve sir Condy but he must be three times a-week at the least with his new friends, which grieved me, who knew, by the captain's groom and gentleman, how they talked of him at Mount Juliet's town, making him quite, as one may say, a laughingstock and a butt for the whole company; but they were soon cured of *that* by an accident that surprised 'em not a little, as it did me. There was a bit of a scrawl[7] found upon the waiting-maid of old Mr. Moneygawl's youngest daughter, miss Isabella, that laid open the whole; and her father, they say, was like one out of his right mind, and swore it was the last thing he ever should have thought of, when he invited my master to his house, that his daughter should think of such a match. But their talk signified not a straw,[8] for, as miss Isabella's maid reported, her young mistress was fallen over head and ears in love with sir Condy, from the first time that ever her brother brought him into the house to dinner: the servant who waited that day behind my master's chair was the first who knew it, as he says; though it's hard to believe him, for he did not tell till a great while afterwards; but, however, it's likely enough, as the thing turned out, that he was not far out of the way; for towards the middle of dinner, as he says, they were talking of stage-plays, having a playhouse, and being great play-actors at Mount Juliet's town; and miss Isabella turns short to my master, and says, "Have you seen the play-bill, sir Condy?" "No, I have not," said he. "Then more shame for you," said the captain her brother, "not to know that my sister is to play Juliet to-night, who plays it better than any woman on or off the stage in all Ireland." "I am very happy to hear it," said sir Condy; and there the matter dropped for the present. But sir Condy all this time, and a great while afterwards, was at a terrible nonplus; for he had no liking, not he, to stage-plays, nor to miss Isabella either; to his mind, as it came out over a bowl of whiskey punch at home, his little Judy M'Quirk, who was daughter to a sister's son of mine, was worth twenty of miss Isabella. He had seen her often when he stopped at her father's cabin to drink whiskey out of the eggshell, out hunting, before he came to the estate, and, as she gave out, was under something like a promise of marriage to her. Any how, I could not but pity my poor master, who was so bothered between them, and he an easy-hearted man, that could not disoblige nobody, God bless him! To be sure, it was not his place to behave ungenerous to miss

7. A hurriedly and poorly written letter.
8. No importance.

Isabella, who had disobliged all her relations for his sake, as he remarked; and then she was locked up in her chamber, and forbid to think of him any more, which raised his spirit, because his family was, as he observed, as good as theirs at any rate, and the Rackrents a suitable match for the Moneygawls any day in the year: all which was true enough; but it grieved me to see, that upon the strength of all this, sir Condy was growing more in the mind to carry off miss Isabella to Scotland,[9] in spite of her relations, as she desired.

"It's all over with our poor Judy!" said I, with a heavy sigh, making bold to speak to him one night when he was a little cheerful, and standing in the servants' hall all alone with me, as was often his custom. "Not at all," said he; "I never was fonder of Judy than at this present speaking; and to prove it to you," said he, and he took from my hand a halfpenny, change that I had just got along with my tobacco, "and to prove it to you, Thady," says he, "it's a toss up with me which I should marry this minute, her or Mr. Moneygawl of Mount Juliet's town's daughter—so it is." "Oh, boo! boo!"* says I, making light of it, to see what he would go on to next; "your honour's joking, to be sure; there's no compare between our poor Judy and miss Isabella, who has a great fortune, they say." "I'm not a man to mind a fortune, nor never was," said Sir Condy, proudly, "whatever her friends may say; and to make short of it," says he, "I'm come to a determination upon the spot;" with that he swore such a terrible oath, as made me cross myself; "and by this book," said he, snatching up my ballad book, mistaking it for my prayer book, which lay in the window; "and by this book," says he, "and by all the books that ever were shut and opened, it's come to a toss-up with me, and I'll stand or fall by the toss; and so, Thady, hand me over that *pin*† out of the ink-horn," and he makes a cross on the smooth side of the halfpenny; "Judy M'Quirk," says he, "her mark."‡ God bless him! his hand was a little unsteadied by all the whiskey punch he had taken, but it was plain to see his heart was for poor Judy. My heart was all as one as in my mouth when I saw the halfpenny up in the air, but I said nothing at all; and when it came down, I was glad I had kept

---

* *Boo! boo!* an exclamation equivalent to *pshaw or nonsense.*
† *Pin,* read *pen.* It formerly was vulgarly pronounced *pin* in Ireland.
‡ *Her mark.* It *was* the custom in Ireland for those who could not write to make a cross to stand for their signature, as was formerly the practice of our English monarchs. The Editor inserts the fac-simile of an Irish *mark,* which may hereafter be valuable to a judicious antiquary—

Her
Judy × M'Quirk,
Mark.

In bonds or notes, signed in this manner, a witness is requisite, as the name is frequently written by him or her.

---

9. Under Scottish law minors didn't require the consent of parents to be married.

myself to myself, for to be sure now it was all over with poor Judy. "Judy's out a luck," said I, striving to laugh. "I'm out a luck," said he; and I never saw a man look so cast down: he took up the halfpenny off the flag, and walked away quite sober-like by the shock. Now, though as easy a man, you would think, as any in the wide world, there was no such thing as making him unsay one of these sort of vows,* which he had learned to reverence when young, as I well remember teaching him to toss up for bog-berries[1] on my knee. So I saw the affair was as good as settled between him and miss Isabella, and I had no more to say but to wish her joy, which I did the week afterwards, upon her return from Scotland with my poor master.

My new lady was young, as might be supposed of a lady that had been carried off, by her own consent, to Scotland; but I could only see her at first through her veil, which, from bashfulness or fashion, she kept over her face. "And am I to walk through all this crowd of people, my dearest love?" said she to sir Condy, meaning us servants and tenants, who had gathered at the back gate. "My dear," said sir Condy, "there's nothing for it but to walk, or to let me carry you as far as the house, for you see the back road is too narrow for a carriage, and the great piers have tumbled down across the front approach; so there's no driving the right way, by reason of the ruins." "Plato, thou reasonest well!"[2] said she, or words to that effect, which I could no ways understand; and again, when her foot stumbled against a broken bit of a car-wheel, she cried out, "Angels and ministers of grace defend us!"[3] Well, thought I, to be sure if she's no Jewish, like the last, she is a mad woman for certain, which is as bad: it would have been as well for my poor master to have taken up with poor Judy, who is in her right mind, any how.

She was dressed like a mad woman, moreover, more than like any one I ever saw afore or since, and I could not take my eyes off her, but still followed behind her, and her feathers on the top of her hat were broke going in at the low back door, and she pulled out her little bottle out of her pocket to smell to when she found herself in the kitchen, and said, "I shall faint with the heat of this odious, odious place." "My dear, it's only three steps across the kitchen, and there's a fine air if your veil was up," said sir Condy, and with

---

* *Vows.*—It has been maliciously and unjustly hinted, that the lower classes of the people in Ireland pay but little regard to oaths; yet it is certain that some oaths or vows have great power over their minds. Sometimes they swear they will be revenged on some of their neighbours; this is an oath that they are never known to break. But, what is infinitely more extraordinary and unaccountable, they sometimes make and keep a vow against whiskey; these vows are usually limited to a short time. A woman who has a drunken husband is most fortunate if she can prevail upon him to go to the priest, and make a vow against whiskey for a year, or a month, or a week, or a day.

1. Wild berries.
2. Joseph Addison, *Cato* 5.1.
3. *Hamlet* 1.4.39.

that threw back her veil, so that I had then a full sight of her face;
she had not at all the colour of one going to faint, but a fine complexion of her own, as I then took it to be, though her maid told me
after it was all put on; but even complexion and all taken in, she
was no way, in point of good looks, to compare to poor Judy; and
with all she had a quality toss[4] with her; but may be it was my over-
partiality to Judy, into whose place I may say she stept, that made
me notice all this. To do her justice, however, she was, when we
came to know her better, very liberal in her housekeeping, nothing
at all of the skin-flint in her; she left every thing to the housekeeper;
and her own maid, Mrs. Jane, who went with her to Scotland, gave
her the best of characters for generosity. She seldom or ever wore a
thing twice the same way, Mrs. Jane told us, and was always pulling
her things to pieces, and giving them away, never being used, in her
father's house, to think of expence in any thing; and she reckoned,
to be sure, to go on the same way at Castle Rackrent; but, when I
came to inquire, I learned that her father was so mad with her for
running off, after his locking her up, and forbidding her to think
any more of sir Condy, that he would not give her a farthing;[5] and it
was lucky for her she had a few thousands of her own, which had
been left to her by a good grandmother, and these were very convenient to begin with. My master and my lady set out in great style;
they had the finest coach and chariot, and horses and liveries,[6] and
cut the greatest dash in the county, returning their wedding visits;
and it was immediately reported, that her father had undertaken to
pay all my master's debts, and of course all his tradesmen gave him
a new credit, and every thing went on smack smooth, and I could
not but admire my lady's spirit, and was proud to see Castle Rackrent again in all its glory. My lady had a fine taste for building, and
furniture, and playhouses, and she turned every thing topsy-turvy,
and made the barrack-room into a theatre, as she called it, and she
went on as if she had a mint of money at her elbow; and, to be sure,
I thought she knew best, especially as sir Condy said nothing to it
one way or the other. All he asked, God bless him! was to live in
peace and quietness, and have his bottle or his whiskey punch at
night to himself. Now this was little enough, to be sure, for any gentleman; but my lady couldn't abide the smell of the whiskey punch.
"My dear," says he, "you liked it well enough before we were married, and why not now?" "My dear," said she, "I never smelt it, or I
assure you I should never have prevailed upon myself to marry you."

---

4. Toss of her hair in an arrogant fashion.
5. Quarter of a penny. Used here to denote the lack of financial support provided by Captain Moneygawl.
6. Stables. "Coach": typically an enclosed four-wheel horse-drawn carriage. "Chariot": an
   open two-wheel horse-drawn carriage.

"My dear, I am sorry you did not smell it, but we can't help that now," returned my master, without putting himself in a passion, or going out of his way, but just fair and easy helped himself to another glass, and drank it off to her good health. All this the butler told me, who was going backwards and forwards unnoticed with the jug, and hot water, and sugar, and all he thought wanting. Upon my master's swallowing the last glass of whiskey punch my lady burst into tears, calling him an ungrateful, base, barbarous wretch! and went off into a fit of hysterics, as I think Mrs. Jane called it, and my poor master was greatly frightened, this being the first thing of the kind he had seen; and he fell straight on his knees before her, and, like a good-hearted cratur as he was, ordered the whiskey punch out of the room, and bid 'em throw open all the windows, and cursed himself: and then my lady came to herself again, and when she saw him kneeling there bid him get up, and not forswear himself any more, for that she was sure he did not love her, nor never had: this we learnt from Mrs. Jane, who was the only person left present at all this. "My dear," returns my master, thinking, to be sure, of Judy, as well he might, "whoever told you so is an incendiary, and I'll have 'em turned out of the house this minute, if you'll only let me know which of them it was." "Told me what?" said my lady, starting upright in her chair. "Nothing at all, nothing at all," said my master, seeing he had overshot himself, and that my lady spoke at random; "but what you said just now, that I did not love you, Bella; who told you that?" "My own sense," she said, and she put her handkerchief to her face, and leant back upon Mrs. Jane, and fell to sobbing as if her heart would break. "Why now, Bella, this is very strange of you," said my poor master; "if nobody has told you nothing, what is it you are taking on for at this rate, and exposing yourself and me for this way?" "Oh, say no more, say no more; every word you say kills me," cried my lady; and she ran on like one, as Mrs. Jane says, raving, "Oh, sir Condy, sir Condy! I that had hoped to find in you—" "Why now, faith, this is a little too much; do, Bella, try to recollect yourself, my dear; am not I your husband, and of your own choosing; and is not that enough?" "Oh, too much! too much!" cried my lady, wringing her hands. "Why, my dear, come to your right senses, for the love of heaven. See, is not the whiskey punch, jug and bowl, and all, gone out of the room long ago? What is it, in the wide world, you have to complain of?" But still my lady sobbed and sobbed, and called herself the most wretched of women; and among other out-of-the-way provoking things, asked my master, was he fit for company for her, and he drinking all night? This nettling[7] him, which it was hard to do, he replied, that as to drinking all

7. Provoking.

night, he was then as sober as she was herself, and that it was no matter how much a man drank, provided it did no ways affect or stagger him: that as to being fit company for her, he thought himself of a family to be fit company for any lord or lady in the land; but that he never prevented her from seeing and keeping what company she pleased, and that he had done his best to make Castle Rackrent pleasing to her since her marriage, having always had the house full of visitors, and if her own relations were not amongst them, he said that was their own fault, and their pride's fault, of which he was sorry to find her ladyship had so unbecoming a share. So concluding, he took his candle and walked off to his room, and my lady was in her tantarums for three days after; and would have been so much longer, no doubt, but some of her friends, young ladies, and cousins, and second cousins, came to Castle Rackrent, by my poor master's express invitation, to see her, and she was in a hurry to get up, as Mrs. Jane called it, a play for them, and so got well, and was as finely dressed, and as happy to look at, as ever; and all the young ladies, who used to be in her room dressing of her, said, in Mrs. Jane's hearing, that my lady was the happiest bride ever they had seen, and that to be sure a love-match was the only thing for happiness, where the parties could any way afford it.

As to affording it, God knows it was little they knew of the matter; my lady's few thousands could not last for ever, especially the way she went on with them, and letters from tradesfolk came every post thick and threefold with bills as long as my arm, of years' and years' standing; my son Jason had 'em all handed over to him, and the pressing letters were all unread by sir Condy, who hated trouble, and could never be brought to hear talk of business, but still put it off and put it off, saying, settle it any how, or bid 'em call again to-morrow, or speak to me about it some other time. Now it was hard to find the right time to speak, for in the mornings he was a-bed, and in the evenings over his bottle, where no gentleman chooses to be disturbed. Things in a twelvemonth or so came to such a pass there was no making a shift to go on any longer, though we were all of us well enough used to live from hand to mouth at Castle Rackrent. One day, I remember, when there was a power of company,[8] all sitting after dinner in the dusk, not to say dark, in the drawing-room, my lady having rung five times for candles, and none to go up, the housekeeper sent up the footman, who went to my mistress, and whispered behind her chair how it was. "My lady," says he, "there are no candles in the house." "Bless me," says she, "then take a horse and gallop off as fast as you can to Carrick O'Fungus, and get some." "And in the mean time tell them to step into the playhouse,

8. A group traveling together.

and try if there are not some bits left," added sir Condy, who happened to be within hearing. The man was sent up again to my lady,
to let her know there was no horse to go, but one that wanted a
shoe. "Go to sir Condy, then; I know nothing at all about the
horses," said my lady; "why do you plague me with these things?"
How it was settled I really forget, but to the best of my remem-
brance, the boy was sent down to my son Jason's to borrow candles
for the night. Another time in the winter, and on a desperate cold
day, there was no turf in for the parlour and above stairs, and scarce
enough for the cook in the kitchen; the little *gossoon** was sent off
to the neighbours, to see and beg or borrow some, but none could
he bring back with him for love or money; so as needs must, we
were forced to trouble sir Condy—"Well, and if there's no turf to be
had in the town or country, why what signifies talking any more
about it; can't ye go and cut down a tree?" "Which tree, please your
honour?" I made bold to say. "Any tree at all that's good to burn,"
said sir Condy; "send off smart and get one down, and the fires
lighted, before my lady gets up to breakfast, or the house will be too
hot to hold us." He was always very considerate in all things about
my lady, and she wanted for nothing whilst he had it to give. Well,
when things were tight with them about this time, my son Jason put
in a word again about the lodge, and made a genteel offer to lay
down the purchase-money, to relieve sir Condy's distresses. Now sir
Condy had it from the best authority, that there were two writs[9]
come down to the sheriff against his person, and the sheriff, as ill
luck would have it, was no friend of his, and talked how he must do
his duty, and how he would do it, if it was against the first man in
the country, or even his own brother; let alone one who had voted
against him at the last election, as sir Condy had done. So sir Condy
was fain to take the purchase-money of the lodge from my son
Jason to settle matters; and sure enough it was a good bargain for
both parties, for my son bought the fee-simple of a good house for
him and his heirs for ever, for little or nothing, and by selling of it
for that same, my master saved himself from a gaol.[1] Every way it
turned out fortunate for sir Condy; for before the money was all
gone there came a general election, and he being so well beloved in
the county, and one of the oldest families, no one had a better right
to stand candidate for the vacancy; and he was called upon by all his

---

* *Gossoon*, a little boy—from the French word *garçon*. In most Irish families there *used*
to be a barefooted gossoon, who was slave to the cook and the butler, and who in fact,
without wages, did all the hard work of the house. Gossoons were always employed as
messengers. The Editor has known a gossoon to go on foot, without shoes or stockings,
fifty-one English miles between sunrise and sunset.

9. Summons.
1. Jail. "Fain": glad.

friends, and the whole county I may say, to declare himself against
the old member, who had little thought of a contest. My master did
not relish the thoughts of a troublesome canvass, and all the ill-will
he might bring upon himself by disturbing the peace of the county,
besides the expence, which was no trifle; but all his friends called
upon one another to subscribe,[2] and they formed themselves into a
committee, and wrote all his circular letters for him, and engaged
all his agents, and did all the business unknown to him; and he was
well pleased that it should be so at last, and my lady herself was very
sanguine about the election; and there was open house kept night
and day at Castle Rackrent, and I thought I never saw my lady look
so well in her life as she did at that time; there were grand dinners,
and all the gentlemen drinking success to sir Condy till they were
carried off; and then dances and balls, and the ladies all finishing
with a raking pot of tea° in the morning. Indeed it was well the
company made it their choice to sit up all nights, for there were not
half beds enough for the sights of people that were in it, though
there were shakedowns[3] in the drawing-room always made up
before sunrise for those that liked it. For my part, when I saw the
doings that were going on, and the loads of claret that went down
the throats of them that had no right to be asking for it, and the
sights of meat that went up to table and never came down, besides
what was carried off to one or t'other below stairs, I could'nt but
pity my poor master, who was to pay for all; but I said nothing, for
fear of gaining myself ill-will. The day of election will come some
time or other, says I to myself, and all will be over; and so it did, and
a glorious day it was as any I ever had the happiness to see. "Huzza![4]
huzza! sir Condy Rackrent for ever!" was the first thing I hears in
the morning, and the same and nothing else all day, and not a soul
sober only just when polling, enough to give their votes as became
'em, and to stand the browbeating of the lawyers, who came tight
enough upon us; and many of our freeholders[5] were knocked off,
having never a freehold that they could safely swear to, and sir
Condy was not willing to have any man perjure himself for his sake,
as was done on the other side, God knows, but no matter for that.
Some of our friends were dumb-founded, by the lawyers asking
them: Had they ever been upon the ground where their freeholds
lay? Now sir Condy being tender of the consciences of them that
had not been on the ground, and so could not swear to a freehold

2. Provide funds and support for Sir Condy's election campaign. "Canvass": personally
   soliciting votes before an election.
3. Makeshift beds.
4. A cheer of excitement.
5. Landowners who therefore have the right to vote and to be elected to Parliament.
   "Browbeating": discouragement.

when cross-examined by them lawyers, sent out for a couple of cleaves-full of the sods[6] of his farm of Gulteeshinnagh:* and as soon as the sods came into town he set each man upon his sod, and so then, ever after, you know, they could fairly swear they had been upon the ground.† We gained the day by this piece of honesty.° I thought I should have died in the streets for joy when I seed my poor master chaired, and he bareheaded, and it raining as hard as it could pour; but all the crowds following him up and down, and he bowing and shaking hands with the whole town. "Is that sir Condy Rackrent in the chair?" says a stranger man in the crowd. "The same," says I; "who else should it be? God bless him!" "And I take it, then, you belong to him?" says he. "Not at all," says I; "but I live under him, and have done so these two hundred years and upwards, me and mine." "It's lucky for you, then," rejoins he, "that he is where he is; for was he any where else but in the chair, this minute he'd be in a worse place; for I was sent down on purpose to put him up,‡ and here's my order for so doing in my pocket." It was a writ that villain the wine merchant had marked against my poor master for some hundreds of an old debt, which it was a shame to be talking of at such a time as this. "Put it in your pocket again, and think no more of it any ways for seven years to come, my honest friend," says I; "he's a member of parliament now, praised be God, and such as you can't touch him: and if you'll take a fool's advice, I'd have you keep out of the way this day, or you'll run a good chance of getting your deserts amongst my master's friends, unless you choose to drink his health like every body else." "I've no objection to that in life," said he; so we went into one of the public houses kept open for my master; and we had a great deal of talk about this thing and that. "And how is it," says he, "your master keeps on so well upon his legs? I heard say he was off Holantide twelvemonth past." "Never was better or heartier in his life," said I. "It's not that I'm after speaking of," said he; "but there was a great report of his being ruined." "No matter," says I, "the sheriffs two years running were his particular friends, and the sub-sheriffs were both of them gentlemen, and were properly spoken to; and so the writs lay snug with them, and they, as I understand by my son Jason the custom in

---

* At St. Patrick's meeting, London, March, 1806, the duke of Sussex said he had the honour of bearing an Irish title, and, with the permission of the company, he should tell them an anecdote of what he had experienced on his travels. When he was at Rome, he went to visit an Irish seminary, and when they heard who he was, and that he had an Irish title, some of them asked him, "Please your Royal Highness, since you are an Irish peer, will you tell us if you ever trod upon Irish ground?" When he told them he had not, "O then," said one of the order, "you shall soon do so." They then spread some earth, which had been brought from Ireland, on a marble slab, and made him stand upon it.
† This was actually done at an election in Ireland.
‡ *To put him up*—to put him in gaol.

---

6. Turf. "Cleaves": baskets.

them cases is, returned the writs as they came to them to those that sent 'em; much good may it do them! with a word in Latin, that no such person as sir Condy Rackrent, bart.,[7] was to be found in those parts." "Oh, I understand all those ways better, no offence, than you," says he, laughing, and at the same time filling his glass to my master's good health, which convinced me he was a warm friend in his heart after all, though appearances were a little suspicious or so at first. "To be sure," says he, still cutting his joke, "when a man's over head and shoulders in debt, he may live the faster for it, and the better, if he goes the right way about it; or else how is it so many live on so well, as we see every day, after they are ruined?" "How is it," says I, being a little merry at the time; "how is it but just as you see the ducks in the chicken-yard, just after their heads are cut off by the cook, running round and round faster than when alive?" At which conceit he fell a laughing, and remarked he had never had the happiness yet to see the chicken-yard at Castle Rackrent. "It won't be long so, I hope," says I; "you'll be kindly welcome there, as every body is made by my master; there is not a freer spoken gentleman, or a better beloved, high or low, in all Ireland." And of what passed after this I'm not sensible, for we drank sir Condy's good health and the downfall of his enemies till we could stand no longer ourselves. And little did I think at the time, or till long after, how I was harbouring my poor master's greatest of enemies myself. This fellow had the impudence, after coming to see the chicken-yard, to get me to introduce him to my son Jason; little more than the man that never was born did I guess at his meaning by this visit: he gets him a correct list fairly drawn out from my son Jason of all my master's debts, and goes straight round to the creditors and buys them all up, which he did easy enough, seeing the half of them never expected to see their money out of sir Condy's hands. Then, when this base-minded limb of the law, as I afterward detected him in being, grew to be sole creditor over all, he takes him out a custodiam[8] on all the denominations and sub-denominations, and every carton and half carton° upon the estate; and not content with that, must have an execution against the master's goods and down to the furniture, though little worth, of Castle Rackrent itself. But this is a part of my story I'm not come to yet, and its bad to be forestalling: ill news flies fast enough all the world over.

To go back to the day of the election, which I never think off but with pleasure and tears of gratitude for those good times; after the election was quite and clean over, there comes shoals[9] of people from all parts, claiming to have obliged my master with their votes, and putting him in mind of promises which he could never remember himself to have made; one was to have a freehold for each of his four sons; another was to have a renewal of a lease; another an abatement; one came to be paid ten guineas for a pair of silver buckles sold my master on the hustings,[1] which turned out to be no better than copper gilt; another had a long bill for oats, the half of which never went into the granary to my certain knowledge, and the other half were not fit for the cattle to touch; but the bargain was made the week before the election, and the coach and saddle horses were got into order for the day, besides a vote fairly got by them oats; so no more reasoning on that head; but then there was no end to them that were telling sir Condy he had engaged to make their sons excisemen, or high constables, or the like; and as for them that had bills to give in for liquor, and beds, and straw, and ribands, and horses, and postchaises[2] for the gentlemen freeholders that came from all parts and other counties to vote for my master, and were not, to be sure, to be at any charges, there was no standing against all these; and, worse than all, the gentlemen of my master's committee, who managed all for him, and talked how they'd bring him in without costing him a penny, and subscribed by hundreds very genteelly, forgot to pay their subscriptions, and had laid out in agents and lawyers' fees and secret service money the Lord knows how much; and my master could never ask one of them for their subscription you are sensible, nor for the price of a fine horse he had sold one of them; so it all was left at his door. He could never, God bless him again! I say, bring himself to ask a gentleman for money, despising such sort of conversation himself; but others, who were not gentlemen born, behaved very uncivil in pressing him at this very time, and all he could do to content 'em all was to take himself out of the way as fast as possible to Dublin, where my lady had taken a house fitting for him as a member of parliament, to attend his duty in there all the winter. I was very lonely when the whole family was gone, and all the things they had ordered to go, and forgot, sent after them by the car. There was then a great silence in Castle Rackent, and I went moping from room to room, hearing the doors clap for want of right locks, and the wind through the broken windows, that the glazier never would come to mend, and the rain coming through the roof and best ceilings all over the house for want of the slater, whose bill was not paid, besides our having no slates or shingles for that part of the old building which was shingled and burnt when the

---

1. A platform on which candidates for Parliament stood while addressing the voters.
2. Typically horse-drawn four-wheeled carriages. "Excisemen": government officials who collect excise duties and prevent infringement of the excise laws.

chimney took fire, and had been open to the weather ever since. I took myself to the servants' hall in the evening to smoke my pipe as usual, but missed the bit of talk we used to have there sadly, and ever after was content to stay in the kitchen and boil my little potatoes,* and put up my bed there; and every post-day I looked in the newspaper, but no news of my master in the house; he never spoke good or bad; but as the butler wrote down word to my son Jason, was very ill used by the government about a place that was promised him and never given, after his supporting them against his conscience very honourably, and being greatly abused for it, which hurt him greatly, he having the name of a great patriot in the country before. The house and living in Dublin too were not to be had for nothing, and my son Jason said, "Sir Condy must soon be looking out for a new agent, for I've done my part, and can do no more:—if my lady had the bank of Ireland to spend, it would go all in one winter, and sir Condy would never gainsay[3] her, though he does not care the rind of a lemon for her all the while."

Now I could not bear to hear Jason giving out after this manner against the family, and twenty people standing by in the street. Ever since he had lived at the lodge of his own, he looked down, howsomever, upon poor old Thady, and was grown quite a great gentleman, and had none of his relations near him; no wonder he was no kinder to poor sir Condy than to his own kith or kin.[†] In the spring it was the villain that got the list of the debts from him brought down the custodiam, Sir Condy still attending his duty in parliament, and I could scarcely believe my own old eyes, or the spectacles with which I read it, when I was shown my son Jason's name joined in the custodiam; but he told me it was only for form's sake, and to make things easier than if all the land was under the power of a total stranger. Well, I did not know what to think; it was hard to be talking ill of my own, and I could not but grieve for my poor master's fine estate, all torn by these vultures of the law; so I said nothing, but just looked on to see how it would all end.

It was not till the month of June that he and my lady came down to the country. My master was pleased to take me aside with him to the brewhouse that same evening, to complain to me of my son and other matters, in which he said he was confident I had neither art nor part; he said a great deal more to me, to whom he had been fond to talk ever since he was my white-headed boy, before he came to the estate; and all that he said about poor Judy I can never forget,

---

* *My little potatoes*—Thady does not mean, by this expression, that his potatoes were less than other people's, or less than the usual size—*little* is here used only as an Italian diminutive, expressive of fondness.

† *Kith* and *kin*—family or relations. *Kin* from *kind*; *kith* from we know not what.

---

3. Contradict.

but scorn to repeat. He did not say an unkind word of my lady, but
wondered, as well he might, her relations would do nothing for him
or her, and they in all this great distress. He did not take any thing
long to heart, let it be as it would, and had no more malice, or thought
of the like in him, than a child that can't speak; this night it was all
out of his head before he went to his bed. He took his jug of whiskey punch—my lady was grown quite easy about the whiskey punch
by this time, and so I did suppose all was going on right betwixt[4]
them, till I learnt the truth through Mrs. Jane, who talked over
their affairs to the housekeeper, and I within hearing. The night my
master came home thinking of nothing at all but just making merry,
he drank his bumper toast "to the deserts of that old curmudgeon[5]
my father-in-law, and all enemies at Mount Juliet's town." Now my
lady was no longer in the mind she formerly was, and did no ways
relish hearing her own friends abused in her presence, she said.
"Then why don't they show themselves your friends," said my master, "and oblige me with the loan of the money I condescended, by
your advice, my dear, to ask? It's now three posts since I sent off my
letter, desiring in the postscript a speedy answer by the return of
the post, and no account at all from them yet." "I expect they'll
write to *me* next post," says my lady, and that was all that passed
then; but it was easy from this to guess there was a coolness betwixt
them, and with good cause.

The next morning, being post-day, I sent off the gossoon early to
the post-office, to see was there any letter likely to set matters to
rights, and he brought back one with the proper post-mark upon it,
sure enough, and I had no time to examine, or make any conjecture
more about it, for into the servants' hall pops Mrs. Jane with a blue
bandbox[6] in her hand, quite entirely mad. "Dear ma'am, and what's
the matter?" says I. "Matter enough," says she; "don't you see my
bandbox is wet through, and my best bonnet here spoiled, besides
my lady's, and all by the rain coming in through that gallery window, that you might have got mended, if you'd had any sense,
Thady, all the time we were in town in the winter." "Sure I could not
get the glazier, ma'am," says I. "You might have stopped it up any
how," says she. "So I did, ma'am, to the best of my ability; one of the
panes with the old pillow-case, and the other with a piece of the old
stage green curtain; sure I was as careful as possible all the time
you were away, and not a drop of rain came in at that window of all
the windows in the house, all winter, ma'am, when under my care;
and now the family's come home, and it's summer time, I never

4. Between.
5. Ill-tempered person.
6. Cardboard box for carrying hats.

thought no more about it, to be sure; but dear, it's a pity to think of your bonnet, ma'am; but here's what will please you, ma'am, a letter from Mount Juliet's town for my lady." With that she snatches it from me without a word more, and runs up the back stairs to my mistress; I follows with a slate to make up the window. This window was in the long passage, or gallery, as my lady gave out orders to have it called, in the gallery leading to my master's bedchamber and hers. And when I went up with the slate, the door having no lock, and the bolt spoilt, was a-jar after Mrs. Jane, and as I was busy with the window, I heard all that was saying within.

"Well, what's in your letter, Bella, my dear?" says he: "you're a long time spelling[7] it over." "Wont you shave this morning, sir Condy?" says she, and put the letter into her pocket. "I shaved the day before yesterday," says he, "my dear, and that's not what I'm thinking of now; but any thing to oblige you, and to have peace and quietness, my dear" —and presently I had the glimpse of him at the cracked glass over the chimney-piece, standing up shaving himself to please my lady. But she took no notice, but went on reading her book, and Mrs. Jane doing her hair behind. "What is it you're reading there, my dear?—phoo,[8] I've cut myself with this razor; the man's a cheat that sold it me, but I have not paid him for it yet: what is it you're reading there? did you hear me asking you, my dear?" "The Sorrows of Werter,"[9] replies my lady, as well as I could hear. "I think more of the sorrows of sir Condy," says my master, joking like. "What news from Mount Juliet's town?" "No news," says she, "but the old story over again, my friends all reproaching me still for what I can't help now." "Is it for marrying me?" said my master, still shaving: "what signifies, as you say, talking of that, when it can't be help'd now?"

With that she heaved a great sigh, that I heard plain enough in the passage. "And did not you use me basely, sir Condy," says she, "not to tell me you were ruined before I married you?" "Tell you, my dear," said he; "did you ever ask me one word about it? and had not you friends enough of your own, that were telling you nothing else from morning to night, if you'd have listened to them slanders?" "No slanders, nor are my friends slanderers; and I can't bear to hear them treated with disrespect as I do," says my lady, and took out her pocket handkerchief; "they are the best of friends; and if I had taken their advice—. But my father was wrong to lock me up, I own; that was the only unkind thing I can charge him with; for if he had not locked me up, I should never have had a serious thought

7. Looking.
8. For Edgeworth's earliest use of this expression, see *The Double Disguise* on p. 109.
9. Johann Wolfgang von Goethe's *The Sorrows of Young Werther*, first translated into English in 1779.

of running away as I did." "Well, my dear," said my master, "don't cry and make yourself uneasy about it now, when it's all over, and you have the man of your own choice, in spite of 'em all." "I was too young, I know, to make a choice at the time you ran away with me, I'm sure," says my lady, and another sigh, which made my master, half shaved as he was, turn round upon her in surprise. "Why, Bell," says he, "you can't deny what you know as well as I do, that it was at your own particular desire, and that twice under your own hand and seal expressed, that I should carry you off as I did to Scotland, and marry you there." "Well, say no more about it, sir Condy," said my lady, pettish like[1]—"I was a child then, you know." "And as far as I know, you're little better now, my dear Bella, to be talking in this manner to your husband's *face*; but I won't take it ill of you, for I know it's something in that letter you put into your pocket just now, that has set you against me all on a sudden, and imposed upon your understanding." "It is not so very easy as you think it, sir Condy, to impose upon *my* understanding," said my lady. "My dear," says he, "I have, and with reason, the best opinion of your understanding of any man now breathing; and you know I have never set my own in competition with it till now, my dear Bella," says he, taking her hand from her book as kind as could be—"till now, when I have the great advantage of being quite cool, and you not; so don't believe one word your friends say against your own sir Condy, and lend me the letter out of your pocket, till I see what it is they can have to say." "Take it then," says she, "and as you are quite cool, I hope it is a proper time to request you'll allow me to comply with the wishes of all my own friends, and return to live with my father and family, during the remainder of my wretched existence, at Mount Juliet's town."

At this my poor master fell back a few paces, like one that had been shot. "You're not serious, Bella," says he; "and could you find it in your heart to leave me this way in the very middle of my distresses, all alone?" But recollecting himself after his first surprise, and a moment's time for reflection, he said, with a great deal of consideration for my lady, "Well, Bella, my dear, I believe you are right; for what could you do at Castle Rackrent, and an execution against the goods coming down, and the furniture to be canted, and an auction in the house all next week? so you have my full consent to go, since that is your desire, only you must not think of my accompanying you, which I could not in honour do upon the terms I always have been, since our marriage, with your friends; besides, I have business to transact at home; so in the mean time, if we are to have any breakfast this morning, let us go down and have it for the last time in peace and comfort, Bella."

1. Childishly.

Then as I heard my master coming to the passage door, I finished fastening up my slate against the broken pane; and when he came out, I wiped down the window seat with my wig,* and bade him a good morrow as kindly as I could, seeing he was in trouble, though he strove and thought to hide it from me. "This window is all racked and tattered," says I, "and it's what I'm striving to mend." "It *is* all racked and tattered, plain enough," says he, "and never mind mending it, honest old Thady," says he; "it will do well enough for you and I, and that's all the company we shall have left in the house by-and-bye." "I'm sorry to see your honour so low this morning," says I; "but you'll be better after taking your breakfast." "Step down to the servants' hall," says he, "and bring me up the pen and ink into the parlour, and get a sheet of paper from Mrs. Jane, for I have business that can't brook[2] to be delayed; and come into the parlour with the pen and ink yourself, Thady, for I must have you to witness my signing a paper I have to execute in a hurry." Well, while I was getting of the pen and ink-horn, and the sheet of paper, I ransacked my brains to think what could be the papers my poor master could have to execute in such a hurry, he that never thought of such a thing as doing business afore breakfast, in the whole course of his life, for any man living; but this was for my lady, as I afterwards found, and the more genteel of him after all her treatment.

I was just witnessing the paper that he had scrawled over, and was shaking the ink out of my pen upon the carpet, when my lady came into breakfast, and she started as if it had been a ghost! as well she might, when she saw sir Condy writing at this unseasonable hour. "That will do very well, Thady," says he to me, and took the paper I had signed to, without knowing what upon the earth it might be, out of my hands, and walked, folding it up, to my lady.

"You are concerned in this, my lady Rackrent," says he, putting it into her hands; "and I beg you'll keep this memorandnm safe, and show it to your friends the first thing you do when you get home; but put it in your pocket now, my dear, and let us eat our breakfast, in God's name." "What is all this?" said my lady, opening the paper in great curiosity. "It's only a bit of a memorandum of what I think becomes me to do whenever I am able," says my master; "you know

---

*   Wigs were formerly used instead of brooms in Ireland, for sweeping or dusting tables, stairs, &c. The Editor doubted the fact, till he saw a labourer of the old school sweep down a flight of stairs with his wig; he afterwards put it on his head again with the utmost composure, and said, "Oh, please your honour, it's never a bit the worse."

It must be acknowledged, that these men are not in any danger of catching cold by taking off their wigs occasionally, because they usually have fine crops of hair growing under their wigs. The wigs are often yellow, and the hair which appears from beneath them black; the wigs are usually too small, and are raised up by the hair beneath, or by the ears of the wearers.

2. Bear.

my situation, tied hand and foot at the present time being, but that can't last always, and when I'm dead and gone, the land will be to the good, Thady, you know; and take notice, it's my intention your lady should have a clear live hundred a year jointure off the estate afore any of my debts are paid." "Oh, please your honour," says I, "I can't expect to live to see that time, being now upwards of fourscore[3] years of age, and you a young man, and likely to continue so, by the help of God." I was vexed to see my lady so insensible too, for all she said was, "This is very genteel of you, sir Condy. You need not wait any longer, Thady;" so I just picked up the pen and ink that had tumbled on the floor, and heard my master finish with saying, "You behaved very genteel to me, my dear, when you threw all the little you had in your own power along with yourself, into my hands; and as I don't deny but what you may have had some things to complain of,"—to be sure he was thinking then of Judy, or of the whiskey punch, one or t'other, or both,—"and as I don't deny but you may have had something to complain of, my dear, it is but fair you should have something in the form of compensation to look forward to agreeably in future; besides, it's an act of justice to myself, that none of your friends, my dear, may ever have it to say against me, I married for money, and not for love." "That is the last thing I should ever have thought of saying of you, sir Condy," said my lady, looking very gracious. "Then, my dear," said sir Condy, "we shall part as good friends as we met; so all's right."

I was greatly rejoiced to hear this, and went out of the parlour to report it all to the kitchen. The next morning my lady and Mrs. Jane set out for Mount Juliet's town in the jaunting car:[4] many wondered at my lady's choosing to go away, considering all things, upon the jaunting car, as if it was only a party of pleasure; but they did not know, till I told them, that the coach was all broke in the journey down, and no other vehicle but the car to be had; besides, my lady's friends were to send their coach to meet her at the cross roads; so it was all done very proper.

My poor master was in great trouble after my lady left us. The execution came down; and every thing at Castle Rackrent was seized by the gripers,[5] and my son Jason, to his shame be it spoken, amongst them. I wondered, for the life of me, how he could harden himself to do it; but then he had been studying the law, and had made himself attorney Quirk; so he brought down at once a heap of accounts upon my master's head. To cash lent, and to ditto, and to ditto, and to ditto, and oats, and bills paid at the milliner's and linen draper's,

---

3. Eighty.
4. A light, two-wheeled vehicle, popular in Ireland, drawn by a single horse.
5. Extortioners. "Milliner" (below): seller of accessories and articles of female apparel, especially hats.

and many dresses for the fancy balls in Dublin for my lady, and all
the bills to the workmen and tradesmen for the scenery of the theatre, and the chandler's and grocer's bills, and tailor's, besides butcher's and baker's, and worse than all, the old one of that base wine
merchant's, that wanted to arrest my poor master for the amount
on the election day, for which amount sir Condy afterwards passed
his note of hand, bearing lawful interest from the date thereof; and
the interest and compound interest was now mounted to a terrible
deal on many other notes and bonds for money borrowed, and
there was besides hush money to the sub-sheriffs, and sheets upon
sheets of old and new attorneys' bills, with heavy balances, *as per
former account furnished*, brought forward with interest thereon;
then there was a powerful deal due to the crown for sixteen years'
arrear of quit-rent[6] of the town-lands of Carrick-shaughlin, with
driver's fees, and a compliment to the receiver every year for letting
the quit-rent run on, to oblige sir Condy, and sir Kit afore him. Then
there were bills for spirits and ribands at the election time, and the
gentlemen of the committee's accounts unsettled, and their subscription never gathered; and there were cows to be paid for, with
the smith and farrier's bills to be set against the rent of the demesne,[7]
with calf and hay money; then there was all the servants' wages, since
I don't know when, coming due to them, and sums advanced for them
by my son Jason for clothes, and boots, and whips, and odd moneys
for sundries expended by them in journeys to town and elsewhere,
and pocket-money for the master continually, and messengers and
postage before his being a parliament man; I can't myself tell you
what besides; but this I know, that when the evening came on the
which sir Condy had appointed to settle all with my son Jason, and
when he comes into the parlour, and sees the sight of bills and load
of papers all gathered on the great dining-table for him, he puts his
hands before both his eyes, and cried out, "Merciful Jasus! what is
it I see before me?" Then I sets an arm-chair at the table for him,
and with a deal of difficulty he sits him down, and my son Jason
hands him over the pen and ink to sign to this man's bill and t'other
man's bill, all which he did without making the least objections.
Indeed, to give him his due, I never *seen* a man more fair and honest, and easy in all his dealings, from first to last, as sir Condy, or
more willing to pay every man his own as far as he was able, which
is as much as any one can do. "Well," says he, joking like with
Jason, "I wish we could settle it all with a stroke of my grey goose
quill. What signifies making me wade through all this ocean of

6. Rent paid to the crown in lieu of services rendered. "Chandler": one whose trade it is to
   make or sell candles. "Note of hand": a written promise to pay (or repay) a specified
   sum of money at a stated time or on demand.
7. Personal estate. "Farrier": one who shoes horses.

papers here; can't you now, who understand drawing out an account, debtor and creditor, just sit down here at the corner of the table, and get it done out for me, that I may have a clear view of the balance, which is all I need be talking about, you know?" "Very true, sir Condy; nobody understands business better than yourself," says Jason. "So I've a right to do, being born and bred to the bar," says sir Condy. "Thady, do step out and see are they bringing in the things for the punch, for we've just done all we have to do for this evening." I goes out accordingly, and when I came back, Jason was pointing to the balance, which was a terrible sight to my poor master. "Pooh! pooh! pooh!" says he, "here's so many noughts they dazzle my eyes, so they do, and put me in mind of all I suffered, larning of my numeration table, when I was a boy at the day-school along with you, Jason—units, tens, hundreds, tens of hundred. Is the punch ready, Thady?" says he, seeing me. "Immediately; the boy has the jug in his hand; it's coming up stairs, please your honour, as fast as possible," says I, for I saw his honour was tired out of his life; but Jason, very short and cruel, cuts me off with—"Don't be talking of punch yet a while; it's no time for punch yet a bit—units, tens, hundreds," goes he on, counting over the master's shoulder, units, tens, hundreds, thousands. "A-a-ah! hold your hand," cries my master; "where in this wide world am I to find hundreds, or units itself, let alone thousands?" "The balance has been running on too long," says Jason, sticking to him as I could not have done at the time, if you'd have given both the Indies and Cork[8] to boot; "the balance has been running on too long, and I'm distressed myself on your account, sir Condy, for money, and the thing must be settled now on the spot, and the balance cleared off," says Jason. "I'll thank you if you'll only show me how," says sir Condy. "There's but one way," says Jason, "and that's ready enough: when there's no cash, what can a gentleman do, but go to the land?" "How can you go to the land, and it under custodiam to yourself already," says sir Condy, "and another custodiam hanging over it? and no one at all can touch it, you know, but the custodees." "Sure, can't you sell, though at a loss? sure you can sell, and I've a purchaser ready for you," says Jason. "Have ye so?" said sir Condy; "that's a great point gained; but there's a thing now beyond all, that perhaps you don't know yet, barring Thady has let you into the secret." "Sarrah bit of a secret, or any thing at all of the kind, has he learned from me these fifteen weeks come St. John's eve,"[9] says I; "for we have scarce been upon speaking terms of late; but what is it your honour means of a secret?" "Why, the secret of the little keepsake I gave my lady Rackrent the

8. Places of trade where one could become wealthy.
9. June 23. "Sarrah": meaning sorrow; often referring in sense to the devil.

morning she left us, that she might not go back empty-handed to her friends." "My lady Rackrent, I'm sure, has baubles[1] and keepsakes enough, as those bills on the table will show," says Jason; "but whatever it is," says he, taking up his pen, "we must add it to the balance, for to be sure it can't be paid for." "No, nor can't till after my decease," said sir Condy; "that's one good thing." Then colouring up a good deal, he tells Jason of the memorandum of the five hundred a year jointure he had settled upon my lady; at which Jason was indeed mad, and said a great deal in very high words, that it was using a gentleman, who had the management of his affairs, and was moreover his principal creditor, extremely ill, to do such a thing without consulting him, and against his knowledge and consent. To all which sir Condy had nothing to reply, but that upon his conscience, it was in a hurry and without a moment's thought on his part, and he was very sorry for it, but if it was to do over again he would do the same; and he appealed to me, and I was ready to give my evidence, if that would do, to the truth of all he said.

So Jason with much ado was brought to agree to a compromise. "The purchaser that I have ready," says he, "will be much displeased, to be sure, at the incumbrance on the land, but I must see and manage him; here's a deed ready drawn up; we have nothing to do but to put in the consideration money and our names to it." "And how much am I going to sell?—the lands of O'Shaughlin's town, and the lands of Gruneaghoolaghan, and the lands of Crookagnawaturgh," says he, just reading to himself,—"and—Oh, murder, Jason! sure you won't put this in—the castle stable, and appurtenances of Castle Rackrent." "Oh, murder!" says I, clapping my hands, "this is too bad, Jason." "Why so?" said Jason, "when it's all, and a great deal more to the back of it, lawfully mine, was I to push for it." "Look at him," says I, pointing to sir Condy, who was just leaning back in his arm-chair, with his arms falling beside him like one stupified; "is it you, Jason, that can stand in his presence, and recollect all he has been to us, and all we have been to him, and yet use him so at the last?" "Who will you find to use him better, I ask you?" said Jason; "if he can get a better purchaser, I'm content; I only offer to purchase, to make things easy and oblige him: though I don't see what compliment I am under, if you come to that; I have never had, asked, or charged more than sixpence in the pound, receiver's fees; and where would he have got an agent for a penny less?" "Oh, Jason! Jason! how will you stand to this in the face of the county and all who know you?" says I; "and what will people think and say, when they see you living here in Castle Rackrent, and the lawful owner turned out of the seat of his ancestors, without a cabin to put his head into, or so much as a

1. Trinkets.

potatoe to eat?" Jason, whilst I was saying this, and a great deal more, made me signs, and winks, and frowns; but I took no heed; for I was grieved and sick at heart for my poor master, and couldn't but speak.

"Here's the punch," says Jason, for the door opened; "here's the punch!" Hearing that, my master starts up in his chair, and recollects himself, and Jason uncorks the whiskey. "Set down the jug here," says he, making room for it beside the papers opposite to sir Condy, but still not stirring the deed that was to make over all. Well, I was in great hopes he had some touch of mercy about him when I saw him making the punch, and my master took a glass; but Jason put it back as he was going to fill again, saying, "No, sir Condy, it sha'n't be said of me, I got your signature to this deed when you were half-seas over: you know your name and handwriting in that condition would not, if brought before the courts, benefit me a straw; wherefore let us settle all before we go deeper into the punchbowl." "Settle all as you will;" said sir Condy, clapping his hands to his ears; "but let me hear no more; I'm bothered to death this night." "You've only to sign," said Jason, putting the pen to him. "Take all, and be content," said my master. So he signed; and the man who brought in the punch witnessed it, for I was not able, but crying like a child; and besides, Jason said, which I was glad of, that I was no fit witness, being so old and doting. It was so bad with me, I could not taste a drop of the punch itself, though my master himself, God bless him! in the midst of his trouble, poured out a glass for me, and brought it up to my lips. "Not a drop, I thank your honour's honour as much as if I took it though," and I just set down the glass as it was, and went out, and when I got to the street-door, the neighbour's childer, who were playing at marbles there, seeing me in great trouble, left their play, and gathered about me to know what ailed me; and I told them all, for it was a great relief to me to speak to these poor childer, that seemed to have some natural feeling left in them: and when they were made sensible that sir Condy was going to leave Castle Rackrent for good and all, they set up a whillalu that could be heard to the farthest end of the street; and one fine boy he was, that my master had given an apple to that morning, cried the loudest, but they all were the same sorry, for sir Condy was greatly beloved amongst the childer, for letting them go a nutting in the demesne, without saying a word to them, though my lady objected to them. The people in the town, who were the most of them standing at their doors, hearing the childer cry, would know the reason of it; and when the report was made known, the people one and all gathered in great anger against my son Jason, and terror at the notion of his coming to be landlord over them, and they cried, "No Jason! no Jason! Sir Condy! sir Condy! sir Condy Rackrent for ever!"

and the mob grew so great and so loud, I was frightened, and made my way back to the house to warn my son to make his escape, or hide himself for fear of the consequences. Jason would not believe me till they came all round the house, and to the windows with great shouts: then he grew quite pale, and asked sir Condy what had he best do? "I'll tell you what you'd best do," said sir Condy, who was laughing to see his fright; "finish your glass first, then let's go to the window and show ourselves, and I'll tell 'em, or you shall, if you please, that I'm going to the Lodge for change of air for my health, and by my own desire, for the rest of my days." "Do so," said Jason, who never meant it should have been so, but could not refuse him the Lodge at this unseasonable time. Accordingly sir Condy threw up the sash, and explained matters, and thanked all his friends, and bid 'em look in at the punch-bowl, and observe that Jason and he had been sitting over it very good friends; so the mob was content, and he sent 'em out some whiskey to drink his health, and that was the last time his honour's health was ever drunk at Castle Rackrent.

The very next day, being too proud, as he said, to me, to stay an hour longer in a house that did not belong to him, he sets off to the Lodge, and I along with him not many hours after. And there was great bemoaning through all O'Shaughlin's town, which I stayed to witness, and gave my poor master a full account of when I got to the Lodge. He was very low and in his bed when I got there, and complained of a great pain about his heart, but I guessed it was only trouble, and all the business, let alone vexation, he had gone through of late; and knowing the nature of him from a boy, I took my pipe, and, whilst smoking it by the chimney, began telling him how he was beloved and regretted in the county, and it did him a deal of good to hear it. "Your honour has a great many friends yet, that you don't know of, rich and poor, in the county," says I; "for as I was coming along the road, I met two gentlemen in their own car-riages, who asked after you, knowing me, and wanted to know where you was and all about you, and even how old I was: think of that." Then he wakened out of his dose, and began questioning me who the gentlemen were. And the next morning it came into my head to go, unknown to any body, with my master's compliments, round to many of the gentlemen's houses, where he and my lady used to visit, and people that I knew were his great friends, and would go to Cork to serve him any day in the year, and I made bold to try to borrow a trifle of cash from them. They all treated me very civil for the most part, and asked a great many questions very kind about my lady, and sir Condy, and all the family, and were greatly surprised to learn from me Castle Rackrent was sold, and my master at the Lodge for health; and they all pitied him greatly, and he had their good wishes, if that would do, but money was a thing they unfortunately had not any of them at this time to spare. I had my journey for my pains, and I, not used to walking, nor supple as formerly, was greatly tired, but had the satisfaction of telling my master, when I got to the Lodge, all the civil things said by high and low.

"Thady," says he, "all you've been telling me brings a strange thought into my head; I've a notion I shall not be long for this world any how, and I've a great fancy to see my own funeral afore I die." I was greatly shocked, at the first speaking, to hear him speak so light about his funeral, and he, to all appearance, in good health, but recollecting myself, answered, "To be sure, it would be as fine a sight as one could see, I dared to say, and one I should be proud to witness, and I did not doubt his honour's would be as great a funeral as ever sir Patrick O'Shaughlin's was, and such a one as that had never been known in the county afore or since." But I never thought he was in earnest about seeing his own funeral himself, till the next day he returns to it again. "Thady," says he, "as far as the wake°*2 goes, sure I might without any great trouble have the satisfaction of seeing a bit of my own funeral." "Well, since your honour's honour's so bent upon it," says I, not willing to cross him, and he in trouble, "we must see what we can do." So he fell into a sort of a sham disorder, which was easy done, as he kept his bed, and no one to see him; and I got my shister, who was an old woman very handy about the sick, and very skilful, to come up to the Lodge, to nurse him; and we gave out, she knowing no better, that he was just at his latter end, and it answered beyond any thing; and there was a great throng of people, men, women, and childer, and there being only two rooms at the Lodge, except what was locked up full of Jason's furniture and things, the house was soon as full and fuller than it could hold, and the heat, and smoke, and noise wonderful great; and standing amongst them that were near the bed, but not thinking at all of the dead, I was started by the sound of my master's voice from under the great coats that had been thrown all at top, and I went close up, no one noticing. "Thady," says he, "I've had enough of this; I'm smothering, and can't hear a word of all they're saying of the deceased." "God bless you, and lie still and quiet," says I, "a bit longer, for my shister's afraid of ghosts, and would die on the spot with fright, was she to see you come to life all on a sudden this way without the least preparation." So he lays him still, though well nigh stifled, and I made all haste to tell the secret of the joke, whispering to one and t'other,

---

* A wake in England is a meeting avowedly for merriment; in Ireland it is a nocturnal meeting avowedly for the purpose of watching and bewailing the dead; but, in reality, for gossiping and debauchery.

2. Edgeworth's father, Richard Lovell Edgeworth, wrote the accompanying Glossary note. See unpublished letter from Maria Edgeworth to Charlotte Sneyd, August or September 1806 (National Library of Ireland, MS. 10, 166/7. Pos. 9029, letter 539).

and there was a great surprise, but not so great as we had laid out it would. "And aren't we to have the pipes and tobacco, after coming so far to-night?" said some; but they were all well enough pleased when his honour got up to drink with them, and sent for more spirits from a shebean-house,*[3] where they very civilly let him have it upon credit. So the night passed off very merrily, but, to my mind, sir Condy was rather upon the sad order in the midst of it all, not finding there had been such a great talk about himself after his death as he had always expected to hear.

The next morning, when the house was cleared of them, and none but my shister and myself left in the kitchen with sir Condy, one opens the door, and walks in, and who should it be but Judy M'Quirk herself! I forgot to notice, that she had been married long since, whilst young captain Moneygawl lived at the Lodge, to the captain's huntsman, who after a whilst listed[4] and left her, and was killed in the wars. Poor Judy fell off greatly in her good looks after her being married a year or two; and being smoke-dried in the cabin, and neglecting herself like, it was hard for sir Condy himself to know her again till she spoke; but when she says, "It's Judy M'Quirk, please your honour, don't you remember her?" "Oh, Judy, is it you?" says his honour; "yes, sure, I remember you very well; but you're greatly altered, Judy." "Sure it's time for me," says she; "and I think your honour, since I *seen* you last,—but that's a great while ago,—is altered too." "And with reason, Judy," says sir Condy, fetching a sort of a sigh; "but how's this, Judy?" he goes on; "I take it a little amiss of you, that you were not at my wake last night." "Ah, don't be being jealous of that," says she; "I didn't hear a sentence of your honour's wake till it was all over, or it would have gone hard with me but I would have been at it sure; but I was forced to go ten miles up the country three days ago to a wedding of a relation of my own's, and didn't get home till after the wake was over; but," says she, "it won't be so, I hope, the next time,† please your honour." "That we shall see, Judy," says his honour, "and may be sooner than you think for, for I've been very unwell this while past, and don't reckon any way I'm long for this world." At this, Judy takes up the corner of her apron, and puts it first to one eye and then to t'other, being to all appearance in great trouble; and my shister put in her word, and bid his honour have a good heart, for she was sure it was only the gout, that sir Patrick used to have flying about him, and he

---

* *Shebean-house*, a hedge-alehouse. Shebean properly means weak small-beer, taplash.
† At the coronation of one of our monarchs, the king complained of the confusion which happened in the procession. The great officer who presided told his majesty, "That it should not be so next time."

---

3. "Taplash": dregs (mentioned in the footnote).
4. Enlisted.

ought to drink a glass or a bottle extraordinary to keep it out of his stomach; and he promised to take her advice, and sent out for more spirits immediately; and Judy made a sign to me, and I went over to the door to her, and she said, "I wonder to see sir Condy so low! has he heard the news?" "What news?" says I. "Didn't ye hear it, then?" says she; "my lady Rackrent that was is kilt° and lying for dead, and I don't doubt but it's all over with her by this time." "Mercy on us all," says I; "how was it?" "The jaunting car it was that ran away with her," says Judy. "I was coming home that same time from Biddy M'Guggin's marriage, and a great crowd of people too upon the road, coming from the fair of Crookaghnawaturgh, and I sees a jaunting car standing in the middle of the road, and with the two wheels off and all tattered. 'What's this?' says I. 'Didn't ye hear of it?' says they that were looking on; 'it's my lady Rackrent's car, that was running away from her husband, and the horse took fright at a carrion[5] that lay across the road, and so ran away with the jaunting car, and my lady Rackrent and her maid screaming, and the horse ran with them against a car that was coming from the fair, with the boy asleep on it, and the lady's petticoat hanging out of the jaunting car caught, and she was dragged I can't tell you how far upon the road, and it all broken up with the stones just going to be pounded, and one of the road-makers, with his sledge-hammer in his hand, stops the horse at the last; but my lady Rackrent was all kilt* and smashed, and they lifted her into a cabin hard by, and the maid was found after, where she had been thrown, in the gripe[6] of the ditch, her cap and bonnet all full of bog water, and they say my lady can't live any way.' Thady, pray now is it true what I'm told for sartain, that sir Condy has made over all to your son Jason?" "All," says I. "All entirely?" says she again. "All entirely," says I. "Then," says she, "that's a great shame, but don't be telling Jason what I say." "And what is it you say?" cries sir Condy, leaning over betwixt us, which made Judy start greatly. "I know the time when Judy M'Quirk would never have stayed so long talking at the door, and I in the house." "Oh!" says Judy, "for shame, sir Condy; times are altered since then, and it's my lady Rackrent you ought to be thinking of." "And why should I be thinking of her, that's not thinking of me now?" says sir Condy. "No matter for that," says Judy, very properly; "it's time you

---

* *Kilt and smashed.*—Our author is not here guilty of an anti-climax. The mere English reader, from a similarity of sound between the words *kilt* and *killed*, might be induced to suppose that their meanings are similar, yet they are not by any means in Ireland synonymous terms. Thus you may hear a man exclaim, "I'm kilt and murdered!" but he frequently means only that he has received a black eye, or a slight contusion.—*I'm kilt all over* means that he is in a worse state than being simply *kilt*. Thus, *I'm kilt with the cold* is nothing to *I'm kilt all over with the rheumatism.*

---

5. Decaying animal.
6. Grasp.

should be thinking of her, if ever you mean to do it at all, for don't you know she's lying for death?" "My lady Rackrent!" says sir Condy, in a surprise; "why it's but two days since we parted, as you very well know, Thady, in her full health and spirits, and she and her maid along with her going to Mount Juliet's town on her jaunting car." "She'll never ride no more on her jaunting car," said Judy, "for it has been the death of her, sure enough." "And is she dead, then?" says his honour. "As good as dead, I hear," says Judy; "but there's Thady here has just learnt the whole truth of the story as I had it, and it is fitter he or any body else should be telling it you than I, sir Condy: I must be going home to the childer." But he stops her, but rather from civility in him, as I could see very plainly, than any thing else, for Judy was, as his honour remarked at her first coming in, greatly changed, and little likely, as far as I could see—though she did not seem to be clear of it herself—little likely to be my lady Rackrent now, should there be a second toss-up to be made. But I told him the whole story out of the face, just as Judy had told it to me, and he sent off messenger with his compliments to Mount Juliet's town that evening, to learn the truth of the report, and Judy bid the boy that was going call in at Tim M'Enerney's shop in O'Shaughlin's town and buy her a new shawl. "Do so," said sir Condy, "and tell Tim to take no money from you, for I must pay him for the shawl myself." At this my shister throws me over a look, and I says nothing, but turned the tobacco in my mouth, whilst Judy began making a many words about it, and saying how she could not be beholden for shawls to any gentleman. I left her there to consult with my shister, did she think there was any thing in it, and my shister thought I was blind to be asking her the question, and I thought my shister must see more into it than I did; and recollecting all past times and every thing, I changed my mind, and came over to her way of thinking, and we settled it that Judy was very like to be my lady Rackrent after all, if a vacancy should have happened.

The next day, before his honour was up, somebody comes with a double knock at the door, and I was greatly surprised to see it was my son Jason. "Jason, is it you?" said I; "what brings you to the Lodge?" says I; "is it my lady Rackrent? we know that already since yesterday." "May be so," says he, "but I must see sir Condy about it." "You can't see him yet," says I; "sure he is not awake." "What then," says he, "can't he be wakened? and I standing at the door." "I'll not be disturbing his honour for you, Jason," says I; "many's the hour you've waited in your time, and been proud to do it, till his honour was at leisure to speak to you. His honour," says I, raising my voice, at which his honour wakens of his own accord, and calls to me from the room to know who it was I was speaking to. Jason made no more ceremony, but follows me into the room. "How are you, sir Condy?" says he; "I'm happy to see you looking so well; I came up to know how you did to-day, and to see did you want for any thing at the Lodge." "Nothing at all, Mr. Jason, I thank you," says he; for his honour had his own share of pride, and did not choose, after all that had passed, to be beholden, I suppose, to my son; "but pray take a chair and be seated, Mr. Jason." Jason sat him down upon the chest, for chair there was none, and after he had sat there some time, and a silence on all sides, "What news is there stirring in the country, Mr. Jason M'Quirk?" says sir Condy very easy, yet high like. "None that's news to you, sir Condy, I hear," says Jason: "I am sorry to hear of my lady Rackrent's accident." "I'm much obliged to you, and so is her ladyship, I'm sure," answered sir Condy, still stiff; and there was another sort of a silence, which seemed to lie the heaviest on my son Jason.

"Sir Condy," says he at last, seeing sir Condy disposing himself to go to sleep again, "sir Condy, I dare say you recollect mentioning to me the little memorandum you gave to lady Rackrent about the 500*l.* a-year jointure." "Very true," said sir Condy; "it is all in my recollection." "But if my lady Rackrent dies, there's an end of all jointure," says Jason. "Of course," says sir Condy. "But it's not a matter of certainty that my lady Rackrent won't recover," says Jason. "Very true, sir," says my master. "It's a fair speculation, then, for you to consider what the chance of the jointure on those lands, when out of custodiam, will be to you." "Just five hundred a-year, I take it, without any speculation at all," said sir Condy. "That's supposing the life dropt, and the custodiam off, you know; begging your pardon, sir Condy, who understands business, that is a wrong calculation." "Very likely so," said sir Condy; "but, Mr. Jason, if you have any thing to say to me this morning about it, I'd be obliged to you to say it, for I had an indifferent night's rest last night, and wouldn't be sorry to sleep a little this morning." "I have only three words to say, and those more of consequence to you, sir Condy, than me. You are a little cool, I observe; but I hope you will not be offended at what I have brought here in my pocket," and he pulls out two long rolls, and showers down golden guineas upon the bed. "What's this?" said sir Condy; "it's long since"—but his pride stops him. "All these are your lawful property this minute, sir Condy, if you please," said Jason. "Not for nothing, I'm sure," said sir Condy, and laughs a little—"nothing for nothing, or I'm under a mistake with you, Jason." "Oh, sir Condy, we'll not be indulging ourselves in any unpleasant retrospects," says Jason; "it's my present intention to behave, as I'm sure you will, like a gentleman in this affair. Here's two hundred guineas, and a third I mean to add, if you should think proper to make over to me all your right and title to those lands that you know of." "I'll consider of it," said my master; and a great deal more, that I was tired listening to, was said by Jason, and all that, and the sight of the ready cash upon the bed worked with his honour; and the short and the long of it was, sir Condy gathered up the golden guineas, and tied them up in a handkerchief, and signed some paper Jason brought with him as usual, and there was an end of the business; Jason took himself away, and my master turned himself round and fell asleep again.

I soon found what had put Jason in such a hurry to conclude this business. The little gossoon we had sent off the day before with my master's compliments to Mount Juliet's town, and to know how my lady did after her accident, was stopped early this morning, coming back with his answer through O'Shaughlin's town, at Castle Rackrent, by my son Jason, and questioned of all he knew of my lady from the servant at Mount Juliet's town; and the gossoon told him my lady Rackrent was not expected to live over night; so Jason thought it high time to be moving to the Lodge, to make his bargain with my master about the jointure afore it should be too late, and afore the little gossoon should reach us with the news. My master was greatly vexed, that is, I may say, as much as ever I *seen* him, when he found how he had been taken in; but it was some comfort to have the ready cash for immediate consumption in the house, any way.

And when Judy came up that evening, and brought the childer to see his honour, he unties the handkerchief, and, God bless him! whether it was little or much he had, 'twas all the same with him, he gives 'em all round guineas a-piece. "Hold up your head," says my shister to Judy, as sir Condy was busy filling out a glass of punch for her eldest boy—"Hold up your head, Judy; for who knows but we may live to see you yet at the head of the Castle Rackrent estate?" "May be so," says she, "but not the way you are thinking of." I did not rightly understand which way Judy was looking when she makes this speech, till a-while after. "Why, Thady, you were telling me yesterday, that sir Condy had sold all entirely to Jason, and where then does all them guineas in the handkerchief come from?" "They are the purchase-money of my lady's jointure," says I. Judy looks a little bit puzzled at this. "A penny for your thoughts, Judy," says my shister; "hark,[7] sure sir Condy is drinking her health." He was at the table in *the room*,* drinking with the exciseman and the gauger, who came up to see his honour, and we were standing over the fire in the kitchen. "I don't much care is he drinking my health or not," says Judy; "and it is not sir Condy I'm thinking of, with all your jokes, whatever he is of me." "Sure you wouldn't refuse to be my lady Rackrent, Judy, if you had the offer?" says I. "But if I could do better!" says she. "How better?" says I and my shister both at once. "How better?" says she; "why, what signifies it to be my lady Rackrent, and no

---

* *The room*—the principal room in the house.

7. Listen.

castle? sure what good is the car, and no horse to draw it?" "And where will ye get the horse, Judy?" says I. "Never mind that," says she; "may be it is your own son Jason might find that." "Jason!" says I; "don't be trusting to him, Judy. Sir Condy, as I have good reason to know, spoke well of you, when Jason spoke very indifferently of you, Judy." "No matter," says Judy; "it's often men speak the contrary just to what they think of us." "And you the same way of them, no doubt," answers I. "Nay, don't be denying it, Judy, for I think the better of ye for it, and shouldn't be proud to call ye the daughter of a shister's son of mine, if I was to hear ye talk ungrateful, and any way disrespectful of his honour." "What disrespect," says she, "to say I'd rather, if it was my luck, be the wife of another man?" "You'll have no luck, mind my words, Judy," says I; and all I remembered about my poor master's goodness in tossing up for her afore he married at all came across me, and I had a choaking in my throat that hindered me to say more. "Better luck, any how, Thady," says she, "than to be like some folk, following the fortunes of them that have none left." "Oh! King of Glory!" says I, "hear the pride and ungratitude of her, and he giving his last guineas but a minute ago to her childer, and she with the fine shawl on her he made her a present of but yesterday!" "Oh, troth,[8] Judy, you're wrong now," says my shister, looking at the shawl. "And was not he wrong yesterday, then," says she, "to be telling me I was greatly altered, to affront me?" "But, Judy," says I, "what is it brings you here then at all in the mind you are in; is it to make Jason think the better of you?" "I'll tell you no more of my secrets, Thady," says she, "nor would have told you this much, had I taken you for such an unnatural fader as I find you are, not to wish your own son prefarred to another." "Oh, troth, *you* are wrong now, Thady," says my shister. Well, I was never so put to it in my life: between these womens, and my son and my master, and all I felt and thought just now, I could not, upon my conscience, tell which was the wrong from the right. So I said not a word more, but was only glad his honour had not the luck to hear all Judy had been saying of him, for I reckoned it would have gone nigh to break his heart; not that I was of opinion he cared for her as much as she and my shister fancied, but the ungratitude of the whole from Judy might not plase him; and he could never stand the notion of not being well spoken of or beloved like behind his back. Fortunately for all parties concerned, he was so much elevated at this time, there was no danger of his understanding any thing, even if it had reached his ears. There was a great horn at the Lodge, ever since my master and captain Moneygawl was in together, that used to belong originally to the celebrated sir Patrick, his ancestor; and his

8. A pledge of fidelity.

honour was fond often of telling the story that he learned from me
when a child, how sir Patrick drank the full of this horn[9] without
stopping, and this was what no other man afore or since could without drawing breath. Now sir Condy challenged the gauger, who
seemed to think little of the horn, to swallow the contents, and had
it filled to the brim with punch; and the gauger said it was what he
could not do for nothing, but he'd hold sir Condy a hundred guineas he'd do it. "Done," says my master; "I'll lay you a hundred golden
guineas to a tester* you don't." "Done," says the gauger; and done
and done's enough between two gentlemen. The gauger was cast, and
my master won the bet, and thought he'd won a hundred guineas,
but by the wording it was adjudged to be only a tester that was his
due by the exciseman. It was all one to him; he was as well pleased,
and I was glad to see him in such spirits again.

The gauger, bad luck to him! was the man that next proposed to
my master to try himself could he take at a draught the contents of
the great horn. "Sir Patrick's horn!" said his honour; "hand it to me:
I'll hold you your own bet over again I'll swallow it." "Done," says the
gauger; "I'll lay ye any thing at all you do no such thing." "A hundred
guineas to sixpence I do," says he: "bring me the handkerchief." I
was loth,[1] knowing he meant the handkerchief with the gold in it,
to bring it out in such company, and his honour not very able to
reckon it. "Bring me the handkerchief, then, Thady," says he, and
stamps with his foot; so with that I pulls it out of my great coat
pocket, where I had put it for safety. Oh, how it grieved me to see
the guineas counting upon the table, and they the last my master
had! Says sir Condy to me, "Your hand is steadier than mine to-
night, old Thady, and that's a wonder; fill you the horn for me." And
so, wishing his honour success, I did; but I filled it, little thinking
of what would befall him. He swallows it down, and drops like one
shot. We lifts him up, and he was speechless, and quite black in the
face. We put him to bed, and in a short time he wakened, raving
with a fever on his brain. He was shocking either to see or hear.
"Judy! Judy! have you no touch of feeling? won't you stay to help us
nurse him?" says I to her, and she putting on her shawl to go out of
the house. "I'm frightened to see him," says she, "and wouldn't nor
couldn't stay in it; and what use? he can't last till the morning."
With that she ran off. There was none but my shister and myself
left near him of all the many friends he had. The fever came and
went, and came and went, and lasted five days, and the sixth he was

* *Tester*—sixpence; from the French word tête, a head: a piece of silver stamped with a
head, which in old French was called "un testion," and which was about the value of an
old English sixpence. Tester is used in Shakspeare.

9. A vessel made from the tusk of an animal, used to hold liquid.
1. Reluctant.

sensible for a few minutes, and said to me, knowing me very well, "I'm in burning pain all withinside of me, Thady." I could not speak, but my shister asked him would he have this thing or t'other to do him good? "No," says he, "nothing will do me good no more," and he gave a terrible screech with the torture he was in—then again a minute's ease—"brought to this by drink," says he; "where are all the friends?—where's Judy?—Gone, hey? Ay, sir Condy has been a fool all his days," said he; and there was the last word he spoke, and died. He had but a very poor funeral, after all.

If you want to know any more, I'm not very well able to tell you; but my lady Rackrent did not die, as was expected of her, but was only disfigured in the face ever after by the fall and bruises she got; and she and Jason, immediately after my poor master's death, set about going to law about that jointure; the memorandum not being on stamped paper,[2] some say it is worth nothing, others again it may do; others say, Jason won't have the lands at any rate; Many wishes it so: for my part, I'm tired wishing for any thing in this world, after all I've seen in it—but I'll say nothing; it would be a folly to be getting myself ill-will in my old age. Jason did not marry, nor think of marrying Judy, as I prophesied, and I am not sorry for it; who is? As for all I have here set down from memory and hearsay of the family, there's nothing but truth in it from beginning to end: that you may depend upon; for where's the use of telling lies about the things which every body knows as well as I do?

The Editor could have readily made the catastrophe of sir Condy's history more dramatic and more pathetic, if he thought it allowable to varnish the plain round tale of faithful Thady. He lays it before the English reader as a specimen of manners and characters, which are, perhaps, unknown in England. Indeed, the domestic habits of no nation in Europe were less known to the English than those of their sister country, till within these few years.

Mr. Young's picture of Ireland,[3] in his tour through that country, was the first faithful portrait of its inhabitants. All the features in the foregoing sketch were taken from the life, and they are characteristic of that mixture of quickness, simplicity, cunning, careless-ness, dissipation, disinterestedness, shrewdness, and blunder, which, in different forms, and with various success, has been brought upon the stage, or delineated in novels.

---

2. Embossed or stamped with a seal for authenticity.
3. Arthur Young, *Tour in Ireland* (1780).

It is a problem of difficult solution to determine, whether an Union will hasten or retard the melioration[4] of this country. The few gentlemen of education, who now reside in this country, will resort to England: they are few, but they are in nothing inferior to men of the same rank in Great Britain. The best that can happen will be the introduction of British manufacturers in their places.

Did the Warwickshire militia,[5] who were chiefly artisans, teach the Irish to drink beer? or did they learn from the Irish to drink whiskey?

1800.

4. Improvement.
5. Part-time military units who served as peacekeepers in Ireland in the 1790s.

Glossary[1]

Some friends, who have seen Thady's history since it has been printed, have suggested to the Editor, that many of the terms and idiomatic phrases, with which it abounds, could not be intelligible to the English reader without further explanation. The Editor has therefore furnished the following Glossary.[2]

Page 11. *Monday morning.*—Thady begins his memoirs of the Rackrent Family by dating *Monday morning*, because no great undertaking can be auspiciously commenced in Ireland on any morning but *Monday morning*. "O, please God we live till Monday morning, we'll set the slater to mend the roof of the house. On Monday morning we'll fall to, and cut the turf. On Monday morning we'll see and begin mowing. On Monday morning, please your honour, we'll begin and dig the potatoes," &c.

All the intermediate days, between the making of such speeches and the ensuing Monday, are wasted: and when Monday morning comes, it is ten to one that the business is deferred to *the next* Monday morning. The Editor knew a gentleman, who, to counteract this prejudice, made his workmen and labourers begin all new pieces of work upon a Saturday.

Page 12. *Let alone the three kingdoms itself.*—*Let alone*, in this sentence, means *put out of consideration*. The phrase, *let alone*, which is now used as the imperative of a verb, may in time become a conjunction, and may exercise the ingenuity of some future etymologist. The celebrated Horne Tooke[3] has proved most satisfactorily, that the conjunction *but* comes from the imperative of the Anglo-Saxon very (*beoutan*) *to be out*; also, that *if* comes from *gift*, the imperative of the Anglo-Saxon verb which signifies *to give*, &c.

---

1. While not without precedence in eighteenth-century novels (see William Beckford's 1787 novel *Vathek*), the inclusion of additional commentary was a rare occurrence. See the preface on pp. viii–x.
2. Editions of *Castle Rackrent* published from 1800 to 1815 saw this prefix printed on a separate page under the title "Advertisement to the English Reader." See the preface on p. ix.
3. John Horne Took (1736–1812), English politician and philologist.

Page 13.   *Whillaluh.*—Ullaloo, Gol, or lamentation over the
dead—

> "Magnoque ululante tumultu."—VIRGIL.
> "Ululatibus omne
> Implevere nemus."—OVID.

A full account of the Irish Gol, or Ullaloo, and of the Caoinan or
Irish funeral song, with its first semichorus, second semichorus,
full chorus of sighs and groans, together with the Irish words and
music, may be found in the fourth volume of the transactions of the
Royal Irish Academy. For the advantage of *lazy* readers, who would
rather read a page than walk a yard, and from compassion, not to
say sympathy, with their infirmity, the Editor transcribes the following passages:

"The Irish have been always remarkable for their funeral lamentations, and this peculiarity has been noticed by almost every trav-
eller who visited them; and it seems derived from their Celtic
ancestors, the primæval inhabitants of this isle . . .

"It has been affirmed of the Irish, that to cry was more natural to
them than to any other nation, and at length the Irish cry became
proverbial . . .

"Cambrensis in the twelfth century says, the Irish then musically
expressed their griefs; that is, they applied the musical art, in which
they excelled all others, to the orderly celebration of funeral obse-
quies, by dividing the mourners into two bodies, each alternately
singing their part, and the whole at times joining in full chorus. . . .
The body of the deceased, dressed in grave clothes, and ornamented
with flowers, was placed on a bier, or some elevated spot. The relations and keepers (*singing mourners*) ranged themselves in two
divisions, one at the head, and the other at the feet of the corpse.
The bards and croteries had before prepared the funeral Caoinan.
The chief bard of the head chorus began by singing the first stanza
in a low, doleful tone, which was softly accompanied by the harp: at
the conclusion, the foot semichorus began the lamentation, or
Ullaloo, from the final note of the preceding stanza, in which they
were answered by the head semichorus; then both united in one
general chorus. The chorus of the first stanza being ended, the
chief bard of the foot semichorus began the second Gol or lamentation, in which he was answered by that of the head; and then, as
before, both united in the general full chorus. Thus alternately
were the song and choruses performed during the night. The genealogy, rank, possessions, the virtues and vices of the dead were
rehearsed, and a number of interrogations were addressed to the
deceased; as, Why did he die? If married, whether his wife was
faithful to him, his sons dutiful, or good hunters or warriors? If a

woman, whether her daughters were fair or chaste? If a young man, whether he had been crossed in love; or if the blue-eyed maids of Erin treated him with scorn?"[4]

We are told, that formerly the feet (the metrical feet) of the Caoinan were much attended to; but on the decline of the Irish bards these feet were gradually neglected, and the Caoinan fell into a sort of slipshod metre amongst women. Each province had different Caoinans, or at least different imitations of the original. There was the Munster cry, the Ulster cry, &c. It became an extempore performance, and every set of keepers varied the melody according to their own fancy.

It is curious to observe how customs and ceremonies degenerate. The present Irish cry, or howl, cannot boast of such melody, nor is the funeral procession conducted with much dignity. The crowd of people who assemble at these funerals sometimes amounts to a thousand, often to four or five hundred. They gather as the bearers of the hearse proceed on their way, and when they pass through any village, or when they come near any houses, they begin to cry—Oh! Oh! Oh! Oh! Oh! Agh! Agh! raising their notes from the first *Oh!* to the last *Agh!* in a kind of mournful howl. This gives notice to the inhabitants of the village that *a funeral is passing*, and immediately they flock out to follow it. In the province of Munster it is a common thing for the women to follow a funeral, to join in the universal cry with all their might and main for some time, and then to turn and ask—"Arrah! who is it that's dead?—who is it we're crying for?" Even the poorest people have their own burying-places, that is, spots of ground in the church-yards, where they say that their ancestors have been buried ever since the wars of Ireland; and if these burial-places are ten miles from the place where a man dies, his friends and neighbours take care to carry his corpse thither. Always one priest, often five or six priests, attend these funerals; each priest repeats a mass, for which he is paid, sometimes a shilling, sometimes half-a-crown, sometimes half-a-guinea, or a guinea, according to their circumstances, or, as they say, according to the *ability* of the deceased. After the burial of any very poor man, who has left a widow or children, the priest makes what is called *a collection* for the widow; he goes round to every person present, and each contributes sixpence or a shilling, or what they please. The reader will find in the note upon the word *Wake*, p. 53, more particulars respecting the conclusion of the Irish funerals.

Certain old women, who cry particularly loud and well, are in great request, and, as a man said to the Editor, "Every one would

4. The passage is quoted from William Beauford's "Caoinan: or Some Account of the Antient Irish Lamentations," *Transactions of the Royal Irish Academy*, 4.41–44.

wish and be proud to have such at his funeral, or at that of his friends." The lower Irish are wonderfully eager to attend the funerals of their friends and relations, and they make their relationships branch out to a great extent. The proof that a poor man has been well beloved during his life is his having a crowded funeral. To attend a neighbour's funeral is a cheap proof of humanity, but it does not, as some imagine, cost nothing. The time spent in attending funerals may be safely valued at half a million to the Irish nation; the Editor thinks that double that sum would not be too high an estimate. The habits of profligacy and drunkenness, which are acquired at *wakes*, are here put out of the question. When a labourer, a carpenter, or a smith, is not at his work, which frequently happens, ask where he is gone, and ten to one the answer is—"Oh faith, please your honour, he couldn't do a stroke to-day, for he's gone to *the* funeral."

Even beggars, when they grow old, go about begging *for their own funerals*; that is, begging for money to buy a coffin, candles, pipes, and tobacco. For the use of the candles, pipes, and tobacco, see *Wake*.

Those who value customs in proportion to their antiquity, and nations in proportion to their adherence to ancient customs, will, doubtless, admire the Irish *Ullaloo*, and the Irish nation, for persevering in this usage from time immemorial. The Editor, however, has observed some alarming symptoms, which seem to prognosticate the declining taste for the Ullaloo in Ireland. In a comic theatrical entertainment, represented not long since on the Dublin stage, a chorus of old women was introduced, who set up the Irish howl round the relics of a physician, who is supposed to have fallen under the wooden sword of Harlequin.[5] After the old women have continued their Ullaloo for a decent time, with all the necessary accompaniments of wringing their hands, wiping or rubbing their eyes with the corners of their gowns or aprons, &c. one of the mourners suddenly suspends her lamentable cries, and, turning to her neighbour, asks, "Arrah now, honey, who is it we're crying for?"

Page 14.   *The tenants were sent away without their whiskey.*—It is usual with some landlords to give their inferior tenants a glass of whiskey when they pay their rents. Thady calls it *their* whiskey; not that the whiskey is actually the property of the tenants, but that it becomes their *right* after it has been often given to them. In this general mode of reasoning respecting *rights* the lower Irish are not singular, but they are peculiarly quick and tenacious in claiming these rights. "Last year your honour gave me some straw for the

5. Comedic servant characters known for their acrobatic skill.

roof of my house, and I *expect* your honour will be after doing the same this year." In this manner gifts are frequently turned into tributes. The high and low are not always dissimilar in their habits. It is said, that the Sublime Ottoman Porte[6] is very apt to claim gifts as tributes: thus it is dangerous to send the Grand Seignor a fine horse on his birthday one year, lest on his next birthday he should expect a similar present, and should proceed to demonstrate the reasonableness of his expectations.

Page 14.   *He demeaned himself greatly*—means, he lowered or disgraced himself much.

Page 15.   *Duty fowls, and duty turkies, and duty geese.*—In many leases in Ireland, tenants were *formerly* bound to supply an inordinate quantity of poultry to their landlords. The Editor knew of thirty turkies being reserved in one lease of a small farm.

Page 15.   *English tenants.*—An English tenant does not mean a tenant who is an Englishman, but a tenant who pays his rent the day that it is due. It is a common prejudice in Ireland, amongst the poorer classes of people, to believe that all tenants in England pay their rents on the very day when they become due. An Irishman, when he goes to take a farm, if he wants to prove to his landlord that he is a substantial man, offers to become an *English tenant*. If a tenant disobliges his landlord by voting against him, or against his opinion, at an election, the tenant is immediately informed by the agent, that he must become an *English tenant*. This threat does not imply that he is to change his language or his country, but that he must pay all the arrear of rent which he owes, and that he must thenceforward pay his rent on that day when it becomes due.

Page 15.   *Canting*—does not mean talking or writing hypocritical nonsense, but selling substantially by auction.

Page 15.   *Duty work.*—It was formerly common in Ireland to insert clauses in leases, binding tenants to furnish their landlords with labourers and horses for several days in the year. Much petty tyranny and oppression have resulted from this feudal custom. Whenever a poor man disobliged his landlord, the agent sent to him for his duty work, and Thady does not exaggerate when he says, that the tenants were often called from their own work to do that of their landlord. Thus the very means of earning their rent were taken from them: whilst they were getting home their landlord's

6. Metonym for the central government of the Ottoman empire.

harvest, their own was often ruined, and yet their rents were expected to be paid as punctually as if their time had been at their own disposal. This appears the height of absurd injustice.

In Esthonia, amongst the poor Sclavonian race of peasant slaves, they pay tributes to their lords, not under the name of duty work, duty geese, duty turkies, &c., but under the name of *righteousnesses*. The following ballad is a curious specimen of Esthonian poetry:—

> "This is the cause that the country is ruined,
> And the straw of the thatch is eaten away,
> The gentry are come to live in the land—
> Chimneys between the village,
> And the proprietor upon the white floor!
> The sheep brings forth a lamb with a white forehead,
> This is paid to the lord for a *righteousness sheep*.
> The sow farrows pigs,
> They go to the spit of the lord.
> The hen lays eggs,
> They go into the lord's frying-pan.
> The cow drops a male calf,
> That goes into the lord's herd as a bull.
> The mare foals a horse foal,
> That must be for my lord's nag.
> The boor's wife has sons,
> They must go to look after my lord's poultry."[7]

Page 16.   *Out of forty-nine suits which he had, he never lost one but seventeen.*—Thady's language in this instance is a specimen of a mode of rhetoric common in Ireland. An astonishing assertion is made in the beginning of a sentence, which ceases to be in the least surprising, when you hear the qualifying explanation that follows. Thus a man who is in the last stage of staggering drunkenness will, if he can articulate, swear to you—"Upon his conscience now, and may he never stir from the spot alive if he is telling a lie, upon his conscience he has not tasted a drop of any thing, good or bad, since morning at-all-at-all, but half a pint of whiskey, please your honour."

---

7. The source of this poem is found in *Varieties of Literature, from Foreign Literary Journals and Original MSS., Now First Published* (1795), pp. 22–44. See Alan S. C. Ross, "An Estonian Quotation in *Castle Rackrent*," *Notes and Queries* (Jan., 1975), p. 26. In the original publication, the editor of *Varieties of Literature* writes of the poem, titled "Song in Spring-Tide," "Can one desire a more just and lively display of the wretched situation of these poor people in regard to their lords, than this ballad, the result of their feelings and their woeful experience?"

Page 16.   *Fairy Mounts*—Barrows. It is said that these high mounts were of great service to the natives of Ireland when Ireland was invaded by the Danes. Watch was always kept on them, and upon the approach of an enemy a fire was lighted to give notice to the next watch, and thus the intelligence was quickly communicated through the country. *Some years ago*, the common people believed that these barrows were inhabited by fairies, or, as they called them, by the *good people*. "O troth, to the best of my belief, and to the best of my judgment and opinion," said an elderly man to the Editor, "it was only the old people that had nothing to do, and got together, and were telling stories about them fairies, but to the best of my judgment there's nothing in it. Only this I heard myself not very many years back from a decent kind of a man, a grazier, that as he was coming just *fair and easy* (*quietly*) from the fair, with some cattle and sheep, that he had not sold, just at the church of ——, at an angle of the road like, he was met by a good-looking man, who asked him where he was going? And he answered, 'Oh, far enough, I must be going all night.' 'No, that you mustn't nor won't (says the man), you'll sleep with me the night, and you'll want for nothing, nor your cattle nor sheep neither, nor your *beast* (*horse*); so come along with me.' With that the grazier *lit* (*alighted*) from his horse, and it was dark night; but presently he finds himself, he does not know in the wide world how, in a fine house, and plenty of every thing to eat and drink; nothing at all wanting that he could wish for or think of. And he does not *mind* (*recollect* or *know*) how at last he falls asleep; and in the morning he finds himself lying, not in ever a bed or a house at all, but just in the angle of the road where first he met the strange man: there he finds himself lying on his back on the grass, and all his sheep feeding as quiet as ever all round about him, and his horse the same way, and the bridle of the beast over his wrist. And I asked him what he thought of it; and from first to last he could think of nothing, but for certain sure it must have been the fairies that entertained him so well. For there was no house to see any where nigh hand, or any building, or barn, or place at all, but only the church and the *mote* (*barrow*). There's another odd thing enough that they tell about this same church, that if any person's corpse, that had not a right to be buried in that church-yard, went to be burying there in it, no, not all the men, women, or childer in all Ireland could get the corpse any way into the church-yard; but as they would be trying to go into the church-yard, their feet would seem to be going backwards instead of forwards; ay, continually backwards the whole funeral would seem to go; and they would never set foot with the corpse in the church-yard. Now they say that it is the fairies do all this; but it is my opinion it is all idle talk, and people are after being wiser now."

The country people in Ireland certainly *had* great admiration mixed with reverence, if not dread, of fairies. They believed that beneath these fairy mounts were spacious subterraneous palaces, inhabited by *the good people*, who must not on any account be disturbed. When the wind raises a little eddy of dust upon the road, the poor people believe that it is raised by the fairies, that it is a sign that they are journeying from one of the fairies' mounts to another, and they say to the fairies, or to the dust as it passes, "God speed ye, gentlemen; God speed ye." This averts any evil that *the good people* might be inclined to do them. There are innumerable stories told of the friendly and unfriendly feats of these busy fairies; some of these tales are ludicrous, and some romantic enough for poetry. It is a pity that poets should lose such convenient, though diminutive machinery. By-the-bye, Parnell,[8] who showed himself so deeply "skilled in faerie lore," was an Irishman; and though he has presented his faeries to the world in the ancient English dress of "Britain's isle, and Arthur's days," it is probable that his first acquaintance with them began in his native country.

Some remote origin for the most superstitious or romantic popular illusions or vulgar errors may often be discovered. In Ireland, the old churches and church-yards have been usually fixed upon as the scenes of wonders. Now the antiquarians tell us, that near the ancient churches in that kingdom caves of various constructions have from time to time been discovered, which were formerly used as granaries or magazines by the ancient inhabitants, and as places to which they retreated in time of danger. There is (p. 84 of the R. I. A. Transactions for 1789) a particular account of a number of these artificial caves at the west end of the church of Killossy, in the county of Kildare. Under a rising ground, in a dry sandy soil, these subterraneous dwellings were found: they have pediment roofs, and they communicate with each other by small apertures. In the Brehon laws[9] these are mentioned, and there are fines inflicted by those laws upon persons who steal from the subterraneous granaries. All these things show that there was a real foundation for the stories which were told of the appearance of lights, and of the sounds of voices near these places. The persons who had property concealed there very willingly countenanced every wonderful relation that tended to make these places objects of sacred awe or superstitious terror.

---

8. Thomas Parnell's (1679–1718) *A Fairy Tale in the Ancient English Style* opens with the line "In Britain's Isle and Arthur's days."
9. Archaic statutes that governed everyday life in early medieval Ireland.

Page 17. *Weed-ashes.*—By ancient usage in Ireland, all the weeds on a farm belonged to the farmer's wife, or to the wife of the squire who holds the ground in his own hands. The great demand for alkaline salts in bleaching rendered these ashes no inconsiderable perquisite.

Page 17. *Sealing money.*—Formerly it was the custom in Ireland for tenants to give the squire's lady from two to fifty guineas as a perquisite upon the sealing of their leases. The Editor not very long since knew of a baronet's lady accepting fifty guineas as sealing money, upon closing a bargain for a considerable farm.

Page 17. *Sir Murtagh grew mad.*—Sir Murtagh grew angry.

Page 17. *The whole kitchen was out on the stairs*—means that all the inhabitants of the kitchen came out of the kitchen, and stood upon the stairs. These, and similar expressions, show how much the Irish are disposed to metaphor and amplification.

Page 19. *Fining down the yearly rent.*—When an Irish gentleman, like sir Kit Rackrent, has lived beyond his income, and finds himself distressed for ready money, tenants obligingly offer to take his land at a rent far below the value, and to pay him a small sum of money in hand, which they call fining down the yearly rent. The temptation of this ready cash often blinds the landlord to his future interest.

Page 19. *Driver.*—A man who is employed to drive tenants for rent; that is, to drive the cattle belonging to tenants to pound. The office of driver is by no means a sinecure.

Page 19. *I thought to make him a priest.*—It was customary amongst those of Thady's rank in Ireland, whenever they could get a little money, to send their sons abroad to St. Omer's,[1] or to Spain, to be educated as priests. Now they are educated at Maynooth.[2] The Editor has lately known a young lad, who began by being a post-boy, afterwards turn into a carpenter, then quit his plane and workbench to study his *Humanities*, as he said, at the college of Maynooth; but after he had gone through his course of Humanities, he determined to be a soldier instead of a priest.

---

1. An English-speaking Catholic seminary in northern France run by the Jesuits.
2. St. Patrick's College. Officially established as the Royal College of St. Patrick by an act of Grattan's Parliament in 1795 to provide a university education for Catholic lay and ecclesiastical students.

Page 21. *Flam.*—Short for flambeau.

Page 22. *Barrack-room.*—Formerly it was customary, in gentle-men's houses in Ireland, to fit up one large bedchamber with a number of beds for the reception of occasional visitors. These rooms were called Barrack-rooms.

Page 22. *An innocent*—in Ireland, means a simpleton, and idiot.

Page 27. *The Curragh*[3]—is the Newmarket of Ireland.

Page 27. *The cant.*—The auction.

Page 30. *And so should cut him off for ever, by levying a fine, and suffering a recovery to dock the entail.*—The English reader may perhaps be surprised at the extent of Thady's legal knowledge, and at the fluency with which he pours forth law-terms; but almost every poor man in Ireland, be he farmer, weaver, shopkeeper, or steward, is, beside his other occupations, occasionally a lawyer. The nature of processes, ejectments, custodiams, injunctions, replevins, &c. is perfectly known to them, and the terms as familiar to them as to any attorney. They all love law. It is a kind of lottery, in which every man, staking his own wit or cunning against his neighbour's property, feels that he has little to lose, and much to gain.

"I'll have the law of you, so I will!" is the saying of an Englishman who expects justice. "I'll have you before his honour" is the threat of an Irishman who hopes for partiality. Miserable is the life of a justice of the peace in Ireland the day after a fair, especially if he resides near a small town. The multitude of the *kilt* (*kilt* does not mean *killed*, but hurt) and wounded who come before his honour with black eyes or bloody heads is astonishing: but more astonish-ing is the number of those who, though they are scarcely able by daily labour to procure daily food, will nevertheless, without the least reluctance, waste six or seven hours of the day lounging in the yard or hall of a justice of the peace, waiting to make some com-plaint about—nothing. It is impossible to convince them that *time is money.* They do not set any value upon their own time, and they think that others estimate theirs at less than nothing. Hence they make no scruple of telling a justice of the peace a story of an hour long about a *tester* (sixpence); and if he grows impatient, they attri-bute it to some secret prejudice which he entertains against them.

3. An area in County Kildare, Ireland, known for horse breeding and training and as the home of the Curragh Racecourse.

Their method is to get a story completely by heart, and to tell it, as they call it, *out of the face*, that is, from the beginning to the end, without interruption.

"Well, my good friend, I have seen you lounging about these three hours in the yard; what is your business?"

"Please your honour, it is what I want to speak one word to your honour."

"Speak then, but be quick—What is the matter?"

"The matter, please your honour, is nothing at-all-at-all, only just about the grazing of a horse, please your honour, that this man here sold me at the fair of Gurtishannon last Shrove fair, which lay down three times with myself, please your honour, and *kilt* me; not to be telling your honour of how, no later back than yesterday night, he lay down in the house there within, and all the childer standing round, and it was God's mercy he did not fall a-top of them, or into the fire to burn himself. So, please your honour, to-day I took him back to this man, which owned him, and after a great deal to do I got the mare again I *snopped* (*exchanged*) him for; but he won't pay the grazing of the horse for the time I had him, though he promised to pay the grazing in case the horse din't answer; and he never did a day's work, good or bad, please your honour, all the time he was with me, and I had the doctor to him five times any how. And so, please your honour, it is what I expect your honour will stand my friend, for I'd sooner come to your honour for justice than to any other in all Ireland. And so I brought him here before your honour, and expect your honour will make him pay me the grazing, or tell me, can I process him for it at the next assizes, please your honour?"

The defendant now turning a quid of tobacco with his tongue into some secret cavern in his mouth, begins his defence with—

"Please your honour, under favour, and saving your honour's presence, there's not a word of truth in all this man has been saying from beginning to end, upon my conscience, and I wouldn't, for the value of the horse itself, grazing and all, be after telling your honour a lie. For, please your honour, I have a dependance upon your honour that you'll do me justice, and not be listening to him or the like of him. Please your honour, it's what he has brought me before your honour, because he had a spite against me about some oats I sold your honour, which he was jealous of, and a shawl his wife got at my shister's shop there without, and never paid for; so I offered to set the shawl against the grazing, and give him a receipt in full of all demands, but he wouldn't out of spite, please your honour; so he brought me before your honour, expecting your honour was mad with me for cutting down the tree in the horse park, which was none of my doing, please your honour—ill luck to them that went and belied me to your honour behind my back! So if your honour is pleasing, I'll tell you the whole truth about the horse that he swopped against my mare out of the face. Last Shrove fair I met this man, Jemmy Duffy, please your honour, just at the corner of the road, where the bridge is broken down, that your honour is to have the presentment for this year—long life to you for it! And he was at that time coming from the fair of Gurtishannon, and I the same way. 'How are you, Jemmy?' says I. 'Very well, I thank ye, kindly, Bryan,' says he; 'shall we turn back to Paddy Salmon's and take a naggin[4] of whiskey to our better acquaintance?' 'I don't care if I did, Jemmy,' says I; 'only it is what I can't take the whiskey, because I'm under an oath against it for a month.' Ever since, please your honour, the day your honour met me on the road, and observed to me I could hardly stand, I had taken so much; though upon my conscience your honour wronged me greatly that same time—ill luck to them that belied me behind my back to your honour! Well, please your honour, as I was telling you, as he was taking the whiskey, and we talking of one thing or t'other, he makes me an offer to swop his mare that he couldn't sell at the fair of Gurtishannon, because nobody would be troubled with the beast, please your honour, against my horse, and to oblige him I took the mare—sorrow take her! and him along with her! She kicked me a new car, that was worth three pounds ten, to tatters the first time I ever put her into it, and I expect your honour will make him pay me the price of the car, any how, before I pay the grazing, which I've no right to pay at-all-at-all, only to oblige him. But I leave it all to your honour; and the whole grazing he ought to be charging for the beast is but two and eightpence halfpenny, any how, please your honour. So I'll abide by what your honour says, good or bad. I'll leave it all to your honour."

I'll leave *it* all to your honour—literally means, I'll leave all the trouble to your honour.

The Editor knew a justice of the peace in Ireland, who had such a dread of *having it all left to his honour*, that he frequently gave the complainants the sum about which they were disputing, to make peace between them, and to get rid of the trouble of hearing their stories *out of the face*. But he was soon cured of this method of buying off disputes, by the increasing multitude of those who, out of pure regard to his honour, came "to get justice from him, because they would sooner come before him than before any man in all Ireland."

Page 38. *A raking pot of tea.*—We should observe, this custom has long since been banished from the higher orders of Irish gentry.

4. Small cup.

The mysteries of a raking pot of tea, like those of the Bona Dea,[5] are supposed to be sacred to females; but now and then it has happened, that some of the male species, who were either more audacious or more highly favoured than the rest of their sex, have been admitted by stealth to these orgies. The time when the festive ceremony begins varies according to circumstances, but it is never earlier than twelve o'clock at night; the joys of a raking pot of tea depending on its being made in secret, and at an unseasonable hour. After a ball, when the more discreet part of the company has departed to rest, a few chosen female spirits, who have footed it till they can foot it no longer, and till the sleepy notes expire under the slurring hand of the musician, retire to a bedchamber, call the favourite maid, who alone is admitted, bid her *put down the kettle*, lock the door, and amidst as much giggling and scrambling as possible, they get round a tea-table, on which all manner of things are huddled together. Then begin mutual railleries and mutual confidences amongst the young ladies, and the faint scream and the loud laugh is heard, and the romping for letters and pocket-books begins, and gentlemen are called by their surnames, or by the general name of fellows! pleasant fellows! charming fellows! odious fellows! abominable fellows! and then all prudish decorums are forgotten, and then we might be convinced how much the satirical poet was mistaken when he said,

> "There is no woman where there's no reserve."

The merit of the original idea of a raking pot of tea evidently belongs to the washerwoman and the laundry-maid. But why should not we have *Low life above stairs* as well as *High life below stairs?*[6]

Page 39. *We gained the day by this piece of honesty.*—In a dispute which occurred some years ago in Ireland, between Mr. E. and Mr. M., about the boundaries of a farm, an old tenant of Mr. M.'s cut a *sod* from Mr. M.'s land, and inserted it in a spot prepared for its reception in Mr. E.'s land; so nicely was it inserted, that no eye could detect the junction of the grass. The old man, who was to give his evidence as to the property, stood upon the inserted sod when the *viewers* came, and swore that the ground he *then stood upon* belonged to his landlord, Mr. M.

The Editor had flattered himself that the ingenious contrivance which Thady records, and the similar subterfuge of this old Irishman, in the dispute concerning boundaries, were instances of *'cuteness* unparalleled in all but Irish story: an English friend,

---

5. The Good Goddess, a divinity in ancient Roman religion.
6. David Garrick's immensely popular late-eighteenth-century stage comedy *High Life below the Stairs*, first performed at the Theatre Royal, Drury Lane, on October 31, 1759.

however, has just mortified the Editor's national vanity by an account of the following custom, which prevails in part of Shropshire. It is discreditable for women to appear abroad after the birth of their children till they have been *churched*.[7] To avoid this reproach, and at the same time to enjoy the pleasure of gadding, whenever a woman goes abroad before she has been to church, she takes a tile from the roof of her house, and puts it upon her head: wearing this panoply[8] all the time she pays her visits, her conscience is perfectly at ease; for she can afterwards safely declare to the clergyman, that she "has never been from under her own roof till she came to be churched."

Page 40.   *Carton, or half carton.*—Thady means cartron, or half cartron. "According to the old record in the black book of Dublin, a *cantred* is said to contain 30 *villatas terras*, which are also called *quarters* of land (quarterons, *cartrons*); every one of which quarters must contain so much ground as will pasture 400 cows, and 17 ploughlands. A knight's fee was composed of 8 hydes, which amount to 160 acres, and that is generally deemed about a *plough-land*."

The Editor was favoured by a learned friend with the above extract, from a MS. of lord Totness's in the Lambeth library.

Page 53.—*Wake.*—A wake in England means a festival held upon the anniversary of the saint of the parish. At these wakes, rustic games, rustic conviviality, and rustic courtship, are pursued with all the ardour and all the appetite which accompany such pleasures as occur but seldom. In Ireland a wake is a midnight meeting, held professedly for the indulgence of holy sorrow, but usually it is converted into orgies of unholy joy. When an Irish man or woman of the lower order dies, the straw which composed the bed, whether it has been contained in a bag to form a mattress, or simply spread upon the earthen floor, is immediately taken out of the house, and burned before the cabin door, the family at the same time setting up the death howl. The ears and eyes of the neighbours being thus alarmed, they flock to the house of the deceased, and by their vociferous sympathy excite and at the same time soothe the sorrows of the family.

It is curious to observe how good and bad are mingled in human institutions. In countries which were thinly inhabited, this custom prevented private attempts against the lives of individuals, and formed a kind of coroner's inquest upon the body which had recently expired, and burning the straw upon which the sick man

---

7. A blessing given to mothers after recovery from childbirth.
8. Covering. "Gadding": going from one place to another without much purpose.

lay became a simple preservative against infection. At night the dead body is waked, that is to say, all the friends and neighbours of the deceased collect in a barn or stable, where the corpse is laid upon some boards, or an unhinged door, supported upon stools, the face exposed, the rest of the body covered with a white sheet. Round the body are stuck in brass candlesticks, which have been borrowed perhaps at five miles' distance, as many candles as the poor person can beg or borrow, observing always to have an odd number. Pipes and tobacco are first distributed, and then, according to the *ability* of the deceased, cakes and ale, and sometimes whiskey, are *dealt* to the company:

> "Deal on, deal on, my merry men all,
>   Deal on your cakes and your wine,
> For whatever is dealt at her funeral to-day
>   Shall be dealt to-morrow at mine."[9]

After a fit of universal sorrow, and the comfort of a universal dram, the scandal of the neighbourhood, as in higher circles, occupies the company. The young lads and lasses romp with one another, and when the father and mothers are at last overcome with sleep and whiskey (*vino et somno*[1]), the youth become more enterprising, and are frequently successful. It is said, that more matches are made at wakes than at weddings.

Page 55. *Kilt.*—This word frequently occurs in the preceding pages, where it means not *killed*, but much *hurt*. In Ireland, not only cowards, but the brave "die many times before their death."—There *killing is no murder.*

---

9. Verse 16 of "Fair Margaret and Sweet William," a traditional song.
1. Wine and sleep.

BACKGROUNDS AND CONTEXTS

The Edgeworth Family (1787) by Adam Buck. *Left to right:* Maria, Emmeline, Henry, Charlotte, Sneyd, Lovell, R. L. Edgeworth, Anna, Bessy, Mrs. E. Edgeworth, William, Honora. Courtesy of the Estate of Michael Butler. Photograph © National Portrait Gallery, London.

Daguerreotype of Maria Edgeworth (1841) by Richard Beard. © National Portrait Gallery, London.

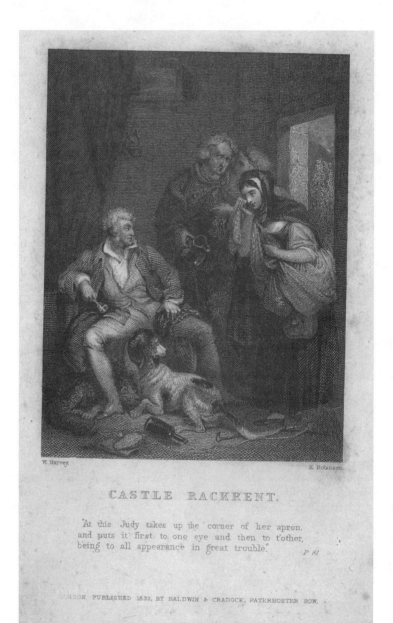

CASTLE RACKRENT.

'At this Judy takes up the corner of her apron.
and puts it first to one eye and then to t'other,
being to all appearance in great trouble.'
                                        p 61

W. Harvey.   H. Robinson.

LONDON PUBLISHED 1832, BY BALDWIN & CRADOCK, PATERNOSTER ROW.

Letters

Maria Edgeworth to Fanny Robinson[†]

August 1782

The Irish are perhaps the laziest civilized nation on the face of the Earth; to avoid a moment's present trouble they will bring on themselves real misfortunes . . . for this indolence peculiar to the Irish Peasantry several reasons may be assigned, amongst others the most powerful is the low wages of labor 6d a day in winter and 8d in summer; the demand for labor must be very little indeed, in a country when the day labourers in it can find it answer to go over to a foreign nation, in search of employment . . .

They live in a hut whose mudbuilt walls can scarcely support their weather-beaten roofs: you may see the children playing before the cabins sans shoes sans stockings sans every thing—The father of the family, on a fine summer's day standing in the sunshine at his door while his house is ready to fall upon his head and is supported only by two or three props of wood; perhaps out of charity you go up to him and tell him he had much better set about repairing his house.—he would answer you 'Oh (pronounced Ho) faith Honey when it falls it will be time enough to think of picking it up' . . .

To conclude their character, the Irish are remarkably hospitable to strangers; friendly & charitable to each other; apropos, about charity, I must observe to you that the charity of the higher class of people in Ireland is one of the greatest checks to industry it encourages Idleness amongst the Poor & increases the numbers, or rather, the swarms of Beggars, which infest the streets of Dublin. Let the rich raise the wages of labor, the rewards of industry, that would be true charity.—The lower class of Irish are extremely eloquent, they have a volubility, a fluency, & a facility of delivery which is really surprising . . . The Irish language is now almost gone into disuse, the class of people all speak English except in their quarrels with each other, then unable to give vent to their rage in any but their

---

† From Marilyn Butler, *Maria Edgeworth: A Literary Biography* (Oxford: Clarendon, 1972), pp. 90–91. Penned by fourteen-year-old Edgeworth shortly after her arrival in Ireland, this letter offers insight into her earliest reflections on the Irish peasantry.

own they have recourse to that and they *throw* it out with a rapidity and vehemence which I can give you no idea of * * *

Maria Edgeworth to Fanny Robinson[†]

September 15, 1783

* * * Moliere's [plays] entertained me much. The plots of all I have yet read of Marivaux I think too much alike & too uninteresting; indeed that is a fault I have met with in most French plays—the waiting women & valets are mere machinery to help the author through his plot and to bring their Masters and Mistresses in spite of fate together.[1]

Maria Edgeworth to Miss Sophy Ruxton[‡]

Edgeworthstown, *January 29, 1800*

*   *   *

Will you tell me what means you have of getting parcels from London to Arundel? because I wish to send to my aunt a few "Popular Tales," which I have finished, as they cannot be wanted for some months by Mr. Johnson. We have begged Johnson to send "Castle Rackrent;" I hope it has reached you: do not mention to any one that it is ours. * * *

Richard Lovell Edgeworth
to David Augustus Beaufort[*]

April 26, 1800

* * * 'We hear from good authority that the king was much pleased with Castle Rack Rent—he rubbed his hands & said what what—I know something now of my Irish subjects.' * * *

---

† From Marilyn Butler, *Maria Edgeworth: A Literary Biography* (Oxford: Clarendon, 1972), p. 150. Edgeworth was just fifteen years old when she wrote to her school friend Fanny Robinson explaining her interest in literary realism.

1. National Library of Ireland, MS collection 21, 826. The punctuation of this copy is not necessarily ME's own.

‡ From J. C. Augustus Hare, ed., *The Life and Letters of Maria Edgeworth*, vol. 1 (Cambridge, MA: Houghton Mifflin, 1895), p. 72. In this letter Edgeworth reveals her anxiety over being discovered as the author of the recently published *Castle Rackrent*.

* From Marilyn Butler, *Maria Edgeworth: A Literary Biography* (Oxford: Clarendon, 1972), p. 359.

Maria Edgeworth to Miss. Mary Sneyd[†]

LONDON, NEROT'S HOTEL, *September 27, 1802.*

* * *

We proceeded to Leicester. Handsome town, good shops: walked, whilst dinner was getting ready, to a circulating library. My father asked for "Belinda," "Bulls," etc., found they were in good repute—"Castle Rackrent" in better—the others often borrowed, but "Castle Rackrent" often bought. * * *

Maria Edgeworth to Michael Pakenham Edgeworth[‡]

February 19, 1834

* * * It is impossible to draw Ireland as she now is in a book of fiction—realities are too strong, party passions too violent to bear to see, or care to look at their faces in the looking-glass. The people would only break the glass, and curse the fool who held the mirror up to nature—distorted nature, in a fever. We are in too perilous a case to laugh, humor would be out of season, worse than bad taste. Whenever the danger is past, as the man in the sonnet says,—

"We may look back on the hardest part and laugh."

Then I shall be ready to join in the laugh. Sir Walter Scott once said to me, "Do explain to the public why Pat, who gets forward so well in other countries, is so miserable in his own." A very difficult question: I fear above my power. But I shall think of it continually, and listen, and look, and read.

* * *

[†] From J. C. Augustus Hare, ed., *The Life and Letters of Maria Edgeworth,* vol. 1 (Cambridge, MA: Houghton Mifflin, 1895), p. 87.

[‡] From J. C. Augustus Hare, ed., *The Life and Letters of Maria Edgeworth,* vol. 1 (Cambridge, MA: Houghton Mifflin, 1895), p. 550. In this letter to her brother, Edgeworth laments the lack of humor and Irish characters in her final novel, *Helen* (1834), attributing their absence to the recent historical changes in Ireland.

Maria Edgeworth to Mrs. Stark[†]

Edgeworthstown, September 6, 1834

"* * * The only character drawn from the life in *Castle Rackrent* is 'Thady' himself, the teller of the story. He[1] was an old steward (not very old, though, at that time; I added to his age, to allow him time for the generations of the family). I heard him when I first came to Ireland, and his dialect struck me, and his character; and I became so acquainted with it, that I could think and speak in it without effort; so that when, for mere amusement, without any idea of publishing, I began to write a family history as Thady would tell it, he seemed to stand beside me and dictate; and I wrote as fast as my pen could go. The characters are all imaginary. Of course they must have been compounded of persons I had seen, or incidents I had heard, but how compounded I do not know; not by 'long forethought,' for I had never thought of them till I began to write, and had made no sort of plan, sketch, or framework. There is a fact, mentioned in a note, of Lady Cathcart[2] having been shut up by her husband, Mr. M'Guire, in a house in this neighbourhood. So much I knew, but the characters are totally different from what I had heard. Indeed, the real people had been so long dead, that little was known of them. Mr. M'Guire had no resemblance, at all events, to my Sir Kit, and I knew nothing of Lady Cathcart, but that she was fond of money, and would not give up her diamonds. Sir Condy's history was added two years afterwards: it was not drawn from life, but the good-natured and indolent extravagance was suggested by a relation of mine long since dead. All the incidents are pure *invention*; the duty work, and duty fowl, *facts*.

---

† From Emily Lawless, *Maria Edgeworth* [English Men of Letters] (London: Macmillan, 1904), pp. 89–90. Edgeworth's letter to Mrs. Stark offers insight into the impetus and production of *Castle Rackrent*.
1. John Langan.
2. See n. 4, p. 24.

Reception and Reviews

THE MONTHLY REVIEW
Ireland[†]

We most heartily offer our best thanks to the unknown author of these unusually pleasing pages, which we have closed with much regret. They are written with singular humour and spirit; and it is seldom indeed that we meet with such flowers in our walks in the rugged and thorny paths of literature, through which we are often obliged to explore our weary way.

In these Hibernian Memoirs, we have been highly entertained with the exhibition of some admirable pictures, delineated (as we conceive) with perfect accuracy and truth of character; and we apprehend that, from a due contemplation of these portraits, many striking conclusions may be drawn, and applications made, respecting the necessity and probable consequences of an union between the two kingdoms.

In his[1] preface; as well as in his title-page, the author has duly warned his readers to note that these are "Tales of other Times:" 'that the manners depicted in the following pages are not those of the *present* age: the race of the Rackrents has long since been extinct in Ireland; and the drunken Sir Patrick, the litigious Sir Murtagh, the fighting Sir Kitt, and the slovenly Sir Condy, are characters which could no more be met with at present in Ireland, than Squire Western or Parson Trulliber in England. There is a time when individuals can bear to be rallied for their past follies and absurdities, after they have acquired new habits and a new consciousness. Nations as well as individuals gradually lose attachments to their identity, and the present generation is amused rather than offended by the ridicule that is thrown on their ancestors.'—

---

† *The Monthly Review* was a successful English periodical founded by the London bookseller Ralph Griffiths in 1749.
1. The reviewer incorrectly assumes the author of *Castle Rackrent* is male.

'When Ireland loses her identity by an Union with Great Britain, the will look back with a smile of good-humoured complacency on the Sir Kitts and Sir Condys of her former existence.'

The Memoirs of the Rackrents are not of a nature to admit of extracts, without injury to the whole; the structure of which is of so peculiar and singular a cast, that the reader, to be himself pleased, and to do justice to the author, must be enabled to judge of the connection and dependencies of the several parts.—The work concludes with the following remark:

'Mr. Young's picture of Ireland, in his *Tour* through Ireland, was the first faithful portrait of its inhabitants. All the features in the foregoing sketch were taken from the life, and they are characteristic of that mixture of quickness, simplicity, cunning, carelessness, dissipation, disinterestedness, shrewdness, and blunder, which in different forms, and with various success, has been brought upon the stage, or delineated in novels.'

We are truly sorry that we have found it impracticable to communicate to our readers, in our usual mode of reviewing productions of merit, any share of that pleasure which this ingenious writer has communicated to us in the perusal of his uncommon performance.

THE BRITISH CRITIC

Novels[†]

This is a very pleasant, good-humoured, and successful representation of the eccentricities of our Irish neighbours. The style is very happily hit off; and the parallel to his[1] story, we apprehend, has been too frequently exhibited. The character of "honest Thady" is remarkably comic, and well delineated; and we are not at all surprised that the publication should, in so very short a time, have passed through two editions.

---

† The *British Critic* was a conservative quarterly publication established in 1793.
1. The reviewer incorrectly assumes the author of *Castle Rackrent* is male.

JOSEPH COOPER WALKER

Letter[†]

November 23, 1800

An Irish production entitled *Castle Rackrent* has lately appeared in London. The pictures of life in this little work are allowed to be equal to any thing that has appeared since the days of Smollett.[1]

EDINBURGH REVIEW

[The Irish Novel][‡]

Ireland, with all which that word suggests—its darkly-chequered and eventful annals—its misery—its gaiety—its turbulence—its humour, and the many eminently characteristic points which mainly distinguish it from other nations, affords so good a field for the range of the novelist, that works, descriptive of those among its peculiarities which it is chiefly the business of the novelist to embody, are, especially when written by Irishmen, reasonably entitled to some attention. For those who can depict the varieties of human character, there are materials copious beyond example. There is a strongly marked national character, full of distinct and salient points, giving to all within its scope one common impress, and yet not to such a degree as to destroy the individuality which prevents the surface of society from being even and monotonous; and there is, in addition to this, a character equally conspicuous, and which furnishes more ample materials for interesting and (we must add) mournful speculation—a character which is produced by circumstances—a character which centuries of subjection and misrule have so deeply imprinted, that we cannot always, without difficulty, distinguish that which is natural from that which is the result of situation. Hence arise some of those anomalies and contrasts which impart such a remarkable degree of picturesqueness to the varied features of Irish life. There is the wild recklessness of those who have little to lose—the fitful bursts of suppressed gaiety—the impulse of a lively temperament to enjoy the brief saturnalia which each slight alleviation of misery may

---

† From Dublin City Libraries, Ms. 146, Walker, letters, letter 48. Walker (1761–1810), an Irish antiquarian. Reprinted by permission of Dublin City Public Libraries.
1. Tobias George Smollett (1721–1771), Scottish poet and author, known for his picaresque novels and influence on Charles Dickens.
‡ Founded in 1802, the second *Edinburgh Review* promoted Romanticism and Whig politics. It became one of the most influential British magazines of the 19th century.

afford—a natural fearlessness, breaking out, ever and anon, into temporary turbulence, and a natural quickness of intellect, subdued into the tortuous ingenuities of slavish cunning. We see the melancholy perversion of much that, under happier circumstances, might have been rendered active only for good—we see the current of naturally ardent feelings too little restrained by the influence of that countercheck which education can afford, and fermenting with the double exasperation of political and religious hate. Delineations of national character in the persons of individuals are too often gross caricatures. Whoever sits down to draw an Irishman—a Scotchman—a Frenchman, will generally either exaggerate, for the sake of effect, some one peculiarity, or try to combine, in the same person, so many qualities not co-existent, that the figure, by being meant to resemble all its countrymen, ceases to be like any. None, perhaps, have been more caricatured than the Irish, but rather by the former than by the latter process. The latter demanded a more intimate acquaintance with them than often existed in their pourtrayers, and the exaggeration of some one peculiarity was easy and effective. Blunders and the brogue have often been considered capital enough for would-be delineators to trade upon; and such have been the capabilities which the character afforded, that the worst sketches have seldom been altogether unamusing. It is only within the last thirty years that the Irish have been very successfully represented. Before that time we had, now and then, cleverly executed single figures by such pens as Farquhar's, Cumberland's, and Sheridan's,[1] which, even if they were incorrect, were not likely to sketch coarsely; but we never saw the Irish grouped—we never trode with them on Irish ground—we never viewed them as natives of a kindred soil, surrounded by the atmosphere of home, and all those powerful accessaries which made *them* natural, and us comparatively strange and foreign. We had seen them alone in English crowds—solitary foreigners, brought over to amuse us with their peculiarities; but we had never been carried to Ireland, and made familiar with them by their own hearths, till, for the first time, they were shown to us by Miss Edgeworth. Perhaps her 'Castle Rackrent' may be considered the first very successful delineation of the Irish character; and our admiration of the force and fidelity of that brief sketch is not diminished by comparison with any that have since appeared. As a pourtrayer of national manners, Miss Edgeworth occupies a high place—clear, lively, and sensible—forcible without exaggeration, and pointed without being affected. Hers is the least dim and distorting mirror in which we ever viewed a reflection of the Irish people. * * *

---

1. Richard Brinsley Sheridan (1751–1816), Irish playwright and poet. George Farquhar (1677–1707), Irish dramatist. Richard Cumberland (1732–1811), English dramatist.

W. B. YEATS

[Miss Edgeworth]†

The one serious novelist coming from the upper classes in Ireland, and the most finished and famous produced by any class there, is undoubtedly Miss Edgeworth. Her first novel, 'Castle Rackrent', is one of the most inspired chronicles written in English. One finds no undue love for the buffoon, rich or poor, no trace of class feeling, unless, indeed, it be that the old peasant who tells the story is a little decorative, like a peasant figure in the background of an old-fashioned autumn landscape painting. An unreal light of poetry shines round him, a too tender lustre of faithfulness and innocence. The virtues, also, that she gives him are those a poor man may show his superior, not those of poor man dealing with poor man. She has made him supremely poetical, however, because in her love for him there was nothing of the half contemptuous affection that Croker and Lover[1] felt for their personages. On the other hand, he has not the reality of Carleton's[2] men and women. He stands in the charming twilight of illusion and half-knowledge. When writing of people of her own class she saw everything about them as it really was. She constantly satirised their recklessness, their love for all things English, their oppression of and contempt for their own country. The Irish ladies in 'The Absentee' who seek laboriously after an English accent, might have lived today. Her novels give, indeed, systematically the mean and vulgar side of all that gay life celebrated by Lever.[3]

† From W. B. Yeats, ed., *Representative Irish Tales* (1891; Gerrard's Cross: Colin Smythe, 1979), pp. 27–28. William Butler Yeats (1865–1939), Irish poet who was awarded the Nobel Prize for literature in 1923.
1. Samuel Lover (1797–1868), Anglo-Irish novelist and painter. John Wilson Croker (1780–1857), Irish author and statesman.
2. William Carleton (1794–1869), Irish writer and novelist.
3. Charles Lever (1806–1872), Irish novelist.

Biography

LORD BYRON

[Reading the Edgeworths]†

* * *

January 19th, 1821.

I have been reading the Life, by himself and daughter, of Mr. R. L. Edgeworth, the father of *the* Miss Edgeworth. It is altogether a great name. In 1813, I recollect to have met them in the fashionable world of London (of which I then formed an item, a fraction, the segment of a circle, the unit of a million, the nothing of something) in the assemblies of the hour, and at a breakfast of Sir Humphry and Lady Davy's, to which I was invited for the nonce.[1] I had been the lion of 1812; Miss Edgeworth and Madame de Staël, with 'the Cossack,'[2] towards the end of 1813, were the exhibitions of the succeeding year.

I thought Edgeworth a fine old fellow, of a clarety, elderly, red complexion, but active, brisk, and endless. He was seventy, but did not look fifty—no, nor forty-eight even. * * * Edgeworth bounced about, and talked loud and long; but he seemed neither weakly nor decrepit, and hardly old.

He began by telling 'that he had given Dr. Parr a dressing, who had taken him for an Irish bog-trotter,'[3] etc. Now I, who know Dr. Parr, and who know (*not* by experience—for I never should have presumed so far as to contend with him—but by hearing him *with* others, and *of* others) that it is not so easy a matter to 'dress him,' thought Mr. Edgeworth an assertor of what was not true. He could not have stood before Parr an instant. For the rest, he seemed intelligent, vehement, vivacious, and full of life. He bids fair for a hundred years.

---

† From George Gordon, Lord Byron, *Lord Byron's Letters, Journals, and Conversations*, vol. 2 (Frankfurt: H. L. Brönner, 1834), 156–58.
1. Particular purpose. Sir Humphry Davy (1778–1829), an English inventor and chemist.
2. An allusion to the visit of Alexander I of Russia.
3. Derogatory term for an Irishman. Samuel Parr (1747–1825).

He was not much admired in London, and I remember a 'ryghte merrie' and conceited jest which was rife among the gallants of the day,—viz. a paper had been presented for the *recall of Mrs. Siddons*[4] *to the stage* (she having lately taken leave, to the loss of ages,—for nothing ever was, or can be, like her), to which all men had been called to subscribe. Whereupon, Thomas Moore,[5] of profane and poetical memory, did propose that a similar paper should be *sub*-scribed and *circum*scribed 'for the recall of Mr. Edgeworth to Ireland.'

The fact was—every body cared more about *her*. She was a nice little unassuming 'Jeanie Deans-looking bodie,'[6] as we Scotch say—and, if not handsome, certainly not ill-looking. Her conversation was as quiet as herself. One would never have guessed she could write *her name;* whereas her father talked, *not* as if he could write nothing else, but as if nothing else was worth writing.

As for Mrs. Edgeworth, I forget—except that I think she was the youngest of the party. Altogether, they were an excellent cage of the kind; and succeeded for two months, till the landing of Madame de Staël.

To turn from them to their works, I admire them; but they excite no feeling, and they leave no love—except for some Irish steward or postillion. However, the impression of intellect and prudence is profound—and may be useful.

GENTLEMAN'S MAGAZINE

Miss Edgeworth[†]

*   *   *

Fifty years or more have elapsed since her Castle Rackrent—the precursor of a copious series of tales, national, moral, and fashion-able (never romantic)—at once established her in the first class of novelists, as a shrewd observer of manners, a warmhearted gath-erer of national humours, and a resolute upholder of good morals in fiction. Before her Irish stories appeared, nothing of their kind—so complete, so relishing, so familiar yet never vulgar, so humorous yet

---

4. Sarah Siddons (1755–1831), Welsh actress. "Ryghte merrie": joke.
5. Thomas Moore (1779–1852), Irish poet.
6. Jeanie Deans is a character in Scott's *The Heart of Midlothian* (1818). Deans, an honest and highly religious character, became so popular that her name was given to paddle steamers, pubs, and railway locomotives.
† *The Gentleman's Magazine,* founded by Edward Cave in London in 1731, was the first periodical to use the term *magazine.*

not without pathos—had been tendered to the public. Their effect was great not merely on the world of readers, but on the world of writers and politicians also.

✳ ✳ ✳

Generally, Miss Edgeworth was happier in the short than in the long story. She managed satire with a delicate and firm hand, as her Modern Griselda attests. She was reserved rather than exuberant in her pathos. She could give her characters play and brilliancy when these were demanded, as in "Lady Delacour;"[1] she could work out the rise, progress, and consequences of a foible (as in Almeria) with unflinching consistency. Her dialogue is excellent; her style is in places too solicitously laboured, but it is always characteristic, yielding specimens of that pure and terse language which so many contemporary novelists seem to avoid on the maidservant's idea that "plain English" is ungenteel. Her tales are singularly rich in allusion and anecdote. In short, they indicate intellectual mastery and cultivation of no common order. Miss Edgeworth has herself confessed the care with which they were wrought. They owed much to her father's supervision; but this, we are assured by her, was confined to the pruning of redundancies. In connexion with Mr. Edgeworth the Essay on Irish Bulls was written; also the treatise on Practical Education. The latter, some years after its publication, was disclaimed by its authors, as having expounded a system which, in place of being practical, proved virtually impracticable. This brings us to speak of that large and important section of Maria Edgeworth's writings—her stories for children. Here, as elsewhere, she was "nothing if not prudential;" and yet who has ever succeeded in captivating the fancy and attention of the young as her Rosamonds and Lucys have done? In her hands the smallest incident riveted the eye and heart,—the driest truth gained a certain grace and freshness. We may, and we do, question some of the canons of her school; but one of her tales for children is not to be laid aside unfinished, let the hands into which it falls be ever so didactic—ever so romantic. ✳ ✳ ✳

If Miss Edgeworth's long literary life was usefully employed, so also were her claims and services adequately acknowledged during her lifetime. Her friendships were many; her place in the world of English and Irish society was distinguished. Byron (little given to commending the women whom he did not make love to, or who did not make love to him) approved her. Scott, when personally a stranger to her, addressed her like an old friend and a sister. There is hardly a tourist of worth or note who has visited Ireland for the last 50 years without bearing testimony to her value and vivacity as one of a large

---

1. A character from Edgeworth's novel *Belinda* (1801).

and united home circle. She was small in stature, lively of address, and diffuse as a letter-writer. To sum up, it may be said that the changes and developements which have convulsed the world of imagination since Miss Edgeworth's career of authorship began have not shaken her from her pedestal nor blotted out her name from the honourable place which it must always keep in the records of European fiction.

[Maria Edgeworth's Publication Earnings][†]

List written by Maria Edgeworth and dated September 1842:

	£	s.	d.
Parent's Assistant	120—	0—	0.
Practical Education	300—	0—	0.
Letters for Literary Ladies	40—	0—	0.
Castle Rackrent	100—	0—	0.
Moral Tales	200—	0—	0.
Early Lessons	50—	0—	0.
Belinda	300—	0—	0.
Bulls	100—	0—	0.
Explanations of Poetry } published under	40—	0—	0.
Letter to Lord Charlemont } RLE's name	3—	12—	0.
Griselda	100—	0—	0.
Popular Tales	300—	0—	0.
Leonora	200—	0—	0.
Fashionable Tales, 1st part	900—	0—	0.
Professional Education	300—	0—	0.
Fashionable Tales, 2nd part	1,050—	0—	0.
Johnson's acct. pd.	78—	16—	10.
Patronage	2,100—	0—	0.
Early Lessons, cont.	210—	0—	0.
Comic Dramas	300—	0—	0.
Harrington and Ormond	1,150—	0—	0.
Memoirs	750—	0—	0.
Rosamond—Sequel—	420—	0—	0.
Frank	400—	0—	0.
Little Plays	100—	0—	0.
Harry and Lucy Concluded	400—	0—	0.
Helen	1,100—	0—	0.
	£11,062—	8—	10.

[†] From Marilyn Butler, *Maria Edgeworth: A Literary Biography* (Oxford: Clarendon, 1972), pp. 492–93.

As usual with the Edgeworths, the money Maria made from her books was carefully accounted for. She made a mark in red ink beside those works written and published after her father's death, and counted these sums earned in difficult times peculiarly her own to spend on her dearest object, the family circle. 'I spent of this sum in delightful travelling to France Switzerland and Scotland and England including nine or ten months residence in France and two winters in England about Two thousand pounds—& I had the pleasure of giving to my brother & sister & near relatives from copyright of *Helen* about £600—and the remaining £500 I used in purchasing principal . . . With Comic Dramas £300 I had the pleasure of paying a debt of my father's to Catherine Billamore [the housekeeper]. He left to me the privilege of paying his personal debts of which this was the only one I ever heard of.'

Edgeworth and Scott

SIR WALTER SCOTT

From A Postscript, Which Should Have Been a Preface[†]

* * * The Lowland Scottish gentlemen, and the subordinate characters, are not given as individual portraits, but are drawn from the general habits of the period (of which I have witnessed some remnants in my younger days), and partly gathered from tradition.

It has been my object to describe these persons, not by a caricatured and exaggerated use of the national dialect, but by their habits, manners, and feelings; so as in some distant degree to emulate the admirable Irish portraits drawn by Miss Edgeworth, so different from the "Teagues" and "dear joys"[1] who so long, with the most perfect family resemblance to each other, occupied the drama and the novel.

I feel no confidence, however, in the manner in which I have executed my purpose. Indeed, so little was I satisfied with my production, that I laid it aside in an unfinished state, and only found it again by mere accident among other waste papers in an old cabinet, the drawers of which I was rummaging in order to accommodate a friend with some fishing-tackle, after it had been mislaid for several years.
* * *

[†] From Sir Walter Scott, *Waverley; or, 'Tis Sixty Years Since* (Edinburgh: Adam & Charles Black, 1871), chap. 72. *Waverley* is an 1814 historical novel by Scott (1771–1832). It is often regarded as the work that established the genre of the historical novel. In the postscript to *Waverley*, Scott acknowledged the debt owed to Maria Edgeworth, even though the two authors had yet to meet or correspond.

1. Appellations for Irishmen.

Maria Edgeworth to the Author of *Waverley*[†]

Edgeworthstown, October 23, 1814

Aut Scotus, aut Diabolus.[1]

We have this moment finished "Waverley." It was read aloud to this large family, and I wish the author could have witnessed the impression it made—the strong hold it seized of the feelings both of young and old—the admiration raised by the beautiful descriptions of nature—by the new and bold delineations of character—the perfect manner in which every character is sustained in every change of situation from first to last, without effort, without the affectation of making the persons speak in character—the ingenuity with which each person introduced in the drama is made useful and necessary to the end—the admirable art with which the story is constructed and with which the author keeps his own secrets till the proper moment when they should be revealed, whilst in the mean time, with the skill of Shakespeare, the mind is prepared by unseen degrees for all the changes of feeling and fortune, so that nothing, however extraordinary, shocks us as improbable; and the interest is kept up to the last moment.

* * *

I tell you without order the great and little strokes of humor and pathos just as I recollect, or am reminded of them at this moment by my companions. The fact is that we have had the volumes only during the time we could read them, and as fast as we could read, lent to us as a great favor by one who was happy enough to have secured a copy before the first and second editions were sold in Dublin. When we applied, not a copy could be had; we expect one in the course of next week, but we resolved to write to the author without waiting for a second perusal. Judging by our own feeling as authors, we guess that he would rather know our genuine first thoughts, than wait for cool second thoughts, or have a regular eulogium or criticism put in the most lucid manner, and given in the finest sentences that ever were rounded.

* * *

Believe me, I have not, nor can I convey to you the full idea of the pleasure, the delight we have had in reading "Waverley," nor of the

---

[†] From J. C. Augustus Hare, ed., *The Life and Letters of Maria Edgeworth*, vol. 1 (Cambridge, MA: Houghton Mifflin, 1895), pp. 239, 242, 244.

1. Either a Scotsman or the Devil. In her letter addressed to the author (but sent to Sir Walter Scott's publisher), Edgeworth playfully acknowledges Scott as being the author of the anonymously published *Waverley* (1814). This letter sparked a lifelong friendship between the two authors.

feeling of sorrow with which we came to the end of the history of persons whose real presence had so filled our minds—we felt that we must return to the *flat realities* of life, that our stimulus was gone, and we were little disposed to read the "Postscript, which should have been a Preface."

"Well, let us hear it," said my father, and Mrs. Edgeworth read on.

Oh! my dear sir, how much pleasure would my father, my mother, my whole family, as well as myself have lost, if we had not read to the last page! And the pleasure came upon us so unexpectedly—we had been so completely absorbed that every thought of ourselves, of our own authorship, was far, far away.

Thank you for the honor you have done us, and for the pleasure you have given us, great in proportion to the opinion we had formed of the work we had just perused—and believe me, every opinion I have in this letter expressed was formed before any individual in the family had peeped to the end of the book, or knew how much we owed you.

Your obliged and grateful

Maria Edgeworth

SIR WALTER SCOTT

From General Preface to the 1829 Edition of *Waverley*[†]

> —And must I ravel out
> My weaved-up follies?
> RICHARD II. *Act IV.*

* * *

Two circumstances in particular recalled my recollection of the mislaid manuscript. The first was the extended and well-merited fame of Miss Edgeworth, whose Irish characters have gone so far to make the English familiar with the character of their gay and kind-hearted neighbours of Ireland, that she may be truly said to have done more towards completing the Union than perhaps all the legislative enactments by which it has been followed up.

Without being so presumptuous as to hope to emulate the rich humour, pathetic tenderness, and admirable tact, which pervade the works of my accomplished friend, I felt that something might be

---

[†] Sir Walter Scott, *Waverley; or, 'Tis Sixty Years Since*, (Edinburgh: Adam & Charles Black, 1871). The "General Preface" was written by Scott for the 1829 edition of *Waverley*.

attempted for my own country of the same kind with that which Miss Edgeworth so fortunately achieved for Ireland—something which might introduce her natives to those of the sister kingdom in a more favourable light than they had been placed hitherto, and tend to procure sympathy for their virtues and indulgence for their foibles. I thought also that much of what I wanted in talent might be made up by the intimate acquaintance with the subject which I could lay claim to possess, as having travelled through most parts of Scotland, both Highland and Lowland; having been familiar with the elder as well as more modern race; and having had from my infancy free and unrestrained communication with all ranks of my countrymen, from the Scottish peer to the Scottish ploughman. Such ideas often occurred to me, and constituted an ambitious branch of my theory, however far short I may have fallen of it in practice.

* * *

Juvenilia

From The Double Disguise†

As with *Castle Rackrent*, Edgeworth's youthful comedic drama, *The Double Disguise*, was produced as entertainment for family and close friends. Written in 1786 and performed at Edgeworthstown at Christmas the same year, *The Double Disguise* marks a literary turning point in Edgeworth's career. It is important that it includes her first surviving Irish sketch, the character of Justice Cocoa, a Tipperary grocer who has risen in social standing to become an officer in the Volunteers.[1] In a 1786 letter to Erasmus Darwin (Charles Darwin's grandfather), Richard Lovell Edgeworth wrote of the recently performed *Double Disguise*:

> We have just been acting a little farce, for our own family and intimate visitors *only*. The piece written, and all the characters filled, by ourselves.
>
> We promised Lord and Lady Longford and their children, who came to stay some days with us, that we would give them a play of *home-manufacture*.[2]

In Marilyn Butler's biography of Maria Edgeworth, she states of *The Double Disguise* and other minor comic dramas written by Edgeworth that "they carry no weight as political statements about Ireland."[3] In part, this is an accurate assessment of *The Double Disguise*. Yet the character portrayals (in particular those of the servant ranks), the employment of plot devices Edgeworth reused in her later work, and the fact that her Irish character of Justice Cocoa shares a distinctively similar brogue and use of Hiberno-English to Thady mean that *The Double Disguise* is not as easily dismissed as

† From Maria Edgeworth, *The Double Disguise*, ed. Christine Alexander and Ryan Twomey (Sydney: Juvenilia Press, 2014). Reprinted by permission of Juvenilia Press.
1. For "Volunteers," see n. 6, p. 104. County Tipperary is located in the province of Munster, Ireland.
2. Richard Lovell Edgeworth, *Memoirs of Richard Lovell Edgeworth, Begun by Himself and Concluded by His Daughter*, vol. 2 (Shannon: Irish University Press, 1969), p. 80.
3. Marilyn Butler, *Maria Edgeworth: A Literary Biography* (Oxford: Clarendon Press, 1972), p. 125.

Edgeworth's other minor works.[4] For the first time in this edition the text of *Castle Rackrent* and excerpts of Edgeworth's *The Double Disguise* are printed together. The text and notes of the latter are excerpted from the Juvenilia Press edition of *Maria Edgeworth: The Double Disguise*, edited by Christine Alexander and Ryan Twomey, 2014.

List of Characters[5]

JUSTICE COCOA, an Irish Volunteer[6]
MISS DOROTHEA COCOA, "Dolly", daughter to the Justice
FANNY, cousin to Miss Cocoa
CHARLES WESTBROOKE (ALSO FORTUNE TELLER, CAPTAIN CAMPBELL)
LANDLADY, MRS THUNDER, landlady of an English Inn, the Pig & Castle
BETTY BROOM, chambermaid
BOOTS, post-boy or driver of a chaise
BLUE COAT BOY, charity scholar who acts as a delivery boy

Minor characters (with no speaking role):

BUTCHER FLY BLOW, butcher at the Pig & Castle
JIM WAITER, waiter at the Pig & Castle
NAN COOK, cook at the Pig & Castle
TIM TROWELL, painter and handyman at the Pig & Castle

[From the opening scenes of *The Double Disguise*, Edgeworth signals her intent to produce recognizable characters, going about their mundane daily activities. Yet, as with Thady's comment that he "thanked [his] stars he was not born a gentleman" (p. 16), those of the lower classes in *The Double Disguise* appear to accept their role in the social hierarchy and are subversive in their commentary on characters of a higher social standing. Further, like Jason in *Castle Rackrent*, Edgeworth presents her middle-class characters as those most desirous to rise in social status. The passages reprinted here provide an example of Edgeworth's earliest surviving attempt at these representations.]

4. See Ryan Twomey, *"The Child Is Father of the Man": The Importance of Juvenilia in the Development of the Author* (Houten, Netherlands: Hes & De Graaf, 2012), pp. 19–52.
5. Edgeworth does not have a list of Dramatis Personae at the beginning of her play, only a partial list of characters and cast at the end with the names of family members who first participated in its performance. This list, together with descriptive information, is derived from several sources, as documented in the Note on the Text.
6. The Irish Volunteers (also known simply as "Volunteers") were local militias raised to defend Ireland from the threat of French and Spanish invasion when British troops were dispatched from Ireland for the American Revolutionary War (1775–83). Throughout the 1760s and 1770s, volunteer units were made up of local landlords in various parts of the country for the preservation of peace and protection of property (Kieran Kennedy, "Limerick Volunteers 1776–93," *The Old Limerick Journal* [winter 1999]: 21–26).

* * *

BETTY BROOM [*behind the scenes*]   Coming Ma'am, coming!
[*Enter* BETTY BROOM]

LANDLADY   Coming, why so is Christmas. Why where have you been gossiping, and what have you been about all this time?

BETTY BROOM   About, Ma'am! Was not I all morning helping Jim Waiter to pick sloes for port wine & pare turnips for cyder?[7] Lord knows I have had enough to be about—had not I a dozen pair of sheets to sprinkle[8] for the stage folks[9] & a whole week's tea leaves to dry and—

* * *

LANDLADY   What rooms have you ready? Hey? Has Tim Trowell finished white washing[1] the Blackmoore's Head?[2]

BETTY BROOM   Yes Madam, he has just done, but it feels so damp & cold, I'm afraid we can't put any body into it tonight.

LANDLADY   What's to hinder it? Twill do well enough for the stage people—and do you hear let the Comet[3] be kept for the job & four[4] that's coming downwards & be sure to keep all the best rooms for last—there's a power of company on the road.

   [*Exit* BETTY BROOM. *A cry of* "Hostler—a light here—the Volunteer has lost his sword & dropt his cockade"][5]

LANDLADY   Lights there—heartily welcome ladies—very long stage the last—I'm afraid you found the roads deadly heavy at this time o'year. Betty, Betty Broom, shew the company into the Blackamores head.

---

7. Sloe, the small ovate fruit of the blackthorn, has a black or dark-purple colour and a sharp sour taste. The Pig & Castle passes itself off as a fine establishment, while cutting corners and using cheap substitutes for food and drink, such as using sloes for port wine and pared (peeled) turnips for cider.

8. Soaking laundry in lye was part of the bleaching process; sometimes cloth was sprinkled in between laundering with water and lye soap to lengthen the process and enhance bleaching ("Washing clothes and household linen").

9. Travellers arriving by stage-coach.

1. To cover or coat with whitewash, a low-cost type of paint made from slaked lime and chalk. The aim is to give an immediate fresh appearance.

2. The name of a room at the *Pig & Castle*; "blackamoor" is an archaic term for a black African or dark-skinned person; also figuratively, a devil. Used here it is a possible reference to the colloquialism "to wash a blackamoor (white)," namely "to labour in vain." Edgeworth uses this term again in *Castle Rackrent* (1800): "What will become of him and his, . . . with this heretic Blackamore [Lord Rackrent's Jewish wife] at the head of the Castle Rackrent estate," p. 22.

3. The Comet, the Sun, the Peacock and the Blackmoore's Head are room names at the *Pig & Castle*. Jane Austen makes the same comic use of room names in eighteenth-century inns in her early "The first Act of a Comedy" (Jane Austen, *Three Mini-Dramas*, ed. Juliet McMaster and Lesley Peterson [Sydney: Juvenilia Press, 2006]).

4. The carriage (job: a cartload) and the number of horses (four) pulling the carriage—and by extension here, its passengers.

5. It is not clear from the manuscript to whom this line is attributed. A hostler is a stableman who attends to horses at an inn. A *cockade* is a knot of ribbons, a rosette, worn in the hat as a badge of office or party, or as part of a livery dress.

BETTY BROOM   Please to walk this way ladies . . .

> [BETTY BROOM *opens a door on one side Stage. The moment*
> MISS COCOA *sees the room—starts back*]

MISS COCOA   Oh horrid! Is that to be our apartment! Our Irish
Inns on the Sligo[6] road are better ten to one than this. Just white
washed all wet! I hope Mrs Landlady you don't mean to put us
into such a room as this?

LANDLADY   [*setting her arms akimbo*] Why Madam for that matter . . .

FANNY   Oh Madam, to be sure the room's as good a room as I could
wish for my own part, but my Cousin has caught a very bad cold
on the road, & I'm afraid sitting so long in a damp room might
increase it.

JUSTICE COCOA   By Jabus[7] Mrs Landlady, if we don't take care I'm
afraid we shall be in a minority, & so, as I perceive it to be the
unanimous opinion of the whole Corps,[8] I give the casting vote
for another & more suitable apartment—we must not let Dolly
catch cold.

                    ☆   ☆   ☆

LANDLADY   Your half Gentry[9] always give one more trouble than
the best quality in the land, I will say that for them. They are so
touchy & dainty forsooth[1] I wish folks would know their places so
I do.

                    ☆   ☆   ☆

MISS COCOA   ☆ ☆ ☆ Lord any thing's good enough you know for a
stagecoach—one's so afraid of being seen—and besides, really
now, to be packed up with all sorts of company without being
able to help oneself. I protest, Papa, I don't think it's fit for young
ladies. Thank God last stage there was nobody but our selves.
But now there was the stage before last, I was nigh stifled to
death by the great fat cheese monger's wife who sat herself plump
down beside me without saying with your leave, or by your leave.

---

6. (Irish: *Sligeach*, meaning "shelly place.") County Sligo is in the northwest of Ireland,
about forty miles from the border with Northern Ireland; it has a county town of the
same name, to which Dolly is referring.

7. Edgeworth's rendering of the Anglo-Irish pronunciation of "Jebus," meaning Jesus
(Flynn, "Dialect as Didactic Tool: Maria Edgeworth's Use of Hiberno-English," 159).
In the seventeenth century, "Jebus" was a nickname for Roman Catholics, especially
Jesuits.

8. A division of the Irish Volunteers: see n. 6, p. 104.

9. Gentry refers to the class in society immediately below the nobility; Maria Edgeworth's family were considered gentry. The Landlady's scorn is directed to those who
ape the Gentry and pretend to this rank through recent acquisition of wealth, rather
like the modern-day *nouveaux riches*. Here we have what appears to be the earliest
surviving commentary on class status by Edgeworth.

1. In truth.

JUSTICE COCOA   Why now upon my conscience, I don't know whether it was'nt more considerate of her to do it without your leave than against it. Besides, where now would you expect her to sit? The other side of the coach was full; would you have had her sit upon your lap?

MISS COCOA   Oh no Papa, but those sort of people should learn to keep their distance you know. And there Fanny, there was the woman & her child that you took such a fancy to & must needs hold upon your lap half the stage. I protest I could see no beauty in it for my part. I thought when the mother offered us almonds & raisins that she would turn out to be some grocer's wife or other.

JUSTICE COCOA   Take care Dolly, you are upon tender ground between you & I, remember what you are some of yourself, Dolly.

MISS COCOA   Dear Sir, if you & my Mother did keep a grocer's shop, it was in wholesale line & besides you know it was before I was born. But now Papa you are a Volunteer you know, & a Gentleman you know, and so do dear Sir let's take a chaise & four[2] next stage. What signifies the expence for the two stages we have to go? At the worst it would be but a guinea[3] extra ordinary, chay boy,[4] hostlers, turnpikes[5] and all. Do dear Papa, let's have a chaise & four?

*   *   *

ACT 2 SCENE 7

[*Enter* WESTBROOKE *as* Cap[n] CAMPBELL *without legs & with a black patch over one eye*]

FANNY   Mercy on us, Cousin, he'es scarcely human!

MISS COCOA   In truth he *is* a little disfigured.

BETTY BROOM   Shall I sit you there, Sir?

WESTBROOKE   Yes my good girl, here if you please. Madam, you see before you the fortunate man whom you have permitted to entertain hopes of becoming pleasing in your bright eyes. I am a little out of breath, Madam, with the fatigue of being carried up stairs— but I shall be able presently to make myself better understood.

---

2. Also "chay & four"; a light open carriage drawn by four horses. Lighter and faster than the stage-coach, the chaise usually held two persons, with a dicky behind for the servants; it was driven by a post-boy or "chay-boy" who rode one of the horses (Rosamond Bayne-Powell, "The Coaches," *Travellers in Eighteenth-Century England* [London: John Murray, 1951] <www.ourcivilisation.com>).
3. An English gold coin, not minted since 1813.
4. See n. 2, above.
5. Roads on which turnpikes were erected for the collection of tolls; hence, a main road or highway formerly maintained by a toll levied on cattle and wheeled vehicles.

MISS COCOA   For heaven's sake Papa, do say something to him for I'm thunderstruck.[6]

*   *   *

WESTBROOKE   Nothing Sir shall be wanting on my part & I hope the young lady will not retract the condescending encouragement she has given me.

FANNY   [aside] For God's sake, Cousin, don't have anything to say?

MISS COCOA   Indeed Sir, I must say that I think myself at liberty to retract. And I must observe that it was not so open, so soldier like of you to prepare me for only a trifling accident, the loss of one limb for instance, when you must have foreseen the shock my nerves were to receive.

WESTBROOKE   Pardon me Miss Cocoa, a fault occasioned by my too great anxiety to please. I could not prevail upon myself to represent my form to your imagination in colors so frightful, before I had the possibility of softening the impression.

MISS COCOA   Possibility!

WESTBROOKE   Madam I can not expect to do that in a first interview which it shall be the business of my life to effect. From the first moment, Madam, that I had the most distant hopes—my whole mind has been intent upon procuring every thing which I thought would please you. The most elegant chariot which could be procured already waits your command.

MISS COCOA   Chariot indeed! You don't think, Sir, I would expose myself continually in a chariot, tête à tête[7] with my husband.

JUSTICE COCOA   Captain, between your two billets, by the wheel of fortune, Dolly's become Mistress of ten thousand pounds of her own; and I assure you she begins to hold her head very high.

WESTBROOKE   I am extremely sorry, Madam, that the idea of favoring me with your company & conversation in an equipage, which I had fondly thought would be agreeable to you, should have such a contrary effect—but my sollicitude to please you in affairs of consequence will I hope be measured by my eagerness to comply with your taste in trifles. I shall write this very night to Hacket[8] to bespeak the handsomest coach he can make.

MISS COCOA   Well to be sure, Captain, that is very obliging.

---

6. Struck with amazement.
7. Together without the presence of a third person; in private (of two persons); face to face.
8. A very Irish name, also the name of a make of coach; but here it may be a play on the verb "to hack," to chop up or mutilate.

WESTBROOKE   If Miss Cocoa would condescend to name the color
of her horses, they shall be bought immediately.

JUSTICE COCOA   Black, white, or pie balled,[9] hey Dolly?

MISS COCOA   Bays Sir, cock tail bees[1] if you please. But Captain, if
ever I should have the misfortune to become attached—my sympathy would be so exquisite—I should be in a perpetual agony of
distress for you in company.

JUSTICE COCOA   [aside] Aye, in company Dolly!

*   *   *

BETTY BROOM   [aside] Well what ladies will do for fortune! Now I
who have my bread to earn would not have him I know . . . Lack-
adaisy it's a strange thing!

*   *   *

ACT I SCENE 3

[The Double Disguise and Castle Rackrent contain verbal and literary
similarities through their employment of Hiberno-English[2] and the
use of analogous quotes and phrases. A representative sample is provided in the excerpts below.]

[JUSTICE COCOA, MISS COCOA, FANNY and BETTY BROOM]

JUSTICE COCOA   [to BETTY] Come my good girl, make us up a good
fire, for faith & troth[3] I'm perished alive. And let me have the
newspaper now as soon as convenient.

MISS COCOA   Oh yes, do pray bring us the newspaper directly, for I
long to know the fate of my ticket in the Lottery.[4]

JUSTICE COCOA   Upon my conscience Dolly, I belave your head
runs on nothing but that same confounded ticket!

---

9. Piebald, a horse having black and white patches.
1. Cocktail horses, i.e. their tails have been docked so that the short stump leaves hair
sticking up like a cock's tail. Dolly's use of the word "bees" is probably an Anglo-Irish
irregular use of "to be" (Joyce Flynn, "Dialect as Didactic Tool: Maria Edgeworth's Use
of Hiberno-English" [Proceedings of the Harvard Celtic Colloquium 2(1982): 115–86]).
2. Examples of Hiberno-English included in the excerpted passages are 'Jabus' (Jesus),
'clane' (clean), and 'belave' (believe). Instances of this use of Hiberno-English in Castle
Rackrent are 'pin' (pen) p. 32, 'Jasus' (Jesus) p. 48, and 'larning' (learning) p. 49. For
more on the "Hibernicized" language in Castle Rackrent see Flynn's, Dialect as a
Didactic Tool pp. 193–198, and Hollingworth's Edgeworth's Irish Writing pp. 199–203,
in this Norton Critical Edition. [Editor]
3. Troth is a "vulgar" word, a corruption of "truth," as in the Irish phrase, "faith and
troth!" (The Vulgarities of Speech Corrected: With Elegant Expressions for Provincial
and Vulgar English, Scots, and Irish; For the Use of Those Who Are Unacquainted with
Grammar, 2nd ed. [London: F. C. Westley, 1829], 166).
4. In 1780 the Irish government initiated the first state-controlled lottery. Tickets in the
Irish lottery were moderately priced, encouraging all levels of society to participate
and newspapers perpetuated interest in the lottery (Rowena Dudley, The Irish Lottery,
1780–1801 [Dublin: Four Courts Press, 2005], 13).

MISS COCOA   Dear Sir, I am so impatient!

JUSTICE COCOA   By Jabus & so am I for my supper, & so pray summons Mrs Landlady. Fanny dear, come in here to the fire & don't stand there sewing that cockade o'mine on. Pooh.[5] leave it there now. Here Waiter, please to take this sword along with you & see to get the hilt[6] of it washed clane. The sword of a Volunteer should never be contaminated.

WESTBROOKE   But Mrs Betty, it's an ill wind, as the saying is, that blows nobody good.[7]

*   *   *

JUSTICE COCOA   Phoo! Phoo! Phoo![8] Arrah, now be quiet. Who do you take me for to be putting your flying mutilation upon me?

*   *   *

5. A "vocal gesture" expressing the action of puffing something away (*Online Etymology Dictionary*). Like the alternatives "pugh" and "phoo," both of which Edgeworth also uses in *The Double Disguise*, it expresses contemptuous rejection, cursory dismissal, impatience or disdain. "Pooh" is first found in Shakespeare's *Hamlet* (Act 1, Scene 3) and all three forms were used in the eighteenth century. The *OED* cites a nuanced meaning of "Phoo," first used by Maria Edgeworth in 1800 in *Castle Rackrent*: "Phoo, I've cut myself with this razor" (p. 44). This usage, "Expressing discomfort, disgust, weariness, or relief," actually occurs before *Castle Rackrent* in *The Double Disguise*: see n. 8 below.

6. The handle of a sword or dagger.

7. Edgeworth reuses this phrase in *Castle Rackrent*. See p. 28. [Editor]

8. Edgeworth's nuanced use of "Phoo." [Editor]

CRITICISM

General Studies

WALTER ALLEN

[*Castle Rackrent's* Originality]†

I

Significant changes, new directions, in literature are rarely so obliging as to coincide in their appearance with such convenient points in time as the turn of a century. The year 1800, however, is a date of the first importance in the history of English fiction, indeed of world fiction, for in that year Maria Edgeworth published her short novel *Castle Rackrent.* Not her first book, it was her first work of fiction proper, and had she written nothing else, P. H. Newby's suggestive remark, in his admirable little book on her, would still hold good: 'Whereas Jane Austen was so much the better novelist Maria Edgeworth may be the more important.' The judgment needs expanding before it makes sense, but Maria Edgeworth herself was nearly a great novelist, and her purely historical importance must not blind us to the positive merit of her own achievement.

Miss Edgeworth occupied new territory for the novel. Before her, except when London was the scene, the locale of our fiction had been generalized, conventionalized. Outside London and Bath, the eighteenth-century novelist rarely had a sense of place; the background of his fiction is as bare of scenery almost as an Elizabethan play; and when landscape came in for its own sake, with Mrs Radcliffe,[1] it was there not because it was a specific landscape but because it was a romantic one. Maria Edgeworth gave fiction a local habitation and a name. And she did more than this: she perceived the relation between the local habitation and the people who dwell in it. She invented, in other words, the regional novel, in which the very nature of the novelist's characters is conditioned,

---

† From Walter Allen, "The Nineteenth Century: The First Generation," in *The English Novel: A Short Critical History* (London: Phoenix House, 1954), pp. 98–100. Reprinted by permission of David Higham Associates. All notes are the editor's.
1. Ann Radcliffe (1764–1823), a pioneer of the Gothic novel known for her vivid descriptions of landscapes and travel scenes.

receives its bias and expression, from the fact that they live in a countryside differentiated by a traditional way of life from other countrysides.

The region she discovered was Ireland, and, with Ireland, the Irish peasant. She was what would now be called Anglo-Irish, one of the ruling class, and she is the first of a long line of Anglo-Irish novelists who have exploited the humours of the Irish peasantry and its relation to the big house: Lover, Lever, Somerville and Ross were her literary descendants. But her influence goes far beyond this, as we may realize when we consider how many of the world's great novelists, from Scott through Flaubert to Mauriac, are regional novelists. Scott made no secret of his debt to her;[2] his aim in fiction, as he said in the postscript to *Waverley*, was 'in some distant degree to emulate the admirable Irish portraits drawn by Miss Edgeworth', and when we read these words we have to remember how enormous was Scott's influence on the novel throughout the western world. But her direct influence goes even beyond Scott. Turgenev[3] is said to have stated that he was 'an unconscious disciple of Miss Edgeworth in setting out on his literary career'.

The originality of Maria Edgeworth's contribution to the novel is apparent as soon as one begins to read *Castle Rackrent*, short as it is. It is not so important, perhaps, that in it she wrote the first of all 'saga' novels, tracing the history of a family through several generations. What matters much more is the way in which the history of the Rackrent family, who are Irish landowners, is told. The story is narrated in the first person by old Thady, a peasant who is the ancient retainer of the family. So we have at once a family history and a vivid self-portrait of an old man, simple, shrewd, possessed of native dignity, told in his own language, which, though naturally a literary version, is close enough to Irish peasant speech to retain the illusion of authenticity. And Thady is a delightful character, rich in what we now think of as typically Irish humour, the more beguiling because it is unconscious. An example is his comment on the death of Sir Patrick Rackrent:

> The whole country rang with his praises. Happy the man who could but get a sight of the hearse! But who'd have thought it? Just as all was going on right, through his own town they were passing, when the body was seized for debt.

At the same time, through Thady's voice, there is summed up the whole social history of a country over four generations. *Castle*

---

2. See Sir Walter Scott on p. 99.
3. Ivan Sergeyevich Turgenev (1818–1883), Russian novelist and playwright.

Rackrent is a very considerable work of art in fiction, and how remarkable Maria Edgeworth was as an innovator in this novel we may probably best estimate at this point in time by setting beside it a novel that did a comparable job for its own national literature eighty years later: Mark Twain's *Huckleberry Finn*, the novel that freed American fiction from the domination of specifically English literature.

W. J. McCORMACK

[*The Black Book of Edgeworthstown*]†

It has often been noted that Edgeworth family lore contains anecdotes which may have been models for some of the more extravagant behaviour of the earlier generations of Rackrent. Maria Edgeworth's biographer, Marilyn Butler, simply accepts that 'the Edgeworths of earlier times are beyond question the real models for the four generations of the Rackrent family', and adds that their careers 'could be paralleled in dozens of anecdotes about the Anglo-Irish squirearchy of the seventeenth and eighteenth centuries'. Mrs Butler is certainly right in observing that 'tracing the history of the direct line gives an inadequate idea' of the novelist's borrowings; what is of interest to the literary historian is the bearing upon *form* of the interactions of method and source in the fiction. Here, the biographer leads us to—but does not exploit—a vital element in the composition of *Castle Rackrent*:

> In her grandfather's narrative in the 'Black Book' Maria had an outline which strongly resembled the plot of *Castle Rackrent*—a family saga compounded of debts and prosperous marriages; successive landlords who were selfishly oblivious of their tenants, and yet were strikingly endowed with personal charm, humour, and finally pathos.[1]

Far from confirming any sturdy sense of succession in Maria Edgeworth's exploitation of family history, the presence of a 'black book' of Edgeworth tradition is an indicator of the novelist's nervous reliance on the privacy of a written text as well as on the publicly recognizable narrative skills of a Thady Quirk. The imposition of that short title, *Castle Rackrent*, upon so complex a narrative is an

---

† From W. J. McCormack, *Ascendancy and Tradition in Anglo-Irish Literary History from 1789 to 1939*, (Oxford: Clarendon Press, 1985), pp. 103–05. Reprinted by permission of the author.
1. Marilyn Butler, "Maria Edgeworth: A Literary Biography (Oxford: Clarendon Press, 1972).

example of the romantic insistence upon a unity which is no more than a (usually degraded) longing for unity. If we note the as yet crudely transcribed material of family history together with the ironies of Thady's narrative, then we have discovered in the backwaters of Anglo-Irish literature a prime example of Walter Benjamin's analysis of romantic symbolism. Illegitimate talk of the symbolic, Benjamin argues, leads to a neglect of a proper discussion of 'content in formal analysis' and of 'form in the aesthetics of content'.[2] Resisting the orthodox pleas to assimilate content and form, we may find in *Castle Rackrent* the origins of an allegorical mode of writing and interpretation which will take us through to the late work of Yeats and Joyce[3] as a characteristic of Anglo-Irish literature.

There is no doubt that *The Black Book of Edgeworthstown*, even in the synthetic edition available to the public, is of compelling relevance to any reading of *Castle Rackrent*. Casually, one reads of Sir John Edgeworth (1638–96) that, having gambled away his wife's most valuable jewels and won them back again 'some time afterwards he was found in a hay yard with a friend, drawing straws out of the hayrick, and betting upon which should be the longest.'[4] Having read the story, Sir Condy's mode of choosing a wife attaches itself to a sequence of such stories. Yet resemblances between the family chronicle and the novel are less significant than silent divergences. *Castle Rackrent* is almost innocent of sectarian allusion, whereas in *The Black Book* the intermarriage of Protestant and Catholic is the marriage of Francis Edgeworth and Jane Tuite sometime around 1590. Their son, John Edgeworth, left his wife and son in their house at Crannelagh 'some days before the fatal 23rd of October, 1641'.[5] In keeping with the long-standing tradition of Papist treachery, rebels suddenly seized the house, humiliated the wife, and made to murder the child: they were prevailed upon to spare the property because 'there was the picture of that pious Catholic, Jane Tuite, painted on the wainscot with her beads and crucifix . . .'.[6] A loyal servant had meantime saved the infant heir by pretending to reserve the privilege of murdering him to himself. Not only are these diverse details of the potency of an image, an illusion in preserving the

2. Walter Benjamin, *The Origins of German Tragic Drama*, trans. John Osborne (London: New Left Books, 1977), p. 160.
3. James Joyce (1882–1941), Irish poet and novelist best known for *Ulysses* (1922). William Butler Yeats (1865–1939), Irish poet and prominent twentieth-century literary figure [editor's note].
4. *The Black Book of Edgeworthstown and Other Edgeworth Memories 1585–1817*, ed. H. J. Butler and H. E. Butler (London: Faber and Gwyer, 1927), p. 19 (quoting R. L. Edgeworth's *Memoirs*).
5. Ibid., pp. 11–12.
6. Ibid., p. 13.

endangered line of the Edgeworths in Ireland but, the chronicler records:

> This event was told me . . . by an eye-witness of the fact, one Simpson, who was a little foot-boy in Captain Edgeworth's family in 1641, being then eleven years old. He came at my request to my house in 1737. He was then a hundred and seven years old; his understanding and memory seemed perfect, though he was not quite sincere in all his relations. His eyes were very dim, his voice a little hollow, but he was strong and walked from his house to mine, upward of a mile, the day I saw him, and refused to ride. He smelt like new-digged earth.[7]

The value of a narrator, less than ingenuous, in holding together the details of a family's varied generations, was evident to Maria Edgeworth whenever she consulted *The Black Book*.

SEAMUS DEANE

[The Irish Novel][†]

Two women, Maria Edgeworth and Lady Morgan,[1] dominate Irish fiction in the first two decades of the nineteenth century. Edgeworth's four Irish novels—*Castle Rackrent* (1800), *Ennui* (1809), *The Absentee* (1812) and *Ormond* (1817)—provide the first serious attempt in fiction to analyse and recommend improvements for Irish society as it was, after the Act of Union in 1800 had extinguished the bright hopes associated with the frail parliamentary independence of 1782 and the dark fears arising from the fierce rebellion of 1798. The price to be paid for the Union with Great Britain was to be Catholic Emancipation. Promised by the British Prime Minister Pitt, it was refused by George III and successive administrations, until it was won by Daniel O'Connell in 1829 after a long campaign of disciplined pressure, exercised through mass meetings and the increasingly organized power of the Catholic clergy. The measure, which would have been politically more effective had it been freely given, had the unforeseen consequence of bringing into being the powerful Catholic nation, which felt little gratitude for what it had been forced to win for itself. Between the Union and Emancipation,

7. Ibid., pp. 13–14.
† From Seamus Deane, "Nineteenth-Century Fiction," in *A Short History of Irish Literature* (London: Hutchinson Education, 1986), pp. 90–97, 116. Reprinted by permission.
1. Née Owenson (1776–1859), an Irish novelist, best known as the author of *The Wild Irish Girl* (1806) [editor's note].

therefore, the Protestant Ascendancy[2] lost its last chance to retain political leadership in Ireland. Maria Edgeworth attempted to show how that leadership could have been preserved; Lady Morgan unwittingly demonstrated in her novels why it could not have been. Both of them finally despaired of writing about the different Ireland that emerged after 1829.[3] Yet each bore witness to the fact that the writing of Irish fiction, like the writing of Irish history in the same period, was inescapably bound up with the increasingly partisan debate about the condition of Ireland and the means of improving it. * * * [Edgeworth] was the first novelist to find an effective means of representing in fiction the subjugation of the individual to social forces. She achieved in the novel what Mme de Stael[4] achieved in her essays and discursive writings, the absorption into literature of the ideas of the great Enlightenment thinkers on the nature of social formations—Montesquieu, Adam Smith, Adam Ferguson, John Miller and Thomas Reid.[5] * * * The romantic hero found his home in poetry, not in the novel. Sir Walter Scott, profoundly impressed by *The Absentee*, followed in Maria Edgeworth's footsteps by portraying a whole community, hitherto ignored or the object of cariacture and antipathy, in its historical reality as reflected through a relatively colourless central character. As a consequence, ancillary groups or characters are often more vividly represented, because they are the object of observation. The observer is always to some degree detached, a commentator as well as a participant.

Yet this is precisely what we do not find in *Castle Rackrent*, the first of Edgeworth's Irish tales. As a tale, it belongs to a specific genre, perfected in the eighteenth century by Voltaire, Dr Johnson and Marmontel[6]—that of the philosophic fable, which is neither novel nor short story but more given than either to didactic illustration. The problem with *Rackrent* is that there has been much dispute about what is being illustrated. Therefore, as a tale, it is not effective. The narrator, Thady M'Quirk, recounts the story of the ruin of the Rackrent family over four generations. He is illiterate, so his story is dictated to the 'Editor', a device for the presentation of dialect

2. Or simply the Ascendancy, a minority group of landowners who dominated the economic, social, and political domains in Ireland between the seventeenth and early twentieth century. All were members of the established church (Church of Ireland and Church of England) while being regarded as exclusionary toward Roman Catholics [editor's note].
3. The Roman Catholic Relief Act was passed by Parliament in 1829 [editor's note].
4. Germaine de Staël (1766–1817), a French woman of letters [editor's note].
5. See especially her *De la littérature considerée dans ses rapports avec les institutions sociales* (Paris, 1800).
6. Jean-François Marmontel (1723–1799), French historian and writer. Voltaire was the *non de plume* of François-Marie Arouet (1694–1778), French Enlightenment writer, historian, and philosopher. Samuel Johnson (1709–1784), highly influential writer and literary critic [editor's note].

speech which Edgeworth made popular. Thady is feudally loyal to his useless masters, whose only skill is in self-destruction—'Sir Patrick by drink, Sir Murtagh by law, Sir Kit by gambling, and Sir Condy, in the amplest portrait of all, by the spendthrift life of politics'.[7] His final loyalty to Sir Condy, the most attractive of the quartet, forces him to choose his master over his son, Jason, Attorney Quirk, who has assumed control of the Rackrent property with that silent rapacity characteristic of the land agent or middleman much used by absentee or feckless landlords in the administration of their Irish estates. The tale is set in the eighteenth century, in the years before the achievement of parliamentary independence in 1782. After that, not much else is certain, except that Thady's voice is a new one in fiction. He has more than a dialect, he has a style— insinuating, colourful and agreeable. But is it also ironic? Is Thady a pseudo-simpleton, taking a degree of pleasure in telling the tale of Ascendancy ruin and the rise of the Irish middle class, represented by his son Jason of whom he pretends to disapprove? If this reading is dismissed, it can quickly be replaced by the more sombre view of the tale as a requiem for the Ascendancy, to which Maria Edgeworth belonged and for which the Union was the final stroke of doom. It could even be a lament for the passing of that ramshackle but warm-hearted Ireland of the early century, replaced now by the more sober and duller society that was still in a state of shock after 1798 and the Union. Or, finally, and perhaps most persuasively, *Rackrent* is the aggressive prelude to Edgeworth's later novels on Ireland, a demonstration of the ruin which an irresponsible aristocracy brings upon itself and upon its dependents. This is a moral judgement not accessible to Thady, who is, bluntly, too stupid and blinded by his pathetic loyalty, to see the significance of the tale he tells. Certainly, Edgeworth's later work supports this last reading, although the other readings are important too in their readiness to see in this work a useful point of origin for the representation of modern Ireland in fiction. The meaning of the relationship between landlord and peasant may be a matter of dispute, but its centrality is not. In that respect, *Rackrent* does point towards the future, even though it is also concerned to dismiss an unfortunate past.

Maria Edgeworth introduced the English public to the Irish problem even more effectively than Arthur Young's brilliant survey, *Tour in Ireland* (1780). Because she was writing fiction in an age which still thought of novels as faintly disreputable and unreliable, she went to some pains to affirm that she was relaying the truth, however improbable it might seem to a non-Irish audience:

---

7. Maria Edgeworth, *Castle Rackrent*, ed. with introduction by George Watson (London, 1964).

> . . . to those who are totally unacquainted with Ireland, the
> following Memoirs will perhaps be scarcely intelligible, or
> probably they may appear perfectly incredible. (p. 6)[8]

This note is to be heard time and again throughout the century in
Irish fiction, even in those numerous forms of memoir, which were
not, consciously at least, offered as fiction. In the preface to *The
Black Prophet* (1847), William Carleton feels bound to assure his
audience that his account of famine conditions is not exaggerated:

> . . . the reader—especially if he is English or Scotch—may rest
> assured that the author has not at all coloured beyond the
> truth.*[9]

W. S. Trench, a land agent anxious to give the English public some
idea of the problems faced by an improving landlord and some hope
that Ireland is 'not altogether unmanageable', prefaces his *Realities
of Irish Life* (1868) with the comment that

> . . . it has been my lot to live surrounded by a kind of poetic
> turbulence and almost romantic violence, which I believe
> could scarcely belong to real life in any other country in the
> world.[1]

The examples could be multiplied. But, along with this problem of
the incredulous audience, went another—the presentation of the
Irish, especially the Catholic Irish, as a people deserving sympathy
and help. Maria Edgeworth, as part of her educational enterprise to
both the Irish and English, wished to demonstrate that the Irish
needed justice and responsible government so that they might become
more recognizably 'civil', inhabitants of the modern world of industrial Britain rather than the eccentric remains of an outmoded past.
She therefore tended to avail of the stereotyped view of the vivacious, endearingly child-like Irish, in order to arouse sympathy on
their behalf. But in doing so, she allowed Celtic Ireland to intrude
upon her fiction and was therefore never quite able to distance her
work from that vast body of writing on the Irish national character,
its habits, inclinations, tendencies, customs, rites and its peculiar
essence, which casts its apologetic shadow over the literature of this
century. Still, she should be rescued from the bondage of too close
an association with Lady Morgan and the Catholic novelists of the
1820–50 period.

---

8. Page numbers throughout refer to this Norton Critical Edition of *Castle Rackrent*.
9. *The Black Prophet*, introduction by Timothy Webb (Shannon, 1972), Author's Preface,
   pp. vii–viii.
1. William Stewart Treuch, *Realities of Irish Life*, 2nd ed. (London: Longmans, Green,
   and Co., 1869).

For Edgeworth is too pragmatic to be persuaded by the almost metaphysical appeal of the idea of national character, which seduced so many of her English and Irish compatriots. As a novelist, she had enough problems to go on with. She had to persuade a disbelieving audience of the truth of Irish conditions; she had to advocate a means to their improvement by allocating responsibility for their creation, among the Protestant Ascendancy, Orange bigots[2] and the Government in London, as well as the Catholic peasantry themselves, though to a lesser degree, since they were the victims of the situation. The representation of daily life was a much more fraught issue for her than for someone like Jane Austen. English commentators, like Coleridge and Southey, and later, Carlyle and de Quincey, were ready to espouse the notion of an Irish national character which was degraded and at the same time, as de Quincey put it, full of 'a spirit of fiery misrepresentation'.[3] It was hard to believe what passed for reality in Ireland, especially if the reporter was Irish and therefore untrustworthy. The untrustworthiness was often confirmed for the English reader by any attempt to blame or even cast in a disobliging light the vagaries of English misrule or cruelty. National character was a perfect escape hatch for those who found the condition of Ireland intractable and would take no responsibility for it. At the same time, it was appealing for those who wanted to exploit Irish difference—as a romantic race—for an English audience. Yet it was also a serious idea, based on the conviction, which Burke[4] had promoted more effectively than anyone else in recent history, that the character of a race was formed by the conditions in which it had developed, the customs to which it had adhered, the mentality which it had inherited. The transition from the analysis of a society to the stereotyping or exploitation of it was rapid in those 'national' novels, which became so popular in the early nineteenth century in Ireland and in Scotland (with Scott and John Galt[5]). For the novelist who subscribed to this idea in any of its forms, the problem of representation was severe, largely because the possibility of misrepresentation was so easy. If the 'people' were to be represented by someone not of them for a foreign audience, and if their situation was an extreme one, the novelist, who was of and not of the people, was in a politically and aesthetically difficult,

2. The Orange Order [editor's note].
3. De Quincey, 'Autobiographic Sketches', in *De Quincey's Works*, 15 vols (Edinburgh, 1863), XIV, p. 285n; Coleridge, *Essays on His Own Times*, 3 vols, ed. D. V. Erdman (London and New Jersey, 1978), I, pp. 106, 120–1; III, pp. 11–12, pp. 238–46; Carlyle, 'Chartism' and 'Downing Street', in *The Works of Thomas Carlyle*, 30 vols (London, 1898–9), XX and XXIX; Southey, 'On The Catholic Question', in *Essays, Moral and Political* (London, 1832), 2 vols, II, pp. 263–433.
4. Edmund Burke (1729–1797), Irish author and politician [editor's note].
5. Sir Walter Scott (1771–1832) and John Galt (1779–1839), Scottish novelists [editor's note].

if not perilous, position. Perhaps only Walter Scott and Turgenev could be said to have mastered it, and both of them claimed to have learned much from Maria Edgeworth.[6]

Yet the 'national' novel, so-called, retains its early intimacy with the didactic tale and Edgeworth set the precedent for this. From the 1820s, Ireland produced a sub-genre of memoirs, sketches, tales, legends, all of which were devoted to the recording of the hitherto occluded life of the Irish peasantry and many of which did so in an antiquarian spirit, setting down what they feared would soon be lost forever. These were sometimes almost indistinguishable from Irish fiction, both in purpose and quality. Among many examples, one could select Gerald Griffin's *Tales of the Munster Festivals* (1827), *Tales of the O'Hara Family* in the same year by the Banim brothers, Crofton Croker's *Fairy Legends and Traditions of the South of Ireland*, Eyre Evans Crowe's *Today In Ireland*, both of 1825, Cesar Otway's *Sketches in Ireland* (1827), Mrs A. M. Hall's *Sketches of Irish Character* (1829) and, later, Sir William Wilde's *Irish Popular Superstitions* (1852), in the preface to which he declared that, 'Nothing contributes more to uproot superstitious rites and forms than to print them'.[7] The recording of oral tradition certainly alters or ends it, but most of these works are impelled by the desire to give the audience a last glimpse of a dying Gaelic civilization which, in its new printed version, resumes a new species of existence as Celtic Ireland. As the didactic intent which Edgeworth had kept preeminent—both in her *Moral Tales for Young People* (1801) and even in her *Essay on Irish Bulls* (1802)—began to give way before the antiquarian or nostalgic spirit, the tale became less like the philosophic fable or *conte*[8] of the eighteenth century, and more a part of the folklore record. However, in the hands of an artist, it could, so to speak, change direction and become more akin to its descendant, the modern short story. Carleton, in his *Traits and Stories of the Irish Peasantry* (1830–3), shows the short story emerging from the original shell of the tale. It may be that the popularity and success of the short story in modern Ireland has a foundation in the blending of the moral tale with the folklorish elements collected as evidence of the forever elusive national character of the forever vanishing Irish. Maria Edgeworth's role in this process is seminal.

But in *Ennui* and *The Absentee*, her will to educate may be felt to have turned potentially brilliant stories into treatises, which unreservedly recommend Irish landlords to return to their estates in

---

6. See Sir Walter Scott on pp. 101–02 [editor's note].
7. Sir William Wilde, *Irish Popular Superstitions* (Shannon: Irish University Press, 1972).
8. Tale [editor's note].

Ireland and forgo the second-rate life of absenteeism in England. In *Ennui*, the Irish-born hero Lord Glenthorn does return to Ireland in a state of vacuous boredom and there undergoes an education in his responsibilities at the hands of his agent, a Scotsman, M'Leod, who is something of a cross between Adam Smith in his ideas and James Mill in his charm. Opposition to the new M'Leod scheme of improvement is provided by the local squire-bigot, Hardcastle. The year is 1798 and Glenthorn is improbably involved in the rebellion, gains a glorious reputation for capturing a band of rebels and then discovers that he is not the rightful heir to the property after all. His Irish nurse turns out to be his real mother, but the newly dis-covered blood bond between them cannot overcome the cultural differences which their different ways of life have created. Glen-thorn, having finally been educated into the problems of Irish life, having given up the useless life of the absentee gentleman for the useful life of a professional and expert improver, is at the end of all forced to retire to England, and the great ancestral house is burned down by its new Irish peasant owner. The reader is left to wonder if this tale is a treatise on the benefits of educated responsibility or a fable about their inapplicability to the Irish situation. *The Absentee*, less celebrated but possibly finer than *Castle Rackrent*, raises no such doubts. It tells the story of young Lord Colambre, the son of the absentee landlord Lord Clonbrony and his giddy wife, who returns incognito to his Irish estates to redeem them from the ramshackle mess, to which they have been reduced by grasping agents, and remodel them on the pattern laid down by Burke, who is that rare specimen, an honest and industrious agent. Colambre, ashamed of the spectacle presented by his mother in London, where she has repaired to forget her accent and her responsibilities together, is given a quick course in Irish history after the Union by a Dublin friend, Sir James Brooke.[9] This is to reassure him that Dublin and Ireland in general have recovered from the shock of the constitu-tional revolution. Thus, in these three works, Edgeworth is careful to associate the story with crucial moments in recent Irish history— the period before 1782, the rebellion of 1798, the Act of Union in 1800—and to suggest that the recovery from these crises can be achieved through a programme of enlightened leadership on the part of the landed gentry, pursued for their own benefit and for that of the peasantry.

In her last Irish novel, *Ormond* (1817), the young hero of the title, orphaned and dispossessed of his property at birth, is faced with a choice between three modes of life, which represent Edgeworth's

---

9. W. J. McCormack, 'The Absentee', and Maria Edgeworth's Notion of Didactic Fiction, *Atlantis*, no. 5 (April, 1973), pp. 123–35.

vision of the three kinds of leadership available to Ireland. Two of these are attractive but delinquent. Ormond's uncle Ulick O'Shane, a corrupt politician and a Rackrent type, belongs to the sophisticated urban world of the Anglo-Irish of the eighteenth century. His brother, Corny O'Shane, King of the Black Islands (anticipated by the sketch of Count O'Halloran in *The Absentee*), is in some ways a noble and in other ways an absurd remnant of the old Gaelic order. Neither can offer Ormond or Ireland a future. The best hope for that lies with the Annaly family, the very epitome of English steadiness and responsibility. Ormond marries the Annaly daughter, Florence, and inherits King Corny's position as ruler and owner of the Black Islands. The Anglo-Irish, the Gaelic and the English elements are thus reconciled in a dapper conclusion. As always, the Edgeworth hero receives an education which helps to extricate him from the past and prepare him for the future. Yet Ormond's growth as an individual is much less programmatic than that of Glenthorn or Colambre. He grows up to become a leader after serving his apprenticeship to the idea of being led.

Leadership is the preoccupation of these novels. The Protestant landlords in their shattered estates, the Catholic aristocrats in their Gaelic time-warp, represent to the peasantry an idea of leadership which has never been embodied in action. Thady M'Quirk in *Castle Rackrent* may be said to insist on the reality of the idea in order to find something worthy of his devotion. His peculiar attraction, though, is scarcely capable of surviving the repellent aspects of his personality. He is a character only a hairsbreadth removed from caricature. Indeed, most of Edgeworth's people are in this condition. Her utilitarians tend to be as prescribed as her peasants. She observes, although she does not respond very interestingly to the observation, that all classes and types behave in a highly histrionic fashion. They are real in so far as they are close to the fulfilling of a stereotype. In that respect, she not only differs from, say, Jane Austen, but points up a difference between the English and the Irish novel at that time (and later). In the Irish colonial situation there was an irresistible temptation to impersonate the idea of oneself which was entertained by others. Landlord or peasant, English improver or Gaelic remnant, played out roles ascribed to them by a situation which had robbed them of the central sense of responsibility, by effectively denying them basic executive power. Thus it was very Irish to be irresponsible and very English to be responsible and very typical of the English–Irish confrontation to find that neither one could learn from or teach the other. This was a paradigm for much of the century's voluminous writings on the issue. It was a stylized representation of a powerless condition.

BRIAN HOLLINGWORTH

[*Castle Rackrent's* Composition]†

The Innocent Text

Castle Rackrent appears to be an innocent text. Although we now
see it as an important development in the regional novel, and
although it remains one of the few major British narratives to use
the vernacular voice as its medium, the author proved singularly
unconscious of its significance, nor did she regard it as part of her
contribution to serious writing.

* * *

Castle Rackrent, in its composition, and narrative form, differs from
her other work, but it should not be regarded as a novel without purpose, a piece of unsophisticated vernacular reportage which chanced
to be published in 1800.

In effect, the narrative structure is carefully organized, the vernacular medium plays a significant part in this organization, and the
'tale' has political purposes which the organized text seeks to serve.

There has always been difficulty in dating the time of composition
accurately. In her letter to Mrs. Stark (6 September, 1834), Edgeworth writes of hearing John Langan 'when first I came to Ireland',
but she does not actually indicate the date when she 'began to
write'. She then compounds our uncertainties by adding that 'Sir
Condy's history was added two years afterwards'.[1]

It is not surprising, therefore, that commentators are undecided
over the issue. Butler locates the text in the middle years of the
1790s. She places the first half of the story, 'probably early in the
period rather than late', between 1793 and 1796, and the second half
two years later, about 1796.[2] Watson (1964), thinks the story was
written 'at any time between 1797 and 1799, or even earlier'.[3]

Such vagueness reflects the lack of documentary evidence in the
family papers concerning the novel. And this lacuna[4] itself supports
Edgeworth's contention that she wrote the story for 'mere amusement', since in other areas there is plenty of detail concerning her

† From Brian Hollingworth, "*Castle Rackrent*," in *Maria Edgeworth's Irish Writing: Language, History, Politics* (New York: St. Martin's Press, 1997), pp. 71–75. Reprinted by
permission of Palgrave Macmillan.
1. Frances Edgeworth, ed., *Memoir of Maria Edgeworth with a Selection from Her Letters*,
vol. 3 (Privately Printed, 1867), p. 153.
2. Marilyn Butler, *Maria Edgeworth: A Literary Biography* (Oxford: Clarendon Press,
1972), pp. 353–54.
3. Maria Edgeworth, *Castle Rackrent*, ed. George Watson (New York: Oxford University
Press, 1964), p. xiii.
4. Gap [editor's note].

writing programme. These were times for her of great literary activity and family letters suggest that her texts were very public events, involving cooperation not only with her father, but with family and friends also.[5] Yet there is no mention of *Castle Rackrent*, either in terms of revision, or of plans for publication. Such silence seems to confirm Edgeworth's claim concerning the unpremeditated nature of the text, a claim which she insistently emphasizes in her letter to Mrs. Stark.[6]

It is also indisputable that in its lack of moral didacticism *Castle Rackrent* differs radically from the other work which Edgeworth was then engaged upon, and from all her later writing. *Practical Education* (1798), is a manual, a work of severe non-fiction. The general title of *Moral Tales* (1801) speaks for itself. *Early Lessons*, also published in 1801, and a continuation of *The Parent's Assistant*, likewise advertises the utilitarian purposes of the writing, and the clear morality which each story will provide. The narrative pattern of *Castle Rackrent*, by contrast, seems discursive, the manners and incidents comic and amoral. It has no message for the reader. Its language is that of the despised vernacular, unsuitable for serious discourse.

So, the case for *Castle Rackrent* as 'accident' is plausible. We are attracted to the argument because Edgeworth's proposition that she never blotted a line supports modern prejudices that this is a likely reason for the story's success. The vatic nature of the text—the artist as the amanuensis[7] of John Langan—makes its claims to uniqueness even easier to accept. Conversely, the apparent absence of the controversial voice of Richard Edgeworth can only confirm such claims.

* * *

Other considerations, however, are even more significant. Firstly a study of the text reveals it to be an organized and sophisticated piece of writing. And, secondly, even if the text was composed with a certain innocence of intention, its date of publication in January 1800, in the midst of the heated Union controversy, cannot have been accidental.

To publish an Irish story in January 1800 was a political act. Though this feature of the story is often ignored today, there is no doubt that its significance was recognized at the time. One of the first notices for the novel came in the May issue of the *Monthly*

---

5. See Letter from Maria Edgeworth to Sophy Ruxton (*But-Edge Corr*: No. 157, March, 1797): Richard Edgeworth to Daniel Beaufort (*But-Edge Corr*: No. 160 April? 1797): Maria Edgeworth to Sophy Ruxton (*But-Edge Corr*: No. 165, Autumn? 1797): *But-Edge Corr*: No. 168, undated.
6. See Edgeworth's letter to Mrs. Stark on p. 86 [editor's note].
7. A person who writes or types what another dictates [editor's note].

Review.[8] It is listed in the 'Monthly Catalogue' of that journal, not among the 'novels' with *Selina* and *The Natural Daughter*, but under the heading of 'Ireland' along with political texts on the Union issue. Moreover, the timing of publication is critical, not only in the general chronology of the movement towards Union, but within the personal Edgeworth contribution to the Union debate.

After the suppression of the rebellion in 1798, Pitt had promptly brought forward a scheme for Union as an answer to the problem of Ireland. Even when the plan was initially rejected by the Irish parliament, it remained clear, that the British would employ all political means to impose their wishes. McDowell describes an 'extraordinary' situation with 'an unusual sense of urgency on the part of the government and a haunting sense of finality among Irish politicians'.[9] This 'haunting sense of finality' is feelingly reflected in the conclusion to the Preface of *Castle Rackrent*, published a full year before the Union became reality, and before deciding votes had been taken:

> Nations as well as individuals gradually lose attachment to their individuality, and the present generation is amused rather than offended by the ridicule that is thrown upon their ancestors . . . When Ireland loses her identity by an Union with Great Britain, she will look back with a smile of good-humoured complacency on the Sir Kits and Sir Condys of her former existence. (p. 7)[1]

Castle Rackrent, therefore, is not a text which accidentally came before the public during this period of anticipation and political dispute in January 1800. Along with the speeches which Richard Edgeworth was soon to deliver in the Irish parliament, it should be seen as part of the Edgeworth contribution to the Union debate.

*　*　*

Castle Rackrent, then, is no innocent text. The timing of the publication was no accident. Though Richard Edgeworth may have been unaware that his daughter had written the book, he was closely involved in its publication. And the text was so presented that it broadcast manifestly Edgeworthian ideas and attitudes towards the forthcoming Union. One strong political purpose of *Castle Rackrent* is that of all Edgeworth's Irish writing. She intends to combat English prejudices against the Irish and to increase understanding between the two kingdoms. In January 1800 it seemed imperative to do so

8. See p. 87 [editor's note].
9. R. B McDowell, *Ireland in the Age of Imperialism and Revolution: 1760–1801* (New York: Oxford University Press, 1979), p. 700.
1. Page numbers refer to this Norton Critical Edition [editor's note].

since the two countries were now heading inexorably towards union—a union which, as the text reveals, the Edgeworths viewed with considerable unease.

JACQUELINE BELANGER

From Educating the Reading Public: British Critical Reception of Maria Edgeworth's Early Irish Writing[†]

Maria Edgeworth's fictional and non-fictional works dealing directly with Ireland—*Castle Rackrent, Essay on Irish Bulls, Ennui, The Absentee*, and *Ormond*—mark an innovation in the development of Anglo-Irish literature because there is an attempt to 'place' the stories within an Irish setting and an attempt accurately to report the speech and customs of all levels of Irish society. Maria Edgeworth portrayed

> a whole community, hitherto ignored or the object of caricature and antipathy, in its historical reality as reflected through a relatively colourless central character. As a consequence, ancillary groups or characters are often more vividly represented, because they are the object of observation. The observer is always to some degree detached, a commentator as well as a participant.[1]

Usually this "colourless" central character through whom objective details about Ireland are filtered is either English or Anglo-Irish. Edgeworth, like many of her literary predecessors, was still writing to and for a primarily English reading public, and this central character is indicative of the audience. It can be argued that many of her innovations arose, at least in part, because Edgeworth was writing for an English audience; in that much of her 'objective' reporting originated from a desire both to dispel prejudices and earlier misrepresentations of Ireland and to portray Ireland sympathetically to the English—particularly after the Act of Union in 1801. As Terry Eagleton points out, nineteenth-century Irish writers were engaged in a complex relationship with their English readership:

[†] From Jacqueline Belanger, "Educating the Reading Public: British Critical Reception of Maria Edgeworth's Early Irish Writing," *Irish University Review* 28.2 (1998): 240–44, 247–50, 252–53, 255. Reprinted by permission of the publisher.
1. Seamus Deane, *A Short History of Irish Literature* (Indiana: University of Notre Dame Press, 1986), p. 91. [See Deane on p. 118—editor.]

We have learnt from Mikhail Bahktin to view the novel as an inherently dialogical form, a conflict or conversation between different codes, languages, genres; but the Irish nineteenth century novel is dialogical in a rather more precise sense of the term. For what we are listening to when we read it is one side of a fraught conversation with the British reading public, the other side of which can only be inferred or reconstructed from the words on the page. Like Irish political rhetoric, which knew that it would be reported and reacted to on the mainland and crafted itself accordingly, Irish fiction constantly overhears itself in the ears of its British interlocutors, editing and adjusting its discourse to those ends, holding the prejudices of its implicit addressee steadily in mind and constituting itself, at least in part, on the basis of that putative response.[2]

While Maria Edgeworth's four novels dealing specifically with Ireland are indeed 'dialogical' in the ways that Eagleton suggests, I will argue that we do hear, at least in part, the other side of the "fraught conversation" between the Irish novelist and the British reading public. More specifically, what is available is a conversation between Maria Edgeworth and her British reviewers, with the reviewers mediating between Edgeworth and the English reading public. While the dialogue between Irish writer and English reader is a characteristic feature of Anglo-Irish literature before Edgeworth's work, the political tensions between Ireland and England in the final years of the eighteenth century spark a form of dialogue between Irish writer and English reader which is complicated by the ways in which Edgeworth's work was reviewed in Britain. This already complex situation is further problematised by the connection between the ways in which Edgeworth's work was reviewed and British counter-revolutionary and imperialist projects in the early years of the nineteenth century.

The relationship between Irish writers, English writers, and an English reading public should, of course, be placed within a much broader literary tradition in which much writing about Ireland and the Irish was connected to an English colonial impulse to 'know' Ireland (and, perhaps through this knowledge, to master Ireland). In Edgeworth's own writing, this impulse is matched by a move to 'explain' Ireland and the Irish to an English audience. Edgeworth's project in writing about Ireland was twofold: to "dispose the English reader in Ireland's favour", and to educate the English reading public about Ireland by providing what she saw as accurate observations (both in her fiction and non-fiction) about all levels of Irish

2. Terry Eagleton, *Heathcliff and the Great Hunger* (London: Verso, 1995), p. 201.

society.[3] As Marilyn Butler observes in her biography of Edgeworth, there were occasionally tensions that arose between these two projects, as sometimes the desire to report accurately and the desire to portray Ireland sympathetically did not always produce a completely coherent result.[4]

This tension is seen in Edgeworth's first text to deal with Ireland. In the case of *Castle Rackrent*, the need for accuracy of representation emerged before the desire to write sympathetically about Ireland for an English audience. When beginning to write *Castle Rackrent*, Maria Edgeworth had been in Ireland for about eleven years; she had arrived to settle permanently at her father's County Longford estate in 1782, aged fourteen, in an Ireland which seemed newly optimistic about the measure of parliamentary independence gained in that year. At the time she began to compose *Castle Rackrent*, there was little of the agrarian violence and political unrest that would culminate in the 1798 United Irishmen uprising, and it is this relative stability which might account for the uniqueness of the story of the Rackrents in terms of the whole of Edgeworth's body of work. The core narrative of *Castle Rackrent* is in many ways free from the sense of purpose, the need to instruct and inform, present in her later Irish works. However, the editorial matter introduced after 1798 in many ways reverses this, and is perhaps indicative of Edgeworth's developing project in representing Ireland in the light of the crucial events of the time period between 1798 and 1800.

Thady Quirk, the narrator of *Castle Rackrent*, is anything but a "colourless" central figure through whom objective details about Ireland are filtered. The complexity of his narrative position in relation to the story he tells has resulted in a degree of critical disagreement as to Edgeworth's attitude to the characters and events portrayed in *Castle Rackrent*. The presence of a framing 'metatext' written by a fictional English editor further complicates any critical approaches to the text; however, it is this 'metatext',[5] addressed directly to an "ignorant English reader" (p. 6),[6] that is crucial in revealing Edgeworth's attitudes towards both her subject matter and her audience. Initially it seems the purpose of the core narrative of the Rackrent family history was simply to tell an amusing story based on the colourful speech of a native Irish figure and to employ some of the

3. Marilyn Butler, *Maria Edgeworth: A Literary Biography* (Oxford: Clarendon Press, 1972), p. 362.
4. When I say 'accurately' here I speak of Edgeworth's view of her own abilities to represent Ireland objectively. This is not to say that I take her representations as accurate, and I am indeed aware that her representations of Ireland were informed by her own political agenda and social position; thus, even before it comes into contact with the impulse to represent sympathetically, the 'accuracy' is already marked by Edgeworth's own subjective interpretations of the Irish.
5. Terry Eagleton, *Heathcliff and the Great Hunger*, p. 202.
6. Page numbers throughout refer to this Norton Critical Edition [editor's note].

stories and dialogue which Edgeworth and her father had heard first-hand in their business dealings with the tenants on their County Longford estate. * * *

The body of the first part of the story was composed between the autumn of 1793 and 1796 (probably earlier in the period rather than later); the second part of *Castle Rackrent*, the "History of Sir Conolly Rackrent", was most likely composed in 1796, as Edgeworth may have used some of her father's parliamentary election experiences from January and February of that year to construct her text. The glossary (and preface) were most likely written in the early half of 1799; the book was published anonymously, complete with the late addition of the glossary, in January 1800.

Thus the explicitly explanatory aspects of the text—the preface, footnotes, conclusion and glossary—were added after the crucial historical point of 1798. What began as an amusing tale suddenly became less amusing in light of the events of 1798 and the following years—Edgeworth seemed to have been concerned with the rather impolitic portrayal of the Irish as drunken, litigious, and generally irresponsible at a time when, if anything, it seemed necessary to portray the Irish in as positive a light as possible to an English audience in order to reconcile her English readership to the Union. Edgeworth's fictional English editor takes great pains to assert that the tale of the Rackrent family is representative of the past, and looks forward to the Union:

> The editor hopes his readers will observe that these are "tales of other times": that the manners depicted in the following pages are not those of the present age: the race of the Rackrents has long been extinct in Ireland. . . . Nations as well as individuals gradually lose attachment to their identity, and the present generation is amused rather than offended by the ridicule that is thrown upon its ancestors. . . . When Ireland loses her identity by a union with Great Britain, she will look back with a smile of good-humoured complacency on the Sir Kits and Sir Condys of her former existence. (p. 7)

While the core narrative itself has a curiously static quality, perhaps reflective of the time period in which it was composed and the initial impulse to represent Irish speech objectively, the editorial matter added at a later date attempts to 'explain' and 'place' the narrative itself by introducing "serious sociological information" about Ireland.[7] In making Irish life explicable, Edgeworth attempts to bring about a sympathetic understanding of the Irish on the part of her English readers. While the editorial matter is not itself as overtly

---

7. Marilyn Butler, p. 356.

sympathetic to the native Irish as some of her later representations
will be, it does represent Edgeworth's developing political and social
views about Ireland in that, in assuming the persona of the male
English editor, she is consciously distancing herself from the authorship of her own text, as well as distancing herself culturally and
historically from Thady's narrative of the Rackrent family. His is a
narrative which seems to endorse traditional stereotypes of the Irish
in a way which did not fit into Edgeworth's aim to dispel prejudices
and misrepresentations of Ireland and the Irish. Whether meant
ironically or not, Edgeworth's fictional editor betrays the ambivalence at the centre of the text of *Castle Rackrent*. The fictional editor
asserts:

> All the features in the foregoing sketch were taken from the life,
> and they are characteristic of that mixture of quickness, sim-
> plicity, cunning, carelessness, dissipation, disinterestedness,
> shrewdness, and blunder, which, in different forms, and with
> various success, has been brought upon the stage, or delineated
> in novels. (p. 61)

So, while distancing herself from the impolitic representations of the
Irish in Thady's narrative, she at once endorses stereotyped representations, and demonstrates the first instance of a contradiction in
her Irish writings which will be unresolved throughout her career.
Often, for Edgeworth, dispelling misrepresentations and representing the Irish sympathetically resulted in the demolishing of one
set of stereotypes only to replace them with another. In using an
English editor to authorise 'authentic' representations of the Irish,
Edgeworth attempts to dissociate herself from (mis)representations
of the Irish as drunken and irresponsible, but in doing so places the
authority to represent the Irish in the hands of the English (or
Anglo-Irish).

*   *   *

Despite the political events which had drawn a good deal of
English attention to Ireland, and which after the Act of Union
increasingly occupied a prominent place in English domestic political affairs, Ireland was very much a 'terra incognita'[8] to the English
reading public; one historian cites, for example, "the general ignorance of Ireland among the British governing class".[9] If this ignorance was prevalent among the "governing class", it might be assumed
that the general British reading public (although made up of a large
part from these governing classes) knew even less. As a reviewer of

8. Unknown land [editor's note].
9. J. C. Beckett, *The Making of Modern Ireland* (London: Faber and Faber, 1981), p. 286.

Patronage wrote, Maria Edgeworth's Irish fiction "enabled her at once to delight and instruct the public, to which, generally speaking, the peculiar manners of Ireland were less known than those of Otaheite".[1] By 1831, in a survey of Irish literature of the previous thirty years, a reviewer in the *Edinburgh Review* can confidently claim:

> Even the most superficial view of the outlines of Irish life—an attention even carelessly turned thitherward for mere amusement, is better than the deep ignorance and callous indifference respecting all that was Irish, with which the English people was once too justly chargeable. Ignorance and indifference on that subject are not among the prevailing sins of the present day.[2]

Although "ignorance" and "indifference" are deemed by the reviewer as no longer characteristic of English attitudes toward Ireland, what is notable about the previous remark is the fact that Ireland is still seen as a place to which readers can turn for amusement.

Interest in Irish subjects can also be seen as arising not only out of a lack of knowledge, but also as a part of larger shift in the tastes of the English reading public. The romantic movement, according to one critic,

> attached a particular value to what was unfamiliar or remote and to ways of life that were regarded as less 'artificial' than those of contemporary society. Thus the British reading public, still largely concentrated in the southern half of England, was in a mood to explore the periphery and to find unsuspected beauty, heroic courage, natural dignity, and domestic virtue in areas and among people hitherto neglected or despised.[3]

The desire to learn about Ireland reflects, at least in part, this new 'mood' on the part of the British public. The irony of this, of course, is that after the Act of Union, Ireland was a 'sister kingdom', a part of the newly-formed United Kingdom of Britain and Ireland, while at the same time very much seen to be foreign. This desire to learn about the 'unfamiliar' was not limited to Ireland, however, as the popularity and critical success of Scott's *Waverley* novels demonstrate. The interest in antiquarianism which grew throughout England, Scotland, Wales and Ireland in the late eighteenth century also attests to this new concern with what was 'unfamiliar' and 'remote'.

1. [J. Ward], *Quarterly Review* 10 (January 1814), p. 309.
2. *Edinburgh Review* 52 (January 1831), pp. 430–31.
3. J. C. Beckett, "The Irish Writer and his Public," *The Yearbook of English Studies* 2 (1981), p. 105.

In the early years of the nineteenth century, the growth of British literary reviews such as the *Edinburgh Review* and the *Quarterly Review* also had a great deal to do with the rise in interest on the part of the English reading public with novels dealing with Ireland. As Marilyn Butler points out, Maria Edgeworth was the first novelist to be "regularly and intelligently reviewed" by these literary journals. Part of this interest reflects the lack of knowledge of Ireland on the part of British readers—"the unusual interest of the subject-matter and the manner of treatment" in Edgeworth's Irish tales appealed to both reviewers and readers.[4] Part of the interest in Edgeworth's work on the part of the reviewers also reflects the growing interest in the novel as a literary form. However, these journals were not solely concerned with literary value. Each had a specific political point of view, a bias which affected how (and perhaps which) books were read and reviewed. Furthermore, Edgeworth's own literary project in representing Ireland suited the political projects of the reviews themselves.

Literary journals of the early nineteenth century have been characterised as "fiercely partisan" in their politics, the *Edinburgh Review* representing Whig interests, the *Quarterly Review* those of Tories. What seems to characterise all of these journals at this time is a fear of the effects of growing societal unrest:

> In these vastly influential journals, the space of the public sphere is fissured and warped, wracked with a fury which threatens to strip it of ideological credibility. It is not, of course, that the class struggle in society at large is directly reflected in the internecine antagonisms between the various literary organs; these unseemly wranglings are rather a refraction of those broader conflicts in ruling class culture, divided as it is over how much political repression of the working class is tolerable without the risk of insurrection.[5]

Connected to this fear of class insurrection were fears about the French Revolution and its aftermath; the republicanism of eighteenth-century France and that of the United Irishmen in Ireland was seen as a great threat to the British church and state. In all of these literary reviews there is the note of concern over the possibility of violent social upheaval and the subversion of British church and state which this would create. In the preface from the *British Critic* of 1800 in which there is a review of *Castle Rackrent*, the editor looks back over the political events of the late eighteenth century and declares:

---

4. Marilyn Butler, p. 338.
5. Terry Eagleton, *The Function of Criticism: From 'The Spectator' to Post-Structuralism* (London: Verso, 1984), p. 37.

The season of gloom is not yet past! Britain, after exhausting her strength to support the liberties of Europe, against an over-bearing and predatory force, seems destined to encounter the assaults of Envy, blindly rushing to its own destruction. The storm lowers on every side . . . with this general aspect opens the nineteenth century; marked in its commencement, throughout the greater part of Europe, by the dejection of the good, and the triumph of the profligate.[6]

In light of these threats to Britain, it is the duty of the critic to "wield the arms that we are competent to use, in defence of a pure church and wisely ordered state".[7] The arms that are wielded at this time by these critics are those of the reviews themselves and the political agenda which informs their work.

In the same way that Ireland, particularly after the Act of Union, was seen to be both familiar and foreign to the English—at once home and Other—it also represented an external and (after union) an internal threat to British security. Ireland was a part of the United Kingdom which had consistently proved itself a strategic weak spot for the rest of Britain, a threat to both the Anglican church and the British state. The fact that the French had aided the United Irish-men in 1798, and had actually landed troops on the west coast of Ireland, only seemed to confirm to some in England that the danger from French and Irish republicanism was real indeed. If the political and literary aims of these reviews are connected to attitudes toward French and Irish republicanism and the threat posed by these to the British state, it can be argued that English criticism of Irish literature itself might be fraught with tensions relating as much to the social and political tensions between Ireland and England as to the writings themselves. Ultimately what these reviews of Maria Edgeworth's work offer is a means of subsuming Ireland into the cultural sphere of the United Kingdom as a substitution for the incorporation which could never be complete in the political realm.

*   *   *

While there is at least a sheen of objectivity in the reviews of Edge-worth's Irish works, in reality those who edited and wrote for the journals at the beginning of the nineteenth century had a profound stake in controlling representations of Ireland.

The review of *Castle Rackrent* in *The Monthly Review* of May 1800 indicates that the Edgeworths' fears about how *Castle Rackrent* might be interpreted were not unfounded. Although the reviewer

6. *British Critic* 14 (November 1800), p. ii.
7. Ibid., p. ii.

acknowledges the fact that the author of *Rackrent* (at this point
the novel was still anonymous) states both on the title page and in
the preface that the stories are "Tales of other times", there still is the
sense that *Rackrent* can provide useful information about the Ireland
of the present:

> In these Hibernian Memoirs, we have been highly entertained
> with the exhibition of some admirable pictures, delineated (as
> we conceive) with perfect accuracy and truth of character; and
> we apprehend that, from a due contemplation of these portraits,
> many striking conclusions may be drawn, and applications
> made, respecting the necessity and probable consequences of
> an union between the two kingdoms.[8]

This is not the picture of Ireland the Edgeworths wished to present
to the English, but it seems that it was taken not only to be accurate
(a note which will be struck consistently in all the reviews of Edgeworth's work), but also more or less contemporary in that it pointed
to the 'necessity' of the union with England. The Edgeworths too saw
the necessity of a union with England, because they believed that
Ireland could benefit economically from a union, and because they
felt that the union would help to bring about religious equality
between Catholics and Protestants in the newly-formed United
Kingdom—but not because Ireland was populated with drunken,
litigious and untrustworthy characters of the Rackrent type.

In a review of *Rackrent* in the *British Critic* of November 1800,
not only was the note of authenticity sounded again, but also there
was an emphasis on the strangeness of the manners described in
Edgeworth's text. The preface to the review states that *Castle Rackrent* "seems to paint with truth, characters that are assuredly not a
little extraordinary". These ideas are echoed in the review itself,
which is worth quoting in full:

> This is a very pleasant, good-humoured, and successful repre-
> sentation of the eccentricities of our Irish neighbours. The style
> is very happily hit off; and the parallel to the story, we appre-
> hend, has been too frequently exhibited. The character of "hon-
> est Thady" is remarkably comic, and well-delineated; and we
> are not at all surprised that the publication should, in so very
> short a time, have passed through two editions.[9]

The emphasis on the "eccentricities" of the Irish here seems again
to indicate that there was a sense of the foreign in British views of
Ireland. It is also interesting that the focus of both reviews is on the
main narrative itself. The very important addition of the glossary is

---

8. *The Monthly Review; or Literary Journal* 32 (May 1800), pp. 91–2. [See p. 87—editor.]
9. *British Critic* 14 (November 1800), p. 555. [See p. 88—editor.]

nowhere mentioned. This omission is particularly telling in that the function of the glossary is to introduce sociological information about Ireland, and to make the narrative seem less 'eccentric'.

* * *

As with attempts to 'regulate' what was read by the public, the attempt to define what was Irish—to 'authorise' certain representations—was a form of asserting power. In selectively sanctioning Edgeworth's representations of the native Irish, the reviews at this time were sanctioning a politically useful definition of Ireland, one in which the Irish were deserving of sympathy because powerless. What the last quotation from the review of *Irish Bulls* also reveals is that the stereotypes of the Irish so prominent in the dramatic works of the eighteenth century are still firmly entrenched—the change seems to be that the Irish are now objects of sympathy rather than merely objects of amusement.

MARILYN BUTLER

Edgeworth's Ireland[†]

* * *

A book that uses literary language and other literary devices demands the attention of its readers. A novel stands or falls by its use of language, narration, and plot—not by who the writer is. "Identity," in the simple sense of national or racial or religious identity, cannot itself explain the allegiances and motivations of even a single writer, especially when the writer consciously addressed a diverse public. Edgeworth from the outset wrote fiction for different audiences—between 1792 and 1801, lively short stories for children of various ages and "lessons" cast as dialogues for parents teaching at home; after 1801, novels and novellas set in English high-life; a sub-genre of these introducing French or Frenchified main characters; and her Irish tales, which also have subplots or substantial episodes introducing English or French characters.

The language Edgeworth uses in these different genres and sub-genres is tailor-made for its imagined audiences. In the children's tales the main child character, who is either decidedly rich and spoilt or decidedly poor and spunky, may be eight, ten, or twelve to

† From Marilyn Butler, "Edgeworth's Ireland: History, Popular Culture, and Secret Codes," *NOVEL* 34. 2(2001): 268–74, 289–92. Copyright 2001, Novel, Inc. All rights reserved. Republished by permission of the copyright holder and the present publisher, Duke University Press.

fourteen—in the last case, he or she is struggling with an often dark adult world, and vocabulary and sentence-lengths adjust accordingly. Edgeworth's adaptability fosters her experimental plotting. She uses non-realistic devices from (say) fairy tale and a playful allusiveness to other texts in both dialogue and third-person narration. Her High Society is sometimes scientifically informed or chic and Parisian, that is, well-read in literary classics in English or French, reaching back to 1600 or before. Or, it can be intermittently raffish, as in *Belinda* (1801), from the introduction of other voices quoting more or less exactly from current newspaper items, fashionable scandals, popular caricature, advertisements, reviews, and the subculture of a big house, the servants' quarters belowstairs.

By characters' easy cross-references to their reading, the Edgeworth text supplies its real-life context. Books by 1800 had a cosmopolitan readership: novels were popular, bookish novels more popular than most. Edgeworth was speedily translated into French from this time, and responded by creating for her readership three socially tiered societies: metropolitan France, metropolitan England, and rural Ireland. Intellectuals of the late Enlightenment were fully aware of the social and political impact of the Europe-wide and Atlantic print network, of belonging to a reading public that knew itself by reading *Reviews*, memoirs, travels, and novels. Dugald Stewart, philosopher and mentor of the early *Edinburgh Review*, considered the circulating print network a guarantee of nineteenth-century progress.

Edgeworth, then, is not narrowly concerned with inventing either the national novel or the naturalistic novel, though she contributes to both; she participates in a historical process by developing a more stylized, consciously intellectual cosmopolitan novel, an intrinsically comparative and interactive exercise. * * *

Edgeworth's Irish tales and the *Essay on Irish Bulls* are among her best, most characteristic writings. All five works are consistently and deliberately historical, but in an idiosyncratic mode that relies on quotation, the naming of authors and books, and allusions to familiar thoughts and ideas. These techniques make characters knowable, but in a new way, by having them reveal their own cultural milieu, deepened for the reader by the use of real-life people and the words they used. Radcliffe's gothic *Mysteries of Udolpho* and Scott's *Waverley* or *Ivanhoe* are obviously historical in that the author dates the action in a past age, but their authors' interests cannot be said to be more historical than those of Edgeworth, whose method is theoretically more organic and intrinsic. Her three later Irish tales all seem to situate the action in 1798 or later; yet the flow of names in narrative and dialogue is topographical, historical, literary, and cultural, embedding the characters richly in their own pasts and giving the reader access to the past. Her invented Ireland is fed by a broad stream of references to the history, personalities, and families of the island, its local place names and topography, its extant documents and archives, especially those bearing on the ownership of land.

Edgeworth's first solo book and for some her masterpiece, *Castle Rackrent* brings together in a narrational *tour de force* the archive of her own extended family, focusing on (yet also masking) its internal quarrels over money, land, and religion in North Longford between 1688 and 1709. Given that this is what Thady's narration actually is, Edgeworth misleads her readers in providing *Castle Rackrent* with the subtitle: "An Hibernian Tale/Taken from Facts, and from the Manners of the Irish Squires before the year 1782." The subtitle makes a point of being historical; yet, since the book was published in the beginning of the year 1800, only eighteen years on, it hardly reaches back into history. Critics beginning with Thomas Flanagan have unsuspiciously connived with her by interpreting *Rackrent* as a study of big historical events, such as the loss of the notionally independent Protestant-Ascendancy parliament, and the incorporation in 1800 of the Irish constituencies and some Irish peers into the parliament at Westminster. It is better to assume Edgeworth was out to puzzle her reader, or even play a joke, as she was doing in the contemporaneous *Essay on Irish Bulls* (1802). This could explain why we have yet to see a satisfactory explanation of how *Castle Rackrent* is supposed to be rendering such public events; or why the manners of squires a generation earlier might be relevant to such a theme; or whether, indeed, *Rackrent* qualifies as either a national tale or historical tale at all.

The story, told by the aged steward Thady M'Quirk, serves as the fictionalized memoir of his service of four successive squires on a remote Irish estate over a period of eighty years. The Rackrent family chronicles, it is now generally conceded, really do derive from a similar family memoir not fictional at all.[1] It was written in the late 1760s by Maria Edgeworth's grandfather Richard Edgeworth (1701–70) from family papers; complete with legal documents, it is available in the National Library of Ireland. Richard Edgeworth stops at the point when both his parents died within a few weeks of each other, that is, in the year 1709, when he was only eight. The orphan boy was left alone as the couple's only surviving child. Half a century later he recalls his father, Frank, dying heartbroken after losing the lands and title deeds to the new house he had built at Edgeworthstown. That dark scene closes the memoir, known in the

---

1. See W. J. McCormack on p. 115–17 [editor's note].

family as the "Black Book of Edgeworthstown," and it also closes
Maria Edgeworth's tale of Sir Condy, last of the Rackrents.

The first Edgeworth to settle near Mastrim, afterwards known
as Edgeworthstown, was the emigré English lawyer Francis Edgeworth. The Dublin-based husband of Jane Tuite, a firmly Catholic woman from nearby County Westmeath, Francis bought a
medium-sized estate at Cranalagh, north of Mastrim, when it
came on the market as part of an official reapportionment in 1619.
The original owners of the property were O'Farrells, still in 1619
the dominant family in a territory known as Annaly until its modernization in 1570 as County Longford. Francis Edgeworth and
others like him benefited from this second wave of anti-baronial
modernization: big Old Irish or Old English estates were reduced
in size as new gentlemen-farmers from further east or from
England were introduced as improvers. Francis Edgeworth was
the first of a line of four squires who lived at Cranalagh, two miles
north of Mastrim, until Frank, the fourth, built his new house at
what became Edgeworthstown.

But Maria Edgeworth changes the real-life story by making the
first of the Rackrents an Irishman by descent. This was a purpose-
ful decision: the central family in all four of her Irish tales is of
Gaelic origin. Sir Patrick O'Shaughlin, a spendthrift and jolly hospitable host, takes over the house and small estate from a relative
on condition he changes to the English name. As a type Sir Patrick
strongly resembles Captain John Edgeworth, who inherited the
property from his father Francis in 1627, a landlord nicknamed by
his tenants "Shaen Mor," Irish for "Big John." The fictional landlords between Sir Patrick and Sir Condy, who are called Sir Murtaugh and Sir Kit, are not specific portraits, but contrasting types
pieced together, without regard for chronology, from one striking
figure in the real memoirs, and one equally notorious neighbor—of
whom more will be said. The original for the mean half-crazy lawyer Murtaugh was not an Edgeworth eldest son, and thus a legiti-
mate heir, but the unfortunate Frank's younger brother Robert,
a Catholic; a still younger brother and another Catholic, Ambrose,
tricked Frank out of his house with the help of a perjured witness,
as one of the glossary notes describes.[2]

Thady's fictional narrative allegedly covers eighty years, with
considerable fidelity to small detail and notable omissions. His life-
story matches landlord régimes spanning eighty-two years in the
Edgeworth family chronicle. Instead of representing the era immediately prior to 1782, as the subtitle claims, the annals recount the

2. "We gained the day by this piece of honesty" (*Castle Rackrent*, p. 39). See glossary note to
   text (p. 75). [Page numbers throughout refer to this Norton Critical Edition—editor.]

eighty years prior to that, ending in 1709. Consequently, they cover Irish history through two periods of religious and dynastic war, followed in the 1690s by William of Orange's penal legislation against the Catholic gentry—the most determined scheme yet devised to break up big Catholic estates and disrupt a basic precept of English law, the rule of inheritance by the eldest son, and thus of ongoing family wealth and power. It is those two civil wars, of 1641 and 1688, that stand as the largest omission from Thady's narrative.

The Irish local historian Raymond Gillespie,[3] editor of a collection of new essays on County Longford (1991), in his own contribution to the volume narrates the real-life slow decline of the county's leading Catholic family, the O'Farrells. He brings out elements in their story—a major schism between two branches of the family; then, incompetence, bad luck, backwardness, absenteeism, and in the senior branch, sterility—factors that regularly appear in Edgeworth's history of the Rackrents. There was, however, a point of difference: whereas the O'Farrells ran out of male heirs in mid-century, the Edgeworths by the 1690s had all too many quarrelsome siblings. Edgeworth holdings in County Longford had once belonged to the northern branch of the O'Farrells, which farmed the more boggy and mountainous terrain between Granard, near the Westmeath border, westward toward Roscommon and northward toward Leitrim. The Edgeworths were sharply reminded of the old owners by a dramatic incident in the house at Cranalagh during the rebellion of 1641. Big John was away from home, as the "Black Book" tells it. Tenants and local men broke into the house, stripped John's wife Mary, English Protestant daughter of Sir Hugh Cullum of Derbyshire, and drove her out naked into the countryside. A family servant, Brian Farrell, seized the couple's child, the future Sir John, then aged three, and fiercely declared he would kill him. He stoutly prevented the mob from proceeding with their main aim after plundering the house, which was to burn it down: the Farrells, he said, the real owners of the estate, might want to live in it. That done, he left with the child and hid him in the bog until he could be spirited away. Brian Farrell's descendents continued to live on the estate into the next century. He was, in his way, a double agent and prototype of Thady, though in a different political cause.

Since Gillespie, another Irish local historian, W. A. Maguire, in a 1996 article on County Longford, decisively re-sources the best-known episode in *Castle Rackrent*, indeed the best-known episode in Edgeworth, that of the "Madwoman in the Attic."[4] In the process

3. Raymond Gillespie and Gerard Moran, eds., *Longford: Essays in County History* (Dublin: Lilliput, 1991).
4. W. A. Maguire, "Castle Nugent and *Castle Rackrent*; Fact and Fiction in Maria Edgeworth," *Eighteenth-Century Ireland* XI (1996): 146–59.

he uncovers an original for the one Rackrent who was not an Edge-worth. In the novel, the third of the dynasty, Sir Kit, incarcerates his Jewish wife for years because she would not give up her jewels. The real story referred to was public knowledge in the late eigh-teenth century, thanks to an obituary in the *Gentleman's Magazine* for Lady Cathcart, once wife of an Irish gentleman, Colonel Hugh Maguire.[5] But the obituary wrongly located their household in County Fermanagh and for two centuries that location, relatively remote from Edgeworthstown, was assumed to be correct.

Maguire shows that the episode occurred in the 1760s in a Cath-olic household four miles north of Edgeworthstown called Castle Nugent. The owner was indeed Colonel Hugh Maguire, who was the nephew on his mother's side of the celebrated Grace Nugent—the subject of an Irish song by the poet and harpist Carolan and the name of the heroine of *The Absentee* (1812), after *Rackrent* the best-known of Edgeworth's Irish tales. The curious intricacy of plot-ting and the localism uncovered by this discovery has consequences for Edgeworth's readers. She can incorporate the history of neigh-boring families; in doing so she merges the real-life experience of Catholic and Protestant Longford gentry. A very high proportion of Thady's narration and many of the yarns that flesh out the glossary notes select archival material from the *Black Book*—not realism, so much as "the real."

Quite separately from these local and family contributions, through the device of allegory the story of *Castle Rackrent* refers to *national* history of the same era. Edgeworth left in a family copy of *Castle Rackrent* a pencilled note of a footnote she intended to add, but never did add, that applies to a line in Thady's narrative, "as I have lived so will I die, true and loyal to the family" (p. 12). Edge-worth's jotting merely says "Loyal High Constable." That ironic allusion to a real title (Lord High Constable) would have brought in James Butler, second Duke of Ormond. By virtue of his office, he carried the crown at the coronation of the Protestant William and Mary, and afterwards at the coronation of Queen Anne. The sec-ond Duke inherited the office, though an altered title, from his grandfather, the first Duke, also James Butler (1610–88), who was elevated both to the Dukedom and to the title of Lord High *Steward* by Charles II at the Restoration—to reward him, gratefully but almost costlessly, for his stalwart support of the Stuart monarchs as their greatest servant in Ireland. As Steward, the first Duke carried the crown at Charles's coronation in 1661 and at the Catholic James II's coronation in 1685, thus beginning the family's tradition of truth and loyalty to four monarchs of the family.

5. See n. 4, p. 24 [editor's note].

Even before the accession of the Protestant Elector of Hanover as George I, however, the second Duke was no longer in favor and may have been planning a secret coup to bring James Edward, the Old Pretender, back to London before the arrival of the Elector of Hanover. Early in 1715, anticipating his impeachment and the sequestration of his vast Munster estates, he fled to the Continent to join James Edward's court in exile and to lead a Spanish fleet that in 1719 attempted to assist the Jacobite rising of 1715 against George I. It was indeed loyalty from the Jacobite perspective: equivocation, followed by treason, for Hanoverians.

Thady's resonant allusion to the second Duke in the novel's first paragraph need not make Thady a Jacobite; Edgeworth's codes tend to be more equivocal than that. Though it can be characterization, it reads better as allegory: Thady's service of the four Rackrents, who are so close to four Edgeworths, is analogous with the two Dukes' service of the last four Stuarts. *Castle Rackrent* reads as the requiem for an unlamented century, that of Europe-wide civil wars driven by religion and devious statecraft. A failed line of English-Irish landlords, disinherited by 1709, replicates the feckless, reckless, amorous Stuart dynasty, whose reign over the Three Kingdoms (England, Scotland and Ireland) ended in 1714.

It is sour and failing family history and national history that graphically merges in *Castle Rackrent*. But even more is perhaps at stake: what the Great House generally signified in feudal times. As it plainly tilts at the irresponsible Stuarts, *Castle Rackrent* also challenges the system—traditional landownership or the aristocratic system of proprietorship, sustained by male primogeniture on the one hand, profitable marriages and the strategic extension of kinship on the other. Great-House stateliness is debunked when Castle Rackrent's annals are handed over to an illiterate Irish chronicler to relate. The entire social system, based on kinship and alliances, is shown crumbling away as, in each generation, wealth-bearing brides make off with what they can salvage in money and durables. Even Thady's granddaughter Judy manages to rescue something from the wreck of Condy's affairs, and to frustrate the schemes of the men of her family, Thady and Jason. Perhaps the social changes posited here would need a time-span longer than 82 years, which may be why Edgeworth in her subtitle gives herself to 1782. Read this way, the glossary note on "the raking pot of tea," served after midnight in the bedrooms where women rule, is a key to *Rackrent*'s radicalism and a useful signpost to the nineteenth-century realist novel that is on its way (74–75). Old aristocratic stories of male dominance and legitimacy are being challenged by democratized women-centered plots of family life in which servants, including female servants, wield power, and almost anything is negotiable.

Castle Rackrent began in 1793–94 as an impromptu act of mimicry, delivered to a family audience that knew the family past, and
made vivacious by being retold in the Hibernian vernacular of an
ancient steward. The annals of the last landlord were added after a
break of two years, and were in place by 1798. At this time, a plan
for an *Essay on Irish Bulls*, to be jointly authored by Maria Edgeworth and her father Richard Lovell Edgeworth, had been in place
since the summer of 1797, but little or no writing on the book-
length *Essay* could have been done.[6] In short, there is a clear break
between *Castle Rackrent* and Edgeworth's other Irish writing,
beginning with the *Essay*. True to its title, the latter serves as a trial
run for Edgeworth's later fictional constructions of Ireland.

Rackrent is already a carefully considered work, as is apparent
from the last-minute framing paratext, consisting of preface, glossary, and probably the first footnote to the text. Despite the spoken
idiom in which it is delivered, Thady's narrative has real claims to
be taken seriously as history, both for its detail based on fact and
for its coolly detached commentary on seventeenth-century Longford and its landlordism. But *Castle Rackent* avoids contemporary
political allusions, except for a sly joke in the closing paragraph at the
expense of the Warwickshire Militia, for (presumably) being drunk
and disorderly and reported as such in the press. In that respect it
differs from the overtly and boldly political *Essay on Irish Bulls*
(May 1802), and from the semi-hidden politics of Edgeworth's elegant later Irish tales.

* * *

6. Letter from Frances Beaufort [from 1798, the fourth Mrs. RLE] to her brother William
Beaufort, 2 July 1797. Her predecessor, Mrs. Elizabeth (Sneyd) Edgeworth was already
at work designing the vignettes (of two bulls) which eventually preceded and followed
the text.

Narrative Voices

STANLEY J. SOLOMON

From Ironic Perspective in Maria Edgeworth's *Castle Rackrent*†

One of the most subtly conceived works of eighteenth-century fiction, Maria Edgeworth's short novel *Castle Rackrent* (published in 1800), has never been fully evaluated in terms of its technical achievement, though its influence and effectiveness in regard to style and content have generally been acknowledged.[1] In the typical neoclassical novel from [Samuel] Richardson to Jane Austen, authors employed irony in the service of their moral interests. The very few exceptions to this generalization, novels like *Tristam Shandy* and *Vathek*,[2] employed irony at the expense of various formal requirements of the genre itself, such as chapter form, chronology, and verisimilitude; moral concerns (if the authors had any) appeared infrequently. Maria Edgeworth's achievement consisted in her using irony for the purpose of both shaping her moral vision and undermining one of the most essential aspects of the developing novel's form, the narrative point of view. The moral vision of *Castle Rackrent* has to do with the nature of passive participation in evil. The ironic perspective develops through an examination of seemingly conventional values presented by the narrator. Here irony undercuts not only the values but the narrative point of view in one of the earliest instances of unreliable narration in the genre.[3]

---

† From Stanley Solomon, "Ironic Perspective in Maria Edgeworth's *Castle Rackrent*," *Journal of Narrative Theory* 2.1 (1972): 68–73. Reprinted by permission of the *Journal of Narrative Theory*.
1. *Cf.* George Sherburn, "The Restoration and Eighteenth Century," *A Literary History of England*, ed. Albert Baugh (New York, 1948), pp. 1198–1199; Walter Allen, *The English Novel* (New York, 1954), pp. 107–109. Joanne Altieri, "Style and Purpose in Maria Edgeworth's Fiction," *Nineteenth-Century Fiction*, XXIII (December, 1968), 265–78.
2. A novel by William Beckford (1760–1844), published in 1786. *Tristram Shandy* is a novel by Laurence Sterne (1713–1768), published in nine volumes (1759–67) [editor's note].
3. This novel is listed—unfortunately without comment—by Wayne Booth in his excellent gallery of unreliable narrators in *The Rhetoric of Fiction* (Chicago, 1961), p. 433.

Before *Castle Rackrent,* first-person narration from *Pamela* to *Evelina* to *Caleb Williams*[4] had sought to establish the narrator's reliability as a filter through which the reader assimilates the author's evaluation of the issues at hand. Where evaluations were erroneous (*e.g.,* Lovelace's letters in *Clarissa*[5]), a center of intelligence was established to serve as a check on the likelihood of a reader's being misled by the wrong judgments. In an eccentric first-person narration, in which a degree of unreliability is not necessarily checked by another character (*e.g.,* Tristram Shandy, Primrose in *The Vicar of Wakefield*[6]), the errors are obviously discoverable by a reader. First-person narrators who, like Tristram, injected their whimsical personalities into the book were on their own terms perfectly honest with their readers, for these characters readily presented their unreliable tendencies as amiable eccentricities of character. But for the most part, the eighteenth-century first-person narrator, a Robinson Crusoe, a Fanny Hill, a Matt Bramble,[7] was motivated by a desire to tell his story accurately, to establish veracity by the use of details, and to conduct the reader to the chief themes of the author.

Thady Quirk of *Castle Rackrent* is an entirely different type of narrator, not only unique for the late eighteenth century but still unusual as a novelistic device even in our age when unreliable narration is commonplace. The whole ironic movement of the novel is involved in the sensibilities of the narrator, but the matter is complicated by a kind of double unreliability. On one level, Thady is, as one critic has noted, disingenuous, shrewd, calculating, and unsentimental.[8] All of these traits are developed through his own revelation, though he appears to us in the guise of the old faithful servant, the family retainer whose entire life is bound up in serving the decaying Irish aristocracy. In his self-professed role as friendly chronologer of the Rackrent family, Thady sets about telling of the Rackrent decline and the (incidental) ironic parallel of the rise of his family—his son Jason eventually takes over the estate, and Thady to

---

4. A novel by William Godwin (1756–1836), published in 1794. *Pamela* (1740) is a novel by Samuel Richardson (1689–1761). *Evelina* (1778) is a novel by Fanny Burney (1752–1840) [editor's note].
5. A novel by Samuel Richardson (1689–1761), published in 1748 [editor's note].
6. A novel by Oliver Goldsmith (1730–1774), published in 1766 [editor's note].
7. A character in Tobias Smollett's *The Expedition of Humphry Clinker* (1771). Robinson Crusoe is the eponymous character in the 1719 novel by Daniel Defoe (1660–1731). Fanny Hill is the eponymous character in the 1748 novel by John Cleland (1709–1789) [editor's note].
8. James Newcomer, "The Disingenuous Thady Quirk," *Studies in Short Fiction,* II (Fall, 1964), 50. The traditional view of Thady as a faithful retainer, blissfully unaware of any irony at all, is in my opinion (and Newcomer's) an oversimplification. But *cf.* Allen, p. 109; Harrison R. Steeves, *Before Jane Austen* (New York, 1965), p. 322; W. L. Renwick, *English Literature, 1789–1815,* Oxford History of English Literature (Oxford, 1963), p. 74.

some extent abets him in his rise.[9] It is a type of plot used later by [Charles] Dickens and [William] Faulkner, though the ironic reversal of fortunes is particularly striking in Maria Edgeworth's age when class mobility was less common than it was to become after the Industrial Revolution.

But the irony of *Castle Rackrent* is complicated by the development of another level of meaning. In detailing the Rackrent decline, Thady supplies us with enough clues to the fact that he very well understands the nature of the family's improvidence. The Rackrents are clearly less competent to control the estate than is Jason, and in a world where only the fit survive, the Rackrents are certain to end in ruin. (The various marks of improvidence include recklessness, drinking, excessive litigation, women, etc.[1] Yet if Thady understands the practical morality of improvidence, the ironic undertone of the author suggests to us that Thady does not at all comprehend the ethical structure of moral values supposedly inherent in the society he represents. For the Rackrents, as their name tells us, are miserly landlords to the Irish peasantry (Thady's class), completely selfish in dealing with tenants, and without interest in them as human beings. Thady's implicit condemnation of the family is based not on their moral shortcomings but on their impractical management of the estate. As far as we can tell, the narrator participates in the moral evils of the family—not by doing any overt evil himself, but by accepting the evil of others as normal behavior of the aristocracy.

*   *   *

The irony of the novel, then, is not limited to the Quirks' rise and the Rackrents' fall, but is also directed against Thady's moral insensitivity in his attitude toward his masters. Maria Edgeworth, however, is in no sense a genial satirist dealing with an old man's moral imperceptiveness. Thady is a symbol of a general attitude, manifest everywhere in the book, of indifference to evil. The ironic condemnation in *Castle Rackrent* is as far-ranging as that of any classical ironist's. It is aimed at all the Irish people by a novelist who spent most of her life in Ireland, and the implications of the irony go even further when in a concluding note (written by the novel's "editor") she adds:

---

9. James Newcomer, "'Castle Rackrent': Its Structure and Its Irony," *Criticism*, VII (1966), 176. The two Newcomer articles and his subsequent book, *Maria Edgeworth, the Novelist, 1767–1849* (Fort Worth, Texas, 1967), make a point of the irony in Thady's awareness of the flaws in the Rackrents' characters. But Newcomer does not see the complexity of the author's irony.
1. Newcomer, "Structure," p. 174.

It is a problem of difficult solution to determine, whether an Union [of Ireland and England just about to occur] will hasten or retard the amelioration of this country. The few gentlemen of education who now reside in this country will resort to England: they are few, but they are in nothing inferior to men of the same rank in Great Britain. The best that can happen will be the introduction of British manufacturers in their places.

Did the Warwickshire militia, who were chiefly artisans, teach the Irish to drink beer, or did they learn from the Irish to drink whiskey? (p. 62)[2]

Maria Edgeworth enlarges the scope of her denunciation of moral laxity by having Thady frequently refer to general opinion as evidence for his own evaluations of the rightness of his master's actions:

My lady had a sort of fit, and it was given out she was dead, by mistake; this brought things to a sad crisis for my poor master—one of the three ladies shewed his letters to her brother, and claimed his promises, whilst another did the same. I don't mention names—Sir Kit, in his defence, said he would meet any man who dared question his conduct, and as to the ladies, they must settle it amongst them who was to be his second, and his third, and his fourth, whilst his first was still alive, to his mortification and theirs. Upon this, as upon all former occasions, he had the voice of the country with him, on account of the great spirit and propriety he acted with. (pp. 25–26)

The upper ranks of society are equally condemned for their failure to exert an effort on behalf of moral truth. After Sir Kit's death, his wife is freed from her seven years' imprisonment:

No sooner was it known for certain that he was dead, than all the gentlemen within twenty miles of us came in a body as it were, to set my lady at liberty, and to protest against her confinement, which they now for the first time understood was against her own consent. (p. 27)

Thady, then, functions as more than an ironic voice detailing the failure of the Rackrents; he is also used by the author as a revelatory device to bring into focus his own moral failure and that of all the other passive participants in the evils of the Rackrents.

The fact that *Castle Rackrent* has always been read as a much simpler book than I have suggested it really is may indicate that Maria Edgeworth's irony actually distracts us from her moral vision, though the two were artistically designed to serve similar purposes. The ironic perspective here works against the reader's ability to

2. Page numbers throughout refer to this Norton Critical Edition [editor's note].

establish the normative values for the author's point of view—in a century which had not yet realized the possibilities of narrative unreliableness. Even today the detached artistry of the ironic perspective makes it difficult to determine with any precision the answers to such questions as: To what extent is Thady conscious of moral ambiguity in his actions? To what extent is he unconscious of even obvious moral failings like drunkenness? How much of his narrative is intended *by him* to inform us obliquely about his attitudes: his condemnation of the Rackrents' incompetency and his approval of his own son's efficiency?

Maria Edgeworth's novel is highly experimental inasmuch as it sets out to destroy the reader's expectations of narrative reliability. That the author's values are probably the same as most other English classicists', such as Fielding's or Smollett's, does not make it the least bit easy to establish these values within the framework of her experiment in ironic perspective. The values can be derived through the work itself, but only by a careful separation of the views of Thady from those of the implied author. Even so, the values develop only in a negative manner: Thady is ultimately to be judged more in terms of his omissions than in terms of what he does. It is no wonder that readers have long accepted him by his own evaluations as "poor Thady," "honest Thady," "old Thady," etc., the loyal family retainer who wrote his history "out of friendship for the family." In applying her irony to the form of first-person narration, Maria Edgeworth explored wide new areas for prose fiction, but at the same time she introduced new possibilities of ambiguity at the moral center of the novel.

SUSAN GLOVER

[Thady and the Editor]†

In his preface to the novel, the "Editor" of Maria Edgeworth's *Castle Rackrent* tells us that a "plain unvarnished tale is preferable to the most highly ornamented narrative" (p. 6),[1] and many readers have been taken in by this claim. Some time ago Thomas Flanagan drew attention to "the curiously enigmatic quality which is a source of the novel's power."[2] Against the conventional view of Thady's naïveté as the basis of the novel's strength, I propose that the narrative

† From Susan Glover, "Glossing the Unvarnished Tale: Contra-Dicting Possession in *Castle Rackrent*," *Studies in Philology* 99.3 (2002): 296–98, 300–11. Copyright © 2002 by the University of North Carolina Press. Used by permission of the publisher.
1. Page numbers throughout refer to this Norton Critical Edition [editor's note].
2. Thomas Flanagan, *The Irish Novelists, 1800–1850* (New York: Columbia University Press, 1959), 77.

tension arising from the competition and "contra-dicting" of two voices, Thady's and the Editor's, is the matrix of this enigmatic qual-ity.[3] This article reads land and text as homologous, each subject to disputed, and ultimately irreconciled, claims of possession.

The critical discussion of Thady Quirk as narrator of the novel has tended to obscure the fact that there is in fact a second dis-course in the novel, that of the Editor.[4] It is the Editor's voice that we encounter first and last in the novel and whose struggle to retain control of the text reflects the author's. The text provides us with a graphically descriptive title for the novel: a short title, *Castle Rack-rent*, followed by

AN
HIBERNIAN TALE
TAKEN FROM FACTS,
AND FROM
THE MANNERS OF THE IRISH SQUIRES,
BEFORE THE YEAR 1782.

The use of the word "Facts" and the explicit dating of the narrative "Before the Year 1782" suggest a verisimilitude and historical accu-racy at odds with the word "Tale." Along with the division between the two-word title and the two-part subtitle, the two etymologically opposed adjectives "Hibernian" and "Irish" and the indicators of two narrative time schemes all signal the division and dualities, the uncertainties about truth that mark the text which follows.

The Editor's voice enters with the preface, which serves as both an elaborate apology for and presentation of a rather unorthodox narra-tor and the first blow in a struggle for control and authority between the two narrative male voices. (The unnamed Editor refers to "his" readers of the novel.) The passive voice of the opening sentence and diction which includes phrases such as "a proper point of view" and "incontestable proof" (p. 5) suggest the Anglocentric, educated voice of authority. He begins an elaborate defense of his choice of narrator by flattering the public on its good sense, and denigrating the "critics"

---

3. Daniel Hack offers an acute reading of this enigmatic quality through the (unresolved) struggle between two nationalisms, Irish and English, in the novel. He concludes that Edgeworth sets in motion "a system of supplementary rationality that endlessly defers complete union even while working towards it" ("Inter-Nationalism: *Castle Rackrent* and Anglo-Irish Union," *Novel* 29.2 [1996]: 162). I suggest that the analysis I offer in this article contributes to an understanding of *how*, narratively, this happens.

4. One of the few critics to discuss the Editor's narrative function is Brian Hollingworth, who reads the Editor's rival role as a reassuring counterweight to Thady's discourse, allowing Edgeworth and her readers to engage safely in the game of enjoying the "vul-gar" tongue (*Maria Edgeworth's Irish Writing: Language, History, Politics* [Houndmills, Basingstoke: Macmillan, 1997]). See also Mary Jean Corbett's "Another Tale to Tell: Post-colonial Theory and the Case of *Castle Rackrent*," *Criticism* 36 (1994): 383–400; and Kathryn Kirkpatrick's "Putting Down the Rebellion: Notes and Glosses on *Castle Rackrent*, 1800," *Éire-Ireland* 30 (1995): 77–90.

and "professed historian" with their "measured prose" (p. 5). He casts doubt on the veracity of even the "best authenticated" histories, suggesting instead that we should look to the private rather than the public life of public men to "discover their real characters" (p. 5). The unsophisticated biographer, lacking the skills to deceive us, can go "behind the scenes" and give us the truth (p. 5). He concludes his introductory remarks with an assertion that the public "judiciously" trusts the artless retailer of anecdotes, even if he is "without sagacity . . . without elegance of style . . . without enlargement of mind" (p. 6). It is in this patronizing and pejorative light that the Editor claims credibility for his author, whom he introduces as "an illiterate old steward" (p. 6). The author is not only illiterate; his language is such as almost to warrant translation into "plain English," but the Editor has chosen instead to include explanatory notes, both to retain the "authenticity of his story" and to inform the "*ignorant* English reader" (p. 6).

The Editor takes full credit for the production of the narrative, noting that it was with some difficulty that "honest Thady" was persuaded to have it committed to writing, and that "his habitual laziness" had to be overcome (p. 7). The Editor hastily adds the reminder that these are "tales of other times," reassuring the contemporary reader that "the race of the Rackrents has long since been extinct in Ireland" (p. 7).

Despite the authoritative and controlling voice of the Editor, several ambiguities undermine his narrative. One of the first is his statement ostensibly arguing for the credibility of the unlettered narrator. "Where we see that a man has the power, we may naturally suspect that he has the will to deceive us, and those who are used to literary manufacture know how much is often sacrificed to the rounding of a period or the pointing an antithesis" (p. 6). Should this be taken as a warning about the intentions of one "used to literary manufacture," the Editor himself? Later he draws our attention to the narrator, "whose partiality to *the family* in which he was bred and born must be obvious to the reader" (p. 6). The use of italics to foreground "the family" and the subsequent reference to the Rackrents lead us to assume that these signifiers have the same referent, but as we shall see it is not entirely clear to which family—the Rackrents, or the Quirks (the one "in which he was bred and born")—Thady's partiality is directed (p. 6).

This sense of ambiguity, of unstable meaning, grows with the conclusion of the preface, as we wonder how we are to take the Editor's statement that the Rackrents are no more to be met with in modern Ireland "than Squire Western or Parson Trulliber in England" (p. 7).[5]

5. See n. 3, p. 7 [editor's note].

The controlling, authoritative voice, which began so confidently, grows more hesitant, suggesting that "probably" we shall be able to verify his observations and that Ireland will contemplate with amusement the stories of the old squires when she "loses her identity by an union with Great Britain" (p. 7). As we are still wondering, more than two hundred years later, when that might be, we cannot help but be conscious of the equivocation. We observe the maneuvering of the Editor as he presents himself as the voice of erudition and textual competence, mediating between a lazy illiterate narrator and the judicious reader. Yet the mask slips, and we glimpse the hesitation and false confidence.

* * *

An examination of Thady's discourse reveals a number of linguistic levels at work simultaneously, and not always harmoniously, which combine to create his "voice" in the novel, and which are set in opposition to the multi-layered presence of the Editor's voice. Thady's story functions as an apologia for his and his son's ascendance over the Rackrent family; a lament for the demise of its mythology; a scathing and brilliantly delivered condemnation of the Rackrents' tenure in Ireland; an expression of his pain, though he does not overtly acknowledge it as such, over his son Jason's ascendance over *him*; and the unwitting textual opposition of his idiolect against that of the Anglocentric Editor.

* * *

A close look at the narrative possibilities in the opening sentence of Thady's discourse will show how some of the tensions are established, how what we are told does not always match what we are shown. In his preface, the Editor carefully positions Thady as a lazy and illiterate old steward, who had with "some difficulty" been prevailed upon to rehearse the history of the Rackrent family. When we turn to Thady's monologue, we see, perhaps not surprisingly, a slightly different presentation. Here is the opening sentence:

> Having out of friendship for the family, upon whose estate, praised be Heaven! I and mine have lived rent free time out of mind, voluntarily undertaken to publish the Memoirs of the Rackrent Family, I think it my duty to say a few words, in the first place, concerning myself. (p. 11)

The first phrase, "out of friendship for the family" has helped to establish the received view of Thady's devotion to the Rackrent family. However, if his opening sentence is unravelled and syntactically re-ordered, beginning with the principal clause, it reads, "I think it my duty to say a few words, in the first place, concerning myself . . .

having . . . voluntarily undertaken to publish the Memoirs of the Rackrent Family." We see that the subject of the sentence, as it will be of the subsequent narrative, is "I," and the subject of his discourse is "myself."

We also see the first example of a rhetorical marker of Thady's discourse, the ritual invocation and praise addressed as an aside to his audience, in the clause "upon whose estate, praised be Heaven! I and mine have lived rent free time out of mind," which modifies "family." These rhetorical markers have been accepted at face value by many critics, and cited as evidence of Thady's continuing devotion and loyalty to the Rackrents. In one of the many cross-currents of dialogue and interpretation resonating through and across the text, we have this mode of discourse set against an explicit explanation of it in the Editor's footnote a few pages later. In his note on the term "Middle men," the Editor explains the Irish system of land tenure where the owner would lease large farms to a middleman, who would in turn sublet them to "under tenants" often at exorbitant rents (p. 19). On occasion the middleman would pocket the rents; as a result the landowner would then seize property of the tenants for his payment, thus forcing the tenants to pay twice. The middleman was characterized by servility towards his superiors and tyranny towards his inferiors, and was detested by the poor. The Editor notes that in speaking to him, however, the poor "always used the most abject language, and the most humble tone and posture—'*Please your honour,—and please your honour's honour,*' they knew must be repeated as a charm at the beginning and end of every equivocating, exculpatory, or supplicatory sentence" (p. 19).

Accordingly, "poor Thady" is employing a customary mode of rhetoric in addressing his story to a "middling" superior who is recording his story. (We assume someone is transcribing his speech, as the Editor says only that Thady "was persuaded to have it committed to writing" [p. 7]). He begins his account with Sir Patrick, and the ritual charm, "the whole country rang with his praises—Long life to him!—I'm sure I love to look upon his picture, now opposite to me," then proceeds to describe an overweight man noted for a short neck and a pimple on his nose who drank himself to death (pp. 12–13). In the midst of a detailed and knowledgeable recounting of Sir Murtagh's ineptness in legal matters and the consequent financial loss of "some hundreds a year of the family estate," Thady interjects "but he was a very learned man in the law, and I know nothing of the matter except having a great regard for the family" (p. 16). He closes a lengthy account of the spendthrift, violent, philandering Sir Kit who brought the estate to complete ruin, and under whose agent the tenants were so hard-driven, with the comment that the estate was "all mortgaged, and bonds out against him, for he was never cured of his gaming tricks—but that was the only fault he had, God bless him!" (p. 25). Too often these asides have been taken as literal expressions of Thady's devotion, rather than the linguistic markers clearly signalled in the footnote.

Several other elements of the opening sentence merit attention. Thady explicitly tells us that he and his family have lived "rent free time out of mind" on the Rackrent estate (p. 11). When we hear about the grasping ways of Sir Murtagh and his wife, who drove their tenants so harshly that they were "always breaking and running away," and of Sir Kit's agent who followed, who was "[b]ad news still for the poor tenants" and would "grind the face of the poor," we wonder at the Quirk family living "rent free" (pp. 15, 18–19). Thady also makes explicit his "voluntarily" undertaking to publish the Memoirs as his "duty," a claim of agency somewhat at odds with the Editor's statement.

There is much of the "exculpatory" in Thady's discourse, which in some ways can be read as a lengthy apologia for the reversal which finds his son Jason in the castle and the last of the Rackrents dispossessed. His remarks are regularly punctuated with the reiterations of his non-involvement: "*I* said nothing" (pp. 14, 19, 22, 32, 38, 42, 56), "I never said any thing" (p. 17), "kept my mind to myself" (p. 22), "I said not a word" (p. 59), right to the future tense of the last paragraph's "I'll say nothing" (p. 61), curious assertions in a lengthy oral discourse. Where blame is attributed, it is usually to the Rackrent wives. When Sir Murtagh's wife left, "to the great joy of the tenantry," she took with her a considerable jointure and most of the movable property in the house (p. 17). As to the long-suffering wife of Sir Kit, "from first to last she brought nothing but misfortunes amongst us," while Sir Condy's wife's few thousand pounds did not last long, "especially the way she went on with them" (pp. 28, 36).

* * *

The representation of an autochthonous and ancient family servant recounting its history, a man who was "not quite sincere or ingenuous in all his relations," and the use of the expression "upwards of" (Thady describes himself as being "upwards of four score and ten years of age" [p. 47]) strongly suggest that Edgeworth drew on more than simply the use of a servant's dialect to create her narrator.

* * *

When the Editor warns us in his preface that he contemplated translating Thady's language into "plain English," the reader assumes he is referring to problems with the dialect. John Cronin points out that Thady's narrative, which is described by the Editor as being "incapable of translation," is in fact nothing of the kind, and moreover does not require translation; his discourse includes very little brogue and shows a surprising facility with legal and technical terminology.[6]

Maria Edgeworth and her father shared a gift for mimicry and a keen interest in the speech of their Irish tenants. Two years after the appearance of *Castle Rackrent*, they published their *Essay on Irish Bulls*. It is a refutation of the Irish bull, or verbal blunder, and a defense of Irish wit and verbal virtuosity. In chapter 12, "Bath Coach Conversation," a Scotchman takes from his pocket a book of rhetoric, and notes that in the long list of tropes and figures one could find explanations for every species of Irish bulls, citing as examples "the oxymoron, as it is a favourite with Irish orators," and noting that the "Irish are particularly disposed to the epizeuxis, as 'indeed, indeed—at all, at all', and antanaclasis, or double meaning."[7] Not surprisingly, we find all of these, the latter in particular, in Thady's speech.

Despite the attention to the dialect of the dominant voice in the novel, the "voice of the land," there is clear evidence from the outset of the struggle for control of the text. Before we get to Thady's words, we are interrupted by the Editor with a note of explanation, in amused, patronizing terms, of the Irish peasants' practice of delaying all work till Monday morning. Thady is hardly into his second, admittedly discursive, sentence when the Editor again intervenes, this time with a learned and lengthy discursive project of his own, elaborating quite gratuitously on the history of "the cloak," even though Thady had used the word "coat" in his discourse.[8] Both texts appear on the opening page of the novel, and while the portion of the text given over to the note is set in smaller type than the text of the main narrative, it is in fact longer, 148 words of note to 100 words of Thady's text. The Editor's note continues on for the better part of the second page, and impresses with its quotation from Spenser, its references to classical and biblical texts, and its scholarly tone.

Julian Moynahan suggests that the first footnote, the extended note on "cloak," adds "stature to the figure of Thady, making him

---

6. John Cronin, *The Anglo-Irish Novel* (Belfast: Appletree Press, 1980), 1:31. Thady's speech poses relatively few problems, and stands in contrast to his reported speech of his great-niece Judy M'Quirk, who, unlike Jason and Thady, has not dropped the Irish prefix. Joanne Altieri compares Judy's dialect to that of Thady, and finds that her speech indicates "the lowest caste," citing as an example the pattern of "omission of the finite verb ('and a great crowd of people too upon the road,' 'and with two wheels off and all tattered')" ("Style and Purpose in Maria Edgeworth's Fiction," *Nineteenth Century Fiction* 23 [1968]: 274). For a helpful discussion of Edgeworth's representation of dialect in Thady's discourse see Hollingworth, *Edgeworth's Irish Writing*. [See Hollingworth on pp. 199–203—editor].

7. Richard Lovell Edgeworth and Maria Edgeworth, *An Essay on Irish Bulls*, vol. 1 of *Tales and Novels* (London, 1832–33), 235.

8. For a discussion of the ideological significance of the "cloak" historically in Anglo-Irish relations see Ann Rosalind Jones and Peter Stallybrass's "Dismantling Irena: The Sexualizing of Ireland in Early Modern England," in *Nationalisms and Sexualities*, ed. Andrew Parker, et al. (New York: Routledge, 1992), 157–71.

a kind of eponym for native Irish tradition, archaic and disregarded by those who hold power in Ireland, but persisting nevertheless, into the latest time."[9] This view introduces another aspect to the Editor-Thady dialogue; while the two voices are usually set in opposition, the tension is complicated by occasional resonances of sympathy, even unity. While the Editor is customarily patronizing in his descriptions of Irish customs and vernacular, at times to the point of ridicule, parts of the discourse exhibit genuine concern or a shared pleasure, such as the footnote on middlemen or the glossary note on the raking pot of tea (pp. 19, 74–75). Occasionally a note is a mixture of both; the long entry on the "Whillaluh" begins respectfully with a quotation from the Transactions of the Royal Irish Academy on funeral lamentation but closes on a sneering note (pp. 64–66). The Editor is constantly intruding, writing over Thady's text, mediating our reception of Thady's discourse with his own.

The first footnote sets up other dynamics in the narrative as well. The passage from Spenser is from a text which itself is two voices: A *View of the State of Ireland written Dialogue-wise, betweene Eudoxus and Irenæus* (1596). The reference in the quoted passage is to outlaws, rebels and thieves, and to the multiple ways they are served by their cloaks. We note that the words "cloak" and "mantle" can function as verbs, in the sense of to cover, to conceal, to disguise, dissemble, and obscure. These allusions serve to further heighten our sense of caution and our awareness of competing voices in the text.

Having firmly established a bulwark against the rambling vernacular of Thady, the Editor frequently re-enters Thady's story in additional footnotes. These usually explain some oddity of "lower Irish" speech or elaborate condescendingly on superstitions, such as in his description of Banshees, whose visits have latterly "been discontinued," or on cultural practices such as the wake, which serve only as an occasion for "gossipping and debauchery" (pp. 16, 53). He explicitly sets his authority against Thady's when he suggests that Thady's account of Sir Kit's treatment of his wife is scarcely credible, but reminds readers of the case of Lady Cathcart and assures the reader that the Editor himself was acquainted with her husband. The Editor's authority is such that his word alone is accepted as sufficient proof where Thady's is not; in order to confirm Thady's claim that voters stood on clods of sod taken from specific properties in order to swear honestly, the Editor simply provides the words, "This was actually done" (p. 39). In the first section of Thady's narrative, the Editor interrupts a total of sixteen times in thirty

---

9. Julian Moynahan, *Anglo-Irish: The Literary Imagination in a Hyphenated Culture* (Princeton: Princeton University Press, 1995), p. 21.

pages of text. The frequency of footnotes in the Continuation is much lower, as are the references to the glossary, yet they remain frequent enough to retain their felt presence in the text.

Surprisingly little attention has been devoted to the rhetorical function of footnotes within a narrative. In his study of fiction, Wayne Booth notes the variety of techniques for providing narrative summary of information the reader could not otherwise easily learn, then wonders, "What, for example, are we to call the device of narrating by footnotes?" but fails to pursue an answer to his question.[1] In his introduction to *Castle Rackrent*, George Watson attributes the footnotes to the novelty of the book's narrative approach: "Rackrent is the first consistent attempt to compose a novel in any dialect of English; and alarmed at her experiment, Maria fitted it out first with explanatory footnotes and then, as an afterthought, with a 'Glossary' (in fact a commentary) as well."[2] Julian Moynahan cites the lengthy passage on Irish knowledge of legal matters and adds that the "Glossary is full of such overkill. Entries on the willalu, on Faery Mounts, on the wake, are nearly article length. One grasps that both Edgeworths were quite anxious about English ignorance of Ireland at this time."[3] As is so often the case in Edgeworth criticism, recourse is made to the Edgeworths' lives, *père et fille*,[4] to explain the text.

Nor does the Editor allow Thady the last word. Appended to Thady's closing question is an epilogue which begins, "The Editor could have readily made the catastrophe of Sir Condy's history more dramatic and more pathetic. . . . He lays it before the English reader . . ." (p. 62). In a curious usurpation of the "author," the Editor takes full possession of and responsibility for Thady's text. Once again we see the pattern of the preface repeated. A forceful, assertive opening soon subsides into a more reflective, humbler mode, acknowledging in a historically resonant comment that Ireland's future is "a problem of difficult solution to determine" (p. 62). It concludes with the curiously ambivalent and interrogative admission of doubt about who will be the real beneficiary of the Union.

Following the end of the much intruded-upon text, the Editor once more addresses the readers in a note explaining that at the suggestion of his friends he has furnished a Glossary of those terms which "could not be intelligible to the English reader without farther explanation" (p. 63). Sixteen pages of additional notes set in smaller type follow, ranging from philological discussions of derivations and

1. Wayne C. Booth, *The Rhetoric of Fiction*, 2d ed. (Chicago: University of Chicago Press, 1983), 171.
2. Watson, introduction to *Castle Rackrent*.
3. Moynahan, *Anglo-Irish* 28.
4. Father and daughter (French) [editor's note].

diction to scholarly accounts of Irish cultural practices, and including quotations ranging from Estonian poetry to Ovid and Virgil.

The glossary, when it is mentioned at all by scholars, is invariably given an historical explanation such as Butler's: "The entire text of *Castle Rackrent*, with its footnotes, was already in print when the family decided that some further explanation for the public was needed." Butler outlines the argument that, with Union imminent, the appearance of a novel presenting Ireland to England in a comic light would undermine Richard Lovell Edgeworth's position of support for the Union, and suggests that "this helps to explain the self-conscious intellectuality and *Englishness* of the Glossary."[5]

If we turn to the paradigm of oppositional discourses, one of the most evident effects of the profusion of footnotes and glossary references is the constant competition for the reader's attention between the two voices. The repeated interruptions of Thady's story require the reader to transfer attention to another discourse, to the bottom of the page or to the back of the book, creating both physical and interpretive breaks in the act of reading Thady's story and making quite explicit the conflicting demands. (This effect is compounded, of course, in modern editions where the twentieth-century editor has superimposed a second layer of footnotes and commentary onto Edgeworth's text.) This oppositional strategy compounds the obstacles in an interpretive process already intensified by the gaps and ambiguities in the text. As W. J. McCormack observes, "the further proliferation of notes, prefaces and glossaries, testifies to the determined refusal of the fiction to mimic a harmony its traditionalist readers desire."[6]

In *Castle Rackrent*, we have a divided title, a divided subtitle, a divided editorial frame, a divided central narrative, two narrators, two families each with two names (O'Shaughlin-Rackrent and M'Quirk-Quirk), two national voices, two religions, and two narrative time frames. It is this struggle for dominance between two voices which leads to both the sense of contra-diction—of speaking-against—in the text, and the consequent sense of an absent center.

Multiple voicing is, according to Bakhtin, the aspect of the novel which distinguishes it from all other genres. By locating meaning in a particular point in space and time, he envisions the working of a novel as a system of intersecting planes. Apart from polyglossia, the influence of a variety of other languages on the structure of a given

5. Marilyn Butler, *Maria Edgeworth: A Literary Biography* (Oxford: Clarendon Press, 1972), 354, 355.
6. W. J. McCormack, "Setting and Ideology: With Reference to the Fiction of Maria Edgeworth," in *Ancestral Voices: The Big House in Anglo-Irish Literature*, ed. Otto Rauchbauer (Hildesheim: Georg Olms, 1992), 45.

language at a given time, he identifies heteroglossia, the condition whereby all utterances are subject to a set of social and historical conditions governing meaning at a particular temporal and spatial instance (chronotope). One consequence of the dual or multiple voices is an apparent loss of authorial control, a notable feature of the ostensibly intentional and "didactic" fiction Maria Edgeworth wrote for children. Elizabeth Harden observes that her "bad" characters are often more forcefully drawn than the "good," that "the indolent, wasteful little boys, peevish little girls, dishonest servants, and drunken butlers frequently succeed in making vice attractive."[7] A similar problem arose with *Castle Rackrent*: Butler speculates that Edgeworth was unhappy with the narrative turn her novel had taken, and that is why she did not use the idiosyncratic narrator again in her fiction.[8]

One frequent explanation for the confusion of voice in Edgeworth's work is a confusion of authorship. Considerable research has been done to determine just how much, and to which works, Maria Edgeworth's father contributed. It is agreed that *Castle Rackrent* is one of the few works she completed independently of her father. While Butler tends to discount much of the earlier critical view that her father interfered excessively with her literary work, a certain tension must have been inevitable. Grace Oliver quotes a passage from a letter by Maria Edgeworth about her work on *Letters for Literary Ladies*, published five years before *Castle Rackrent*: "they are not as well as can be expected, nor are they likely to mend at present. They are now disfigured by all manner of crooked marks of papa's critical indignation, besides various abusive marginal notes, which I would not have you see for half a crown sterling."[9]

In light of this, it is perhaps not surprising that one curiously absent voice in *Castle Rackrent* is that of the author. The diegetic level of discourse, the author-narrator speaking to the reader, is not found in the novel (quite literally in the first edition, which was published anonymously). Butler has remarked on Maria Edgeworth's "fondness for male narrators, and her . . . penchant for invisibility; nowhere more than in *Castle Rackrent*, that best sustained of masquerades."[1] In an oft-quoted reply to her publisher's request for a

---

7. O. Elizabeth McWhorter Harden, *Maria Edgeworth's Art of Prose Fiction* (The Hague: Mouton, 1971), 27.
8. Butler, *Literary Biography*, 306.
9. Quoted in Grace Oliver, *A Study of Maria Edgeworth with Notices of her Father and Friends* (Boston, 1882), 99. Butler summarizes and discusses scholarship on the question of Maria Edgeworth's father's involvement in her writing (*Literary Biography*, chap. 6).
1. Marilyn Butler, introduction to *Castle Rackrent and Ennui*, by Maria Edgeworth (London: Penguin, 1992), 53. Butler makes this remark in the context of a comment on gender and narration. For a helpful discussion of the intersecting of gender and the politics of the impending union of Great Britain and Ireland in Edgeworth's narration see Mary Jean Corbett, "Another Tale."

biographical note, Edgeworth said, "As a woman, my life, wholly domestic, cannot afford anything interesting to the public: I am like the 'needy knifegrinder'—I have no story to tell."[2] Perhaps, like Thady who can "say nothing" for the length of a novel, Edgeworth's story lies hidden in the spaces.

Anthony Mortimer, in an article on the historical contexts surrounding the novel, concludes that the novelist "may shrink from the image of ideology" emerging from his [sic] fiction and may seek to "remystify what his own narrative tends to demystify. And yet he has no ultimate escape, because his evasive strategies will leave their mark on the text as absences that the reader can transform into interrogations."[3] Maria Edgeworth's "evasive strategies" are displaced into the dialogical narrative of the novel, the struggle between Thady and the Editor for control of the text. We see the evasiveness of Thady's discourse, reading in the gaps to learn that Thady and Jason appear to have been working together to take advantage of the Rackrents' dissolution. And when Thady recalls the succession of Sir Patrick to the estate, we are left to wonder just whose family he means when he says, "I ought to bless that day, for the estate came straight into *the* family" (p. 12).

Despite the confident beginnings, both discourses end in ambiguous uncertainty and interrogation of the reader. Thady's apology-memoir ends with the equivocal query, "where's the use of telling lies about the things which everybody knows as well as I do?" (p. 61). The Editor speculates on the future of Anglo-Irish relations, and can only ponder, in that most eloquent of questions, "Did the Warwickshire militia, who were chiefly artisans, teach the Irish to drink beer, or did they learn from the Irish to drink whiskey?" (p. 62). We are left to ask whether this dialogical opposition is presented as a failure of discourse, or as evidence of Maria Edgeworth's acute capacity to represent a living narrative process in what Stanley Solomon calls one of the "most subtly conceived works of eighteenth-century fiction."[4]

The Edgeworths worked towards an "improving" approach to landownership on their property in Ireland, but the inherent conflicts arising from cultural, political, and historical clashes rendered illusory such a goal. When he took over his estate in Ireland, Edgeworth would take Maria with him on the rounds of his tenants and properties. She would take notes and keep records for him,

---

2. Butler, *Literary Biography*, 9.
3. Anthony Mortimer, "*Castle Rackrent* and Its Historical Contexts," *Études Irlandaises* 9 (1984): 111.
4. Stanley J. Solomon, "Ironic Perspective in Maria Edgeworth's *Castle Rackrent*," *Journal of Narrative Technique* 2 (1972): 68. [See Solomon on p. 145—editor.]

observing and documenting the exchanges of landlord and tenant.[5]
At the close of the eighteenth century, on the brink of a union
between Great Britain and Ireland, it is likely that neither appreci-
ated how well she succeeded.

KATHERINE O'DONNELL

[Oral Culture][†]

* * *

To call the narrator, Thady Quirk, an unreliable narrator fails at
marking how fundamentally his narration undermines every convention of the realist novel. *Castle Rackrent* is best understood as
owing a profound debt to the virtuoso oral performance of Anglo-
Gaelic culture.[1] * * *

* * *

Despite the disclaimer of the subtitle that it is "An Hibernian Tale
taken from the facts, and from the manners of the Irish squires,
before the year 1782," the text is a performance given in the present
tense, and the pages are left to the Hiberno-English or Anglo-Gaelic
voice of Thady. The narration of the "illiterate Thady," who can
certainly read and possibly write, works as a brilliant deconstruc-
tion of the English language. His syntax reworks the grammar of
English, the symbolic law of English, where the repudiated identification of (non)sense is recovered to be sensible with a laugh, cry,
shout, or question: the law of the English language is thus exposed
as no longer being in control of the terms of its own discourse. The
text is propelled forward by the Anglo-Gaelic voice, which anarchi-
cally disturbs the English language, as the "Hibernian Tale" of
Castle Rackrent disturbs the genre of social realism.

---

† From Katherine O'Donnell, "Castle Stopgap: Historical Reality, Literary Realism, and
  Oral Culture," *Eighteenth-Century Fiction* 22.1 (2009): 115–16, 123–26, 128–30.
  Reprinted by permission of *Eighteenth-Century Fiction.* www.humanities.mcmaster
  .ca/~ecf.
5. In an incisive article on women and property in the novel, Kathryn Kirkpatrick
   observes that the thousands of pounds Edgeworth earned through the sale of her literary works remained her property, as she remained unmarried (legally, a *feme sole*), but
   that she managed the Edgeworthstown estate for her brother, "an estate she would
   never own" (Kathryn Kirkpatrick, "'Going to Law About that Jointure': Women and
   Property in *Castle Rackrent*," *Canadian Journal of Irish Studies* 22 [1996]: 27). [For
   Edgeworth's earnings, see p. 96—editor.]
1. Brian Hollingsworth discusses Thady's "idolect" and "fluent oral vernacular" but sees
   Edgeworth's deploying it as a method to consolidate the political position of the ruling
   Protestant Ascendancy. Hollingsworth, *Maria Edgeworth's Irish Writing: Language,
   History, Politics* (Basingstoke: Palgrave, 1997), 71–107. [See Hollingsworth on pp. 199–
   203. O'Donnell's use of Anglo-Gaelic here is her own neologism—editor.]

This distinctly reflexive form of narrative anarchy exhibits a pervasive cultural concern, which we often characterize as post-
modernist: things are not only what they seem, what they seem is
what they are. There is no unity of word or image or thing. Words
and images wander free without things or exist as things themselves,
as effects of narrative form and nothing else, unstable, unfixed, and
ungrounded in any reality, truth, or identity other than those that
Thady's voice provides. The editorial gesture of relocating the speech
of the Hibernian to a past era by defining it as a discontinued mode
of discursive value production is not a neutral act of identification.
This editorial gesture might be seen to be a dominant gesture of
incorporation meant to muzzle the disruptive voice of Hiberno-
English/Anglo-Gaelic, a voice, which in its dialect—its pronunciation, punctuation, and idiom—disturbs the homogeneous category
of English. However, the multifaceted editorial edifice of title page,
preface, footnotes, closing advertisement,[2] and the long, fractured
commentary of the glossary, accentuates the sublime achievement of
the power of Thady's articulation to grip our imagination and dazzle
our senses.

The eighteenth century is marked by the concerted efforts of public men to systematize and regulate all knowledge by identifying
what John Locke called "the horizon . . . which sets the bounds
between the enlightened and dark part of things."[3] Seeing and knowing were intrinsically linked; eighteenth-century thought was concerned with perspective, the light of reason, the clarity of the
mind's eye, distinguishing shadow from substance. In *Castle Rackrent*, speech creates reality and totally subsumes the power of sight
to know reality. The reality of the text is utterly dominated by the
mouth in all its most voracious guises, and all the Rackrent lords
are consumed by their uncontrolled lips. Thady, when a little boy,
held a bumper of claret to Sir Patrick's mouth because he could not
hold the vessel "on account of the great shake in his hand" (p. 13).[4]
Sir Patrick sang a loud and hearty chorus, and, as the company gave
three cheers, he fell into a fit and promptly died. The next lord, Sir
Murtagh, "overstrained his chest with making himself heard in one
of his favourite causes" (p. 17), and he ruined the family finances by
constantly arguing and too often losing in the courts; he died shout-
ing at his wife. His brother, Sir Kit, inherited the estate. Sir Kit fought
a number of duels, but in his last duel, Thady tells us, he was
unlucky—"hitting the toothpick out of his adversary's finger and
thumb, he received a ball in a vital part, and was brought home, . . .

2. See the preface on p. ix [editor's note].
3. John Locke, *An Essay Concerning Human Understanding*, ed. Peter H. Nidditch (1690;
   Oxford: Clarendon Press, 1979), book 1, chap. 7.
4. Page numbers throughout refer to this Norton Critical Edition [editor's note].

speechless, on a hand-barrow" (p. 26). In a circular movement, the final Rackrent, Sir Condy, who has metaphorically drunk his estate, gets Thady to feed him drink from the great bowl used by his ancestor Sir Patrick: "He swallows it down, and drops like one shot.—We lifts him up, and he was speechless" (p. 60); and he dies shortly after. Every moment of Thady's narration, conducted through the constant performance of pipe-smoking, is concerned with the mouth and its capacity to consume and create, to bring what is outside to the insides, and to establish an outside according to interior desires. The glossary reminds us that in Ireland, "Canting does not mean talking or writing hypocritical nonsense but selling substantially at auction" (p. 67).

A vivid demonstration of how it is the mouth rather than the eye that establishes the values of the text can be seen in Thady's interaction with Sir Kit and his new English wife. Thady's heart is in his mouth as he walks after Sir Kit because he can see that Sir Kit is not pleased: "'Is the large room damp, Thady?' said his honor—'Oh, damp, your honor! how should it but be as dry as a bone, (says I) after all the fires we have kept in it day and night—It's the barrack room your honor's talking on'" (p. 22). Thady intuits that Sir Kit is referring to the (presumably damp) barrack room and answers his question with an assurance that the large room is not only not damp but is also not the barrack room. Thady continues: "'And what is a barrack room, pray, my dear'—were the first words I ever heard out of my lady's lips—'No matter, my dear,' said he, and went on talking to me, ashamed like I should witness her ignorance" (p. 22). In a hilarious inversion of the usual colonial paradigm, Thady declares himself astounded at the ignorance of the English woman: "it was 'what's this, Sir Kit? and what's that, Sir Kit? (said she) that, that looks like a pile of black bricks, pray Sir Kit?' 'My turf stack, my dear,' said my master, and bit his lip—Where have you lived, my lady, all your life, not to know a turf stack when you see it thought I, but I said nothing" (p. 22). The logic whereby seeing is believing is further undermined as the English lady "takes out her glass, and begins spying over the country":

> "And what's all that black swamp out yonder, Sir Kit?" says she—"My bog, my dear" says he, and went on whistling— "It's a very ugly prospect my dear," says she— "You don't see it, my dear, (says he) for we've planted it out, when the trees grow up, in summer time," says he— "Where are the trees, (said she) my dear," still looking through her glass— "You are blind, my dear, (says he) what are these under your eyes?"— "These shrubs?" said she— "Trees," said he— "Maybe they are what you call trees in Ireland," my dear, (says she) but they are not a yard high, are they?'" (p. 22)

The English wife sees shrubs, yet Sir Kit describes them as trees; the words "shrubs" and "trees" have significance because of the narrow gap between the signifiers "shrubs" and "trees," a gap that is stopped by Sir Kit's iteration. Thady attempts to find a middle ground between Sir Kit's trees and his wife's shrubs: "'They were planted out but last year, my lady' says I, to soften matters between them, . . . —'they are very well grown for their age, and you'll not see the bog of Allyballycarricko'shaughlin at all at all through the skreen, when once the leaves come out—'" (p. 23). Thady's attempt at bridging the gap fails: "but she fell to laughing like one out of their right mind, and made me say the name of the bog over for her to get it by heart a dozen times—then she must ask me how to spell it, and what was the meaning of it in English—Sir Kit standing by whistling all the while—I verily believe she laid the corner stone of all her future misfortunes at that very instant—but I said no more, only looked at Sir Kit" (p. 23). We may presume this silent look speaks volumes. Sir Kit's English wife is also Jewish and is subsequently terrorized by Sir Kit, who insists that pork be brought daily to the table; she retires to her room and is promptly locked in there by Sir Kit, who will not let her out until she surrenders her diamond cross. All of the Stopgap/Rackrent wives endure miserable marriages and gladly embrace their liberty on the deaths of their husbands, but the fate of the Jewish wife (who, true to the ambivalent signifiers of *Castle Rackrent*, wears a cross) is particularly grim as she remains in captivity for seven years.[5]

* * *

Castle Rackrent allowed the family to stage a theatrical stopgap in the midst of fluctuation, uncertainty, and dramatic change, where all signifiers of allies and enemies were open to change. The Edgeworths rejoiced in the linguistic devices of their servant, John Langan, whose Anglo-Gaelic *ancien régime*[6] world of service, loyalty, and community was a high-culture verbal performance. In this world, genealogy was highly prized, and local memory was a collective enterprise of story-telling and the public performance of poetry and song, often performed at ritualized events such as funerals and pattern days.[7] This collective oral enterprise resulted in a rich oral culture that keenly maintained its records, but rather than prizing

---

5. For a discussion of anti-Semitism in Edgeworth's novels, see Susan Manly, "*Harrington* and Anti-Semitism: Mendelssohn's Invisible Agency," in *An Uncomfortable Authority: Maria Edgeworth and Her Contexts*, ed. Heidi Kaufman and Chris Fauske (Newark: University of Delaware Press, 2004), 235–49.
6. Old regime [editor's note].
7. From the Irish *pátrún* (patron). Most Irish parishes had a patron saint; on the saint's feast day, the parishioners celebrated what came to be known as Pattern Day [editor's note].

an ideal of objectivity, so valued in print culture, the record was retold in performances designed to provide a gloss or balm that suited the emotional, social, and political needs of the audience present.[8] We might argue that in the voice of Thady we hear the voice of a consummate verbal performer: he establishes distinct and discreet narrative codes in which events are recorded, while he evades or humorously euphemizes some unflattering implications, and we might say that Thady's voice maintains a studied unawareness, or rather a refusal to cast judgment or make distinctions in favour of maintaining flexible bonds of affection or leaving as many options open in time of revolution. However, the voice of John Langan/Thady Quirk might also be read as inherently untrustworthy: he designs to please and affirm the status quo, he claims his loyalty is to "the family" of the Castle, but as the novel closes do we really believe that he will forsake his blood bond to his son Jason in order to uphold the claim of the Rackrents that Jason usurps? *Castle Rackrent* opens with the declaration that: "A plain unvarnished tale is preferable to the most highly ornamented narrative. Where we see that a man has the power we may naturally suspect that he has the will to deceive us" (p. 6). Thady, who was reluctantly "persuaded to have [his story] committed to writing" (p. 7), gives us anything but a plain tale. During the years of *Castle Rackrent*, the Edgeworths could trust no one but the immediate family: they could not know how they would be perceived, who would defend them, or where an attack might come from. Identities are formed in relation to other groups, but, in the Irish 1790s, secret societies and dramatic shifts in power were the norm: ongoing revolution rolled the end of the century to a close. The family drama that is *Castle Rackrent*, inspired by their past chronicles, marked by their perilous present, and impelled by their uncertain future, provided an opportunity for

---

8. Critics often read *Castle Rackrent* in conjunction with *An Essay on Irish Bulls* (1802), which Maria and her father wrote to counter the English tendency to mistake the Irish or rather Hiberno-English play with figurative language and varieties of humour as evidence of stupidity. Perhaps the Edgeworths' much-neglected two-volume work from 1798, *Practical Education*, might prove a more useful foil for *Castle Rackrent*, as it is a ground-breaking work that recounts in detail the innovative method of respectful record keeping of children's entry into language. Richard Lovell Edgeworth's second wife, Honora Sneyd, first started the Edgeworth project of carefully recording actual conversations between herself and the children (Richard Lovell Edgeworth eventually fathered 22 children with his four wives) in order to maintain records of children's thought processes that could be analysed by parents and educators as a means to understanding how children develop their own chain of reasoning. This early work on educational psychology proved to be immensely influential throughout the nineteenth century. Measures that interrupted or modified the child's own narratives of meaning and location were strongly denounced; the authors demanded that parents and educators allow the individual child to find and develop their own place in language and the practice of learning. See Mitzi Myers, "'Anecdotes from the Nursery' in Maria Edgeworth's *Practical Education* (1798): Learning from Children 'Abroad and At Home,'" *Princeton University Library Chronicle* 60, no. 2 (Winter 1999): 220–50.

the Edgeworths, during these years of familial and public death, new alliances, uncertainty, confusion, and terror, to act out and release their anxiety, and in their shared laughter affirm their own bonds of love and affection.[9]

Castle Rackrent ends with the abrupt, curious question: "Did the Warwickshire militia, who were chiefly artisans, teach the Irish to drink beer, or did they learn from the Irish to drink whiskey?" (p. 62). This strange open-ending is perhaps an apt close to such an unusual verbal text. It is at once a reference to, but also an occlusion of, the brutal years of the Irish 1790s, where some 80,000 militia were brought from England to maintain the rule of the British Crown. It suggests an ecumenism through mutual commerce and more specifically the rituals of public drinking, the quaffing, swallowing of liquids designed for the shared performance of celebration, commemoration, and forgetting: the very practice and achievement of *Castle Rackrent*.

---

9. In a brilliant reading of *Castle Rackrent*, Daniel Hack argues that the endless approach to and deferral of complete political certainty in the novel "helps ensure the survival and authority of those whose identity is equally threatened by both assimilation and separation: the Anglo Irish." Hack's thesis is that Edgeworth's project "is quintessentially Anglo-Irish: her novel works to install a system whereby an ongoing process of Union gives the Anglo-Irish a place and English fear of the duplicity and sheer unreadability of the Irish gives them a function. The Anglo-Irish, in short, feed off the very anxiety of empire *Castle Rackrent* feeds." Hack, "Inter-Nationalism: Castle Rackrent and Anglo-Irish Union," *Novel: A Forum on Fiction* 29, no. 2 (1996): 147–48. In contrast to Hack, I do not see the English as ever exhibiting fear of Ireland: Irish illegibility is routinely read as an Irish failure to be ontologically coherent rather than an English problem of epistemology. *Castle Rackrent* reveals the Anglo-Irish identity, rather than the English Empire to be an inherently anxious state. Ina Ferris argues in a similar vein to Hack that Edgeworth's "Irish" novels have a pragmatic function in that they seek to generate sympathy for Ireland in English readers. Ferris, *The Romantic National Tale and the Question of Ireland* (Cambridge: Cambridge University Press, 2002). Ferris, however, does not include *Castle Rackrent* in discussing and elucidating this argument, possibly because, as Hack puts it, "it is impossible to determine at whose expense the text's ferocious irony operates" (147).

Patriarchy and Paternalism

ELIZABETH KOWALESKI-WALLACE

[Patriarchal Complicity]†

* * *

Gilbert and Gubar's feminist appreciation of *Castle Rackrent* in *The Madwoman in the Attic* is only one version of a reading that celebrates Thady Quirk, finding in him fascinating psychological depth and complexity—evidence of Edgeworth's ability to project into and to sympathize with Thady's character. Gilbert and Gubar believe that Edgeworth specifically identifies with Thady's ambivalence in the face of exploitative male power; to them, *Castle Rackrent* is "a critique of patriarchy." They assert that Edgeworth criticizes the "male aristocratic line" because "it exploits Ireland, that old sow, leaving a peasantry starved and dispossessed. Rackrent means destructive rental, and *Castle Rackrent* is a protest against exploitative landlords."[1] Yet *which* patriarchy is being critiqued here? As Richard Edgeworth's improvements at Edgeworthstown suggest, patriarchal authority could have several different faces, and the several generations of Rackrents represent different phases of Irish history as well as different models for landlord-tenant relations; the ascendancy of Thady's own son Jason at the end of the novel is only the most recent historical phase of patriarchy, one to which Edgeworth responds ambivalently.[2]

The notion that *Castle Rackrent* protests against "exploitative male power" makes most sense when applied to Thady's narrative about Sir Kit, the third master, and his "Jew Lady Rackrent" (p. 28)[3]

---

† From Elizabeth Kowaleski-Wallace, "Good Housekeeping: The Politics of Anglo-Irish Ascendency," in *Their Fathers' Daughters: Hannah More, Maria Edgeworth, and Patriarchal Complicity* (New York & Oxford: Oxford University Press, 1991), pp. 150–59, 227. © 1991 by Oxford University Press. Reprinted by permission of Oxford University Press, USA.
1. Sandra Gilbert and Susan Gubar, *The Madwoman in the Attic* (New Haven: Yale University Press, 1979), p. 150.
2. Marilyn Butler, *Maria Edgeworth: A Literary Biography* (Oxford: Clarendon Press, 1972), 357.
3. Page numbers throughout refer to this Norton Critical Edition [editor's note].

Indeed Sir Kit personifies the worst of the landlords; he bleeds the tenants and practices many of the abuses Richard Edgeworth had so wisely eschewed. When unable to raise any more funds off the land, he marries abroad, choosing a rich Jewish heiress as his bride. Thady's narrative of her experiences—of the mental and physical tortures to which her husband subjects her because she will not relinquish to him a valuable diamond cross—conveys a strong degree of sympathy for her plight. As Gilbert and Gubar write, "Starving inside the ancestral mansion, the literally imprisoned wife is also figuratively imprisoned inside the husband's fictions" (Gilbert and Gubar, 55).

However, if Thady's narrative allows insight into a situation where patriarchal prerogatives exploit and victimize an innocent woman, that insight is problematized by Thady's split loyalties. On the one hand, he cannot help but feel sorry for the wife, and he clearly believes her imprisonment is an extraordinary cruelty. He writes, for example, that "When she was lying, to all expectation, on her deathbed of a broken heart, I could not but pity her, though she was Jewish. . . ." (p. 25). On the other hand, his ability to sympathize with her plight is limited by his persistent loyalty to the Rackrent family. This loyalty precludes any explicit criticism of Sir Kit (as Thady admits on several occasions). Moreover, the narrator's anti-Semitism frequently colors his response to the foreign bride.

Thady's attitude toward the wife's religious difference provides Edgeworth with the material for comedy at his expense, as when Thady passes the wife for a "nabob" in the kitchen in order to account "for her dark complexion and everything" (p. 22). In the process of exposing the wife's ignorance about indigenous Irish practices, Thady more often exposes his own. For example, he is astonished that Lady Rackrent has never heard of a "barrack-room," a word that is then defined in the glossary for the British audience. Edgeworth here satirizes Thady's inability to perceive the strangeness of his own culture to an outsider. Ultimately, Thady is not the opponent of patriarchal exploitation because of his investment in the very system whose abuses he registers and, in the end, he blames Lady Rackrent for the demise of Sir Kit.

> But from first to last she brought nothing but misfortunes amongst us; and if it had not been all along with her, his honour, Sir Kit, would have been now alive in appearance. Her diamond cross was, they say, at the bottom of it all; and it was a shame for her, being his wife, not to show more duty, and to have given it up when she condescended to ask so often for such a bit of a trifle in his distresses, especially when he all along made it no secret he married for money. (p. 28)

Through the absurdity of the last comment, Edgeworth effectively conveys her own critique of the way property figures into marriage, and the story of Sir Kit's Jewish wife can be read, as Gilbert and Gubar suggest, as a protest against the powerlessness of women caught and imprisoned through the dishonest and unscrupulous practices of corrupt patriarchs.

Yet the fact that *Castle Rackrent* is radical in its perception of women's social and economic victimization does not mean that it is radical on all levels. The narrative of Sir Kit and his Jewish wife is only one of many stories told in *Castle Rackrent*. If, at times, Thady exposes his masters, offering subversive readings of their actions in spite of himself, at other times the function of his narrative is still more complicated. While he implicitly attacks some aspects of the Rackrents' patriarchal power, Thady facilitates other aspects, namely their efficacy as colonialist rulers. In an essay entitled "The Significant Silences of Thady Quirk" Maurice Colgan describes the "large opaque area" in the center of Thady's transparent narration—"an area which covers everything relating to the colonial status of the country."[4] To render visible that which *Castle Rackrent* does *not* say or makes obscure, as does Colgan, is to reconstruct the ideological thrust of the novel and to expose the ways in which the novel structures class relations. It is, furthermore, to suggest the shortcomings of a reading that posits Edgeworth's inimical relationship to patriarchy in general and patriarchal class relationships in particular.

Colgan points to important distortions or "anachronisms" in the text. First, Thady relates that the Rackrents are descended from the ancient kings of Ireland. Yet, "As a matter of fact, by mid-century, few native landed families survived in Ireland. Like the Edgeworths themselves, most gentry were of English origin, and such strong concentration in the vicinity of Castle Rackrent of Gaelic 'survivors' calls for explanation."[5] Second, through significant details Edgeworth gives the impression that the Rackrents were Catholics. Yet, "despite this, Sir Condy is elected to parliament, at a time when Catholics were barred from both Houses of Parliament, and did not even have a vote." Surely, Colgan maintains, if Sir Condy's religion were different from that of his ancestors, or if

4. Maurice Colgan, "The Significant Silences of Thady Quirk," *Social Roles for the Artist*, eds. Ann Thompson and Anthony Beck (Liverpool, England: The University of Liverpool Press, 1979), pp. 41–45. Also reprinted in *Family Chronicles: Maria Edgeworth's* Castle Rackrent, ed. Coilin Owens (Totowa, N.J.: Barnes and Noble Books, 1987), pp. 57–61.

5. Of course, Colgan does not entertain the possibility that this genealogy is another one of Thady's mistaken notions, one to which Edgeworth herself does not subscribe. Nonetheless, the point still seems valid in that through Thady's narration—whether accurate or not—Edgeworth creates the impression of a purely Irish ancestry for the Rackrents.

he had recanted, Thady would have mentioned this fact. Third, Colgan believes that, if indeed we are to assume that the Rackrents are Catholic, then the representation of their inheritance is historically inaccurate, since the family fortune would have been dissipated "by the law of gravelkind (which divided Catholic estates equally among the sons) or by the laws which enabled Catholic heirs to be disinherited." Fourth, Edgeworth allows Thady's son Jason, once destined for the priesthood, to become an attorney despite the fact that Catholics could not enter the legal profession until after Langrishe's Relief Act of 1792. (As Colgan reminds us, the title page of the novel indicates it is set in the period preceding 1782.) Fifth, Colgan maintains that Thady's narrative ignores the effects of the penal laws: "the fact that Catholics were not allowed to purchase land, and were not allowed to obtain leases for longer than thirty-one years must have been an important factor in keeping many families on or below the poverty line." In short, Edgeworth "presents a picture which obscures the realities of the Irish situation" (Colgan, 42–43).

Colgan further refutes the premise of loyalty on which the representation of Thady's character depends. Suggesting that his relationship to the Rackrents is more typical of an English feudal situation than an Irish context, he asserts that Edgeworth resolves the real and historical tensions that would have existed between landowners and tenants "by making the Rackrents an ancient Gaelic, Catholic family, and giving them, throughout the novel, the status and privileges of the Protestant Anglo-Irish" (Colgan, 43). The point, then, of Colgan's essay is to reveal the ways in which *Castle Rackrent* functions as an implicit defense of Anglo-Irish Ascendancy through the creative "repression" of important political tensions that would have seriously challenged Edgeworth's own vested interests in the status quo.

The editorial apparatuses—the preface, notes, and glossary—appended to Thady's narrative provide further testimony to a process of representation consistent with Colgan's critique. Many readers have chosen to repress the editorial rubric and to treat the novel as if it consisted of Thady's narration alone, for editorial commentary seems to dampen the spirit of Thady's engaging first-person narrative. Yet to do so is to read only a portion of the text, while to foreground the authorial voices introduced in the editorial commentary is to reconsider the larger social and political context in which the novel functions; Edgeworth's decision to append the glossary in particular demonstrates the process of class and racial positioning that underlies the act of writing the narrative.

According to Marilyn Butler, Edgeworth and her father compiled the glossary after returning from a trip to England in 1799. She suggests that the purpose of this addition to Thady's narrative was to answer the issues recently raised by the possibility of union with England: "Suddenly it must have seemed to the Edgeworths that the onus was on the Irish to prove that the English were getting a bargain; so that the light entertainment Maria was about to produce, which presented the Irish as comic and irresponsible, was anything but timely." In addition, the Edgeworths feared that British readers would fail to detect irony in Thady's curious assertions, and they wanted "to disassociate themselves from his primitive attitudes" (Butler, 354–355). Only by means of an additional voice, this one decidedly not Irish, could the necessary sense of distance be created. Through the authority established in the editorial persona of the glossary, an authority borrowed from literary tradition, Maria Edgeworth first disassociates herself from, and then controls and circumscribes, the problematic tensions—for example, the fierce irrational loyalties or the implicit validation of dissipation—that Thady's narrative brings into play. As the final word on Thady's eccentric observations, the glossary thus reminds the reader of the "appropriate" moral response to his narration.

The significance of the glossary is best seen by means of a specific example of the interplay between Thady's narrative and the editorial commentary: the discussion of Sir Patrick's funeral. This example serves as a brief, yet important, representative moment in which a class voice makes itself audible. In fact, the Irish wake had been, for some time, an issue for English observers of Irish culture.[6] However, by calling attention to the event, Castle Rackrent participates in and perpetuates a tradition that divides one culture from another along the lines of bodily expression. In this instance, Maria Edgeworth borrowed her father's voice, as he contributed the notes intended to supplement Thady's narration of the wake. Yet, regardless of its origin, that voice contextualizes Thady's commentary, and it establishes a characteristic opposition between the perspective of the authors and the perspective of the character.

Thady's description of the funeral of the well-beloved Sir Patrick reads as follows.

> Never did any gentleman live and die more beloved in the country by rich and poor—his funeral was such a one as was never known before or since in the country! All the gentlemen in the three counties were at it—far and near, how they flocked! my great-grandfather said, that to see all the women, even in their red cloaks, you would have taken them for the army drawn out.

---

6. The Irish wake was often cited by Anglo-Irish observers as an example of the Irish tendency to extreme dissipation (as it still is today). See also Arthur Young, *A Tour of Ireland 1776–1779*, I, 249.

Then such a fine Whillaluh! you might have heard it to the farthest end of the country, and happy a man who could get but a sight of the hearse! (p. 13)

From Thady's perspective, the funeral and wake are social events of legendary status. According to his cultural belief, the greatest testimony to a man is to be found in the way he is mourned, and the very dimensions of this funeral attest to the dimensions of the man. The event is memorable as a public event—it is a colorful, celebratory, even joyous occasion. In the context of Thady's narration, the lawmen's seizure of Sir Patrick's corpse for debt comes across ironically; the reader recognizes that the great man does not even "own himself" in death. Thady sees no significance in the seizure, nor does he read a connection between the melodramatic entrance of the law and the elaborate funeral of a man who lived—and died— beyond his means. Thady undergoes no moment of enlightenment concerning the possible ostentation of the celebration; he never perceives in the very dimensions of the funeral the metaphoric expression of Sir Patrick's extravagance. In fact, he actively resists finding meaning in the juxtaposition of the funeral and the seizure of the body: "It was whispered, (but none but the enemies of the family believe it) that this was all a sham seizure to get quit of the debts which he had bound himself to pay in honour" (p. 14).

In contrast to Thady, the editorial comment conveys an awareness of the ironies inherent in the situation and makes explicit a moralistic assessment of the circumstances surrounding the funeral. This note, which far exceeds in length the incident itself, begins with a brief explanation of the word "Whillaluh, Ullaloo, Gol, or lamentation over the dead" and continues to include a history of the funeral song. Quoting the fourth volume of the *Transactions of the Royal Society*, which in turn cites Cambrensis in the twelfth century, the note describes the rituals of mourning in their ancient forms. Such description affords a certain dignity to the older practices; under the direction of the Celtic bards, mourners were said to have followed a highly ritualized format that allowed for the expression of the "genealogy, rank, possessions, virtues and vices" of the deceased. The balance of the note concerns the decline of the practice of Ullaloo from ancient times to the present—a decline that culminates, much to the editor's dismay, in the mock representation of the practice in comic theatrical entertainments in Dublin.

The editor writes, "It is curious to observe how customs and ceremonies degenerate. The present Irish cry, or howl, cannot boast of such melody [as in ancient times], nor is the funeral procession conducted with much dignity" (p. 65). The cacophony of the mourners is cited as proof of a decline in custom; in another context their voice would overwhelm his own, thereby subverting his authority. The voice of certain women in particular testifies to their power within the community: "Certain old women, who cry particularly loud and well, are in great request, and as a man said to the Editor, 'Every one would wish and be proud to have such at his funeral, or at that of his friends.'" Yet the voice of the women must also be effectively quieted—if not altogether silenced if the editor's perspective is to prevail. The persistent discrediting of funereal practices is thus a strategy for containing a competing voice. For example, the editor accuses the women of viewing the wake not as an ancient, hallowed practice but as an opportunity for public display of sentiment as well as an escape from everyday tedium. Moreover, he exposes a "spurious" sense of connection beneath their social and familial ties: "The lower Irish are wonderfully eager to attend the funeral of their friends and relations, and they make their relationships branch out to a great extent" (p. 66).

In other words, the editor finds more than one critical difference between the ancient practice and its modern version; to his eye, what was once a carefully orchestrated ritual of great cultural significance has now degenerated into an excuse for licentiousness. The discipline that marked the ancient practice of mourning has collapsed into public dissolution. In the editor's account, the movement from the authority of the Celtic bard to the Catholic priest mirrors the demise of a culture, as cultic celebration yields to superstitious indulgence. The editor registers his indignation over the changes in practice.

> To attend a neighbor's funeral is a cheap proof of humanity, but it does not, as some imagine, cost nothing. The time spent in attending funerals may be safely valued at half a million to the Irish nation; the Editor thinks that double that sum would not be too high an estimate. The habits of profligacy and drunkenness which are acquired at *wakes* are here put out of the question. When a labourer, a carpenter, or a smith, is not at his work, which frequently happens, ask where he is gone, and ten to one the answer is, "Oh, faith, please your honour, he couldn't do a stroke today, for he's gone to *the* funeral." (p. 66)

In a subsequent note, he elaborates on the ways in which the wake has become the occasion for the collapse of moral restraint: "In Ireland a wake is a midnight meeting, held professedly for the indulgence of holy sorrow, but usually it is converted into orgies of unholy joy" (p. 76). Although he concedes the ways in which "good and bad are mingled in human institutions" (e.g., the burning of the straw on which the sick man lay is a preservation against infection), his attention remains directed to the sensual indulgences incited by the wake itself: "After a fit of universal sorrow, and the comfort of a universal dram, the scandal of the neighborhood, as in higher circles, occupy the company. The young lads and lasses romp with one another, and when their fathers and mothers are at last overcome with sleep and whiskey (*vino et somno*), the youth become more enterprising and are frequently successful. It is said more matches are made at wakes than at weddings" (p. 77). Thus, according to the editor, if the ancient rituals of mourning helped to consolidate community, modern practices contribute to its disruption.

Here, however, the narrator's logic contradicts itself: whereas he raises the issue of lascivious behavior at the wakes in order to prove his assertion that funerals contribute to the dissolution of community, in fact he cites the very evidence suggesting that, to the contrary, such conduct enhances the community. The innumerable "matches" to which he alludes could also be seen as sexual couplings that occur as a result of the festive atmosphere. Such couplings are likely to lead to a growth in population and the expansion of the communal boundaries. In other words, the narrator's rhetoric represses an underlying concern with the reproductive proclivities of the Irish poor. Like much of his commentary, his reference to the lascivious conduct of the mourners discloses his fundamental discomfort with the sexuality of the peasants.

What, however, is the overall effect of the editor's discourse on Thady's narration? What, moreover, is the *author's* relationship to the editorial comments? In answer to the first, in providing the larger history for an event such as the Whillaluh, the editor contextualizes Thady's more localized, idiosyncratic commentary; Thady's description of Sir Patrick's wake is infused with additional meaning when seen against the backdrop of history. Thady's narration suddenly expands to encompass new ironies beyond his comprehension. Knowing what we do about the abuses associated with the Whillaluh, readers further question Thady's interpretation of the event as a tribute to a great man himself. In short, the editor's discourse provides another means for exposing Thady's limitations as a narrator. But if the glossary contextualizes Thady's narrative authority, it also allows for the representation of the editor's own authority, an authority that only assumes significance in opposition to Thady's limited viewpoint. In addition, the glossary makes visible the ways in which issues of the body can provide the opportunity for the constitution of authority. The editor's authority characterizes itself as being in control of what Thady cannot possibly know but, in this instance, what eludes Thady is the way in which the body has been lived differently; Thady's localized perspective on the wake precludes his awareness of the extent to which the contemporary

Irish Ullaloo signals the collapse of bodily restraint, the demise of a disciplined, ancient culture.

What Maria Edgeworth thought of her father's editorial comments can only be an occasion for speculation. If Butler is correct that both Edgeworths wished to "disassociate" themselves from Thady, then certainly his voice would have spoken for her as well. I have been suggesting that Maria's Anglo-Irish interests involved her in a series of attitudes toward indigenous Irish culture and that, although much about that culture intrigued her, much also seemed to demand that she distance herself from the "otherness" on display before her. It seems that, at the moment of union with England, Anglo-Irish Protestants such as the Edgeworths defined themselves as a class not necessarily in terms of "superior blood," or even in terms of economic privilege (although these continued to be a factor) but, instead, in terms of a particular awareness of how the body was to be lived—a knowledge that was thought to be the product of a superior culture and education.

* * *

MARY JEAN CORBETT

[Patriarchy and the Union][†]

In the linguistic project Edgeworth undertakes, we may also find, I think, a fitting emblem for Union itself in this period: like that perceived solution to the political impasse between England and Ireland, *Castle Rackrent* reinscribes Ireland's dependent and inferior status by linguistic means, even as it attempts to establish a basis for merging or marrying two unlike entities so that they would become part of a national or imperial whole. The historian Oliver MacDonagh interprets the consequences of the Union in a similar light when he writes that "the need to treat Ireland as a subordinate collided constantly" over the course of the nineteenth century "with the policy of converting her into a component of an integrated society in the British Isles."[1] In an imperial union of unequals, only

---

† From Mary Jean Corbett, "Public Affections and Failed Politics: Burke, Edgeworth, and Ireland in the 1790s," in *Allegories of Union in Irish and English Writing, 1790–1870: Politics, History, and the Family from Edgeworth to Arnold* (Cambridge and New York: Cambridge University Press, 2000), pp. 44–49, 192–93. Copyright © 2004 Mary Jean Corbett. Reprinted with the permission of Cambridge University Press.

1. Oliver MacDonagh, *Ireland: The Union and Its Aftermath* (London, 1977), 33. For some provocative reflections on the mix of identity and difference that Union implies, see Terry Eagleton, *Heathcliff and the Great Hunger* (1995), 129–38.

one partner can take precedence, as Burke[2] would argue, and that one must be English. Yet Edgeworth wonders, near the conclusion of the novel, "whether an Union will hasten or retard the melioration of this country," with its most likely immediate result being that "the few gentlemen of education, who now reside in this country, will resort to England" (p. 62).[3] Such a claim betrays her sense that "melioration" will necessarily be carried out by a very few men like her own father, and by herself: hence the anglicizing fervor of all Edgeworth's "Irish" fiction, as well as the need to persuade her English readers to value the nation they will, she hopes, come to incorporate within a greater Britain. Perhaps paradoxically, the first step in Ireland's becoming a part of a united kingdom, and more fit according to Burkean criteria for full partnership in it, would be to recognize and represent its linguistic and cultural difference, as Edgeworth does, not so as to preserve it, but in order gradually to erode it.

As some critics of *Castle Rackrent* have recognized, the disorderly transmission of family property in the novel signals, from an English point of view, a serious disturbance in the Irish social order. In its linking of familial stability to social reproduction of the established relations of property and authority, Burke's celebrated discussion of inheritance in the *Reflections* may serve as the exemplary Whig[4] statement on the matter:

> The power of perpetuating our property in our families is one of the most valuable and interesting circumstances belonging to it, and that which tends the most to the perpetuation of society itself. It makes our weakness subservient to our virtue, it grafts benevolence even upon avarice. The possessors of family wealth, and of the distinction which attends hereditary possession (as most concerned in it), are the natural *securities* for this transmission. (45)[5]

For Burke, familial inheritance, proceeding from father to son through the law of primogeniture,[6] secures "the perpetuation of society." In *Castle Rackrent*, however, "weakness" and "avarice" rule without benefit of "benevolence," as the estate rarely passes on in orderly patriarchal fashion. As W. J. McCormack and Ann Owens Weekes have been first to argue in a systematic way, the disorder of

2. Edmund Burke (1729–1797) [editor's note].
3. Page numbers throughout refer to this Norton Critical Edition [editor's note].
4. A British political party that contested power with the Tories from the 1680s to the 1850s [editor's note].
5. Edmund Burke, *Reflections on the Revolution in France*, ed. J. G. A Pocock (Indianapolis, IN, 1987), 45.
6. The right of the firstborn, especially a firstborn son, to inherit property and/or title [editor's note].

family and property relations, judged by an English standard for measuring stability, marks an important node in Edgeworth's critique of the Rackrents, and here an essential field for anglicizing Irish life by establishing proper gender norms comes into view.[7] For in representing the Rackrents as bad husbands and reckless masters, Edgeworth suggests that the absence of sufficient means for perpetuating the transmission of property in the English style, and the parallel absence of appropriately English familial and marital relations, issue in the need for Union itself, which may assist in the regeneration of Irish society.

That Irish society fell short of the Burkean standard for order before and after 1800 was owing in good part, of course, to the legacy of the penal laws, which had delegitimated traditional Irish land practices even as they had also prevented catholic men from enjoying the protection of the private property rights extended to protestant subjects. Penal restrictions indeed generate the very "family" whose uneven history Thady traces: "by act of parliament," and "seeing how large a stake depended upon it," sir Patrick O'Shaughlin chose to "take and bear the surname and arms of Rackrent" (p. 12) in order to inherit. Thus, as Catherine Gallagher points out, "the O'Shaughlins . . . only possess their legal identity and estate by renouncing their Irish name," and, by implication, their (Irish) religion as well.[8] So the bad behavior of the Rackrents can be directly related to the disturbance in indigenous familial and communal practices that English law had created, and that Burke hoped to amend by instituting gendered English norms for the preservation and transmission of property at the heart of an improved Irish society. Edgeworth's Irish Rackrents in no way live up to the model of English gentlemanliness, with its attendant concerns for property, duties, and continuity, that could secure both familial and social stability; what is missing from her analysis, however, is precisely Burke's insistent awareness that English penal intervention has produced in part the instability *Castle Rackrent* chronicles.

Edgeworth's narrative is, rather, far more focused on revealing the patriarchal deficiencies and economic improvidence of the Rackrent men than on analyzing the legal and political factors that

7. See W. J. McCormack, *Ascendancy and Tradition in Anglo-Irish Literary History from 1789 to 1939* (Oxford, 1985), 108–22; but for a more thorough (and more feminist) reading of the Rackrent men as husbands and masters, also consult Ann Owens Weekes, *Irish Women Writers: An Uncharted Tradition* (Lexington, KY, 1990), 41–59, to which my own argument is indebted.

8. Catherine Gallagher, *Nobody's Story: The Vanishing Acts of Women Writers in the Marketplace, 1670–1820* (Berkeley, CA, 1994), 295. While I subscribe to Gallagher's view that conversion is the unspoken fact here, some other critics are somewhat more tentative on this point. McCormack, for instance, writes that "the change of name is maybe the mute signal of a change of sectarian allegiance" (*Ascendancy and Tradition*, 108); for his further qualifications, see 118–20.

helped to create their situation: *Castle Rackrent* is, as Tracy describes it, "a chronological account of four successive owners of the Rackrent estates, whose follies and extravagances become an object lesson in how *not* to be an Irish landlord."[9] The mistreatment of their dependents implied by their name aside, the Rackrents and their story achieve a measure of coherence—are indeed primarily constituted as a "family"—only in Thady's recounting of their history, for their actual relations to each other are tenuous at best. The drunken sir Patrick gives up his religion and his name so as to secure the Rackrent estate and pass it on to his son Murtagh; after his sudden death, Patrick's body is "seized for debt" in what those whom Thady terms "the enemies of the family" suspect to be "a sham seizure" arranged by Murtagh "to get quit of the debts" (p. 14) outstanding against the estate. Sir Murtagh proceeds to exploit his tenants to the utmost without mercy, pursues expensive and unsuccessful lawsuits, and sires no heir; upon Murtagh's demise, his younger brother, sir Kit, an inveterate gambler and absentee, inherits and squanders what is left of the family fortune, rackrenting the tenants and behaving dishonorably all around. Finally, the estate passes to sir Condy, the "heir at law," who belongs to "a remote branch of the family" (p. 28); raised among the common Irish catholic children of the town, with an inveterate devotion to whiskey punch, his character is consequently formed far below what his adult station will require. What links these masters is less their common blood than a common inadequacy to their appointed tasks.

Joseph Lew notes that the Rackrents are virtually "incapable of producing direct heirs; the estate always descends to a junior branch, in a process of irreversible decline."[1] The breaks in the transmission of the estate signal the concomitant degeneracy of the family itself, Edgeworth implies, and contribute to the social instability of the world she portrays: "the generations of Rackrent do not need generation to propagate themselves," as with the exception of Murtagh, Rackrent men inherit only by "claims traced along precarious routes of male protestant descent," as well as through the original dispossession of the nameless catholic landholder that the penal laws induce.[2] Each of the heirs, with the partial exception of Condy, is far more concerned with the conditions of his own present possession than with the prospects for future inheritors of the estate. * * *

9. Robert Tracy, "Maria Edgeworth and Lady Morgan: Legality Versus Legitimacy," *Nineteenth-Century Fiction* 40.1 (June 1985): 3.
1. Joseph Lew, "Sydney Owenson and the Fate of Empire," *Keats-Shelley Journal* 39 (1990), 61–62.
2. Gene W. Ruoff, "1800 and the Future of the Novel: William Wordsworth, Maria Edgeworth, and the Vagaries of Literary History," *The Age of William Wordsworth: Critical Essays on the Romantic Tradition*, eds. Kenneth R. Johnston and Gene W. Ruoff (New Brunswick, NJ, 1987), 309.

"One of the first and most leading principles on which the commonwealth and the laws are consecrated," writes Burke in the *Reflections*, has been put in place

> lest the temporary possessors and life-renters in it, unmindful of what they have received from their ancestors, or of what is due to their posterity, should act as if they were the entire masters, that they should not think it among their rights to cut off the entail or commit waste on the inheritance by destroying at their pleasure the whole original fabric of their society, hazarding to leave to those who come after them a ruin instead of an habitation. (p. 83)

Narratively, then, as well as socially, the Rackrent "story" features discontinuity both within the Irish context and between the Irish world and the English one, a discontinuity emblematized by the failure of succession that only (English) patriarchal intervention can repair.

In its focus on unmanly Irish improvidence, however, Thady's chronicle—like the *Reflections*—tends to obscure the place of women in the reproduction of heirs and transmission of property: the degeneracy of the Rackrent men, foregrounded by Edgeworth (and by most of her critics), also entails a less visible but no less vital absence of "generation" on the part of their wives, a point Edgeworth makes with considerable irony throughout the text.[3] Rackrent marriages are made for money, not for love, yet the women who make these marriages are no mere victims; as Weekes observes, "each wife escapes upon her husband's death, her fortune intact and indeed in two cases increased."[4] Sir Murtagh chooses his wife, for example, on the basis of the fortune she will bring: he "looked to the great Skinflint estate," p. 14) as a means of enhancing his own purse. But his wife is every bit as grasping as he is, and runs a so-called charity school only so her duty-yarn may be spun *gratis* by its pupils (p. 14). As Edgeworth herself did in fictionalizing John Langan for the market, many of the novel's women seek to make material profit from the colonial project and so are directly implicated in it. Like their husbands, Rackrent women display a decided preference for portable property and no interest in securing the means of its transmission; with no commitment to "the family," they simply leave it behind when their husbands die or when things go bad. That they do not reproduce biologically may be taken as emblematic of the

---

3. By contrast with Weekes's careful detailing of the ways in which women do (and do not) matter to *Castle Rackrent*, McCormack terms the "repression" of the female line "deliberate if arbitrary" (*Ascendancy and Tradition*, 110).
4. Ann Owens Weekes, *Irish Women Writers: An Uncharted Tradition* (Lexington: University Press of Kentucky, 1990), 32.

disorder Edgeworth locates in familial and social relations: themselves treated as the site and medium for property exchange between
men, the ladies Rackrent fetishize what they accumulate, seeing
self-interest as the limit of their interest.

Within the family economy, these women thus exercise several
different kinds of power. Despite the fact that they are largely used
as a means of access to property, they resist husbandly efforts at
economic and personal control and appropriate whatever resources
they can. For example, sir Murtagh's nameless lady exacts from the
tenants everything owing to her—"duty fowls, and duty turkies,
and duty geese" (p. 15)—for as long as she remains their mistress, and
carries off all the household furnishings along with her when her
tenure ends; sir Kit's wife—whom Thady calls "the Jewish"—survives
seven years' imprisonment without ever surrendering her diamond
cross to her importunate spouse.[5] Their ostensible dependency on
men masks the fact that the patriarchal system of property transmission, properly ordered, depends in great part on women, yet not
one of the three Rackrent wives to whom we are introduced bears a
child, with Patrick's (presumed) wife, mother to Murtagh, going
entirely unmentioned by Thady, and Condy's mother similarly unrep-
resented. Within the constraints of patriarchal limitations on femi-
nine agency, the Rackrent women thus resist their subordination by
spurning their "natural" reproductive role and remaining childless.
The lack of female subordination in this important arena of patriarchal control is another sign of how far short Irish affairs fall of the
Burkean model Edgeworth implicitly supports.

The Rackrent wives are neither all-powerful nor utterly powerless: they simply take advantage, when they are able, of what rights
they do have in order to secure their own futures. Unlike their husbands, not one of them dies in the course of the novel—although
the last, Isabella, is "disfigured in the face ever after by the fall and
bruises" (p. 61) she incurs on her departure from house and husband
in returning to her family of birth, in what Thady seems to portray
as fit punishment for her lack of loyalty to "the family." But female
disorder, licensed by patriarchal misrule, is only one of the forces
that unsettles the Rackrent settlement, for the hereditary improvidence of the Rackrents does have its price. The ultimate passing of
the estate from sir Condy's hands into Jason Quirk's, expedited by
Condy's indifference and Jason's unerring sense, makes for one of

---

5. In the case of Kit's wife, as Thomas Flanagan points out, "Kitt [sic] cannot touch [her
fortune] without her consent" because her family has entailed it, thereby providing her
with an effective legal means of resistance to his efforts (The Irish Novelists, 1800–
1850 [New York, 1958] 73). For more on Thady's relation to "the Jewish," see my
"Another Tale to Tell: Postcolonial Theory and the Case of Castle Rackrent," Criticism
36 (1994), 383–400.

Castle Rackrent's few acts of primogeniture, with an odd twist. Giving up his former religion to become an attorney, just as old sir Patrick renounced his so as to inherit in compliance with the penal laws, the conforming protestant son receives the legacy of land and family that is just as much—if not, in a sense, more—the creation of his poor catholic father as of his equally impoverished protestant master.[6]

What Iain Topliss calls the "self-impelled extinction" of the Rackrents thus ostensibly marks the beginning of a new line, the Quirks, which with Jason at its head promises to be far more provident in conserving, or even expanding, its property: Jason puts aside the degenerate decadence of the Rackrents in favor of the rationalizing and legalistic power to which he gains access.[7] Some critics have read Jason's assumption of the Rackrent estate rather as a return of the Gaelic repressed: for Dunne, the concluding movement of the novel suggests that "the Quirks achieved the common peasant dream, noted in many contemporary accounts, of repossessing the land which they believed historically and rightfully theirs," while Tracy suggests that such an ending brings on "the nightmare of Anglo-Ireland," in which "one way or another, the Irish peasants will take back the land from its Anglo-Irish owners."[8] But here the impending passage of the Act of Union may help us to read other meanings into Edgeworth's final narrative act in *Castle Rackrent*. For if the future of Ireland indeed lay with the Jason Quirks of the culture, that future would not consist of a peasant society under the improved and improving rule of the Anglo-Irish—to which the Edgeworths, for all their differences with the ascendancy, had always subscribed as the solution to the Irish "problem"; it would be led instead by the emergent catholic Irish middle classes, of which Jason is undoubtedly an avatar Edgeworth cannot approve. In setting even the final actions of *Castle Rackrent* "before the year 1782," or nearly twenty years before the time of writing, Edgeworth implicitly acknowledges the growth of one of the rival powers to Anglo-Irish supremacy which the Act of Union worked to contain, newly literate and partially enfranchised catholic men of increasing property and proportionate disaffection. That acknowledgement,

6. Colin Graham concludes much the same, in his assertion that "Jason's triumph is achieved through the tactics and strategies he has learnt from his father" ("History, Gender and the Colonial Moment: *Castle Rackrent*," *Gender Perspectives in Nineteenth-Century Ireland: Public and Private Spheres*, eds. Margaret Kelleher and James H. Murphy [Dublin, 1997], 102).
7. Iain Topliss, "The Novelist and the Union," 275. This is the view of Jason to which McCormack also subscribes (*Ascendancy and Tradition*, 121–22).
8. Tom Dunne, "Colonial Mind," 10; Tracy, "Legality versus Legitimacy," 4. For a similar line of argument, see Julian Moynahan, *Anglo-Irish: The Literary Imagination in a Hyphenated Culture* (Princeton, NJ, 1995), 27.

however, by no means implies anything but uneasiness about the prospect.[9]

*　*　*

JULIE NASH

[Servants and Paternalism]†

> The Irish are perhaps the laziest civilized nation on the face of the Earth.
>
> Maria Edgeworth, age 14[1]

* * * No doubt, the 14-year-old Maria Edgeworth held her share of prejudices against the Irish people when she first arrived at her new home in Edgeworthtown from England, prejudices she had acquired in England, and that she had every expectation of seeing confirmed by experience. But Edgeworth does not make the logical leap that the inferior legal and political status of the Irish is justified by their idleness, as many did. Instead, she asserts that "for this indolence peculiar to the Irish Peasantry several reasons may be assigned, amongst others the most powerful is the low wages of labor 6d a day in winter and 8d a day in summer"[2] (Kowaleski-Wallace 142). As she would later do in her fictional depictions of the servant class, Edgeworth invokes a familiar stereotype in order to undermine it, laying the responsibility for a lazy nation at the door of its parsimonious rulers.

Despite her initial misgivings about the country, Edgeworth would eventually grow to love Ireland and identify with its people. During the famine of the 1840s, she suffered hunger and deprivation along with her tenants, and the people of Ireland came to regard the famous writer as one of their own—a friend and champion. Yet

---

† From Julie Nash, "'True and Loyal to the Family': Servants in Maria Edgeworth's Irish Novels," in *Servants and Paternalism in the Works of Maria Edgeworth and Elizabeth Gaskell* (Hampshire, UK & Burlington, VT: Ashgate, 2007), pp. 75–83. Reprinted by permission of Ashgate.

9. See Flanagan for a similar conclusion about Edgeworth's Jason as demonstrating a "shrewd understanding . . . of the new class which was rising to power" (*Irish Novelists* 78). In *The Absentee*, Edgeworth presents a view of Dublin immediately after the Union that expresses her fears of class mobility: "commerce rose into the vacated seats of rank[, and] wealth rose into the place of birth," and so "the whole *tone* of society was altered," with the *nouveaux riches* of the merchant class vulgarly aspiring to the status of gentlemen and gentlewomen (*The Absentee*, eds. W.J. McCormack and Kim Walker [Oxford and New York, 1988] 85).

1. See Edgeworth's letter to Fanny Robinson on p. 83 [editor's note].

2. Elizabeth Kowaleski-Wallace, *Their Fathers' Daughters: Hannah More, Maria Edgeworth, and Patriarchal Complicity* (Oxford: Oxford University Press, 1991), 142. [See Kowaleski-Wallace on pp. 167–75—editor.]

Edgeworth never completely lost her early ambivalence about the Irish. A poem that she wrote and enclosed in a letter in May of 1849, shortly before her death, reflects a combination of affection for and frustration toward her country:

> Ireland, with all thy faults, thy follies too,
> I love thee still: still with a candid eye must view
> Thy wit, too quick, still blundering into sense
> Thy reckless humour; sad improvidence,
> And even what sober judges follies call,
> I, looking at the Heart, forget them all! (*Chosen Letters*)

Edgeworth's Irish novels contain a similar contradiction in which criticism of Ireland's "faults" masks a clear admiration for Irish intelligence and resourcefulness. Like the "sober judges" of her poem, Edgeworth finds much to criticize about Ireland, but she ultimately affirms her faith in the Irish people. Her novels, too, reveal a close identification with the Anglo-Irish aristocracy and a paradoxical subversion of that class's social position.

As a writer and an estate manager, Edgeworth worked to reform the exploitative landlord/tenant relationship that structured life in the Irish "Big House." The Edgeworths provided educational opportunities for their tenants; they developed a system that would enable workers to profit from improvements they made to the estate; and they took a personal interest in their tenants' lives, helping their children find jobs and staying in touch with them after they left Edgeworthstown. This system became a model of progressive paternalism in Ireland. In return for their reforms and support, the Edgeworths expected and received their tenants' loyalty and gratitude.

For Maria Edgeworth, "paternalism" had personal as well as political implications. Her intense relationship with her father is well documented. Elizabeth Kowaleski-Wallace describes Edgeworth as "a particularly strong example" of a "daddy's girl," for whom "identification with patriarchal politics provided an opportunity for self-definition . . . [a] chance for authority and for limited empowerment" (96). Gary Kelly writes that Edgeworth's novels "followed plans and themes suggested by her father, corrected according to his criticisms, and published under cover of prefaces by him."[3] Yet like critics of Elizabeth Gaskell, Edgeworth's readers have consistently noted the curious tension between Maria Edgeworth the dutiful daughter of patriarchy and Maria Edgeworth the progressive iconoclast. Mark Hawthorne writes that her novels should be read on

---

3. Gary Kelly, "Class, Gender, Nation, and Empire: Money and Merit in the Writing of the Edgeworths," *The Wordsworth Circle* 25:2 (spring 1994): 91.

two levels: the first, "didactic, purely and simply. It is this level which repels many 20th century scholars, for she could be . . . crudely dogmatic. . . . On the second [level] she advanced her own doubts . . . [creating] a form of fiction that is at once outspoken and subdued."[4] Similarly, Kowaleski-Wallace, who closely associates Edgeworth with patriarchal values, nevertheless comments upon "the persistent shadows of an irrational force, one that never quite disappears from her work" (104). Marjorie Lightfoot describes Edgeworth's outlook as "that of a radical and conservative Anglo-Irish woman, as she questions colonialism, traditional male/female relationships, and styles of art and life while trying to preserve moral boundaries"[5]. Each of these critics approaches Edgeworth's writings from a different perspective, yet they share the common view that Edgeworth's life and work—at once moralistic and doubting, conservative and radical—resist easy categorization.

Although Edgeworth never sought a direct role in politics, her choice to write about Ireland was, by definition, a political decision in a period of dangerous tensions between Protestants and Catholics. Her family's Protestant loyalties were questioned by their Anglo-Irish peers, but the Edgeworths could not (nor did they wish to) assimilate with the Catholic nationals. Her novels about Ireland reflect a similar ambivalence about the relationship between England and Ireland that her English novels do about the relationship between master and servant. But when Edgeworth shifted her focus from the domestic sphere to a changing Ireland, she continued to use servant characters to embody the instability of social and national roles. Throughout these novels, servant characters often function as one of those "irrational" forces that enable Edgeworth to question both tradition and the possibilities for change. In the case of three of Edgeworth's novels that take place (at least partly) in Ireland, Edgeworth extends her examination of class to issues of nationality. In these Irish novels, Edgeworth's most important servant characters, *Castle Rackrent*'s Thady and *Ennui*'s Ellinor, are also frequently characterized as typically and distinctly Irish. Looked at another way, Edgeworth's most important Irish characters also happen to be servants. Their dependent roles, as family steward and nurse respectively, are inseparable from their nationality. In choosing to foreground the lives of these servant characters, she also boldly foregrounds the colonized peasants upon whose labor the Irish ascendancy depended. Through a number of plot twists in which servants assume the roles of their masters or double

4. Mark Hawthorne, *Doubt and Dogma in Maria Edgeworth*, (Gainesville: Florida University Press, 1967), 3.
5. Marjorie Lightfoot, "Morals for Those That Like Them: The Satire of Edgeworth's *Belinda*, 1801," *Eire-Ireland: A Journal of Irish Studies* 29:4 (1994): 119.

as their mistresses, Edgeworth invites her readers to consider some potentially uncomfortable questions: who is worthy of wealth and power? How significant are differences in nationality and ethnicity? Despite Edgeworth's attraction to a socially hierarchical society, her Irish novels reveal a changing world in which—to quote *Ennui*—"Any man can be made a lord; but a gentleman, a man must make himself."[6]

Late eighteenth-century Ireland was plagued by conflict between the Irish Catholic natives and ruling English Protestants. The draconian Penal Laws of 1695 ensured the continual oppression of the Irish peasantry and kept the ownership of land in Protestant hands. By the time Edgeworth wrote the final section of *Castle Rackrent*, the already tense political climate in Ireland was exacerbated by the French Revolution and then by England's war with France. A successful peasant uprising was a pervasive and realistic fear, and the Edgeworth family narrowly escaped personal violence at the hands of both Catholic and Protestant mobs.

It is therefore especially remarkable that Edgeworth's most revolutionary novel would be written and published during this time. *Castle Rackrent* details the debaucheries and decline of an aristocratic Irish family. The book is more than a radical critique of the people who shared Edgeworth's status; it makes a bold statement about the business class destined to replace them. The Rackrents are supplanted by Jason Quirk, son of Thady Quirk, the novel's narrator and longtime Rackrent family steward. As Gilbert and Gubar point out, "whether consciously or unconsciously, this 'faithful family retainer' manages to get the big house."[7]

With its multiple glosses by a fictionalized English editor, a parade of landowners, and the ultimate reversal of the social order, *Castle Rackrent* would certainly qualify as a work with an "irrational force," written on "more than one level," to quote Kowalski-Wallace. Taken at face value, Thady is the type of loyal servant any master could hope for. Although Thady's own son Jason has become master of Castle Rackrent by the time the tale begins, Thady *appears* not to have benefited by that fact, stating,

> To look at me, you would hardly think "poor Thady" was the father of Attorney Quirk; he is a high gentleman, and never minds what poor Thady says, and having better than fifteen hundred a year, landed estate, looks down upon honest Thady;

6. Maria Edgeworth, *Ennui*, ed. Marilyn Butler (New York: Penguin Classics), 290.
7. Sandra Gilbert and Susan Gubar, *The Madwoman in the Attic: The Woman Writer and the Nineteenth-Century Literary Imagination* (New Haven, CT, and London: Yale University Press, 1979), 151.

but I wash my hands of his doings, and as I have lived so will I die, true and loyal to the family. (p. 12)[8]

This passage resembles other moments in the novel where Thady denounces the rise of his son to wealth and power and affirms his complete allegiance to the Rackrents.

*   *   *

The novel is laden with examples of Thady's seemingly incomprehensible loyalty to the Rackrents at the expense of his resourceful, if calculating, son Jason. By the novel's end, Thady laments the fact that Jason has acquired the Rackrent estate, profiting from the neglect and errors of his masters. "[T]o his shame be it spoken," says Thady, "I wondered for the life of me, how he could harden himself to do it" (p. 47). Thady goes so far as to describe Jason as "very short and cruel" (p. 49) to Sir Condy Rackrent and he claims that he is "grieved and sick at heart for my poor master" (p. 51) as Jason assumes Sir Condy's place as owner of the Rackrent estate. Thady pronounces this reversal a "murder" (p. 50); he more appropriately called it a "treason," since a servant's usurpation of power had larger implications for the paternal social order. When he tells Jason to "recollect all he has been to us, and all we have been to him" (p. 50), Thady asserts his belief that traditional roles should continue to dictate relationships between the two families. What Thady appears to forget (or what he ignores) is that Jason only ascends to power because the Rackrents have abdicated their role as caretakers of the castle, land, and tenants. Condy will always be a Rackrent and Jason will always be a Quirk, and those facts are apparently enough to secure Thady's loyalty, even though the Rackrents never gave their loyal steward more than the occasional tip.

Judy, Thady's niece, challenges her uncle's worldview by pointedly asking him how he could be "such an unnatural fader . . . not to wish your own son preferred to another" (p. 59). Even Thady is perplexed at this question. Judy's use of the word "unnatural" underscores the divided loyalties of the paternalist subject. Unlike Judy and Jason, Thady confuses his socially constructed position of servant with his "natural" role as father. He responds to Judy's accusation with a moment of rare self-doubt: "Well, I was never so put to it in my life: between . . . my son and my master, and all I felt and thought just now, I could not, upon my conscience, tell which was the wrong from the right" (p. 59).

This crisis of conscience, which comes toward the end of Thady's tale, marks one of the few instances in which Thady openly

---

8. Page numbers throughout refer to this Norton Critical Edition [editor's note].

questions his loyalty to the Rackrent family. But Thady actually identifies more with Jason than he may be willing to admit to his readers and possibly to himself. In fact, Thady's loyalty to Jason is at least as powerful as his loyalty to the Rackrents, but his life-long position as a servant prevents him from expressing his honest views in language other than that of a grateful dependent.

*   *   *

Is Thady an ignorant servant, stupidly loyal to undeserving masters and unfair to his own hardworking son? Or is he a shrewd manipulator, claiming a loyalty he doesn't feel while damning the Rackrents with faint praise? Perhaps both characterizations tell a partial truth. Having lived so long as a dependent in a paternalist society, he has internalized the belief that his masters' good is his own good, but he is also well aware of their degeneracy and his son's industriousness. William A. Dumbleton looks at it this way:

> [T]hady's been in the big house family service for four generations, and on the surface his anecdotes seem to say how wonderful the family is, but the ultimate revelation is how mean-spirited and profligate they are. Thady, an Irish peasant, is uneducated, but he is very shrewd and knowledgeable in the way of Irish life. He has what some call soft blarney. The reader recognizes that he gets along well by saying positive complimentary things. The peasant-landlord relationship makes it necessary to take this stance.[9]

According to Dumbleton, genuine honesty between landlords and peasants and between masters and servants is impossible in a paternalist system. Thus, Thady's nickname, "Honest Thady" is the first and biggest lie of all. Clearly Edgeworth recognizes this irony and creates a loyal servant-narrator who is not always honest with his readers, and who is not always honest with himself. Outwardly denouncing his son's triumph over the Rackrents, he nevertheless consistently expresses his pride in Jason's achievements, defends Jason's right to own property, and assists him every step of the way until the reversal of roles is complete.

A close examination of Thady's relationship with Jason reveals that his allegiance to the Rackrents instead of his son is more uncertain than it at first appears. Though the novel's editor sets Thady up to be a stereotypical ignorant Irish stooge, the steward's shrewdness and Quirk family pride come across throughout his narrative. Thady began his tale by claiming, "I wash my hands of [Jason's] doings," yet his descriptions of his son indicate the two have a much closer

---

9. William Dumbleton, *Ireland: Life and Land in Literature* (Albany: State University of New York Press, 1984), 22.

connection. Nearly every reference to Jason is prefaced with the possessive phrase, "my son," and many of Thady's stories reveal that he is as "true and loyal" to the Quirks as he claims to be to "the family." When unscrupulous agents are exploiting tenants in the name of the absentee landlord Sir Kit Rackrent, Thady is unmistakeably critical of his master:

> [T]here was no such thing as standing it. I said nothing, for I had great regard for the family; but I walked about thinking if his honour Sir Kit knew all this, it would go hard with him, but he'd see us righted; not that I had any thing of my own share to complain of, for the agent was always very civil to me, when he came down to the country, and took a great deal of notice of my son Jason. Jason Quirk, though he be my son, I must say, was a good scholar from birth, and a very 'cute lad: I thought to make him a priest, but he did better for himself: seeing how he was as good a clerk as any in the county, the agent gave him his rent accounts to copy, which he did first of all for the pleasure of obliging the gentleman, and would take nothing at all for his trouble, but was always proud to serve the family. By-and-bye a good farm bounding us to the east fell into his honour's hands, and my son put in a proposal for it: why shouldn't he, as well as another? (p. 19)

The passage begins with an expression of sympathy for the oppressed peasants and a half-hearted defense of Sir Kit who *would* rectify the situation were he at his estate. The unstated criticism behind this defense, of course, is that Sir Kit *should* be overseeing the activities of the agents on his own property. Practically in the same breath that Thady once again affirms his "great regard for the family," he describes with pride the first time *his* son (described as such three times) remedied the abuses against the peasants and how *his* son acquired property of his own. This early land acquisition is just the first in a series that will end in Jason's ultimately owning the estate. Although Thady will later profess "shame" at this final result, here—*knowing full well how the story will end*—he defends Jason. He describes Jason's intelligence, his hard work, and, more importantly, his *right* to acquire property "as well as another." He also attributes honest motives to Jason, claiming in language similar to that with which he describes himself, that his son "was always proud to serve the family." Clearly, Thady approves more of Jason, taking pride in his financial and social advancement, than he does Sir Kit, the absentee landlord who cheats his tenants out of what little they have.

Together, father and son collude in Jason's progress and exchange information about the Rackrent's problems. After the same unscrupulous agent writes a letter to Sir Kit explaining that he can not extract any more money from his tenants (a letter which implicates Sir Kit in these abuses), Thady writes, "I saw the letter before it ever was sealed, when my son copied it. When the answer came, there was a new turn in affairs, and the agent was turned out; and my son Jason, who had corresponded privately with his honour occasionally on business, was forthwith desired by his honour to take the accounts into his own hands, and look them over till further orders" (p. 20). Here Thady acknowledges that he has had access to his master's private correspondence via his son, an admission of collusion, and a confession of violating his master's privacy, an infraction that the ruling class feared most from their servants. Far from "washing his hands" of Jason's "doings," Thady's fingerprints are all over Jason's advancement.

Thady's sympathy with the Rackrents is tested most acutely when Sir Kit returns to Ireland with his Jewish bride and promptly locks her up until he can steal her diamond cross. "I could not but pity her," admits Thady, "though she was a Jewish: and considering too it was no fault of hers to be taken with my master so young as she was at Bath, and so fine a gentleman as Sir Kit was when he courted her, and considering too, after all they had heard and seen of him as a husband, there were now no less than three ladies in our country talked of for his second wife" (p. 25). Not only does Thady make the traitorous admission of sympathizing with a foreigner at the expense of a member of the family, he goes on to criticize Sir Kit's behavior as a husband and to wonder how any woman could wish to be next in line. Following Sir Kit's death, Thady says, "We got the key out of his pocket the first thing we did, and my son Jason ran to unlock the barrack room" (p. 26) where Lady Rackrent had been imprisoned. Again, Thady's choice of pronouns reveals his loyalties: twice he uses the word "we" to indicate that the two are a team, and twice he refers to Jason as "my son." Clearly, Thady and Jason share a mutual understanding about Lady Rackrent's predicament; their first thoughts are with her, rather than with their dead master, when Sir Kit is killed in a duel.

Sir Kit is replaced as master of Castle Rackrent by Sir Connolly (or Condy) Rackrent, the last Rackrent to own the estate and, despite his profligacy, the most sympathetic of Thady's masters. He is clearly Thady's favorite. It is Sir Condy whom Thady finally does choose over Jason, but Thady remains firm in his defense of his son until the end. As Thady first describes Condy to the reader, he writes with pride that as a child, "my son Jason was a great favorite with him" (p. 29). Thady notes that Condy and Jason were educated together as children, but that Condy ceased to apply himself to his studies once it was clear he would inherit Castle Rackrent. These childhood friends are reunited as master and agent, and Jason increasingly bails Condy out of financial difficulty by buying Rackrent property. Thady seems to have no problems with this land acquisition, telling us at one point that Jason "got two hundred a year profit rent; which was little enough, considering his long agency" (p. 30). Even this late in the narrative, as Jason succeeds at the expense of Sir Condy's fall, Thady defends his son's right to profit as a landowner and suggests that Jason has not been adequately compensated for his years of service. Thady's loyalty to the Rackrents is based on the fact that they are his masters, but his loyalty to Jason is repeatedly justified on the basis of his son's intelligence and hard work.

Edgeworth gives the Quirks another reason to resent their master: Sir Condy chooses to sell a hunting lodge to his neighbor, Captain Moneygawl, despite the fact that Jason had initially made it clear that he was interested in the property. Thady points out that the decision to favor "a stranger" made Jason "jealous" (p. 30). This slight against the Quirks was followed by another in which Sir Condy rejects Thady's niece Judy in favor of the weepy Isabella Moneygawl. Despite his professed regard for the family, Thady maintains that "Judy McQuirk . . . was worth twenty of Miss Isabella" (p. 31). Thady clearly thinks his niece will be a suitable match for Condy Rackrent. Rather than insisting on maintaining the feudal relationship that had governed these families in the past, Thady admits to hopes of allying himself through marriage to the Rackrent estate, thus putting the Quirks and the Rackrents on equal footing. He later confesses to an "over-partiality to Judy, into whose place I may say [Isabella] stept" (p. 34). In Thady's opinion, his niece's rightful place has been ironically usurped by a wealthy heiress. Thady's insistence that Judy's rightful place is mistress of Castle Rackrent is antithetical to a paternalistic notion of predetermined social roles. He takes these slights to his family seriously, and it is shortly after they occur that Thady (supposedly) unwittingly introduces one of Condy's creditors to Jason, who provides him with a list of Condy's creditors, initiating the final stage of the Rackrent decline. Thady denies any intentional complicity, saying, "Little did I think at the time I was harbouring my poor master's greatest of enemies myself" (p. 40), but the timing seems more than coincidental.

Thady cooperates and colludes with Jason throughout *Castle Rackrent* until the moment that Jason finally comes into possession of the estate. At that turning point, Thady's affection for Condy—or the tradition he represents—trumps his paternal feelings and he regrets seeing "the lawful owner turned out of the seat of his ancestors" (p. 50). Even Jason is surprised by his father's sudden change of heart. While Thady expresses sympathy for Sir Condy, Jason tries to signal his father with "signs, and winks, and frowns"

(p. 51) but Thady ignores him, "grieved and sick at heart for my poor master" (p. 51).

While Thady's behavior toward his masters can be read as disingenuous throughout most of the novel, his loyalty to Condy and rejection of Jason in the end seem sincere. Through Thady's grief, Edgeworth expresses her ambivalence about the social destabilization that she sensed was taking place. Having internalized certain attitudes and behaviors suited to their roles, the novel's characters are lost when those roles are reversed. Sir Condy pathetically clings to a belief in himself as the beloved master though he has been banished to a cottage and dies unmourned. Jason becomes master of the estate, though Thady suggests that he, too, is alone, having alienated himself from his father and his peasants, many of whom, we learn, do not want him to have the land. As for Thady, he says, "I'm tired of wishing for anything in this world, after all I've seen in it" (p. 61).

What Thady has seen has been no less than the complete overthrow of an antiquated system, one touted by rulers and dependents alike for its success in maintaining order. Edgeworth's novel radically attacks that system and exposes it as one that perpetuates alcoholism, spousal abuse, violence, and the starvation of workers. By foregrounding a servant character who is necessary to the functioning of the Irish big house, but whose conflicting sense of duty places him in an impossible situation, Edgeworth reveals that within the system lie the seeds of its own destruction. In her portrayal of Jason and Thady, Edgeworth complicates the literary stereotypes of servants as *either* loyal family vassals *or* malicious schemers, making their conflicts and their personal lives real. W. J. McCormack describes all of Edgeworth's writings as "an imaginative historical projection of Enlightenment values in crisis."[1] Edgeworth was preoccupied with economic, social and political changes throughout her career. With the help of a "loyal" servant, the Rackrent family has destroyed itself and been replaced by a member of the professional class, the son of a servant. In an article on Edgeworth's nationalism, Marilyn Butler writes, "*Castle Rackrent . . .* challenges the system—the traditional landownership or aristocratic system of proprietorship, sustained by male primogeniture on the one hand, profitable marriages and the strategic extension of kinship on the other. Great-house stateliness is debunked when Castle Rackrent's annals are handed over to an illiterate Irish chronicler to relate."[2] Edgeworth saw these social and economic

---

1. W. J. McCormack, "Setting and Ideology: With Reference to the Fiction of Maria. Edgeworth," *Ancestral Voices: The Big House in Anglo-Irish Literature*, ed. Otto Rauchbauer (Zurich and New York: Georg Olms Verlag, 1992), 52.
2. Marilyn Butler, "Edgeworth's Ireland: History, Popular Culture, and Secret Codes," *Novel* 34.2 (Spring 2001): 274. [See Butler on p. 143—editor.]

changes coming, and in *Rackrent*, she critiques the ruling class as unworthy of their status and never mourns the destruction of the Rackrents and what they represent. Still, she never really celebrates the Rackrent's destruction either. Jason is too cold and too self-interested to be a laudable representative of the next social order. Significantly, he does not marry, and his rule over the land is neither popular nor regenerative.

Hiberno-English

JOYCE FLYNN
[Edgeworth's Use of Hiberno-English]†

* * *

Maria Edgeworth's career as a writer spans the changing fortunes and ambivalent attitudes of the Irish Protestants, for her first novel *Castle Rackrent* was written in 1793–1795[1] and appeared in 1800. Her last "Irish" work *Ormond* was completed in 1817, the year of publication of her "Irish" plays (*Love and Law,* and *The Rose, The Thistle and the Shamrock*) and the year of her father's death. Excluding such children's pieces as *Garry-Owen, Little Plays for Children,* and *Orlandino,* Edgeworth's vastly reduced literary output after 1817 dealt only with upper- and upper-middle-class English protagonists, as had such earlier works as *Belinda* (1803), *The Modern Griselda* (1805), *Leonora* (1806), *Almeria* and *Manoeuvering* (1809), *Vivian* (1812), and *Patronage* (1814). For Maria Edgeworth, who was born in England in 1768 but took up permanent residence in Ireland at the age of fourteen, the process of emotional identification may have run counter to political realignment of her class: at least one authority, Vivian Mercier, judges that Edgeworth wrote "the best satire on the Protestant Irish after Swift . . . in *Castle Rackrent* while she was still English enough not to feel that she was betraying her own kind. . . . Edgeworth's long silence on Ireland after *Ormond* is explained by Mercier as due to her growing involvement in that land's tragic drama: ". . . perhaps she came to feel implicated in the guilt of Irish landlords, or grew too emotionally involved in the sufferings of the Irish peasantry."[2]

† From Joyce Flynn, "Dialect As Didactic Tool: Edgeworth's Use of Hiberno-English," in *Proceedings of the Harvard Celtic Colloquium,* Vol. 2 (Cambridge: Harvard University, 1982), pp. 115–18, 120–23, 178, 180–01. Reprinted by permission of the author and the Department of Celtic Languages and Literatures, Harvard University.
1. Marilyn Butler, *Maria Edgeworth: A Literary Biography* (Oxford, 1972), 174.
2. Vivian Mercier, *The Irish Comic Tradition* (London, 1962), 86 and 197.

This identification with Ireland and its problems combined with a self-conscious English heritage led Maria Edgeworth and her father, Richard Lovell Edgeworth, to assume a sort of middleman status between Ireland and the British reading public, to whom Edgeworth addressed herself as apologist and interpreter of the Irish situation. This intention is obvious in *Castle Rackrent*, where notes are added "For the information of the *ignorant* English reader" (p. 6);[3] it is schematized in story form in "The Limerick Gloves" ("But paps," said Phoebe, "why should we take a dislike to him because he is an Irishman? Cannot an Irishman be a good man?"),[4] one of a collection of *Popular Tales* intended for the edification of England's less-than-well-to-do readers.[5] But it is the implicit intention in all of Edgeworth's writings on Ireland, especially *An Essay on Irish Bulls*.

The didactic, mediating purpose of Edgeworth's "Irish" writings is perhaps best expressed by an invitation of her father's to William Strutt of Derby, a publisher who was to become a close family friend:

> Few Englishmen are acquainted with the inhabitants of this country, and very few of the Irish country gentry are acquainted with their inferiors. Do me the favour and the justice . . . to visit Edgeworthstown, where I can show you the real character of the people.[6]

It is significant that Edgeworth's father sees the emissary as having a dual role, interpreting the people to their own landlords in Ireland and representing Ireland in a fair but favorable light to English opinion. Given the divergence of native Irish and landlord interests, it was almost inevitable that an attempt to represent the interests of both classes sympathetically would involve contradiction and strain. * * *

A major avenue for exploration and opportunity for national definition presented itself in the examination of the speech of Ireland's inhabitants, whose English (let alone the Irish Gaelic spoken by the vast majority of the peasant population) differed noticeably from the King's English. Edgeworth had fortunately been given an early opportunity to observe the Hiberno-English eloquence of the Edgeworthstown tenants while serving as her father's secretary-bookkeeper[7] when she was frequently treated to chaotic scenes of massed pleaders and petitioners airing their cases in the backyard or on the front lawn of the big house itself.[8] Later at home, her father would

---

3. Page numbers throughout refer to this Norton Critical Edition [editor's note].
4. Maria Edgeworth, "The Limerick Gloves," *Popular Tales* (London, 1895), 110.
5. Butler, *Maria Edgeworth*, 125.
6. Richard Lovell Edgeworth as quoted in the "Introduction" to *Popular Tales*, x.
7. Butler, *Maria Edgeworth*, 87–88.
8. See Chapter 1 of Maria Edgeworth's portion of the *Memoirs of Richard Lovell Edgeworth* (Boston, 1821), 7. Lord Glenthorn in *Ennui* encounters a similar scene whenever he ventures out for a ride.

entertain the family with impressions of the Irish characters they had encountered during the day. It was her father's talent for mimicry which led Edgeworth to write her first Irish sketch, *The Double Disguise*, in the form of a dialogue about Justice Cocoa, a former Tipperary grocer turned Volunteer.[9] *The Double Disguise* is thought to have been staged by the family during Christmas, 1786, with Mr. Edgeworth taking the parts of Justice Cocoa and the servant girl at the inn. The text of the play, which has never been published, survives in two manuscripts held by the Bodleian Library.[1]

Maria herself acquired from her father both the practice of collecting specimens of Irish speech and the mimicry which recreated them. It was her droll impressions of John Langan, her father's steward, that led Mrs. Sophy Ruxton to insist that Maria make a written copy of her dramatic monologue, which became the novel known known as *Castle Rackrent*.[2] The fact that Mr. Edgeworth admittedly spoke English with a brogue[3] probably indicates that Maria, too, was detectable in her conversation as an Anglo-Irishwoman. * * *

Of the so-called Anglo-Irish dialect of English, Edgeworth was to make much wider and more complex use, constructing in the "Irish" novels and plays a social hierarchy systematically stratified in terms of pronunciation and idiom. Edgeworth's first-hand observation of her father's tenants in Edgeworthstown undoubtedly provided most of her characters' Hibernicisms, but she could have turned for verification of her own findings to several nearly contemporary sources.

* * *

Edgeworth's first partiality was for passages of natural, everyday speech. In the preface which accompanied the 1800 publication of *Castle Rackrent*, Edgeworth praised the prevailing taste of the public for anecdote as an "incontestable proof" of the reading public's good sense, and she harshly criticized the unrealistic presentation of heroes who

> are so decked out by the fine fancy of the professed historian; they talk in such measured prose, and act from such sublime or such diabolical motives, that few have sufficient taste, wickedness, or heroism, to sympathize in their fate. (p. 5)

9. Butler, *Maria Edgeworth*, 125. [See *The Double Disguise* on p. 103–10—editor.]

1. Christina Colvin, "Maria Edgeworth's Literary Manuscripts in the Bodleian Library," *Bodleian Library Record* 8(1970):199. Another play for children with a more international theme, *Whim for Whim*, was acted in 1799 and rests unpublished in the same collection. [The text has since been published; see Maria Edgeworth, *The Double Disguise*, ed. Christine Alexander and Ryan Twomey (Sydney: Juvenilia Press, 2014)—editor].

2. Butler, *Maria Edgeworth*, 174.

3. Ibid.

After this attack on the elevated style prized by the century just ended, the preface progresses toward a nineteenth-century view of art with its defense of the lives "not only of the great and good, but even of the worthless and insignificant" as appropriate subject matter for literature (p. 5). Innovative technique necessarily follows upon the new subject matter, and the author asserts that insight into characters cannot be accurately gleaned "from their actions or their appearance in public; it is from their careless conversations, their half-finished sentences, that we may hope with the greatest probability of success to discover their real characters" (p. 5).

The combination and collision of these early theories with conventional notions of appropriate diction already mentioned produced after *Castle Rackrent* a series of works (*An Essay on Irish Bulls* and the so-called "Irish" novels), of which the liveliest portions were dialogues attempting to represent English as spoken by the lower classes of the Irish population. * * *

Edgeworth's first novel, *Castle Rackrent*, was a monologue which seemed to have happened in real life. The narrative of Thady M'Quirk represents Edgeworth's longest sustained use of the Anglo-Irish dialect and a convincing reconstruction of the idiom that O'Faolain later called "speech language, rasped by many tongues, made smooth, like an old penny, by the thousands of lives its has touched."[4] Thady's speech, though containing some archaisms from the English language of an earlier time, demonstrates substantial Gaelic influence in both pronunciation and syntax although probably considerably less than that found in the peasant speech of Edgeworth's time since "at the best . . . the dramatist or novelist is restricted to what will be fairly readily intelligible," especially in a first-person account like *Castle Rackrent*, where the speaker is the reader's sole source of information and commentary.[5] * * *

"Hibernicized" pronunciations in *Castle Rackrent* include the use of [d] or [t] for [ð] ("fader" p. 59, "t'other" pp. 38, 54, 61); [ʃ] for [s] in the vicinity of what Irish Gaelic defines as a "front" vowel ("shister" pp. 53, 54, 56, 58, 59, 60, "Jewish" for "Jewess" pp. 21, 28, 33); [ɪ] for [ɛ] ("pin" for "pen" p. 32), pronunciations probably prompted by the influence of Gaelic. Tudor pronunciations include the use of the tense [ē] for [ī] ("cratur" pp. 15, 35, "plase" p. 59, "Jasus" p. 48), of *ar* for *er* ("larning" p. 49 vs. "learnt" p. 56; "sartain" p. 55, "prefarred" p. 59) and of [t] for [d] in final position, a tendency probably evident in Thady's use of the past participle forms "kilt" (p. 55), "learnt" (p. 56), "dropt" (p. 57), and "lit" (the last for

---

4. Sean O'Faolaoin, "Written Speech," *The Commonweal* 27 (5 November 1937): 35.
5. J. J. Hogan, "Notes on the Study of Anglo-Irish Dialect," *Bealoideas* 14 (1944):188.

"alighted") although the retention of archaic forms may also be advanced as an explanation. (Note also the habitual intrusive *t* in such words as "betwixt" p. 43 [twice], "amongst" pp. 29, 47, and "whilst" pp. 37, 51, 54, 56.) Thady's accidence preserves intact at least two characteristics of the Northern dialect of Middle English: the plural form "childer" instead of "children" (pp. 17, 29, 51, 56, 58, 59, 73) and the present indicative plural form ending in -*s* ("many wishes it" p. 61, "we lifts" p. 60).[6] The formation of the adverb from the adjective without suffixing -*ly* ("smack smooth" p. 34) is also archaic, deriving from the loss in the Middle English period of the Old English adverbial suffix -*e* and preceding the universal adoption of -*ly* from the suffix -*lich*. Other examples of this usage in *Castle Rackrent* are "behave ungenerous" (p. 31), "behaved very genteel" (p. 47), "noise wonderful great" (p. 53), but two other cases seem to echo the Middle English formation with -*lich*: "walked away quite sober-like" (p. 33), and "said my lady, pettish-like" (p. 45). "Afore" used in the sense of "before" by both Thady and Condy (pp. 46, 53, 58, 60) is also an obsolete English usage. Thady's use of such verbal phrases as "a-laughing" (p. 40) and "a-nutting" (p. 51) may derive from Middle-English or Irish-Gaelic usage. Near-archaic and now dialectal, although still of limited use in Edgeworth's time, are the compound forms "withinside" (Condy's "pain all withinside of me" p. 61) and "howsomever" (p. 42), the employment of "barring" as a conjunction (p. 49), and the frequent use of the aphetic form "em" for "them" (pp. 35, 36, 38, 45, 52), apparently by both Thady and Condy. (Because Thady delivered the entire narrative, the differentiation of other characters' pronunciation or accidence is necessarily conjectural since Thady might logically tend to follow his own speech patterns even where quoting others.)

Irish Gaelic idiom is recognizable in such phrases as "at all-at all" (p. 23), "out of the face" (pp. 56, 73, 74, cf. "in the face of" p. 50), "in it" with indefinite reference (pp. 38, 60, 61), "white-headed boy" (pp. 29, 42), and the stereotypical oath, "by all the books that were ever shut or opened" (Condy p. 32), and exclamations, "Long life to him," "God bless him" (Thady, p. 13). Though foreign-sounding, Thady's "Sarrah bit of secret" (p. 49) is, in fact, a special use of the English word "sorrow" found in a number of English dialects (Appendix V). Strange to an English reader and taken directly from Irish Gaelic are Thady's use of periphrastic constructions involving the verb "to be" for simple present and past and imperative forms.

6. See Thomas Pyles, *The Origins and Development of the English Language*, 2nd ed. (New York, 1971), 157–58, for a discusson of these and other characteristics of the Northern dialect of Middle English, which through the Scots dialect influenced Hiberno-English in the early modern period of English.

Vocabulary borrowed from Irish Gaelic includes "shebeen-house" (p. 54, Irish Gaelic *síbín*) and "gossoon" (p. 58, Irish Gaelic *garsúin*).[7]

Significantly, in the conversations recounted by Thady, neither Sir Condy nor Thady's son Jason—with the single exception of Condy's possibly insincere use of "pin" for "pen"—employs the Irish-influenced pronunciations and idioms used by Thady, Thady's sister, and Judy. Jason, a man of few words, speaks those few in Standard English, for he has risen far from his father's world. On the other hand, Sir Condy's Anglo-Irish is marked not by Hibernian influences from the language of his tenants,[8] but by archaic and near-archaic usages which serve as a reminder that he is the last of a decaying aristocracy, which has outlived its usefulness if it ever had one. Unfortunately, many readers took Thady's sentimental eulogy of Sir Condy at face value,[9] for the reason stated by Stanley J. Solomon: "The ironic perspective here works against the reader's ability to establish the normative values for the author's point of view—in a century which had not yet realized the possiblities of narrative unreliableness."[1] Despite *Castle Rackrent*'s success in recreating dialect speech and despite its popularity with English readers, Edgeworth was greatly concerned at the widespread misinterpretation of her own position on the Irish landlord questions.[2] After *Castle Rackrent* she never again wrote a work touching on Ireland or the Irish without including at least one clearly normative character whose virtue, practical wisdom, and fidelity to the King's English articulated the author's point of view.

✻   ✻   ✻

---

7. For discussions of the origins of this apparent borrowing from the French, see P. W. Joyce, *English as We Speak It in Ireland* (Dublin, 1910), 266, and *Castle Rackrent*, 35n.
8. Except for the pronunciation of "pen" already noted, Condy's usage and pronunciation ("Jasus" for "Jesus") represent archaic English whenever a deviation from late eighteenth-century Standard English occurs.
9. Concerning the contemporary interpretation of *Castle Rackrent*, Butler, 360, notes: "The ironic message of the first half is cancelled out by the pathos of the second. The result is that *Castle Rackrent* has always been taken to mean the opposite of what the Edgeworths believed: that the passing of thoroughly selfish and irresponsible landlords is to be regretted when they come from a native Irish family and can command a feudal type of loyalty from some of their peasants."
1. Stanley J. Solomon, "Ironic Perspective in Maria Edgeworth's *Castle Rackrent*," *Journal of Narrative Technique* 2 (1972): 72. [See Solomon on pp. 148–49—editor.]
2. Butler, *Maria Edgeworth*, 358–59.

BRIAN HOLLINGWORTH

From Maria Edgeworth's Irish Writing[†]

The Innocent Voice

Castle Rackrent is unique in Edgeworth's work in adopting a first person narrative, and innovative in its use of a regional vernacular for the 'voice' of this narrative. * * *

In the text, two language features are evident—the informal oral code narrative of Thady Quirk and the contrasting formal written code editorial apparatus which surrounds it. Neither of these modes of discourse is used innocently, and both interact to serve the intentions of the text.

In studying Thady's oral narrative as a sample of Hiberno-English, any assertion that Edgeworth's account is artless must be instantly qualified. Critics have been happy to accept that Thady's voice does represent a genuine local vernacular, but this is true only with reservations. It is plain that, even by comparison with some of the examples offered in the *Essay on Irish Bulls*, the vernacular has been modified so that it is more easily accessible to the English reader. As Todd points out Edgeworth 'does not overdo her representation of dialect'.[1] She is careful not to alienate her readers by making the Irish vernacular accurate but unintelligible.

Edgeworth indicates the speaking voice in three principal ways—by pronunciation, by the use of dialectal vocabulary, and by idiom. Close study of the text will reveal that the first two of these are used very sparingly indeed.

Variation from standard pronunciation would normally be indicated by variant spellings of words common to standard speech. These are few and far between in *Castle Rackrent*. The most common indicator, which is rather an indicator of spoken English in general than of Hiberno-English in particular, is the omission of 'th' in 'them' when it is the object of a verb.[2] 'Them', following a preposition, however, is always given in full. Other variants which are presented with some consistency, but less frequently, are 'afore' (pp. 46, 53, 58) and t'other (pp. 21, 38, 48, 53, 61).[3] Neither of these can be considered a strong marker of Hiberno-English alone.

---

† From Brian Hollingworth, *Maria Edgeworth's Irish Writing: Language History, Politics* (New York: St. Martin's Press, 1997), pp. 86–92, 225–26. Reprinted by permission of Palgrave Macmillan.
1. Loreto Todd, *The Language of Irish Literature* (London 1989), 128.
2. The inclusion of *th* was made standard from the 1804 edition [editor's note].
3. Page numbers throughout refer to this Norton Critical Edition [editor's note].

Occasionally more obviously 'Irish' pronunciations are fore-grounded, for example 'Jasus' (p. 48), 'sacret' (p. 49),[4] 'plase' (p. 59), 'prefarred' (p. 59). All indicate a familiar variation in Irish speech—but this is not a consistent feature of the text. 'Pin' is also offered as a pronunciation of 'pen' at one point (p. 32), but this idiosyncrasy is never repeated.

There are indications, indeed, that, as the story proceeds, Edge-worth more deliberately impresses variations of pronunciation upon the reader. The majority of references given above come from the latter half of the narrative, and pronunciation indicators become most frequent in the last fifty pages of first edition text.

Three are particularly interesting. Although 'sister' is given a standard spelling earlier in the story (p. 31), the Irish pronuncia-tion as a palato-alveolar fricative (sh) appears for the first time on page 53. It is then employed fourteen times in the last fifteen pages—a feature which is difficult to ignore. Similarly the dialectal 'childer' for the plural of child occurs once (p. 17) in the earlier part of the story, but seven times from page 51 onwards. Partly this may be explained as the consequence of Thady speaking more fre-quently about his relatives towards the close, but the feature seems also to suggest Edgeworth's growing self-consciousness in convey-ing idiosyncrasies of pronunciation.

This self-consciousness is also indicated by the presentation of the dialectal use of the unvoiced alveolar plosive ('t'), where the standard speaker uses an unvoiced alveolar fricative ('th'). For much of the story she ignores this distinction, until Sir Condy (p. 49) speaks of 'bringing in the tings for the punch', and a little later Thady asks Jason 'what will people tink and say, when they see you living here in Castle Rackrent?' (p. 50). The first of these was made standard ('th') in the 1804 edition, while the second had been standardized as early as the second edition of 1800. It seems that in the later stages of the narrative Edgeworth decided to draw attention to this feature of Irish speech, but later changed her mind.

In general we can say that Edgeworth's representation of Irish pronunciation is arbitrary and inconsistent. It is intended to give a flavour of Irishness, but in no way to interfere with the readers' easy comprehension of the narrative.

It is the same with Edgeworth's use of dialectal vocabulary. Excluding technical terms to do with estate management, such as 'herriot' (p. 15) or 'custodiam' (e.g. pp. 40, 49) there are very few dialectal terms indeed. Perhaps there are six—'Whillaluh' (p. 13, spelt 'Whillalu' p. 51), 'Banshee' (p. 16), 'aims ace' (p. 26), 'gossoon'

---

4. Hollingworth is referencing the 1800 second edition of *Castle Rackrent* that included "Sacret" ("Secret") and, on occasion, the omission of 'th' in "things" ("tings") and "thinks" ("tinks"). See n. 2, p. 199 [editor's note].

(p. 37), 'sarrah' (p. 49), 'shebean house' (p. 54). To list these words is to cast further doubt on Watson's conjecture[5] that the Glossary and footnotes were added at the last minute because of panic concerning the dialectal form of the narrative. Though most of these terms are indeed annotated by the 'editor', they are, in any case, not sufficient in number to cause a problem for the reader. In fact there is likely to be more difficulty with the financial language of the various land deals which punctuate the story of the Rackrents' decline. The Hiberno-English presented here provides no barrier to Edgeworth's economic and political message.

On the other hand, a feature of dialectal vocabulary which she *does* foreground is the regional use of the word 'kilt'. When Lady Rackrent, in conflict with Sir Condy, but also as part of a scheme to stave off penury, returns to her parents, her jaunting car crashes. She is left 'kilt and lying for dead' (p. 55):

> My lady Rackrent was all kilt and smashed, and they lifted her into a cabin hard by, and the maid was found after, where she had been thrown in the gripe of the ditch, with her cap and bonnet all full of bog-water—and they say my lady can't live any way.
>
> (p. 55)

The context makes it clear that Lady Rackrent is not, in the standard usage, 'killed', and in fact she recovers. But it does point to a perceived ambiguity in dialectal speech, which Edgeworth frequently foregrounds.[6]

In *Castle Rackrent*, the term pursues a remarkably ambiguous path. Not only does it threaten to deceive the English reader, it half-deceives Judy M'Quirk, who builds up her hopes of marriage to either Sir Condy or Jason on the conviction that Lady Rackrent is indeed 'killed'. A feature of the ending is that Lady Rackrent's 'killing' lays a false trail, for both reader and participants in the plot, which is never resolved. The final paragraph (p. 61) becomes a series of denials—'my Lady Rackrent did not die, 'Jason won't have the land at any rate', 'Jason did not marry, nor think of marrying Judy'. Through the vernacular usage, as well as narrative situation, the tale ends in an indeterminacy which reflects a familiar Edgeworth ambivalence concerning the status of the relationship between Ireland and England.

---

5. Maria Edgeworth, *Castle Rackrent*, ed. George Watson (New York: Oxford University Press, 1964).
6. Hollingworth identifies two other occasions on which Edgeworth employs the term *kilt*, *An Essay on Irish Bulls* (1802) and *Ormond* (1817) [editor's note].

If differences of pronunciation and vocabulary play such a small part in the presentation of the vernacular voice of *Castle Rackrent*, then the feature which identifies this voice as unmistakably Hiberno-English is the use of idiom. Here Edgeworth's ear for language—her ability to 'think and speak' in the Langan idiolect—enables her to present the regional dialect with convincing verisimilitude:

> Having out of friendship for the family, upon whose estate, praised be Heaven! I and mine have lived rent free time out of mind, voluntarily undertaken to publish the Memoirs of the Rackrent family, I think it my duty to say a few words, in the first place, concerning myself.—My real name is Thady Quirk, though in the family I have always been known by no other than *honest Thady*—afterwards, in the time of Sir Murtagh, deceased, I remember to hear them calling me *old Thady*; and now I'm come to 'poor Thady'—for I wear a long great coat winter and summer, which is very handy, as I never put my arms into the sleeves, (they are as good as new,) though come Holantide next, I've had it these seven years, it holds on by a single button round my neck, cloak fashion, to look at me, you would hardly think 'poor Thady' was the father of attorney Quirk; he is a high gentleman, and never minds what poor Thady says, and having better than 1500 a-year, landed estate, looks down upon honest Thady, but I wash my hands of his doings, and as I have lived so will I die, true and loyal to the family.
>
> (pp. 11–12)

A marked feature of this opening narrative is its discursiveness. It refuses to stick to the point. So the long apparent digression concerning Thady's great-coat[7], and even his relationship with Jason, immediately interrupts the serious business of telling the family history. This might well be a feature of oral discourse in general rather than a feature of Irish speech in particular, but certain regional features *are* registered. The most obvious are interjections such as 'praised be heaven!'. In the first section of the story we meet 'Long life to him' (p. 12), 'his honour God bless him' (p. 13) and 'Here's my thanks to him' (p. 13). However, more subtly, it is the turn of phrase which marks the particular Irish idiom—in the passage quoted above, phrases such as 'I wear a long great coat winter and summer' or 'I wash my hands of his doings, and as I have lived so will I die'. From time to time Edgeworth provides examples of Irish bulls. For example, shortly after the passage quoted, Thady describes the death of Sir Tallyhoo Rackrent: 'he lost a fine hunter and his life . . . all in one

---

7. The Irish cloak, however, has considerable symbolic value as identifying indigenous Irish custom. It is the 'red-rose-bordered hem' of Yeats's 'To Ireland in the Coming Times'. Even such discursiveness is not as innocent as it may appear.

day's hunt' (p. 12). At one point, discussing Sir Murtagh's law cases, Thady comments 'Out of forty nine suits which he had, he never lost one but seventeen' (p. 16). Such blunders are relatively infrequent however. Irish speech is not caricatured, and overall the impression is given of the natural flow of regional spoken language.

Such an idiomatic use of the vernacular offers no threat to comprehension. With variations in pronunciation muzzled, and dialectal vocabulary confined, the reader can enjoy the pleasures of novelty without enduring its pains.

Even then, it is wrong to assume that the idiom is consistent, or a verbatim copy of the Anglo-Irish dialect. Occasionally the register shifts quite markedly, under the influence of more literary models. For instance, at the beginning of the Second Part the language becomes more formal for a time (p. 28). And again, when Jason is pressing Condy to pay his debts, the language becomes, not that of the old retainer, but that of the ledger book:

> To Cash lent, and to ditto, and to ditto, and to ditto, and oats, and bills paid at the milliner's, and linen draper's and many dresses for the fancy balls in Dublin for my lady, and all the bills to the workmen for the scenery of the theatre, and the chandler's and grocer's bills, and taylor's, besides butcher's and baker's, and worse than all, the old one of that base wine-merchant's, that wanted to arrest my poor master for the amount on the election day.

> (pp. 47–48)

Such an accumulation of impositions, in the mode of the accountant, seems intended in Thady's eyes, to conjure up sympathy for 'poor' Sir Condy. For the reader it is a reminder of Rackrent profligacy and lack of foresight.

It is clear, therefore, that the first person narrative has purposes well beyond a naive intention to record the rhythms of vernacular speech. It changes register artfully to reflect the circumstances of the plot, and to foreground certain moral attitudes. In emphasizing the giddiness of Sir Condy's young wife, for instance,—she has a fondness for the theatre and for romantic situations in the midst of family squalor and bankruptcy—the faithful old retainer displays a remarkable capacity to recall allusions to Addison and Shakespeare (p. 33).

In summary, then, though the narrative voice is presented with the appearance of innocence, it is carefully crafted. Every care is taken that John Langan's tale should present no problem of comprehension to the reader. All vernacular signifiers are made transparent. Moreover, the oral register may shift, picking up echoes from more formal, written codes, to emphasize the local meanings of the text.

* * *

Maria Edgeworth: A Chronology

1768	Maria Edgeworth born January 1 in Black Bourton, Oxfordshire, the third child of Richard Lovell Edgeworth (RLE) (1744–1817) and Anna Maria Edgeworth (née Elers).
1773	Ten days after giving birth to her third daughter (Anna), Anna Maria dies. On July 17, within four months of becoming a widower, RLE marries Honora Sneyd. Family relocates to Edgeworthstown, marking Maria's first visit to Ireland.
1775	Sent away to Mrs. Latuffière's school in Derby.
1777	Family moves back to England (Hertfordshire).
1779	RLE begins to set Maria writing tasks.
1780	April 30, Honora Sneyd dies; RLE marries his third wife, Elizabeth Sneyd, Honora's sister, on Christmas Day. Maria attends school in Upper Wimpole Street, London.
1781	Maria stays with Thomas Day in July and September.
1782	Entire family moves to Edgeworthstown in County Longford. Ireland achieves legislative independence. RLE sets Maria to work translating Madame de Genlis's *Adèle et Théodore: ou lettres sur l'éducation.*
1783	Reads widely throughout the year and is engrossed in French theater, in particular Molière and Marivaux. Completes the translation of *Adèle et Théodore,* even though a rival edition had been published.
1784	Writes the didactic tale "The Mental Thermometer."
1786	Writes her comedic drama *The Double Disguise*; it is performed at Edgeworthstown for Lord and Lady Longford at Christmas.
1787	Writes "The Bracelets," later published in *The Parent's Assistant* (1796).
1788	Begins recording RLE's oral tales, titled *The Freeman Family,* later used as the foundation of her longest novel, *Patronage* (started in 1809, published 1814).
1791	Visits Clifton; writes more tales later published in *The Parent's Assistant.*

1793–94	Begins writing *Castle Rackrent*.
1795	Publishes first book, *Letters for Literary Ladies*. It includes the satirical "An Essay on the Noble Science of Self-Justification," which she later expanded into *The Modern Griselda* (1804).
1796	Publishes *The Parent's Assistant*, a collection of short stories for children.
1797	Elizabeth Sneyd, RLE's third wife, dies in November.
1798	RLE marries his fourth wife, Frances Beaufort, in May. *Practical Education*, written in partnership with RLE and other family members, is published in June. Two months later, on August 22, General Humbert's French forces land in County Mayo, Ireland; by the end of the first week of September, the family is forced to flee Edgeworthstown in fear of a rebel attack. The French are defeated by an Anglo-Irish army under Lord Carhampton. RLE elected to Irish parliament.
1800	*Castle Rackrent*, Maria's first novel, is published anonymously in January. In August the Union of Great Britain and Ireland is passed in Parliament.
1801	A number of key works are published: *Early Lessons*; *Moral Tales*; Maria's first society novel, *Belinda*; and her juvenilia piece *The Mental Thermometer*.
1802	In collaboration with RLE, *Essay on Irish Bulls* is published in May. Maria and RLE travel to Brussels before arriving in Paris on October 23. In December, Chevalier Edelcrantz proposes marriage to Maria and is refused.
1803	On January 21 Maria and RLE are confronted by police and forced to leave Paris. March 5, they arrive in Dover from Calais; arrive in Edinburgh on March 19.
1804	Publishes *The Modern Griselda,* originally intended for publication in *Tales of Fashionable Life*, and a collection of stories included in *Popular Tales*.
1806	Publishes *Leonora*, an epistolary novel.
1809	With RLE, *Essays on Professional Education*; *Tales of Fashionable Life* (vols. i–iii), including *Ennui*, is published.
1812	*Tales of Fashionable Life* (vols. iv–vi), including *The Absentee*, is published.
1813	Visits London and meets Byron and Humphry Davy.
1814	*Patronage* (as with *The Modern Griselda*), originally produced for publication in *Tales of Fashionable Life*, is published along with *Continuation of Early Lessons*

(3 vols.). Edgeworth family reads *Waverley,* and Maria begins her correspondence and friendship with Walter Scott.

1817   RLE dies in June; in July, *Harrington* and *Ormond* published (which contains some material written by RLE).

1820   An autobiography started in 1808–9 by RLE and finished by Maria in 1819, titled *Memoirs of Richard Lovell Edgeworth, Begun by Himself and Concluded by His Daughter,* is published in March.

1821   Publishes *Rosamond: A Sequel to Early Lessons.*

1822   Publishes *Frank: A Sequel to Frank in Early Lessons.*

1823   Travels to Edinburgh for her first meeting with Walter Scott. During August she spends two weeks as Scott's guest at Abbotsford.

1825   Publishes *Harry and Lucy Concluded.* The first collected edition appears: *Tales and Miscellaneous Pieces* (14 vols.). Scott visits Edgeworthstown.

1826   After continual financial mismanagement, Maria takes control of the Edgeworthstown estate from her brother, Lovell.

1832   The eighteen-volume Baldwin & Cradock *Tales and Novels by Maria Edgeworth* is printed—the last edited by Maria.

1833   Visits Connemara.

1834   Publishes her last novel, *Helen.*

1848   Publishes her last moral tale, "Orlandino."

1849   Dies May 22 and is laid to rest in a vault in Edgeworthstown.

Selected Bibliography

• indicates works included or excerpted in this Norton Critical Edition.

Bibliography and Letters

Butler, Harriet J., and Harold Edgeworth Butler, eds. *The Black Book of Edge-worthstown and Other Edgeworth Memoirs, 1585–1817.* London: Faber & Gwyer, 1927.

• Butler, Marilyn. *Maria Edgeworth: A Literary Biography.* Oxford: Clarendon Press, 1972.

Butler, R. F. "Maria Edgeworth and Sir Walter Scott: Unpublished Letters, 1823." *The Review of English Studies* n. s., 9.33 (February 1958): 23–40.

• Byron, George Gordon, Lord. *Letters, Journals, and Conversations.* Vol. 2. Frankfurt: H. L. Brönner, 1834.

Colvin, Christina. *Maria Edgeworth in France and Switzerland: Selections from the Edgeworth Family Letters.* Oxford: Clarendon Press, 1979.

———, ed. *Maria Edgeworth: Letters from England, 1813–1844.* Oxford: Clarendon Press, 1971.

Edgeworth, Frances, ed. *Memoir of Maria Edgeworth with a Selection from Her Letters.* 3 vols. Privately printed, 1867.

Edgeworth, Richard Lovell. *Memoirs of Richard Lovell Edgeworth, Begun by Himself and Concluded by His Daughter.* 2 Vols. Shannon: Irish University Press, 1969.

Hamilton, C. J. *Notable Irishwomen.* Dublin: Sealy, Bryers & Walker, 1904.

• Hare, Augustus J. C, ed. *The Life and Letters of Maria Edgeworth.* 2 vols. Cambridge: Houghton, Mifflin, 1895.

Lawless, Emily. *Maria Edgeworth.* New York: Macmillan, 1905.

• Scott, Sir Walter. *Waverly or 'Tis Sixty Years Since.* Edinburgh: Adam & Charles Black, 1871.

• Yeats, W. B., ed. *Representative Irish Tales.* Foreword by Mary Helen Thuente. Gerrards Cross: Colin Smythe, 1979.

Criticism

• Allen, Walter. *The English Novel: A Short Critical History.* London: Phoenix, 1954.

Altieri, Joanne. "Style and Purpose in Maria Edgeworth's Fiction." *Nineteenth Century Fiction* 23.3 (December 1968): 265–78.

• Belanger, Jacqueline. "Educating the Reading Public: British Critical Reception of Maria Edgeworth's Early Irish Writing." *Irish University Review* 28.2 (Autumn–Winter 1998): 240–55.

Bellamy, Liz. "Regionalism and Nationalism: Maria Edgeworth, Walter Scott and the Definition of Britishness." In *The Regional Novel in Britain and*

Ireland, 1800–1990, edited by K. D. M. Snell, 54–77. Cambridge: Cambridge University Press, 1998.

Botkin, Frances. "Edgeworth and Wordsworth: Plain Unvarnished Tales." In *Ireland in the Nineteenth Century: Regional Identity,* edited by Glenn Hooper and Leon Litvack, 140–55. Dublin: Four Courts Press, 2000.

• Butler, Marilyn. "Edgeworth's Ireland: History, Popular Culture, and Secret Codes." *Novel* 34.2 (Spring 2001): 267–92.

Cary, Meredith. "Privileged Assimilation: Maria Edgeworth's Hope for the Ascendancy." *Éire-Ireland* 26.4 (Winter 1991): 29–37.

Clarke, Isabel C. *Maria Edgeworth, Her Family and Friends.* London: Hutchinson, 1949.

Cochran, Kate. "The Plain Round Tale of Faithful Thady: *Castle Rackrent* as Slave Narrative." *New Hibernian Review* 5.4 (Winter 2001): 57–72.

• Corbett, Mary Jean. *Allegories of Union in Irish and English Writing, 1790–1870: Politics, History and the Family from Edgeworth to Arnold.* Cambridge: Cambridge University Press, 2000.

———. "Another Tale to Tell: Postcolonial Theory and the Case of *Castle Rackrent.*" *Criticism: A Quarterly for Literature and the Arts* 36.3 (Summer 1994): 383–400.

Croghan, Martin J. "Swift, Thomas Sheridan, Maria Edgeworth and the Evolution of Hiberno-English." *Irish University Review: A Journal of Irish Studies* 20.1 (Spring 1990): 19–34.

• Deane, Seamus. *A Short History of Irish Literature.* London: Hutchinson, 1986.

Eagleton, Terry. *Heathcliff and the Great Hunger.* London: Verso, 1995.

Fauske, Christopher, and Heidi Kaufman, eds. *An Uncomfortable Authority: Maria Edgeworth and Her Contexts.* Newark: University of Delaware Press, 2004.

Ferris, Ina. *The Romantic National Tale and the Question of Ireland.* Cambridge: Cambridge University Press, 2002.

Flanagan, Thomas. *The Irish Novelists, 1800–1850.* New York: Columbia University Press, 1959.

• Flynn, Joyce. "Dialect As Didactic Tool: Maria Edgeworth's Use of Hiberno-English." *Proceedings of the Harvard Celtic Colloquium* 2 (1982): 115–86.

Gilbert, Sandra, and Susan Gubar. *The Madwoman in the Attic: The Woman Writer and the Nineteenth-Century Literary Imagination.* New Haven, CT, and London: Yale University Press, 1979.

Gilmartin, Sophie. *Ancestry and Narrative in Nineteenth-Century British Literature: Blood Relations from Edgeworth to Hardy.* Cambridge: Cambridge University Press, 1998.

• Glover, Susan. "Glossing the Unvarnished Tale: Contra-Dicting Possession in *Castle Rackrent.*" *Studies in Philology* 99.3 (Summer 2002): 295–311.

Gonda, Caroline. *Reading Daughters' Fictions, 1709–1834: Novels and Society from Manley to Edgeworth.* Cambridge: Cambridge University Press, 1996.

Graham, Colin. "History, Gender and the Colonial Moment: Castle Rackrent." *Irish Studies Review* 4.14 (Spring 1996): 21–24.

Hack, Daniel. "Inter-Nationalism: *Castle Rackrent* and Anglo-Irish Union." *Novel: A Forum on Fiction* 29.2 (Winter 1996): 145–64.

Hawthorne, Mark. *Doubt and Dogma in Maria Edgeworth.* Gainesville: Florida University Press, 1967.

• Hollingworth, Brian. *Maria Edgeworth's Irish Writing: Language, History, Politics.* London: Macmillan, 1997.

Hurst, Michael. *Maria Edgeworth and the Public Scene: Intellect, Fine Feeling and Landlordism in the Age of Reform.* London: Macmillan, 1969.

Kelly, Gary. "Class, Gender, Nation, and Empire: Money and Merit in the Writing of the Edgeworths." *The Wordsworth Circle* 25.2 (Spring 1994): 89–93.

Kirkpatrick, Kathryn. "'Going to Law about That Jointure': Women and Property in *Castle Rackrent.*" *The Canadian Journal of Irish Studies* 22.1 (July 1996): 21–29.

————. "Putting Down the Rebellion: Notes and Glosses on *Castle Rackrent*, 1800." *Éire-Ireland* 30.1 (Spring 1995): 77–90.

• Kowaleski-Wallace, Elizabeth. *Their Fathers' Daughters: Hannah More, Maria Edgeworth, and Patriarchal Complicity*. Oxford: Oxford University Press, 1991.

• McCormack, W. J. *Ascendancy and Tradition in Anglo-Irish Literary History from 1789 to 1939*. Oxford: Clarendon Press, 1985.

Maguire, W. A. "Castle Nugent and Castle Rackrent: Fact and Fiction in Maria Edgeworth." *Eighteenth-Century Ireland* 11 (1996): 146–59.

Moynahan, Julian. "Maria Edgeworth (1768–1849): Origination and a Checklist." In *Anglo-Irish: The Literary Imagination in a Hyphenated Culture*, 12–42. Princeton, NJ: Princeton University Press, 1995.

Murphy, Sharon. *Maria Edgeworth and Romance*. Dublin: Four Courts Press, 2004.

Murray, Patrick. "The Irish Novels of Maria Edgeworth." *Studies: An Irish Quarterly Review* 59.235 (Autumn 1970): 267–78.

————. "Maria Edgeworth and Her Father: The Literary Partnership." *Éire-Ireland* 6.3 (1971): 39–50.

• Nash, Julie. *Servants and Paternalism in the Works of Maria Edgeworth and Elizabeth Gaskell*. Aldershot: Ashgate, 2007.

Newcomer, James. "*Castle Rackrent*: Its Structure and Its Irony." *Criticism: A Quarterly for Literature and the Arts* 8.2 (Spring 1966): 170–79.

• O'Donnell, Katherine. "Castle Stopgap: Historical Reality, Literary Realism, and Oral Culture." *Eighteenth-Century Fiction* 22.1 (Fall 2009): 115–130.

Ó Gallchoir, Clíona. *Maria Edgeworth: Women, Enlightenment and Nation*. Dublin: University College Dublin Press, 2005.

• Solomon, Stanley J. "Ironic Perspective in Maria Edgeworth's *Castle Rackrent*." *The Journal of Narrative Technique* 2.1 (January 1972): 68–73.

Tracy, Robert. "Maria Edgeworth and Lady Morgan: Legality Versus Legitimacy." *Nineteenth-Century Fiction* 40.1 (June 1985): 1–22.

Wohlgemut, Esther. "Maria Edgeworth and the Question of National Identity." *Studies in English Literature, 1500–1900* 39.4 (Autumn 1999): 645–58.